MAN MADE GOD 005

By Brandon Varnell

Art by Lonwa

Man Made God 005
Copyright © 2023 Brandon Varnell & Kitsune Incorporated
Illustration Copyright © 2023 Lonwa
All rights reserved.

To see Brandon Varnell's other works, or to ask for permission to use his works, visit him at www.varnell-brandon.com, facebook at www.facebook.com/AmericanKitsune, twitter at www.twitter.com/BrandonbVarnell, Patreon at https://www.patreon.com/BrandonVarnell, and instagram at www.instagram.com/brandonbvarnell.

If you'd like to know when I'm releasing a new book, you can sign up for my mailing list at https://www.varnell-brandon.com/mailing-list.

ISBN: 978-1-951904-71-5 (Paperback)
978-1-951904-72-2 (eBook)

DEDICATION

This page is made in dedication to my amazing patrons. Without them, my characters would never get lewded by so many wonderful artists:

Michael Sexton; IronDan; Davgj; Boots; harley; Kenneth tate; Nicholas Heppelle; Ayce-o-Spades; Eduardo Mejia; Julian Sanchez; AceandTanis; Drunkenbiker; Zeus aka Matt; Jacob Brokenwolf; Jonathan Kautz; Alec Watson; Chris Atkinson; Damen Hailey; cj savage; Kconraw; Charles Savage; Casey Simpson; Iron Akela; Brendan Kane; Bart Ursulla Van de Velde aka High Four; randgofire23; MrRedSkill; Rob Hammel; Jim Payne; Thomas Oconnell; Jordan McDonald; Robert Shofner; Mike Dennehy; Alex Burt; Green and Magenta Beast; Paigeon; Tanner Lovelace; Daniel Glasson; robert warnes; Forrest Hansen; Benjamin Collins; TheGothFather72; Christopher Gross; Scott Turner; Joshua Kern; IronKing; Mark Frabotta; Samuel Donaldson; Bruce Johnson; Nathan S; Thomas Jackson; Sean Gray; Chace Corso; ToraLinkley; Dominic Q Roddan; Aaron harris; max a kramer; victor patrick bauer; William Crew; Aesh; Michael Moneymaker; James Rowland

CONTENT

TITANIA

A mysterious fairy who Adam meets in a dungeon. Guardien of the spear. She hates it when people talk about her height.

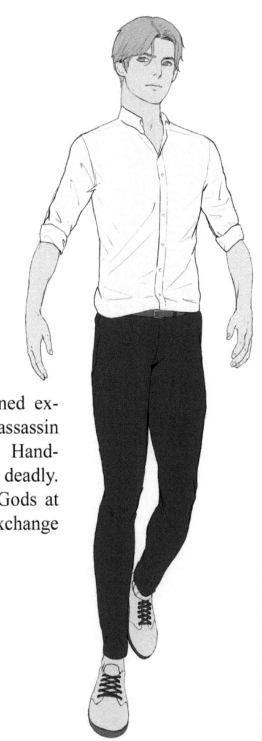

ADAM

A young man trained extensively as an assassin since childhood. Handsome, confident, deadly. He enters Age of Gods at Fayte's behest in exchange for her curing Aris.

SUSAN

Fayte's best and only friend. Genius hacker. Incredibly shy. Has trouble telling people no.

FAYTE

Daughter of the Dairing Family. Fayte is intelligent and determined to fight against her fate. She is the one who pulls Adam into Age of Gods.

LILITH

Adam's most loyal suborddinate. She is a highly skilled and quiet assassin who will do anything Adam asks without question.

ARIS

Adam's lover. She used to
be rambunctious and wild,
but she became a cripple
after contracting mortems
disease. Currently in stasis.

KUREHA

A fox's yokai that Adam
 found. Her human form
looks like a child.

ARIS

MESSES UP

"I WANT YOU THREE TO FORM A HAREM WITH ME!"

Aris knew she had messed things up in a big way immediately after she finished speaking. She didn't even need to look at the others to know how badly she had messed up. Just listening to the stifling silence was enough.

Dang it, Aris! What were you thinking?! You weren't supposed to even mention joining Adam's harem yet! All you were supposed to do was see how interested they are in Adam! You screwed up big time. What was that phrase Dad always used to say? Screw the pooch? Yeah, that's what you did. You screwed the pooch.

Aris had always been reckless. In grade school, she had done all kinds of things that drove her parents up the wall. In second grade, she brought home a baby alligator. In third grade, she snorted dirt on a dare, which required a hospital visit. In fourth grade, she rummaged through her parents' bedroom and found her father's secret stash of porn. Her dad had been very upset with her.

Come to think of it... that was probably what turned me into such a horny woman... wait. Never mind that! I'm dealing with a crisis right now!

Aris's own reckless tendencies hadn't been stymied with age. They had actually become worse. She blamed Adam. He would often tell her something was a bad idea and that she shouldn't do it, but then he would indulge her because he couldn't say no.

Out of morbid curiosity, Aris looked at the others in the room. The three other women wore vastly different expressions. Lilith was completely silent. Aris couldn't tell what she was thinking. Susan's cherry-red face was amusing enough. It was quite cute, and Aris really wanted to tease the girl, but there was something else that stopped her.

The expression on Fayte's face.

I don't think I've ever seen someone look that cold before. Yeesh. That face could freeze the deepest pits of Hell.

Aris felt a chill run down her spine as Fayte stared at her with a hard expression. Her face was like a frozen tundra.

"Uh…"

For the first time in her life, Aris didn't know what to say, but she knew she had to say something. She needed to somehow salvage this situation.

She didn't think saying *"I'm just kidding! That was a joke! Were you surprised?!"* would cut it. No, from the look on Fayte's face, that might make the situation worse. Did that mean she had to be honest? But that would involve telling them her darkest fears. Aris didn't know if she was ready for that.

Even so, Aris did her best to explain herself.

"I, um… what I mean is…"

"Aris."

Fayte's voice stopped her cold. Aris straightened in her seat. She felt like a student who had been caught cheating by her teacher and was about to suffer a harsh reprimand.

"Y-yes?"

"Why would you say something like that? And don't try to worm your way out of this by pretending that was a joke. I like to think I know you pretty well by now. You're mischievous, but I can't imagine you would pull a prank like this. I need you to explain yourself," Fayte said.

"I want to have a threesome with you and Adam?"

"Aris!"

"Sorry! I'm sorry! I'll be serious! I promise!"

"You had better."

Ah. She's got this really commanding presence when she's mad. That's... kind of hot. Wait. Bad Aris. Bad. Don't think about how you want Fayte to tag team you with Adam, strip you down, tie you up, and punish you.

Aris took several deep breaths to calm down. Now wasn't the time to get lost in her fantasies. Fayte had just called her out, and she knew this woman wouldn't accept anything less than the truth. Right now, the only thing Aris could do was be completely open and honest about her feelings.

Man... this sucks.

"So, um... you know I had Mortems Disease," Aris began.

"I know. I am the one who helped cure you, after all," Fayte said.

Aris nodded and clenched her thighs to keep her nerves from getting the better of her. "Right. Well, Mortems Disease is normally one hundred percent fatal. I'm the only person to date who has survived. I have you to thank for that, so thank you."

"You're welcome. Now, stop stalling for time."

"Okay. Okay. Just... give me a second. This isn't easy for me to talk about." Aris closed her eyes and took several deep breaths. When she opened them, her expression was calm, though her insides felt like they were turning to jelly. "When I had Mortems Disease, I had a lot of time to think. Mostly, I thought about how helpless I was. My muscles had atrophied to the point where I couldn't move, and my body was slowly beginning to shut down. I've never felt more helpless in my entire life, and, well, it made me realize how fragile my life really is. I could die at any time. It could be tomorrow. It could be a decade from now. There's no telling when or how you might die. It's not fun to think about."

Part of the reason Aris had become even more reckless than when she was younger was that she had realized how nebulous her life was. She could get hit by a truck tomorrow, or get caught up in a gang shootout, or even catch another disease that would kill her. Aris didn't want to die with regrets, so she lived as if every day was her last one.

She took another deep breath.

"More importantly than my own life, I think a lot about Adam and what would happen to him if I died. You've lived with Adam for a while now. You should know what I'm talking about."

Aris eyed Fayte as the other woman slowly nodded.

"Adam is… very dependent on you," she said.

Aris smiled, but it was wan and brittle. "Yeah. I don't think Adam could live without me anymore."

She thought back on the past. It hadn't occurred to her back then, but after seeing how desperately Adam had struggled to keep her alive, she understood.

"When I first met Adam, he had given up on living. He was alive… but he wasn't living, if that makes any sense. He was like… like… a walking corpse." She paused long enough to shudder. "You should have seen him. He was in really bad shape."

For the first several months after Aris took Adam to her home, he wouldn't talk or respond to anything anyone said. It took shoving a spoon into his mouth just to get him to eat. She didn't even want to talk about how difficult it had been to make him go to the bathroom. Adam had been, for all intents and purposes, a living corpse, a body without a soul.

She understood now that the reason he had been like that was because his best friend, the person for whom he had survived going through hell for so long, the girl he loved with all his heart, had been declared dead. She had been his purpose before Aris. He had endured nightmarish torture and inhumane experiments all for the sake of seeing someone who, upon his return, was no longer present. She could only imagine what kind of hole her death had left in his life.

"It took months before he began responding to me. I thought everything had gotten better after that, but looking back on it, I don't think he ever fully recovered. He just latched onto me. He made me his reason for living."

While it made her feel good to know there was someone so dedicated to her, it also worried her immensely, especially now that she possessed a firm understanding of her own mortality.

"What do you think would happen to Adam if I were to suddenly die?" Aris asked Fayte.

Fayte didn't answer right away. She bit her lower lip and thought about it. Susan and Lilith were both quiet. Aris glanced at them to see that Lilith, at least, seemed to understand what Aris was getting at. Susan just looked confused.

"I understand where you are going with this," Fayte said at last with a sigh. "If you died, Adam would no longer have anyone anchoring him to this world. He would probably stop caring about whether he lived or died and just wither away. Is that why you want us to form a harem with you?"

"I wasn't lying when I said I wanted to have a threesome with you and Adam, but, well, that's more or less the reason." Aris shrugged when Fayte frowned at her. "Look, I can't help it. You three are hot. If I wasn't completely head over heels for Adam, I would have done my best to get in your pants."

Reactions to her words varied. Susan looked like she might pass out. All the blood had rushed to her face and she was swaying in her seat. Lilith, on the other hand, did not appear to even care.

Fayte just sighed. "I hate to break this to you, but I'm straight."

"I know. And I'm disappointed."

"Back to our main topic…"

"Right." Aris sighed, shoulders slumping. "You're not wrong. I'm very worried about what would happen to Adam if I died, so I thought if he had more people he was attached to, he would continue having something to live for even if I kick the bucket. Adam has sacrificed years of his life for me, and I love him so very much. I can't stand the thought of him losing the will to live just because I'm no longer around."

Aris had no intention of dying, of course, but that didn't mean she wouldn't or couldn't die. It was just like she had told Fayte. She understood the fragility of life better than most. She would even go so far as to say no one understood how fragile life was more than her.

The tension eased out of Fayte's shoulders as she sighed and slumped backward, looking exhausted. She ran a hand through her hair, stopped after pushing the bangs away from her eyes, then completed the action.

"Well… I understand why you would feel this way. It's not like I begrudge you for wanting to help Adam form bonds with more people… and they do say that love is the greatest bond of all." She furrowed her brow to glare at Aris. "But did you stop to consider that some of us might not be interested in polyamory?"

"I… well… not really," Aris confessed. She looked away. She didn't want to see the expression on Fayte's face.

Adam had warned her that this might happen, of course, but Aris had pushed ahead anyway. Perhaps her own desperation to prevent Adam from losing his will to live if something happened to her had caused her to act even more recklessly than was her wont. Regardless, Adam's warning had basically gone in one ear and out the other.

"I'm going to pretend that our discussion today never happened," Fayte said at last. "I like you, Aris, and I like and respect Adam, but you have to understand something. I don't want to be in a polyamorous relationship. When I find my partner, I want to be his one and only. So, let's pretend that today didn't happen and continue on as we always have. Sound good?"

"I… yeah, okay," Aris said at last.

"Good," Fayte said with a smile.

Aris wasn't happy with the results, but she knew this was probably the best she could expect, just like she knew this whole situation was her fault. She had ignored Adam's warning and rushed headlong into a situation she couldn't control and didn't take Fayte's feelings into account. Thinking about it, most people wouldn't want to be in a polyamorous relationship. Most people wanted to be the only person in their partner's life. There was probably something fundamentally wrong with Aris for even thinking this way.

Well, it's not like I didn't already know that I was broken.

She had no qualms about who she was. Adam loved her. That was enough. But now she realized that she couldn't just rush into things like she had been. She needed to think about her decisions before she made them.

I'm not going to give up on making Adam grow attached to more people, but I do need to rethink my strategy.

Deciding not to think about this right now since it wouldn't do any good, Aris tried to recapture the joy they had before her faux pas. It was much harder than she thought. Fayte was cordial, but there was a clear wariness in her responses now, and Susan was just a mess. Lilith rarely talked to begin with, but now she was brooding even more than usual.

Whether by fortune or fate, the sound of a door opening and closing came from the entrance hall shortly after their conversation.

"I'm back," Adam announced after stepping into the living room. As always, Titania sat on his shoulder and Kureha, currently in her fox form, was using his head as a burrow.

"Welcome back," Fayte said with a smile. "How did your meeting with Clarise go?"

"It went well," Adam said as Kureha hopped off his head and transformed.

Kureha was an adorable girl with long black hair and skin like freshly fallen snow. Her big eyes were wide and innocent. Aris knew this game was a fantasy setting, and thus the countries on Earth didn't exist, but she looked like someone of Asian descent.

Aris had always thought Asians were super pretty. There was something about them that she found captivating. Kureha was no exception. This girl was gonna be a knockout when she grew up.

It's too bad she's so young. I don't think adding her to Adam's harem would be a good idea, but maybe if we find her mother...

Aris entertained the thought for a few moments before shaking her head. She had just gotten schooled for talking about giving Adam more lovers, so now wasn't the time for such thoughts.

"You say it went well, but once again, you have done something incredibly reckless." Titania floated over to the table and sat down with a huff, while Kureha hopped onto Lilith's lap, finally snapping the woman out of her daze. She looked down at the young child and began petting her head and rubbing her ears. Kureha sighed and melted as though she was experiencing heaven.

"What did Adam do this time?" asked Fayte.

Titania crossed her arms as Adam sat beside Aris. He placed an arm around her shoulder, and she leaned into him without thinking. He was so warm. Even though this was just a game and their bodies were made up of polygons and pixels, his warmth remained the same.

"Hmph. Listen to this. Adam just decided to accept a suicidal commission from the Guild Association to kill the [War Demon's] commanders."

"Adam…"

"Don't look at me like that," Adam shrugged when Fayte stared at him. "I didn't say we would do it right now. We'll level up more, gather intel, and only attack when we're certain of our victory. However, I have determined this is something we need to do. Your reputation in the game will soar if our guild defeats the [War Demon's] commanders."

"You're not wrong. I do wish you would discuss this with me first, but I understand that you're only thinking about how to help me win my bet," Fayte said with a gentle smile. Aris locked onto that smile.

She definitely loves him.

It was clear to Aris that Fayte loved Adam. The only reason she didn't act on her feelings was because he was already in a relationship with Aris. Fayte said she didn't want to be in a polyamorous relationship, and Aris could accept that even if she only had a vague understanding of why, but that didn't mean she would just give up. Wouldn't it be a win-win situation if they could both be with Adam?

I won't do anything right now. I'll be patient and slowly unlock Fayte's heart. I'll wear down her resistance until she's ready to accept a relationship with me and Adam.

Aris nodded several times. She wouldn't give up, but she would learn prudence.

"You're being awfully quiet, Aris. Did something happen?" asked Adam.

"No. Nothing happened. I was just thinking about something Fayte told me," Aris said with a cheerful smile.

***

The sound of the heater hummed through the living room as Adam sat on the couch, sipping a cup of coffee as he read the latest news about *Age of Gods.*

It was December 25. All players had been asked to log off so the updates could be installed. They would be able to log back in on January 1. Adam still had his reservations about implementing a Time Compression System, but this would work out to his advantage. After all, if he could stay in the game for several days at a time, he could increase his level much more quickly.

"What are you reading?" asked Aris.

He looked over at the young woman who, up until just a few seconds ago, had been stuffing her face with pancakes. She had some syrup on her face. He grabbed a napkin and wiped it off for her.

Aris was a young woman with brown hair, innocent blue eyes that reminded him of the sky, and skin like fresh snow. Her face still retained the youth of someone just coming out of their teen years. That made sense. She was barely eighteen now. The form-fitting pants hugged her hips and she wore a shirt that showed off her flat belly.

"Just checking the latest news on *Age of Gods.* At last estimate, 3.5 billion people are now playing it. That's almost the world's entire population," Adam said.

"That's a lot of people," Aris murmured.

"That makes this the most-played game in history," Fayte said on Aris's left. Unlike his girlfriend, Fayte ate with poise and elegance, gracefully cutting her pancake into bite-sized pieces before placing them almost delicately into her mouth.

If Adam considered Aris to be as pretty as a porcelain doll, then Fayte was as seductive as a succubus. The blonde hair descending from her crown was like waves of golden thread. She had blue eyes, but unlike Aris's sky-blue, hers were a darker shade that complemented their narrower, more seductive shape. She didn't wear makeup, but her pink lips still stood out starkly on her white skin. Adorning her body were yoga pants and a turtleneck sweater that hid a buxom figure.

"I think the only gave that ever came close to getting this level of reception was *Final Frontier XXI*," Adam said, nodding.

Final Frontier XXI was a game created by a company stationed out of what had formerly been Japan. The game had combined realistic graphics with a beautiful fantasy-esque setting and an in-game character customization system that a lot of players really enjoyed. There were still many people playing the game even to this day, though it had far fewer players now. While it might have been a great game, it couldn't stand up to the sheer realism of *Age of Gods,* which felt almost indistinguishable from real life.

Aris finished eating, set her place down, then picked up a steaming cup of hot chocolate. She tucked her feet underneath her bum and leaned into him as she took a slow sip of her drink.

"Doesn't it feel weird not to be playing right now?" asked Aris.

Adam nodded. "I'd normally have been playing for several hours already."

"It can't be helped. The updates are going to take five days to implement, which means no one can play right now," Fayte said.

"Uuuuuugh…" Aris groaned.

Adam studied Aris and Fayte with a small frown. He had noticed the distance that had suddenly opened between them. Most people probably wouldn't have noticed at all, but Adam had been watching them for a long time now. Up until his meeting with Claire from the Guild Association, Aris and Fayte had seemed to be as close as real sisters, but something had changed.

He couldn't say whether the change was bad yet, but there was no denying it either. The way they talked to each other was more awkward than it used to be.

He thought about asking, and yet, he refrained for fear that it would only cause the rift between them to widen.

"Hey, we should go out tonight," Aris suddenly said.

"What?" asked Fayte.

"If we stay here, we're just going to get bored. Let's have a night on the town! We can also invite Susan and Lilith!"

"I don't think that's such a good idea…" Adam said.

"Awwwwww. Come on, Adam? Please? I don't want to stay cooped up here all day!"

Aris leaned into him even more, allowing her chest to come into contact with his torso. He gave the young woman a complacent smile as she rubbed herself against him. Maybe if he was a blushing virgin, her attempts would have worked on him, but the two of them had sex regularly, and while he certainly wasn't immune to Aris's charms, he knew when to resist and when to let that resistance crumble.

"Adam is right," Fayte said. "Levon Pleonexia has people everywhere and his family has several government officials in their pocket. It's just a rumor, but I've heard they are allowed access to the surveillance cameras. The last thing we want is for Levon to discover who you are."

While violence was technically illegal, that did not mean nobles wouldn't engage in it. Money was power. And when you had power, you could do whatever you wanted... within reason. Levon might not be able to assault them in a full-on confrontation, but he was more than capable of sending assassins after them. That was the kind of power the nobility possessed.

"Couldn't we go somewhere without surveillance cameras like we did last time?" asked Aris.

Aris was referring to when he, Aris, and Fayte went to the New York Strip. It used to be a popular place, but its popularity declined after World War III, and now it was a hole in the wall. The people who knew of it loved going there. However, most people preferred New York City Town Square Mall, which had many more luxuries and high-end boutiques.

Adam tried to resist the impulse to let Aris do what she wanted. Maybe he was being overly cautious, but in this day and age, he felt like caution was necessary. The last thing they needed was for Levon to find out about him and Aris in the real world. There wasn't a doubt in his mind that the man would stop at nothing to remove them.

Strong as he might be, Adam could not stand up to the power of a noble family. It was better to remain under the radar.

"Adam... please? I really want to go out." Aris clasped her hands together.

"I can't... there's something I need to do today," Adam said, still resisting, though he felt the walls he had built up crumbling. Aris was staring at him with those big, blue eyes and her lips turned into a pout. The look on her face should have been illegal.

"Then it can just be me, Fayte, and Susan," Arith exclaimed.

"Aris..." Fayte said, a warning in her voice.

"Ah! No! Don't worry, Fayte! I promise not to do a repeat of what happened last time!" Aris waved her hands back and forth as though trying to supplicate the other woman.

Adam raised an eyebrow. "Last time? Did something happen?"

"Nothing that you need to worry about," Aris said quickly—a little too quickly. "Anyway, please let us go out? I understand why you wouldn't want us to, but if it's just us girls, there shouldn't be a problem, right? We can even go to New York Town Square Mall where the surveillance cameras are since you won't be with us."

He was about to tell her no again, but then he paused.

No one had seen Aris's face in *Age of Gods* because she wore a veil like Fayte, so it wasn't like they would automatically be able to tell who she was. But it was possible to find out who she was if someone decided to run a background check. That was his biggest worry. He didn't want Levon running a background check on Aris. It wouldn't take much digging to discover her adopted older brother.

But it's not like he would know where to find us. I changed our home address to an abandoned apartment not long after Fayte discovered my location, and now we're living here. Even if he's part of the Pleonexia Family, he can't use the surveillance cameras too freely for fear of being discovered and suffering public backlash. Maybe... it will be fine.

"Well... I suppose, it's okay if you go out," Adam said at last.

"Really?!" Aris looked like she'd just won the lottery. Her eyes were sparkling.

"Are you sure about this, Adam?" asked Fayte. She still seemed concerned.

"Well, no, I'm not really sure about this, but... I think Aris has been confined long enough," Adam said.

Aris had been confined to a bed for years thanks to Mortems Disease. It would be a shame if she couldn't go out and stretch her legs now that she was cured. He didn't think he would be able to handle the guilt of forcing her to remain indoors after everything she had already suffered through.

"Thank you, Adam! I love you!"

He should have expected her pounce, but he was completely unprepared for Aris's surprise kiss. She knocked him onto his back, pressed her hands against his chest, and kissed him hard enough to leave him dizzy.

She's gotten stronger... is this natural?

She wasn't nearly as strong as him, of course, but the strength of her pounce still surprised him. Not only had Aris regained her previous athletic abilities, but she seemed to be even stronger now than she was before. He didn't think that would be possible after she had Mortems Disease.

Is this the effect of consuming my blood, or is it something else?

"I'll call Susan and ask her if she'd like to join us," Fayte said, standing up.

Adam finally managed to pry Aris off his lips. He ignored the woman's whining as he sat them up and looked at Fayte.

"I'll call Lilith and tell her to tag along with you," he said.

Fayte raised an eyebrow. "You have Lilith's contact information?"

"Yes, but you already knew that, didn't you?" said Adam. He posed it like a question, but it was more of a statement.

Fayte turned away.

***

Susan sat on a couch across from her father. Eugine Forebear was a tall man with a charismatic presence. His brown hair was the same shade as his daughter's, but his broad shoulders, thick chest, and strong facial features were the exact opposite of her delicate countenance, which she got from her mother.

Right now, he was looking at her with a mixture of concern and resignation.

"Are you sure about this, Pumpkin? I know that the rumors surrounding Connor Sword are unpleasant at best, but none of them have been proven. They really are just rumors."

"I'm sure, Father. Even if the rumors were not true, I would not feel comfortable with that man as my husband," Susan said. Her voice quaked a little, but she still stood firm.

The two of them were currently sitting inside her father's private office. The centerpiece of the office were the two couches and coffee table made from thick mahogany. Her father's desk was near the back, in front of a window that showed an expansive view of New York City. Bookshelves on either side contained many old tomes that her father had collected. While any book could not be read on the web, her father loved collecting old books. It was his hobby.

"Well… if you don't want to marry him, then I won't force you to." Her father sighed. "I'll tell the Sword Family that our marriage talks are being called off."

"I'm sorry for causing you trouble." Susan bowed her head.

Eugine reached out to rub his daughter's head. She looked startled at first, but he just smiled and ran his hand over her hair.

"Nonsense. This is the first time my daughter has firmly told me what she wants. There's no way I could be angry with you for that." Her father smiled kindly at her. "You are always doing your best not to cause me problems, and you have a strong sense of obligation. I've always worried that your desire not to cause a ruckus would prevent you from being able to seek your own happiness. I'm glad to know that isn't the case."

Susan smiled slightly at her father's words, though it hid the guilt she felt.

While her father acted like this wasn't a big deal, she knew it was. The Sword Family was powerful and influential. They might not have the same political influence as the Pleonexia Family, but they had enough power within the American Federation to put undue pressure on a simple politician like her father. That was, in fact, the reason Eugine had been willing to marry her off.

He hadn't been forced to. However, he knew they could force the issue if they really wanted. In the end, it was simply easier to go along with them than fight a prolonged battle that might end with their family in a worse position than before.

Susan eventually left the office as her father put in a call to the Sword Family. The last she heard was her father addressing the Sword Family head before the door shut behind her.

She walked down the hall and soon entered her room, which was located just a few minutes' walk from her father's office. A noise caused her to pause before closing the door. She looked at her nightstand, where her phone, sitting upon the charger, was ringing. The song belonged to her favorite old video game.

Closing the door, she walked to the nightstand, picked up her phone, and placed it against her ear. She already knew who was calling thanks to the caller ID.

"Fayte? What's going on?"

"Hey, Sue! I was wondering when you would pick up. This is my fifth time calling."

"I-I'm sorry. I was talking to my father…"

Fayte just laughed. *"It's okay. I'm sure whatever you were talking about was important. Anyway, I wanted to know if you were doing anything for Christmas today?"*

"No." Susan shook her head, even though she knew Fayte

couldn't see it. "Mother and Father are attending an important function. I was going to go with them, but we decided at the last minute that I shouldn't."

Connor Sword would be there along with his family, and her father didn't want her meeting with him right now, especially after she informed him of what happened between them in *Age of Gods.*

"In that case, how would you like to come with me, Aris, and Lilith to celebrate?"

"Wait. Really? We're meeting IRL?"

"We are. I hope that's not a problem."

"No. It's no problem at all. I'd love to go."

"Good. We're meeting at New York City Town Square Mall at noon."

"I'll be there," Susan assured her.

"See you then."

After Fayte hung up, Susan stared at the phone for a second, then fell backward onto the bed, clutching the phone to her chest. She was excited to meet with the others in real life. Even though they had only met together in the game so far, she felt more comfortable with them than she did anyone she knew in real life save her parents.

"Celebrating Christmas with friends, huh? That'll be nice." Susan smiled, but then furrowed her brow. "Fayte didn't mention Adam. Is he not coming?"

She hoped he would. Susan secretly wanted to meet with the mysterious masked member of their group in real life. It would be disappointing if he didn't come.

TAKEN

HOLIDAYS HAD ALWAYS BEEN IMPORTANT, but after World War III, their importance had reached new heights. The amount of effort governments around the world put into making their holidays the biggest and best they could was phenomenal. Every time one came around, there would be live shows, TV broadcasts, in-game holiday events, virtual events, and so much more to give the people something festive to celebrate.

Christmas and the new year were the two most important holidays.

Aris remembered her father once telling her the real meaning of Christmas, but the knowledge had since been lost to time. She thought it was something about a person who lived a really long time ago. Not that she particularly cared about such things. For her, Christmas was a time to celebrate merely being alive.

Or it had been.

Now, it meant something more.

"Woooooow! Look at all the decorations! Are the images changing? I'm not hallucinating, am I?"

Aris was in awe as she and Fayte stood outside New York City

Town Square Mall. Having come from a small town, she had never seen such a large structure, nor one adorned with so many extravagant Christmas decorations. It looked like someone had turned the entire building into a holographic display that was lit up with various effects. One moment, the walls would be decorated with Christmas trees. The next, fireworks were going off.

"You're not hallucinating," Fayte answered. "Embedded into the building are over one million holographic nodes. During important holidays, those nodes will activate and coat the entire building in holographic decorations to celebrate whatever important holiday is happening at the time."

It wasn't just the building that was decorated with holographic displays. Many holographic signs floated in the air. Each one contained themes that were common with Christmas and New Year's like Christmas trees, fireworks, candy canes, nut crackers… and like the building, they were constantly changing what they displayed.

"That. Is. So. Cool!"

Aris couldn't see Fayte's face because she was wearing a veil, but she was certain the other woman was giving her an amused smile. That was the impression she gave off. But Aris didn't care. It didn't matter to her if people thought she looked like a hick.

I mean, they're technically not wrong.

The town that Aris came from was way out in the countryside and had no more than around four or five thousand residents. It was a very small place. She would have even said it was confining.

While Aris admired the holographic decorations, Fayte pushed up the sleeves of her overly large cloak to glance at her watch.

It was cold outside. Aris's breath came out in white puffs. Oddly, she didn't feel cold at all. Had this been before she had gotten Mortems Disease, Aris would have been complaining to the heavens about how cold she was, but now all she felt was a refreshing briskness.

"Aris. Fayte," someone suddenly said behind them.

"Gyaaaaa!"

Aris screamed and whirled around to find Lilith standing not a meter from them.

"Jeez, Lilith! Are you trying to give me a… heart… oh…"

Her complaint died in her throat as she stared at the woman standing before her. Unlike Fayte, who wore baggy clothes to hide all of her features, Lilith did no such thing. The black pants that hugged her hips were tight enough to show off every curve of her bountiful bottom. She wore a long-sleeved black shirt, but it showed off her stomach, which didn't contain a single ounce of fat. Aris could only stare at the tight abs this woman had. Her outfit was topped off with fingerless black gloves, black boots, and a black jacket.

Oh… oh my. She's hot. Aris very nearly licked her lips. *And Adam hasn't been pounding that? Really? Really, really? Why not? I'd tap that ass if I had a cock. What is wrong with him?*

"Damn, you look really sexy," Aris blurted.

She covered her mouth when Fayte and Lilith looked at her strangely. She was fortunate they didn't call her out on her faux pas. As her ears burned a fierce red, Fayte turned back to Lilith.

"It's good to see you, Lilith. This is our first time meeting outside of the game, isn't it?"

Lilith nodded. "It is."

"Now all we're waiting for is Su… ah. Speak of the devil."

A limousine pulled up and the doors automatically opened. A young woman with brown hair, large brown eyes, and bundled up in winter clothes stepped out. Susan looked at them all with a smile.

"Aris. Fayte. L-Lilith?! Is that you?"

"Yes. It is a pleasure to see you, Susan," Lilith said in her usual tone.

"I didn't realize you'd be coming…"

"Is that a problem?"

"N-no! It's not a problem at all!"

Susan waved her hands back and forth as though warding something off. Aris wondered if the others had seen the way Susan looked at Lilith. Had they also noticed the insecurity in the young woman's eyes? Well, not that she was all that surprised. Lilith was so hot that even Aris felt her confidence waver.

Though it's not like she's the only one…

Aris glanced at Fayte. The woman might have been decked out in the ugliest outfit she had ever seen, but underneath that baggy exterior was a banging body she would love to seduce into bed.

"Take care of the young lady," said the old man driving the limo.

"We will. I'll call you when it's time to pick Su up, Sebas," Fayte said.

So his name is Sebas. Is that short for Sebastian? What a typical butler name. Are all butlers named Sebastian?

The limousine drove off, and Aris, Fayte, Lilith, and Susan entered the mall.

If the outside was impressive, the inside was even more amazing. Aris could only stare in awe at the many holographic decorations floating in the air. Holographic snowflakes floated from above. Even the floor seemed to have been embedded with holographic nodes. Right now, the floor had been made to look like a winter wonderland, snow as far as the eye could see.

"Incredible…" Aris breathed softly.

"Isn't it?" asked Fayte. "I suppose, I tend to forget how amazing this is because I've seen it so often, but seeing your reaction, I have to admit, it's pretty awe-inspiring to see how much effort went into all this. Anyway, let's do some Christmas shopping."

"Yeah! I want to get Adam something for Christmas!"

The group went off together, drawing a crowd wherever they went. Aris was used to it by this point. She ignored them, or rather, she didn't even see them.

"What do you think Adam would like for Christmas?" asked Fayte.

"Uh... um... that's a very good question."

"You don't know?"

"J-just gimme a minute! I need to think about this!"

"Well, while Aris is thinking, why don't we go into some boutiques and see what new clothes are in stock?"

"Let's do it!"

At Fayte's suggestion, the group traveled to Auspicious Imported. Even Aris knew about this store, or to be more specific, she knew the clothing brand. The Chrysos Family had been well-known clothing makers for generations. Aris used to watch the fashion shows they put on when she was a kid, and she would even wrap herself in various blankets and pretend she was walking across a stage. One time, she had tripped and split her head open on the corner of her parents' coffee table.

That had required stitches.

Auspicious Imported seemed like a modestly sized store. Many different articles of clothing stood on display for their customers' perusal. Aris had never seen so many different outfits in one place.

"Good afternoon," a beautiful lady greeted them with a smile. Her eyes were on Lilith as she spoke, however, making it clear who had attracted her attention. "Welcome to Auspicious Imported. If you need any help, please let me know. I would be happy to assist you."

"Uh... are you... talking to me?" Lilith pointed to herself.

"I am talking to all of you," the woman said.

"Really? You're staring at Lilith awfully hard," Aris added.

The woman just smiled. "That's just your imagination."

"Sure…"

Aris didn't believe that for one second, but she didn't feel like arguing. Fayte and Susan were already moving deeper into the store. She and Lilith shared a look before walking quickly to catch up with them.

The group tried on many different outfits. Fayte was the one who chose most of the clothing. She had a keen eye for fashion, which must have been her noble upbringing at work. Aris couldn't figure out what was in and what wasn't. It all looked amazing to her.

"Aris, try this on."

"Okay."

Taking the outfit Fayte handed her, Aris went into the unoccupied changing room next to the one Lilith was already inside. The other woman had already been roped into Fayte's dress-up game. Susan was also inside one of the changing rooms.

Aris stripped, then began putting on each article. The pants were easy enough to slide up her hips, though they felt a little tight. Her butt felt constricted. However, the top was fine. It was a golden bikini top and a strap that went around the stomach. She rather liked it and wondered if Adam would appreciate it too. An idea came to her as she threw on the red jacket with gold shoulder stripes.

I think I have the perfect idea for Adam's Christmas present!

Feeling quite pleased with herself, Aris stepped out of the changing room. Lilith and Susan were already outside. They couldn't have looked more different if they tried.

Susan was adorable in her black mesh shrug with shoulder cutouts, split sleeves, and black metal D-rings. It was the perfect top to go over her leather shirt. Adorning her hips was a lovely pink semi-translucent skirt that showed off what she was wearing underneath—

black booty shorts. Knee-high boots with zippers finished the outfit.

She's very cute too. Hm hm. I really want to tease Susan right now.

Lilith's outfit had decidedly less fabric. It looked like a neon kimono with shoulder cutouts, but it was far shorter than most kimonos. It stopped around mid-stomach and was open to reveal the tube top wrapped around her chest. This outfit seemed to really highlight her stomach, which Aris approved of. That stomach was worthy of taking shots off of. Come to think of it, Aris had only been able to drink once when she snuck into her father's alcohol stash. The last item of clothing was a pair of kemono cyberpunk boots with glowing soles that changed color with every step.

"You three look amazing!" Fayte said.

"Heck yeah, we do!" Aris agreed, placing her hands on her hips as she thrust out her chest.

"Hmm. I suppose… this doesn't show as much skin as the stuff you normally put me in," Susan added.

Lilith had a completely different opinion. "I'm not sure this is something I should be wearing. These boots are particularly hard to move around in."

"But you look great," Fayte commented. "Fashion is important for a woman. Your style reflects what you stand for."

"I'm not sure if there's anything I stand for, so…"

"It can boost your confidence and make you feel good."

"But I feel perfectly fine."

"Ugh! Whatever! Look, stop being so stubborn! You look great!"

"I-I don't know…" Lilith murmured.

Seeing Fayte and Lilith like this, Aris decided to help out. "Adam would like you in those clothes."

Lilith perked up. "Really?"

"Mhhmmm. Really."

"Then… maybe I should buy them?"

"Definitely."

Fayte sighed and palmed her face. "That's what it took to convince you to buy clothes?"

They bought several different outfits. Fortunately, Adam was not hurting for cash, and Aris had been given access to one of his throwaway accounts for this excursion. She bought hers and Lilith's clothing. The assassin had protested, but Aris would hear none of it.

After they were done shopping, Aris asked them to travel to another store, which sold a different sort of clothes. Susan's face had nearly burst when she saw the store, but Fayte just smiled wryly before following the younger woman inside.

Time passed and Aris's stomach soon told her it was time for food. They traveled to the food court, where Aris ordered enough food to feed a family of five. The other three could only gawk as she scarfed down the junk food like it was going out of style.

"How can you eat so much?" asked Fayte.

"What do you mean? Doesn't everyone have a second stomach for junk food?"

"I'm pretty sure no one has a second stomach for junk food. Also, the phrase you're looking for is a second stomach for dessert."

"Then I have a third stomach—one for junk food."

"Sure. Let's just go with that."

Aris had been unable to eat junk food ever since she contracted Mortems Disease. Adam had carefully regulated her diet. She hadn't minded because she knew he was just looking out for her well-being, and the food he made *was* delicious, but she had terribly missed the taste of greasy pizza and hamburgers.

"I wish I could eat that much. Aren't you worried about gaining weight?" asked Susan.

"Not at all. Adam will love me even if I gain a few pounds," Aris proudly declared. Susan could only wryly smile at that.

Several more hours passed after they finished lunch, and before Aris knew it, the time to leave had come. Susan called Sebas to let him know. Then they traveled outside to wait for the limousine, which pulled up after about fifteen minutes.

"Strange," Fayte murmured.

"What is?" asked Aris.

"Sebas is normally outside before we even arrive," she said, then shook her head. "I'm sure it's nothing."

The doors opened, Susan said goodbye to everyone—and became shocked when Aris hugged her—then stepped inside the limo, which closed behind her.

Aris watched as the limousine pulled away, but her attention was taken from the disappearing vehicle when Lilith tugged on her sleeve.

"I have something I would like to speak to you about," the quiet woman said.

"All right." Aris turned to Fayte. "Would you mind waiting for a moment, Fayte? Lilith wants to talk to me about something?"

"Huh?" Fayte's head snapped up, but then she nodded. "Oh, yeah. Sure. I'll be right here."

Aris and Lilith walked far enough from Fayte to give themselves some privacy. Lilith seemed oddly nervous. It was hard to tell because her expression hadn't changed, but something about her posture made her seem restless.

"Is everything okay?" asked Aris.

Lilith took a deep breath before staring at her with a serious gaze. "Were you serious about forming a harem for Adam? Are you still interested in doing that?"

Aris blinked. She blinked again. Then she pinched herself.

"Ow!"

"What are you doing?"

"Just checking to make sure I'm not dreaming."

"Why would you be dreaming?"

"Because this seems too good to be true." Aris laughed before slowly looking at Lilith with the gravitas she believed this conversation warranted. "I still plan on getting Adam a harem. I have every intention of creating a group of women who can keep Adam motivated to live. You were actually the first person I thought of asking to join when I decided on this."

"I was?" Lilith's eyes widened.

Aris smiled kindly. "I know of your history with Adam. I know what he means to you, and how loyal you are to him. Adam can't take that next step with you because the guilt he feels about abandoning you eats away at him. That's why I want to help."

"But he never abandoned me. He never abandoned any of us," Lilith murmured, frowning. The sadness in her eyes made Aris hold her breath.

Lilith definitely needs to be a part of this. Her dedication alone makes it necessary for her to join Adam's harem.

"I'll contact you when I'm ready to initiate my plan. I need a few days to prepare," Aris said.

Lilith nodded. "I can wait. I've been waiting for several years already. A few more days won't make much difference."

Aris felt a small thrill as they ended their conversation. She was happy that Lilith had come to her since it made initiating the first step of her "Create a Harem for Adam" plan much easier, but that happiness was short-lived when Fayte called over to them. She looked worried.

"Hey! You two! We have a problem!" she said.

"What's wrong, Fayte?" asked Aris.

"Susan and I have a shared app that allows us to track each other's location. Something about the way she left bothered me, so I decided to check the app. It's shut off," Fayte said.

Aris shrugged. "Maybe she turned her phone off?"

Fayte shook her head. "Susan wouldn't do that. She has never turned her phone off before because her father has requested she leave it on at all times in case of emergencies. Also, just before it shut off, her limo was going in the opposite direction of her house."

Aris was about to suggest there might have been an accident or construction work that forced the car to take another route, but she didn't. If Fayte was telling them this, it meant she had already checked that option. This woman was nothing if not thorough in her research.

"Do you mean to say that Susan has been kidnapped?" asked Lilith.

"Yes, and I have no idea who took her," Fayte said, the worry in her eyes evident.

***

La Nouve was a high-end bar located in the ritzier part of New York City. Known by many as the rich district because everything was so expensive, this section of the city was the first to have been rebuilt after World War III.

Many of New York City's once-famous skyscrapers had been destroyed during the war. The ones here had been built afterward at the expense of several noble families who rose to prominence after the war's end. Now, several towering skyscrapers dominated New York City's skyline, their exteriors awash with holographic projections meant to dazzle the eyes. It was a symbol of the nobility's wealth.

Adam sat at a small table inside one of La Nouve's VIP booths, staring out the window on his left. From so high up, he could see everything New York City had to offer, and because the window's placement took the city's still deconstructed state into account, it only revealed the parts that had been rebuilt, leaving only the most aesthetically pleasing parts of the city. It was evening right now. That meant his view was dominated by the gorgeous sight of the sun setting over the city.

Disgusting. Adam thought with a snort. *The nobles wish to pretend the destruction of this city doesn't affect them, so they hide it from view, ignoring its existence like they do those left destitute by war and disease.*

Adam was not a fan of establishments created by nobles, but he was meeting someone, and this was one of the most private establishments available.

A drink sat on the table. Its deep purple color glowed neon in the overhead lighting. Crushed ice filled most of it. The ice was blue and caused the drink to change colors, becoming a deeper shade as more of it melted.

Adam took a sip of the cocktail with a sigh. The burning sensation traveling down his throat was not pleasant. He did not particularly enjoy alcohol, but the slight sweetness that accompanied it wasn't bad. They must have used some kind of artificial sweetener since it didn't taste like sugar.

A hydraulic hiss echoed within the room, but Adam didn't look away from the window, not even at the sound of footsteps drawing near.

"Master."

Adam finally turned to find a man kneeling before him. He was an older man with graying hair, sharp features, and dark eyes. Fitting him like a glove was a sophisticated duster suit that showed off his powerfully built body.

"Don't do that in public. Take a seat, Asmodeus."

"Yes, Master."

Asmodeus stood to his full height, taller than Adam by at least two heads, and sat in the chair indicated. He sat with his back ramrod straight. He said nothing and merely waited for Adam to speak.

"It's time to begin making moves on the Pleonexia Alliance. I'd like you to have Belphegor infiltrate their ranks."

"Belphegor, is it? He is certainly our best at infiltration and intelligence gathering, but it will be hard even for him to infiltrate the Pleonexia Alliance. Will our false IDs hold up to their scrutiny?"

Belphegor was one of the seven most skilled operatives under Asmodeus's command. His specialty lay in infiltration. Whenever Adam had a mission from Lucifer, he was the first one on the scene, infiltrating the target's inner sanctum and gathering all the intel Adam could possibly need for his assassination.

But for however talented Belphegor was, there were limits to what even he could accomplish. These limits were beyond his control. Security checks, for example.

The world after World War III had been unstable. Everyone was picking up the pieces and trying to rebuild, famine and disease had swept across the world like a plague, and the various world governments were still struggling to create international laws that would prevent this from happening again. It had taken over a decade before even a semblance of normality returned to the world.

Adam and his squadron of assassins had been created a mere few years before the world stabilized, and during that time, they had been able to infiltrate the residence of many high-profile targets. This was because security measures still hadn't been put in place. Unfortunately, sometime after they began their work, the various government officials and high-ranking members of society had tightened their security. While their IDs would hold up to a standard inspection, they were unlikely to pass muster during an inspection from someone under the Pleonexia Family's employ.

"You don't need to worry about that. I know someone who I think can help us slip past the Pleonexia Alliance's security checks," Adam said.

Asmodeus took a moment before responding. "Very well. I'll let Belphegor know of his new mission. You have the details?"

"I do," Adam said.

They spent the next hour going over every facet of the mission that Adam could think of. Most of what he focused on was what he wanted to learn. Adam's biggest concern was knowing when and how Levon Pleonexia planned to attack Fayte and their guild, but he also wanted Belphegor to watch for signs that Levon was close to discovering his real-world identity.

"Should that happen, I would like Belphegor to do what he can to erase any evidence of my existence from their database— preferably before Levon has a chance to verify the info's authenticity."

"I understand." Asmodeus nodded. "I will head back now and—"

The sound of something in Adam's pocket vibrating interrupted Asmodeus before he could finish. Adam fished out his phone, looked at the caller ID, and accepted the call.

"Lilith, what is it?"

"Master, I apologize for interrupting your mission briefing with Asmodeus, but something major has happened. We believe Susan has been kidnapped."

Adam pursed his lips. "You believe? It has not been confirmed?"

"Correct. However, Fayte noticed that Susan's transportation was moving in the opposite direction of her house. Her phone was also turned off a few seconds later. According to Fayte, Susan never

turns off her phone. We also checked in with Susan's father one hour ago. She should have been home by now, but she hasn't returned."

"How long has it been since you parted ways with her?"

"About three hours."

Adam closed his eyes and ran some calculations in his head. He already knew where Susan lived. She was a very prominent figure since her father was the pre-eminent politician of the Atlantic Federation. Even accounting for traffic and accidents, it should not have taken Susan more than half an hour to arrive home from New York City Town Square Mall.

Susan also isn't the type to be late without saying something. She would have called her dad to let him know she was being delayed at the very least, but her phone was shut off.

"Where was Susan's last known location before her phone shut off?" he asked.

"Flatbush Avenue and Quentin Road."

"I understand. Stay with Aris and Fayte tonight. Let them know I won't be home."

"Understood... and sorry. This only happened because I was careless."

"None of us could have known this would happen. Don't blame yourself. Anyway, don't worry. I'll get Susan back." Adam hung up the phone, pocketed it, and looked at Asmodeus. "You heard that, right? Susan has gone missing. I want everyone involved in this."

"Yes, Master."

Adam drained his glass as Asmodeus stood up, leaving his own glass unfinished. He gestured to the glass.

"You're not going to finish that?" he asked.

Asmodeus smiled wryly. "Unlike you, Master, I cannot drink to excess without getting drunk, and I suspect I'll need my wits about me."

Adam's body had undergone intense and inhumane enhancements that turned him into something more than human. His body regenerated from almost any wound. His metabolism was powerful enough to burn away any toxic substances, including every known poison. Alcohol was a poison, so naturally, his body did not allow it to stay in his system for long.

"Fair. Anyway, let's go," Adam said, standing up and following Asmodeus out the door.

***

Befitting their status as a unit of assassins, Adam's group had several hideouts located throughout New York City. The one Adam and Asmodeus traveled to was located close to Susan's last known coordinates.

Their hideout looked like a normal apartment building. Like most, it was practically abandoned. Few people lived on the outskirts like this. Most of the people living here were the dredges of society. However, the reason this complex was abandoned had nothing to do with no one wanting to live there. This place had originally been owned by Lucifer. Adam and his group took it over after breaking free from the mad scientist who created them.

Like its exterior, the interior appeared reminiscent of a standard apartment—so long as one ignored all the high-tech equipment stashed inside the living room. Several advanced reclining chairs sat in a row. They were the chairs these people used when logging into *Age of Gods*. There was also an advanced computer system against the far wall, which Adam's group used for various purposes, including but not limited to hacking social cameras, forging documents, erasing evidence, and tampering with government files.

Everyone was already there when he and Asmodeus entered. They all bowed like knights greeting their lord.

"Get up, everyone. Time is ticking and I'd rather not waste it on formalities. What have you got for me?" Adam ordered.

The only woman in their unit aside from Lilith—Leviathan—stood up. She was a tall woman with a lithe build. A black enhancement suit covered her body and left little to the imagination.

Due to their intense training in Eden, Leviathan possessed muscles that looked like they might tear her clothes. She had black hair, dark eyes, and pale skin. The shape of her face denoted her Asian descent.

"We swept the area where Susan's last known coordinates were and discovered an abandoned limousine several kilometers south of it. The license plate matches the one Susan's chauffeur, Sebas, drives."

"If they abandoned the limo, it means they had another vehicle waiting for them. Whoever did this was very thorough," Adam murmured.

Leviathan nodded. "The limo was abandoned in a place where there are no social cameras. However, we did follow the limo through the social cameras until it reached that point. We also scoured the records of every social camera within that general vicinity and discovered that another vehicle entered this zone several days ago and never left… until just two hours ago."

A holographic screen appeared between Leviathan and Adam as Beleth, their tech specialist, manipulated a computer to their left. The screen revealed a large van painted black appearing from a no-camera zone and heading south.

"This 2032 RAM ProMaster was seen leaving the no-camera zone fifteen minutes after Sebas's limousine arrived. We conclude that Susan's kidnappers changed to this vehicle and fled south."

"I assume you're tracking their location even now?" Adam asked Beleth.

"We are," answered Beleth.

Perhaps due to his role as a tech specialist, Beleth was not as built as the other members of their unit. He wore gray slacks, a black turtleneck, and large headphones. A pair of glasses sat upon a studious face. He looked more like a scholar than an assassin.

"As of this moment, they are traveling down Marine Parkway Bridge across the Rockaway Inlet."

"Can you think of anything there that might be their destination?" asked Adam.

"We believe their destination is Breezy Point," Leviathan said. "I suspect their goal is to smuggle Susan out of the state. They can't take a plane. Security is too tight. Traveling by boat is also risky, but Breezy Point is the only location where police patrols happen just once every four hours. As you know, police departments between states aren't always on good terms. Breezy Point borders New York and New Jersey, which have a particularly bad history thanks to an incident several years ago involving a high-profile Redline dealer. If they want to make a clean getaway, traveling from there is their best bet."

Redline was a powerful drug that induced an incredible high at the cost of a person's sanity. The person who took it would experience sensations similar to sexual fulfillment, but would also be left in a state of rage and increase their strength severalfold. They would have no idea that they were going on a rampage.

There had been an incident two years ago where a young woman had been forced to take some and let loose into Los Angeles. She killed thirteen people with her bare hands before being put down by the police.

Because time was of the essence, Adam didn't take more than a second to think about what needed to be done.

"I'll go on this mission alone since I can move faster by myself. I want you to monitor the situation. If possible, hack into the Orion Observatory Satellite to observe the situation."

"Understood!" everyone present, including Asmodeus, said.

Since Adam didn't have any weapons on him, he went over to a solid-looking wall that appeared normal at a glance, but soon revealed a hidden compartment of weapons when he pressed his hand against a hidden panel.

He quickly stripped his clothes and changed into a dark bodysuit that was not quite black. Pure black clothes actually made you more visible at night due to the light from the moon and stars. He slid a combat knife into his left boot, attached a pistol with a silencer to his right hip, strapped a bandolier with several magazines across his shoulder, and placed a dark blue helmet on his head. The helmet activated with a hiss. His vision, once dark, suddenly lit up and revealed not just the room he was in but also an advanced heads-up display that provided detailed information about his environment.

Now properly equipped for his mission, Adam raced out the door and traveled toward the basement garage beneath the complex.

He was going to need a fast vehicle if he wanted to arrive in time to rescue Susan.

RESCUE

IT WAS CALLED THE 2V AGUSTA SUPERVELOCE AGO, a high-tech motorcycle that was once used in the Grand Prix before racing sports went out of business. Powered by a mini four-cylinder nuclear engine that put out 350 horsepower at 34,000 rpm, it was easily the most overpowered motorcycle on the current market. Not only was it powerful, but it came with a setting that allowed Adam to connect his helmet's HUD to the motorcycle's advanced AI.

Adam raced down Maine Parkway Bridge at 240 kilometers per hour. Barely five minutes had passed since he left the hideout and he was already more than halfway there.

The bike tried several times to slide off course, but the inbuilt stabilization systems helped it maintain this speed without going into an out-of-control slide.

"How much further do I have to go before I reach my destination?" asked Adam.

A voice echoed from inside his helmet.

"You have fourteen more miles to go. At the current speed you are traveling, you should reach your destination in less than five minutes."

The voice sounded very much like a British butler. Beleth must have been messing with the AI's settings.

The bridge soon ended and Adam tilted the bike into a sharp turn without losing his speed. Despite how hard he was pushing it, the bike remained silent. This motorcycle ran on nuclear power rather than a standard engine and thus did not make any noise like the vehicles of yesteryear.

Adam soon reached Breezy Point after passing through a suburb full of small houses. He slowed down, turned off his lights, and relied on his helmet's night vision display to show him what he needed.

He did not travel into the parking lot. Instead, he parked his motorcycle behind a series of buildings, then walked across a dirt field until he reached the parking lot. There were no cars to hide behind, so he crouched behind a series of shrubs and observed the situation.

The RAM ProMaster that Beleth had been tracking was exactly where they predicted. It sat in the center of the parking lot. Several people carrying guns stood around it, dressed in worn-out military fatigues and wearing balaclava helmets to hide their faces.

He counted six people.

As Adam had expected, this group did not have a standard uniform nor were they all using the same guns. One of the men near the side door carried a Tavor TAR-66—an older assault rifle developed during World War III. Another man standing just outside the driver's door had a standard-issue 9mm pistol strapped to a holster resting against his right thigh. Still, there was one guy who carried an oscillation knife, which relied on high-frequency oscillations to cut through most substances known to man. It was frequently used to slice apart tungsten and chromium.

"I've arrived at my destination and have found the vehicle in question. It's guarded. However, I haven't been able to confirm Susan's location yet," Adam said.

A smooth click echoed in his ear.

"Copy that. Wait until you confirm the target's location and safety before engaging the enemy. Also, be sure to take one of them alive for interrogation," said Mammon. He was their communications officer.

"Don't worry. It's been a while since I've done this, but I still remember how to properly operate during a mission."

"Just wanted to make sure you haven't gone soft, Boss."

As Adam continued to study the situation, the man standing on the driver's side reached into his pocket and pulled out a phone. Adam could not hear what was being said. However, he could read lips, and what he read caused him to purse his own.

"You're at the rendezvous point? Very well. We'll move out now."

The call ended fast and the leader began barking out orders. One of the men slid the passenger door open, and Adam was finally able to confirm that Susan was indeed there, tied up, mouth bound shut, and eyes wide in terror.

***

Everything had happened too fast.

After saying goodbye to Aris, Fayte, and Lilith, Susan had entered her limousine and settled in as the vehicle began moving. She hadn't paid much attention to what was happening at the time, busy as she was texting her father to let her know she would be home soon. Her father always worried about her and asked that she let him know her situation as often as possible.

It wasn't until several minutes passed that she realized

something strange was going on.

"Sebas? Are we… traveling in the right direction?" asked Susan.

"…"

Sebas did not answer.

Now worried, Susan reached out to open the tinted glass blocking her view of the driver's seat.

"Sebas? Is everything o… kay…? Who are you?!"

The person who greeted Susan was not Sebas, but a man dressed in camo fatigues and a mask covering his face. The only thing she could see was his pale skin and dark eyes. He stared at her with a hard edge that caused Susan's heart to leap into her throat.

"Sorry, hon. But Sebas is no longer with us, but don't you worry, I'll be your chauffeur from now on."

Susan scrambled back and reached for the door. In the back of her mind, she knew it was no use. The vehicle was moving, but her instincts told her that she needed to get away from this man now. Yet before her hand could touch the door, a thick mist seeped in through the limo's ventilation system.

Limousines like hers came with an advanced ventilation system that was designed to remove harmful bacteria and properly ventilate cigarette smoke to avoid stinking up the vehicle. That same system was now backfiring on Susan. Instead of preventing harmful substances from getting in, it was being used to vent those substances into the limo.

Susan felt her eyes grow droopy. She struggled to stand up, but her legs wobbled as the strength began leaving them. It wasn't long before she had fallen back onto the couch. Her head tilted left to right. Her eyes fluttered rapidly as she struggled to remain awake, but it was no use, and darkness soon engulfed her.

When next Susan woke up, she found herself disoriented. It felt like everything in her mind was jumbled together and her body felt like led. It took her several minutes just to become fully alert.

She almost wished she hadn't.

"Are you finally awake, Princess?" asked a gruff voice to her left.

Susan shrieked, but it was muffled, and she soon realized the cause. Her mouth had been covered with a thick cloth and there was something lodged inside to prevent her from speaking. Her arms and legs were similarly bound. She was also lying on her side.

The man who had spoken wore a mask and fatigues just like the other man, but he wore dark blue colors instead of camo. A gun of some sort sat across his legs. She didn't recognize it. Susan was not interested in guns. But she didn't need to recognize what a weapon was to know that she was in danger.

Tears formed in her eyes.

"Now, now. There's no need to cry. We ain't bad guys. Heh heh. We're just delivering you to your new husband. Some rich brat is paying an awful lot of money for you. Guess that makes you a hot commodity. Ain't you a lucky girl?"

The man spoke with an accent. She thought he might be from Boston, but in her panicked state of mind, she could only register the accent as a side note.

She quickly struggled to remove her bonds, but it was no use. Her arms were tied behind her back in such a way that she couldn't move them. The ropes binding her legs were so tight it felt like they were cutting off her circulation.

"Hey! Stop squirming! You want me to blow out that pretty brain of yours?!" the man shouted when she accidentally kicked him. Susan froze when the muzzle of a gun was pointed at her head.

"Oi. Don't threaten the merchandise. We're being paid a lot of money to deliver her unharmed," said the driver. She recognized his voice. It was the man who had been driving her limousine.

Sebas...

Susan choked back a sob as something inside of her snapped. For some reason, she couldn't help but think of her butler, who had been with her for as long as she could remember. He was like a second father to her.

Now he was gone.

Whoever these people were, it was clear they had killed Sebas.

She didn't know how long the drive lasted, but Susan was somehow able to observe more of her situation through her panic. There were a total of six people in this vehicle with her. Each of them wore different colored fatigues and carried different weapons. They were a ragtag group. Probably mercenaries.

Mercenaries had been used a lot during World War III. Most of them had been hired by third-world countries, which had weak militaries and therefore not a strong enough force to protect themselves. Those same countries were absorbed after the war and no longer existed. Thus, mercenaries were no longer needed.

Or so the world thought.

Plenty of nobles used mercenaries as part of their private militia. They were called private security forces, but Susan didn't delude herself into believing they were anything less than an army. Her father was a strong advocate against letting nobles have such a force. He often told her that the nobles shouldn't need such a force because they had entered an age of peace.

The vehicle she was in eventually stopped. Susan was jolted out of her reverie as the doors opened and everyone stepped out. The doors closed again, leaving her in darkness.

Left to her own thoughts, Susan's mind became overwhelmed with fear.

What was going to happen to her?

Who were these people?

Who hired them to kidnap her?

Her mind looped over and over again, asking these questions as various scenarios played out in her head, each one more horrifying than the last. She felt trapped. She felt helpless. She felt like the entire world was conspiring against her.

Was this because she had decided she didn't want to marry Connor Sword?

Was this the world's way of punishing her?

As she struggled to contain her tears, the door suddenly opened and the man who had been sitting next to her leaned in.

"Time to go, Princess. You're gonna meet your new husband."

No... I don't want this! No!

Susan backed away as much as she could, but her back soon ran into the vehicle's other door.

"There ain't no use trying to escape. Just give up and make things easier for me."

The man climbed in and grabbed her leg. Susan's shriek was muffled. Her feet were bound, but she still managed to lash out. A loud crack echoed around the vehicle as her feet slammed into the man's mask. His head snapped back, but then he tilted it back down and glared at her.

Susan shuddered.

"That does it! Fucking little twat! Screw what the boss says! I'm gonna teach you a lesson!"

The man grabbed her legs again, his grip like a vice. It hurt. Susan struggled more. She screamed and tried to fight, but the man's grip grew tighter and tighter as he dragged her over to him.

Someone... please! Anyone! Help!

Susan could do nothing more than scream in her mind, praying for a miracle.

And then a miracle occurred.

Several sounds echoed from outside, followed by even more sounds. The man froze. Susan was so terrified that she couldn't figure out what the sounds were, but then someone outside shouted, "We're under attack!"

"Tch!"

The man who had been grabbing her clicked his tongue as he let go of her legs, grabbed his rifle, unlatched the safety, and stepped outside.

He fell to the ground a second later.

Susan could only blink in shock.

What was happening?

***

Adam was able to put three of the six men down before the rest were able to find cover. One of those men was the guy who had been hurting Susan. Adam had wanted to kill him first, but he thought it would have been traumatic for the girl if he shot the guy while he was still inside. Nothing could be more frightening for a normal person than having a bleeding corpse fall on top of you.

Since he was unable to kill the remaining three from this position, Adam decided to get in close. He holstered his pistol and, still crouching, ran across the grounds in a wide arc that let him avoid the enemies' line of sight.

The three men were huddled against the other side of the vehicle. They looked from around the cover, trying to locate him. It was clear they only had a general idea of where he'd been shooting from. All they had to do was look at how the bodies of their comrades had fallen to at least get a direction.

Too bad he was already behind them.

"Do you see 'em?" asked one of them. It was the one with the oscillation knife. He was holding the weapon in a reverse grip.

"No. I didn't even see the flash from their gun. They must be using a suppressor," said the leader. He gripped the assault rifle firmly in his hands and peered out from behind the vehicle.

"Dammit! I thought this was going to be an easy job! Everything was going so smoothly!" another complained.

"Now Biggs, Wedge, and Jake are gone. Shit. Whoever's attacking us is obviously a pro."

"Stop bitching and help me find this fucker," the leader snapped.

Adam waited for one second longer and, just as the group looked out to try and spot him, he made his move.

The first to die was the one wielding the knife. That was the most dangerous weapon in close quarters. Adam rushed in behind him and jabbed his own knife into the man's neck, just about even with the Adam's apple. His attack cut the carotid artery. Blood gushed from the wound as he removed his knife and the man fell back with a dull thud.

He would bleed out in five to fifteen seconds.

The others proved their experience by turning around barely a second after Adam stabbed the man. They aimed their weapons at him, but Adam leaped into the air and landed on top of the vehicle.

Both remaining mercenaries tried to track him, but Adam threw his knife, impaling the man holding a pistol in the forehead. Such an attack would normally not do much damage, especially since this man was wearing a metal-reinforced mask. Adam's knife went through easily, however. It was a testament to the strength he could bring to bear.

"Shit! Shit, shit, shit!"

The remaining man shouted. He was the one Adam singled out as the leader of this group. He held his finger on the trigger, firing at Adam, who landed on the ground and outran the bullets with his superhuman strength.

A clicking noise soon echoed around them.

The gun was out of bullets.

"Fuck! Dammit! Fucking dammit!"

The man threw his weapon aside and tried to pull out a secondary weapon, but Adam slammed into him before that happened. He whacked the man in the temple with the butt of his knife. The mercenary dropped like a sack of bricks.

Adam quickly pulled some rope from inside his suit and used it to bind the man's arms and legs. Then he contacted his group.

"I've killed all the enemies but one. Get someone out here to interrogate him. I'm going to check on Susan."

"Roger that. Good job."

The communication ended and Adam moved around to the vehicle's other side. The door was already open. Susan was at the other end with her back pressed against the wall. She tried to move even further back as he climbed in.

"Relax, you're safe now," Adam said.

But Susan either hadn't heard him or was too frightened to register his words. Her muffled scream was the very definition of terrified.

I guess... there's no choice.

With a sigh, Adam removed his helmet, revealing his face to Susan.

"Su, it's me. Adam."

Susan stopped the moment he removed his mask. She seemed stunned. Of course she was, he thought. Not only was this their first time meeting in the real world, but this was also the first time she was seeing his face. He had never shown it to her before now.

"You probably can't recognize my face, but you should recognize my voice," Adam said. Susan nodded. "I'm going to untie you now. Just hang on."

Adam used his knife to cut the binds on her legs, then her arms. He reached up, about to undo the binds on her mouth, but Susan lunged at him the moment she was free.

"Su! Hey, I still need to remove... oh..."

Adam lost his words as Susan bawled into his chest. Her voice was muffled, but her cries were clear. She was a very kind and innocent girl. Even though her father was a prominent figure, she had probably never been actively targeted like this since it generally wasn't worth incurring the wrath of a man like Eugine Forebear. It was only natural she would be frightened out of her mind.

And so Adam said nothing. He wrapped his arms around Susan's tiny body and allowed the woman to stain his clothing in her tears.

A FAMILY

REUNITED

SUSAN HAD FALLEN ASLEEP ON HIS LAP.

Adam could do nothing but stare helplessly at the young woman sleeping on him as though he was a giant pillow. He had attempted to set her down, but as if she could sense what he was doing, Susan had latched onto him like a leech. She was stronger than she looked too. It was strength fueled by desperation. Adam eventually gave up and let the brunette sleep on him.

Still, this is awkward...

To make himself more comfortable, Adam was sitting on the rear chair and had adjusted the back to have a slight incline. Susan's head rested on his shoulders and her legs hung off his lap. He was running his hands though her hair because she seemed to like it. Her body would tense whenever he stopped, so continued this action as he waited for Asteroth to arrive.

"Master," someone said from outside the van.

It was Asteroth. The man in charge of interrogating captives. He was middle-aged, had brown hair flecked with gray around the sideburns, and a few wrinkles lining his face.

This man was the oldest among all those who had been trained by Lucifer. He had also been Adam's instructor in the way of killing.

Adam possessed a great deal of respect for this man.

"Asteroth, I'm glad you made it. I need help," Adam said.

"I can see that, though I'm not sure how you want me to help you with this," Asteroth chuckled.

Adam scowled. "Not with this. I need you to interrogate the man I captured. He's around the other side."

Asteroth was the only one among those who survived Eden that had a playful side. He sometimes enjoyed cracking jokes at the expense of others, especially Adam. Perhaps that was why Adam kept him around. The ability to joke in a high-tension situation was invaluable for many reasons.

"I understand. I'll interrogate the man who kidnapped Susan."

"Be sure to take him further away. I don't want Susan waking up to screaming."

"Of course."

Asteroth vanished from the open doorway. Adam heard the sound of his footsteps, followed by a pause, and then the sound of something being dragged across the ground.

"Hssssssss… haaaaaah… hssssssss… haaaaaaaah…"

Adam blinked as Susan tensed, her breathing suddenly heavy. He realized he had stopped stroking her hair, so he started up again, sighing in relief as the young woman settled down.

With nothing to do but wait, Adam pondered the people who had kidnapped Susan. He didn't want to theorize who the mastermind behind this was without solid evidence. At the same time, he couldn't

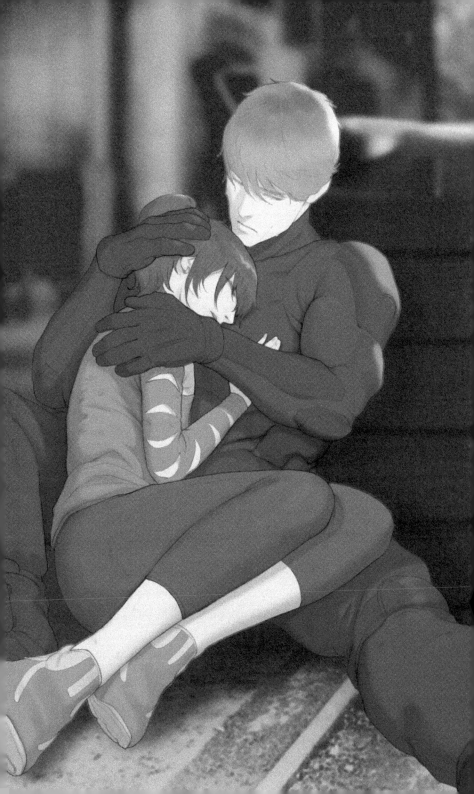

help but wonder if Connor Sword might be the one who orchestrated the kidnapping. He had the power, the influence, and the connections to do it.

But it's possible whoever kidnapped her wants us to think that way. Much as I want to blame him, there's still no guarantee he's the one responsible.

Asteroth returned before Susan woke up. He knelt before the entrance, his head bowed.

"What did you find out?" asked Adam.

"As we've already surmised, the man was hired to kidnap Susan. The person who employed him is a woman named Catherine Herring."

"A name I don't know. Haaah. Very well. I want you to find out what you can about Catherine Herring. We need to work fast. I suspect she's just a frontman for the true mastermind. Also, is the cleanup crew already here?"

"They shall be here in less than five minutes."

"Good," Adam nodded, then paused. "Did you come in a car?"

"I did."

"Give me the keys. I want you to take the motorcycle back."

Adam tossed the keys to his bike at Asteroth, who caught the keys before giving him the ones to the car he drove here in. The man soon vanished. Adam remained silent for a moment before sighing and looking at the girl on his lap.

"You can stop pretending to be asleep now."

Susan slowly opened her eyes, looking abashed as she stared at his face. Her pink cheeks made her quite fetching.

"How did you know I was awake?"

"It's easy to tell when someone is awake based on how they are breathing. I knew the moment you woke up."

Susan had woken up shortly after Asteroth had returned from his interrogation. Adam hadn't said anything.

"Um… I'm sorry."

"It's fine."

"But… you don't want anyone to know about, uh, who you are, right?"

Susan squirmed in his lap as Adam studied her. She was a smart girl, so she must have a few guesses as to his identity, though whether she realized he was a former assassin was still up in the air. He was certain she had at least realized he was someone who operated under the radar.

"You're right. I don't want people knowing about me. The more people who know I exist, the harder it will be to hide myself from people like Levon Pleonexia." Susan flinched, but Adam smiled as he gently stroked her head. "But I've decided to trust you. You're already helping me, right? How can I ask for your assistance if I'm not willing to extend my trust to you?"

Partnerships on any level required a certain amount of trust. If you could not trust the person you were working with, it would make accomplishing your goals more difficult. That was why Adam had extended his trust to Fayte as well. He had allowed her to listen in on his conversation with Aris that night when he told her about Alexis.

"… Thank you for trusting me," Susan said after a short pause.

"You are welcome. In either event, I really need to get you home. I'm sure your father is worried about you."

Adam slid an arm under Susan's legs and another around her back. The timid woman squeaked when he lifted her into a princess carry.

"I-I can walk on my own," Susan murmured.

Adam shrugged. "You probably can, but there's no need to be shy now. You've been sleeping on my lap for the past two hours. Sticking close a little longer won't hurt."

Susan's cheeks turned a shade so vibrant that Adam thought they were glowing in the dark. He now understood why some men enjoyed teasing timid women like Susan. Their reactions were adorable.

The car Asteroth had used to drive here was a Z-69 Subaru. While it was a nicer car than the average income family could afford, it was unassuming enough that no one would suspect it belonged to a group of former assassins.

Adam tapped the bottom with his foot, unlatching the passenger side door, which hissed as it opened upward instead of out. He placed Susan gently on the seat and closed the door as she strapped herself in. Then he went around the other side, entered the vehicle, and started it up. A soft whine echoed around them as he flipped several switches to engage the CO-O8 engine.

As he drove out of the parking lot, he spoke to Susan without turning his head. "You should probably call your father to let him know you're safe. I imagine he's out of his mind with worry right now."

"Oh. You're right. I'll do that now—uh... where is my phone?"

Adam cursed as he realized he'd forgotten to grab Susan's phone. With a sigh, he pulled back into the driveaway, got out, and grabbed Susan's phone. He also grabbed his helmet and placed it back on his head. Adam might have decided to trust Susan with his identity, but he didn't want her father or anyone else to learn about him.

He handed it to her after he sat back down. The girl scrolled through her list of contacts as he drove out of the parking lot once more. They passed a large gray van on the way here. He nodded at the familiar face in the driver's seat.

"Hello, Father—" Susan began after making the call.

"Susan?! Is that you?! Oh, thank God you're safe! I didn't know what to do when your location suddenly vanished from the app! Are you okay?!"

Most people in this day and age used phone apps to track the location of their family members. It was an extra security measure many people implemented to ensure the safety of their loved ones, though not everyone used it. Some people thought it was a gross violation of privacy. It was clear that Susan's father was not one of those people—and with good reason given what just happened.

"I'm okay, Father. Sorry for worrying you."

"What happened?!"

Susan did her best to explain what happened over the phone, but it was difficult for the poor girl. Eugine kept interrupting the girl with startled exclamations and cries of despair. Adam could feel the sweat building up on his forehead just listening to this man. It was no wonder Susan was such a meek girl. Her father was quite possibly the most doting man in the entire world.

"So you're coming home?"

"Yes. Ad—I mean, the friend who rescued me is driving me home right now."

"Very well. I will wait for you outside."

"Th-there's no need for that, Father. It's very late."

"Nonsense! My daughter who was kidnapped is being returned to me! How can I sleep at a time like this?! I will be outside! See you soon!"

"Father! But—"

Susan was unable to get a word in edgewise as the call ended. She stared helplessly at her phone.

Adam chuckled. "Your father loves you very much."

"Sometimes… I feel like he loves me too much," Susan confessed with an embarrassed smile. "Don't get me wrong. I love my father with all my heart, but… I feel guilty because of how much he dotes on me."

"I can see how that might be a problem."

Eugine gave his daughter whatever she wanted. While some might grow up spoiled from being treated this way, Susan had grown soft and meek. She was unable to tell her father not to waste money on her. At the same time, she felt guilty that he gave her whatever she asked for, and even things she didn't ask for. That was also why she never went against her father when he wanted something from her.

"It's hard to say no when you are treated with such kindness and don't feel like you deserve it," Susan confessed. Then she smiled. "But… I do feel like I am getting better. Just the other day, I told Father I didn't want to marry Connor Sword, and he agreed to cancel our marriage talks."

"Oh? That's good. I'm glad you were able to tell your father how you felt about Connor. He's not a very good man."

"I agree. I don't have any proof, but there are just so many rumors about the way he treats women. The fact that they all get swept under the rug has made me suspicious of him."

Adam had not known this, and now that he did, Connor Sword had risen to the top of his list of potential suspects behind Susan's kidnapping.

"Um… Adam?" Susan began as they drove across Queensboro Bridge. It was still late, so the waters below were so dark as to be invisible.

"Yes?"

"… No… never mind."

Adam didn't look away from the window, but he did glance at Susan out of the corner of his eye. She was blushing. Even the tips of her ears were red. He wondered what she was thinking about, but he didn't want to push the girl into answering after what she had been through.

It took another fifteen minutes to reach Susan's house, though calling her mansion a house was a misnomer if there ever was one. The massive, four-story building spanned several acres of land and contained at least three wings.

This place had once been the location of many tall skyscrapers. Those had been destroyed during the bombings in World War III. Eugine had paid many contractors to clear out this space and built his estate atop it. This had happened after his inauguration as one of the American Federation's leading politicians.

A man stood outside in nothing but his expansive silk pajamas, shivering from the cold. Adam could only imagine he'd been there for the past half an hour it took them to reach her home. The color of his hair was just like Susan's, but his face was masculine. He had sky-blue eyes, a refined goatee, and was a little on the heavy side.

"Suuuuuu!" The man was sobbing as he threw himself at the young woman mere moments after she emerged from the car. "My little girl has returned! Oh! I'm so grateful!"

"F-Father… I… I…"

Her father's emotions must have caused her own to boil over once more, for she latched onto her father and began crying seconds later. Her wails might have been even louder than after Adam had rescued her.

Adam stood off to the side and awkwardly watched the bawling pair. He glanced at the sky. The twinkling stars spread across the black canvas, but the dull light of the sun was beginning to shine from the east, signifying the start of a new day.

EVERYONE
LOVES PANCAKES

ADAM ARRIVED HOME IN THE EARLY MORNING, just as the sun was beginning to rise. He wasn't tired despite having stayed up all night—at least, not physically. His mentality was a different story.

Eugine Forebear had been far too enthusiastic about repaying his debt to Adam. He had offered all kinds of rewards, from staying the night to marrying his daughter to offering Adam untold riches. That second offer had caused poor Susan to blush from the roots of her hair all the way to her chest.

The ding of the elevator snapped Adam out of his stupor. He exited after the door slid open, walked down the hallway, and entered the apartment room.

"I'm home," he said to no one in particular. It was late, and he was certain Fayte and Aris were asleep.

"Welcome back."

That was why he felt surprised when someone answered him.

After removing his shoes and setting them aside, he walked into the living room to find Fayte sitting on the couch. He thought she was alone at first. Then he saw Aris sleeping with her head on Fayte's thighs. The blonde woman was stroking the brunette's hair. Adam wondered if the woman realized she looked like an older sister doting on her younger sibling.

"I didn't expect you to still be up. Couldn't sleep?" asked Adam as he wandered into the kitchen.

"How can you expect me to sleep with the current circumstances?" Fayte asked back.

"I suppose... I can't," Adam acknowledged.

He opened a cabinet, pulled out two cups, and set about making coffee. Fayte had a very nice coffee maker that didn't require much effort. Just place a pod inside the machine and let it do its thing. The coffee took less than five minutes to prepare, and then he was bringing both cups into the living room.

"Thank you," Fayte said as he set a cup down in front of her.

"You're welcome," Adam replied with an easygoing smile.

He sat down and sighed as he allowed all the tension to drain from his muscles. Adam had been very high-strung ever since he learned Susan had been kidnapped. Now that the situation had been resolved, his body felt like jello.

"Also... thank you for saving Susan," Fayte added in a soft voice. "That girl means more to me than anyone else in the world. I'm... I'm very grateful to you."

Adam pretended not to hear the hitch in her voice or the tears in her eyes. Fayte liked to act strong in front of others. That was how she had survived this long in a world where women like her were used as pawns to form alliances through marriage. He took a sip of his coffee, sighing as he realized it tasted better when Fayte prepared it.

I don't understand. She doesn't do anything differently, so why does it taste so much better when she makes it?

"It was no trouble. Susan has become important to me too. She's a member of our group. I wasn't about to let someone take her away from us," Adam said.

Fayte smiled at him. Her tears had dried. Unlike Susan, who had bawled her heart out and clung to him after her rescue, this woman did no such thing.

A long silence that was neither uncomfortable nor stifling passed between them. Adam considered telling Fayte what he knew about the kidnapping, but he currently didn't have any info on the kidnappers themselves.

However, he did have a name.

"Does the name Catherine Herring ring any bells?" he asked.

"I'm afraid not." Fayte shook her head as she set down her now empty mug and shook her head. "Why do you ask?"

"The person who kidnapped Susan said he was hired by a woman named Catherine Herring," Adam admitted.

Fayte frowned. She began stroking Aris's hair again. Adam wondered if it was an unconscious gesture that helped calm her down. If so, this woman was more like Adam than either of them realized.

"The name doesn't ring any bells, but it's possible the name is just an alias," Fayte said.

Adam nodded. "I considered that possibility, but I don't think it's likely."

"Can you tell me why?"

"Because mercenaries are cautious people. They have to be in this day and age where they're basically considered criminals."

Mercenaries might have been widely used back in World War III, but after the war, their use was banned and anyone caught hiring them was sentenced to life imprisonment and slave labor. The mercenaries themselves would follow the one who hired them. Any merc worth their weight in gold would do an extensive background check on whoever wanted to hire them before accepting a job.

"If nothing else, I believe Catherine Herring is a real person," Adam continued, only to pause. "Of course, I don't expect this woman to be the one who ordered the kidnapping. She's most likely a middleman."

"So her purpose is to hide the true kidnapper's identity," Fayte said.

"Yes."

"Can you find out who was responsible?"

"I'm going to try my best, but I suspect I'll hit a dead end. Whoever wanted Susan has to be a fairly powerful individual with a lot of influence, and people don't become influential or powerful by being stupid. I'm certain whoever did it will have covered their tracks well."

"I see. Well, at least Susan is safe."

"For now," Adam added to Fayte's blanket statement.

Adam didn't think this would be the last time someone tried to kidnap Susan, but they wouldn't try something again for a while. Eugine Forebear would now be on guard for any potential kidnappers. He suspected the man would also place several restrictions on Susan's movement and who could see her.

She probably won't be allowed to go outside for a while.

Adam glanced at the sleeping Aris, then smiled wryly as he said, "I should probably put that one to bed."

"I would appreciate that. My legs are going numb," Fayte admitted with a wry smile of her own.

Adam scooped Aris into his arms and carried her like a princess to their room. He needed to use his toes to pull back the covers, but he soon set Aris on the bed, then crawled in himself. Aris, as if sensing his presence, rolled over onto her side and wrapped an arm and leg around him. He almost chuckled when she hooked her leg around his.

It took him some time to fall asleep, but darkness did eventually consume him. It only felt like he had slept for a few seconds before he was woken up again by the sound of his phone vibrating in his pocket. He must have forgotten to place it on the charger.

"Astaroth? What do you have for me?" asked Adam after accepting the call.

"We sought out the woman called Catherine Herring," Astaroth began without preamble. *"She is not located in New York City. She owns a small house outside city limits. Belial took a team to confront her, but…"*

"She was dead when you arrived?" Adam asked.

Aris shifted against him, crawling over his body until she was pressing her entire front against his chest. He stifled a smile to focus on his conversation with Astaroth.

"She wasn't even there."

Adam closed his eyes for a moment and pondered that. There were only a few reasons Catherine would not be at this location if she lived there, and none of them were good.

"Are there any social cameras in the area?" he asked.

"There are, and we checked them. According to the social cameras, Catherine arrived at her home at exactly 1500 yesterday. Our research indicates she works the morning shift at a convenience store on Greenpoint Avenue and Kingsland. She never left her house during that time. However, there was a brief period of five minutes when the social cameras shut off. It took some effort to discover this. Whoever shut off the cameras made it so those five minutes looped."

The social cameras contained advanced security measures to prevent tampering, which meant whoever had tampered with them was either a master at hacking or had government aid. Either one of those was bad for them.

Creating a repeating loop within a social camera was done when someone wanted to enact a covert operation. It was a standard procedure for anyone who wanted to accomplish an objective that was against the law… such as assassinating someone who had become a liability.

"Was there any evidence that she had been assassinated?"

"Negative."

Adam gnawed on his lower lip. "Meaning either the people responsible for her assassination are pros like us, or she was never assassinated to begin with and Catherine Herring is just an alias. Either way, it looks like investigating further will prove fruitless."

"I concur."

The world of intelligence gathering was a constant battle between people trying to gather intel and those trying to hide it. Sadly, the ones trying to hide something often held the initiative. While that didn't mean much if the person in question was careless, it would prove fruitless to the opposing side if the person they were trying to gather intel on was an expert at covering their tracks.

Yet even covering their tracks like this gave Adam several ideas as to the identity of this person.

"Whoever was responsible for this not only has a lot of power, but either has access to the underworld, government aid, or both," Adam said at last.

The underworld was what they called the world of crime. No matter the laws, no matter the era, crime would always exist so long as humans continued to exist. There were many people who did not care for society's laws. Murderers, thieves, spies, rapists. It was impossible to remove people like that forever. Even if you went around and killed every criminal in the world, more would just appear to take their place eventually.

"In other words, a noble," Astaroth said.

"Yes, a noble." Adam paused for a moment to gather his wits about him. "I'd like you to create two teams. Send one to investigate the criminal underworld for signs of activity that could provide a lead to Susan's would-be kidnapper. The other should investigate the American Federation's government."

"It shall be as you command," Asteroth said before hanging up.

Adam sighed as he set his phone on the charging stand. Susan might have been saved, but that didn't mean their problems had ended. He needed to figure out who had tried to kidnap her, which meant utilizing the Soul Reapers in the real world.

Soul Reapers always acted in squads of four. One person gathered intelligence, one person watched the intelligence agent from afar in case they needed rescue, another acted as general support, and the last acted as either a bodyguard or body double depending on the situation. This was how they managed to avoid getting caught for so long.

To further ensure their success and safety, all of them were masters of disguise and had several IDs they could use to throw anyone off their trail. These IDs were technically real. The people in the IDs did exist. They were just no longer of this world, their identities subsumed by the Soul Reapers.

If there was any information to be found, they would find it.

"It sounds like you're dealing with something serious," a voice said.

Adam looked down to find doe-like blue eyes staring at him. He reached out and stroked Aris's hair. It was soft like silk, parting as he threaded his fingers through it. Aris hummed contentedly.

"It's not polite to listen in on a private conversation," Adam teased.

Aris grinned. "Hee-hee. If you really didn't want me listening, you would have said something when I woke up." Her grin left. "Do you think Susan is still in danger?"

"She's not in any immediate danger," Adam confessed. "But yes, she is still in danger. I doubt whoever attempted to kidnap her will give up."

"Is there anything we can do to protect her? I don't want my friend getting kidnapped again," Aris said.

"There's nothing we can do right now," Adam said with a sigh as Aris began drawing circles on his chest. "Whoever kidnapped her will go off the radar for now. I doubt even the Soul Reapers will find anything right away. But I'll have my people infiltrate the dregs of society so that when the kidnapper makes another attempt, we'll catch them in the act."

That was Adam's plan for now. Infiltrate the criminal underworld, gather information on the most likely candidates for someone looking to hire a kidnapper, and watch them for any signs of someone contacting them to kidnap Susan. They would need to be fast. Once someone made contact and hired them, the Soul Reapers would have to act even before the kidnapping attempt occurred to trace the middleman back to the real culprit before they could remove all the evidence.

An operation like this could take months or even years.

He sighed.

This would cut down the Soul Reapers' efficiency within the game by at least thirty percent.

As Adam lamented the loss of his forces' prowess in *Age of Gods*, a loud gurgling erupted from the young woman lying on top of him. He blinked. Then he looked down at Aris, who stared at him with those imploring eyes of hers.

He sighed several seconds later.

"I'll go make us some breakfast," he said at last.

"Yay! I want pancakes."

"Pancakes it is."

RECRUIT-
MENT DRIVE

HE STARED AT THE OBJECT RESTING ON A PEDESTAL BEYOND THE
WINDOW.

The window itself was quite thick. It wasn't made of glass either.
He had created this window by mixing a variety of substances that
couldn't be produced by anyone but him. It blocked out all forms of
energy and radiation.

Given the amount of energy the object was radiating, such
precautions were necessary.

"How are the energy readings?" he asked.

"Energy readings are fluctuating, but they are within our
expectations. There's no danger of The Arch overloading," someone
said. It was one of the workers sitting at a computer station. The
holographic monitor before him displayed all kinds of information.
Even though the way he rapidly typed on the computer made him
seem lively, his eyes were dead like a corpse's.

He nodded. "Good. Good. And how's the time compression process coming along?"

"Proceeding smoothly."

"How much energy did it use up?"

"It used up more than ninety percent of the energy we gathered from players."

"Ninety percent." He sighed. "Meaning I am still far from my goal. Well, that's fine. That's fine. The game has just started, after all, and my plans are nowhere near finished. Continue the operation."

"Yes, sir."

***

Twice a year, the Pleonexia Alliance held a recruitment drive to bring fresh blood into their guild. The drive was held at the same place every time.

Belphegor woke up early that morning and made his way to a place called South Cove. It was located on the tip of what had once been Lower Manhattan, past the now-destroyed Chinatown.

This place used to contain several memorials and museums, but those had been destroyed during the bombings in World War III. The Pleonexia Family had bought the area at some point. Now it was used by their guild to recruit new people who would be placed in various positions within the guild.

Belphegor stood within the sea of people. Despite being surrounded on all sides, with people jockeying around to get a better position as if that would somehow give them an advantage, Belphegor remained untouched. He casually dodged bodies with ease. It was like he was a ghost.

He was in the middle of this massive tide of humanity. Near the front, toward the tip of the straight just before the Diamond Reef was a platform upon which a dozen people stood.

These people were middle management and in charge of recruiting. While they weren't important in the grand scheme of things, Belphegor still made sure to memories their names, along with their hobbies, interests, likes, dislikes, what kind of foods they ate, and even their morning routines. Thanks to Belial's intelligence, he knew everything there was to know about the group in charge of allowing new members to join.

"I can hardly wait to show these people what I'm made of! I'm sure to impress them with my incredible talent!" someone to his left suddenly said.

"Ha! You think you're talented? Bitch, you've only just reached level 12 in *Age of Gods*. I'm already close to reaching level 14."

"That's because you joined a smaller guild! I worked my butt off all by myself! That's way more impressive!"

"As if! I suppose we'll just have to leave it to the judges to decide."

"Bring it on!"

Belphegor sighed as he listened to these people get into a dick-fighting contest. Why so many humans felt the need to compete against each other was beyond him. It was a huge waste of time.

"Settle down, everyone!" one of the people said into a microphone that was attached to several speakers hovering in the sky.

The person who spoke was older than most. He had gray hair, wrinkles around his eyes, and stood with a stoop. His name was Kalvin Hobbs. He was sixty years old, but he would turn sixty-one next month. Not only was he the oldest among the recruiters, but he had worked for the Pleonexia Family since before Levon took over it.

Out of all the people present, he was the one Belphegor wanted to impress the most.

The group of people quieted down.

"Excellent. My name is Kalvin Hobbs, and I'm in charge of recruitment. Behind me are my assistants, who will be helping me determine which among you are good enough to join the Pleonexia Alliance."

No one said anything, but many of the people present shifted on the balls of their feet, listening with anticipation.

"The Pleonexia Alliance has a long and storied history. Our group rose from the ashes of the American Federation in the wake of World War III and have helped rebuild this nation from the ground up. As the most powerful guild within the American Federation, we only accept the best and the brightest into our ranks. I can see there are at least several thousand of you here, but only several hundred will be selected to join. If you fail to join now, don't worry. You can wait for another six months and try again, or you can always join one of the branch guilds."

Due to their size and strength, the Pleonexia Alliance had the right to be picky with who they recruited. Belphegor had done his research. Only one to two hundred people were chosen per recruitment drive out of the tens of thousands who participated.

"Now, then. Allow me to explain the test for those of you who are participating for the first time. There are three trials you must complete. The first trial is a written test. This test will ask a number of questions about different scenarios you may find yourselves in as part of the Pleonexia Alliance. It's designed to see your problem-solving skills and deductive reasoning. The second test is a physical examination. Because we are more than just a guild that plays video games, there will be times when you must use your physical body to accomplish a task. We want to make sure you are healthy enough to complete the tasks required of you. The third trial will be to compete against one of our members in a duel within a virtual simulator that has been created based on *Age of Gods*. I'll warn you now, all of our members are experts who have reached level 17 in *Age of Gods*. You won't have an easy time fighting against them."

Several people gulped. Belphegor could only assume most of these people were still at level 15 and below. He had reached level 18 by the time *Age of Gods* shut down to implement its new time compression system.

"If you're all ready, then I want you to form twelve lines. Remember to have your documents prepared. We don't accept anyone who doesn't have proper documentation," Kalvin said.

Belphegor lined up with everyone else. Because he was somewhere in the middle, it took several hours before it was his turn.

He eventually reached the front. The assistant he stood before was a young woman in her early twenties. She had mousy brown hair, brown eyes, and pale skin. She looked like those unassuming librarian types, especially with the large wire-rimmed glasses sitting on her nose.

Optical technology had advanced significantly within the last ten years. Not only could a person's vision be healed with a single surgery, but it was very cheap. This woman didn't wear glasses because she needed them. It was a style she liked.

Her name was Ophelia. She was twenty-four years-old, never had a boyfriend, and her parents had died of Mortems Disease when she was fourteen. She joined the Pleonexia Alliance two years ago. Her hobbies outside of gaming were reading and playing erotic reverse harem visual novels.

She also only liked 2D men.

"Identification?" Ophelia asked.

Belphegor said nothing as he handed his identification documents over to Ophelia. She ran a scanner over the documents, which flashed red several times before lighting up green.

"You're all clear. Go wait over there," she said, handing the documents back to Belphegor.

"Understood."

Belphegor moved off to the side where several dozen people were being directed toward a building some distance away by another assistant.

The building looked like a square. It had no windows and only a single door. The interior was as bare as the exterior. Several computer stations were lined up in rows of ten. Belphegor and the others were directed to sit at the computer stations.

"The test will begin in fifteen minutes," the assistant said. He was a middle-aged man whose hair had not yet begun to gray. The shirt he wore was filled out with muscles, the fabric stretching taught across his shoulders and chest.

His name was Anton Demascus. He was thirty-five and his hobby was sleeping with women. According to Belial's report, this man had convinced several women into providing sexual favors in exchange for being let into the Pleonexia Alliance, though he was careful to never force anyone into it. That was how he managed to avoid getting arrested.

"The test is beginning now," Anton announced. "Turn on your computers and begin."

A holographic screen appeared as he turned on the computer. He typed in the basic information about himself when requested, then began going through the test.

***

"I'm so glad you're okay, Su. You can't imagine how worried I was when I realized you'd been kidnapped," Fayte said as she hugged the girl.

"I-I'm sorry for worrying you," Susan returned the hug.

"What are you apologizing for? If anything, we should be the ones saying sorry. We didn't even realize what was happening until it was too late," Aris said. She was not part of the hug, but that was only because she was waiting her turn.

Adam stood off to the side, leaning against the wall with his arms crossed as he watched the proceedings. His face was covered by a mask just like in the game.

The three of them had left early this morning and gone to Susan's house. Aris and Fayte wanted to check on their friend, worried about how she was doing after such a harrowing experience.

Adam had been reluctant to go at first, but he capitulated when Aris gave him her infamous puppy dog eyes. He couldn't deny her anything. And to be fair, he had also been worried about Susan.

"A-Adam?" Susan suddenly called out to him.

"Hmmm?" Adam looked up.

"Thanks again... for rescuing me," Susan said with flushed cheeks.

Adam smiled even though he knew Susan couldn't see it. "You're very welcome."

They were inside one of the many rooms located in the Forebear Family estate. This particular room was obviously meant for gaming. It not only contained six different holographic televisions, but there was even an advanced gaming PC—the kind that had once been used for gaming before the age of virtual reality. Adam couldn't figure out the make. It was clear from the various parts visible beyond the glass panel that it was a custom creation.

Su probably made it herself.

It was December 31, the last day of the year, and the last day

Age of Gods would be down. Susan had convinced her father to let him, Aris, and Fayte come over to celebrate the new year with her.

All three ladies were hardcore gamers. They not only played VR games, but they had a burning passion for old console and PC games.

Which explained why they spent the last few hours of the year competing in various games.

"All right! Time to show you what I'm made of!" Aris declared, controller in hand.

Fayte smiled. "What say we add some stakes to make this competition more interesting?"

"What do you have in mind?" asked Susan.

"Hmmm. How about the winner gets to make one request from Adam?" suggested Aris.

"And why do I have to be the one fulfilling your request?" asked Adam. He was also holding a controller. "Also, what do I get if I win?"

"Uh... you can... make a request from... yourself?"

"I'm gonna pretend you didn't say something really stupid just now."

"Hey!"

While the idea of forcing Adam to do one request from the winner was rejected, they did eventually settle on an appropriate reward for the winner, which was the winner would be able to make the losers do one thing they asked, so long as it was within reason.

Of course, Adam won.

"Uuuuuuuugh... I forgot how good Adam was," Aris moaned.

"How can you forget something like that? He beats us almost every day. I've rarely ever won against him," Fayte said.

"What should I make you girls do... I wonder," Adam pondered out loud. He wanted to diabolically rub his chin, but his mask was in the way.

"It can't be anything perverse," Fayte said.

"I don't mind if he requests something perverted," Aris admitted.

Fayte rolled her eyes. "Of course you wouldn't."

Susan just blushed.

"How about you three—" Adam began, only to pause when his phone began vibrating. He glanced at the caller ID, then sighed. "Hold on for just a moment. I'll tell you my request after I take this call."

"Don't take too long," Aris said.

Adam waved at her as he left the room, leaned against the wall, and placed the phone to his ear.

"Astaroth?"

"Master, Belphegor has successfully managed to infiltrate the Pleonexia Alliance."

"Nice. How did he do?"

"He placed in the top ten, though he made sure to hold back every test accept the physical one."

"Good. We want him to stand out, but the nail that stands out the furthest gets hit the hardest. Have they given him an official position within the guild yet?"

"Negative, but they will give him a position within the next two days. They've currently got him moving into the Pleonexia Alliance's dormitories."

"All right. Keep me posted on his situation."

"Of course."

"And how are the other two missions going?"

"Abaddon, Mammon, Beelzebub, and Abyzou have successfully infiltrated the criminal underworld. They are currently out of contact, but we are keeping taps on them. Mephisto, Andras, Baal, and Balam have all managed to get jobs within the government thanks to Susan, though it will take a while for them to rise to a high enough position to prove useful."

"That's fine. We have time. Susan's kidnappers won't make another move for a while yet. Anyway, I want bi-weekly updates on how everyone is doing. You can send them through the usual means."

"Understood."

Adam hung up, pocketed the phone, and stepped back into the game room, where Susan and Aris were competing in a game called *DDR*. It was a dancing game that involved stepping on pads timed to the rhythm of whatever song was playing on the screen. Both of them were grinning. Fayte stood off to the side and watched with a smile.

With a smile of his own, Adam closed the door and spent the rest of the new year with the three young women.

TIME COM-
PRESSION

ADAM WOKE UP AT FOUR O'CLOCK OF THE NEW YEAR. He was fully clothed, an odd turn of events considering he normally woke up naked these days. Aris had a voracious sexual appetite and would often ask him to perform all kinds of acts on her—not that he was complaining. Her libido was a good match for him.

A weight on his stomach caused him to look down, where he found Susan and Aris curled up. Aris was resting in the crook of his left arm, but Susan was lying with her head on his stomach. She was facing him as she lay on her side. Her eyelashes weren't very long. Her innocent sleeping face caused warm feelings to rise within him.

I wonder if she has some kind of esper power to make people feel the desire to protect her. Wouldn't surprise me.

Esper powers were very different from the classic magic found in video games and the fantasy stories of yore. There were some esper powers that could create elemental attacks, but most were far more bizarre, like the power to control static electricity or the ability to release pheromones. Adam had once fought an esper who could manipulate oils by breaking down and reconstructing them.

The more bizarre the power, the rarer it was.

A power like Susan's—if she did indeed have esper powers—would be considerably rare.

Shaking his head, Adam glanced at the clock once more. Barely a minute had passed. He looked around and eventually found Fayte sleeping on a couch to his left.

They had stayed up until around two o'clock. The only reason Adam had woken up after barely getting two hours of sleep was because his body didn't need much rest to function. He felt fully refreshed despite the previous night.

What should I do now? I guess I can check out Age of Gods...

The new update should have been fully installed. He wanted to see what sort of changes had been made. The device needed to log in was already around his neck, and thus he shut his eyes and logged in.

Adam materialized in the game world exactly where he had logged off—inside Destiny's Overture's guild house. Titania and Kureha were exactly where he last saw them. The young fox yokai was sleeping on the couch, her cute snores echoing around the room as she curled up into a little ball. She was somehow more adorable now that she was in her human form. Titania was sitting on the couch's armrest closest to him.

She looked up when he appeared.

"That was fast. I thought you would have spent more time in your world," Titania said.

"What are you talking about? It's been almost a week," Adam said.

Titania furrowed her brow. "You must be mistaken. It's only been a few hours since you returned to your world."

"Huh?"

"Huh?"

Adam's mind moved a mile a minute as they stared at each other.

I get it. The game must have shut down while the updates were being installed, so to her, it feels like only a bit of time has passed.

The Time Compression System extended how much time passed in the game world compared to the real world by 1:14, meaning one day in the real world was fourteen days in *Age of Gods*. It had been installed at 0000 hours. He imagined it had taken a good amount of time for the updates to finish, so the likelihood that Titania and Kureha had yet to feel the effects of the Time Compression System was quite high.

"Well... maybe it just feels like a long time to me," Adam said after a moment.

"Weirdo," Titania muttered.

"Anyway, I'd like to head out and get some training done. Would you and Kureha like to—"

Adam didn't get to finish his sentence before someone else appeared in the room. Long hair the color of midnight was tied into a ponytail on her head. Her eyes were so dark they looked black, and her pale face was covered with a mask. She wore skin-tight clothes and armor befitting her Demon Knight Assassin class.

"Lilith," Adam greeted.

"Master." Lilith paused. "I did not expect to see you so soon. I figured you would be spending this time with Aris."

"Aris is still asleep. Figured I'd check out the updates that had been made to *Age of Gods*. Anyway, I was just about to head out and do some training. Wanna join?"

"Of course, Master."

"Must we begin training so soon?" asked Titania.

"Yes," Adam said.

"It is important to train every day," Lilith added.

"Haaaaaah. Very well, but at least let me prepare myself."

They woke up Kureha, who began excitedly running around Adam when she noticed him, then made their way out of the guild house.

Adam took a deep breath as he stepped outside. The Suncrest Mountain Range loomed in front of them and a forest blocked the base of the mountain from view. Nothing had changed visually about the game world. Even the scent of grass and leaves remained the same. Adam had almost forgotten how realistic this game was, but the scent carried on the breeze, which rustled through his hair, reminded him once again that this game was as close to reality as a VR world would ever get.

With Lilith, Titania, and Kureha in tow, Adam set off toward the Suncrest Mountain Range, where they battled several monsters to refresh themselves. Adam had worried his skills in the game might have atrophied, but he found it easy to pick up right where he left off. The spear felt familiar in his hands. Not even being away for a week was enough to dull his senses.

The one thing Adam was unable to wrap his head around was the concept of compressed time. If fourteen days here equaled one day in the real world, then it meant one day in *Age of Gods* was about two hours in the real world. It was hard to conceive how such a thing was possible.

"Do you think we have time to complete a quest?" asked Adam.

Lilith tilted her head. "I do not know."

"You want to complete a quest before the others arrive? I don't think we have time," Titania said. She didn't know about the Time Compression System, so she would obviously say something like that.

"We might as well try," Adam said.

"Sure. Why not?" Titania agreed with a sigh.

***

All quests were handed out by the Guild Association. Adam headed over to the Guild Association's main headquarters in Solum, where he met with Clarise, the Guild Association in charge of Destiny's Overture, and accepted a quest.

The quest he accepted was to teach a noble's son how to wield a spear. The reason he accepted this quest even though it didn't grant him very many experience points was because the quest was located in Solum, the amount of money offered was impressive, and Adam mostly wanted to see if he could complete a quest before Aris and the others woke up.

It was a relatively easy quest. His student was a noble who lived in a mansion on the outskirts of Solum. He was a slightly arrogant but good-natured boy in his early teens, and while Adam didn't think he would ever become a master spearman, he was diligent enough to pick up the basics.

Adam did not teach him the Seven Phoenix Forms Style that was his signature, but he instilled the basics of spearmanship, which involved primarily thrusting.

Spears were one of the earliest weapons devised by man, though it was originally just a wood stick with a sharpened point. Primitive peoples used spears primarily as thrown weapons. When military practice evolved from the independent action of individuals to the group movements of masses of soldiers, the spear became a thrusting weapon.

The weapon eventually evolved further to take on several different forms. There was the pike, the lance, the axe-bladed halberd, and numerous other variations. The spear-carrying phalanx was used by the Sumerian armies. Two thousand years later, the Greeks refined the concept, using 1.8 to 2.7-meter-long pikes.

The spear the boy used was a standard kind with a pointed metal tip at the end, meaning it was meant to be used only as a thrusting weapon. Adam had the boy learn several stances that would help him put as much power into his thrusts as possible. The boy, one Michael Sunsettia, was able to pick up the basics within a single day of training.

Adam netted himself 30,000,000 gold coins from that one quest, which he placed in Destiny's Overture's treasury, to be used as a means of furthering their net worth. One of the conditions of Fayte's bet was to accrue half the Dairing Family's annual income within three years.

Sadly, 30,000,000 gold coins were just a drop in the ocean for a family like that.

"I cannot believe you completed a quest within a day. Also, where are the others? Should they not have arrived already?" asked Titania after they returned to the guild house.

Adam wasn't sure if it was a good idea to tell her how time had changed, so he shrugged. "I don't know, but I'm heading back to my world, so I'll check on them."

"You do that."

"You're leaving already, Big Brother? But we barely got to do anything," Kureha muttered, shoulders dejectedly slumping.

"We can play more when I get back. I'll also bring Aris with me, so you two can play together."

"Yay! I like Big Sis Aris!"

Once he mollified Kureha, Adam said goodbye to Lilith and Titania, then logged off *Age of Gods.*

And woke up to someone poking his cheek.

"Adaaaaaaam. Hey, Adam! You awake yet?"

"I-I don't think you should poke him like that while he's sleeping."

"Why not? I poke him all the time."

"You do?"

"Of course. One of my favorite past times is poking him like this."

"Liar," Adam said as he opened his eyes.

"Oh, so you're awake. Good morning, sleeping beauty," Aris said with a grin. She filled up most of his vision, but he could see Susan behind her, though she "eeped!" and stepped back when their eyes met.

"I wasn't asleep. I was playing *Age of Gods.*"

"How was it?" asked Fayte. She was awake as well, sitting on the couch where she'd fallen asleep.

"Interesting. I managed to complete a quest. It took a full day, but... it seems only two hours passed in the real world," he said, glancing at the clock, which now read 6:00 a.m.

"Sounds like the Time Compression System is working," Fayte muttered. She shook her head and stood up. "Anyway, why don't we all have breakfast?"

Susan called for several maids to deliver them breakfast. Adam kept his mask on when the maids arrived, but he removed it to eat. Susan had already seen his face, so there was no point hiding it from her. However, he didn't want anyone else to see his face. The only reason he was willing to show her was because he trusted Susan to keep quiet.

Adam, Aris, and Fayte left not long after breakfast. Susan looked sad to see them go, but they promised to log into *Age of Gods* when they arrived home. Eugine Forebear also saw them off despite his busy schedule.

"Thank you again for saving my daughter," he said to Adam.

They arrived home an hour later. After showering and getting changed into comfortable pajamas, the group was ready to log into *Age of Gods.*

Adam's phone vibrated before they could, however. He glanced at his phone to find Dr. Julia Sofocor had sent him a message.

"It looks like Dr. Sofocor wants to schedule a time she and her team can conduct research on the healing capsule," Adam said after reading the message. "She's sent me a list of people she'd like to join her."

"I understand," Fayte said. "Forward me the list. I'll have Susan run an extensive background check on each person to make sure they're trustworthy."

"Will do."

Adam sent the list over to Fayte, who then sent it to Susan with a request to run background checks on the people on the list. She received a reply a few seconds later. Adam was surprised since he expected Susan would have already logged into *Age of Gods.*

"Are you two ready?" asked Adam.

"You know I am," Aris said with a cheer.

"Of course. I'm excited to see what sort of changes have been made to *Age of Gods,*" Fayte added.

All three of them got comfortable on the couches. The world around them soon disappeared as they logged into *Age of Gods.*

***

The Time Compression System changed the way *Age of Gods* was played. Now that one day in the real world was the same as fourteen days in the virtual world, people had begun spending far more time in-game to gain experience, explore dungeons, take on quests, and level up.

Adam was one of those people. He woke up at 2:00 a.m. every morning and stopped only for breakfast, lunch, and dinner. All around, he probably spent close to twelve days in the virtual world.

Several problems did crop up with the Time Compression System. The biggest among them was that several people ended up losing track of time and nearly starved to death. This would have kicked up a big commotion, but luckily, the creator had already installed a solution into the game's programming. Anyone who remained in-game for more than six real-world hours was automatically logged off and couldn't log back in for another hour.

Adam avoided that by staying in-game for exactly five hours and fifteen minutes.

With the new Time Compression System, Fayte's guild had far more time to gain experience and level up than before. They had decided to change the way they did things. Working on a two-week system, they would take high-paying quests on Mondays, Wednesdays, and Fridays, then travel to instance dungeons to grind their levels and gain extra experience points on Tuesdays, Thursdays, and Saturdays.

They took Sundays off to avoid burnout.

Instance dungeons were a game concept as old as MMOs. Adam couldn't remember when the idea was first created, but it had been an MMO staple for far longer than he had been alive.

Everyone wanted to be The Hero, slay The Monster, rescue The Princess, and obtain The Magic Sword. It became clear that not everyone could be the hero when thousands of players played the same game. Before the creation of instance dungeons, it had not been unusual for players raiding the same dungeon to compete and harass each other to acquire the item drops left by monsters and dungeon bosses.

The instance dungeon fixed that by creating a new copy of a dungeon for each group that entered.

Adam had curiously asked Titania about instance dungeons in this world, wondering how the NPCs felt about them, and the answer had not really surprised him.

"After the Age of War, many people would travel into dungeons in order to acquire powerful treasures and artifacts. This led to people fighting even more. The bloodshed eventually became so bad the goddesses created dungeons that exist within a pocket dimension. Whenever someone enters a dungeon, they are entering a copy of that dungeon. When another person or party enters the same dungeon, another copy is made. In this way, the goddesses ensure that everyone can obtain whatever valuable treasures are inside."

Adam felt he should have suspected the goddesses would be woven into the creation of instance dungeons. It only made sense to include them.

Because of their higher-than-average levels, Adam and the others didn't travel to any of the already-known instance dungeons, and instead explored a dungeon they had discovered near Suncrest Pass.

Suncrest Pass was the mountain pass anyone wanting to reach the next area of the Sun Continent needed to travel through. It was littered with monsters between levels 30 and 40, making it impassable to just about everyone at the moment.

Adam was sure they could have passed through, but he wanted them to increase their level much more before heading to the next area. The monsters beyond the pass would be far more powerful if *Age of Gods* followed video game logic.

The dungeon they had discovered was located in a small, almost unnoticeable passage that branched off from the main pass. During their explorations, they had discovered a cave, which, after exploring, they had realized was an instance dungeon.

There were four different types of enemies in this instance dungeon: level 45 Elementals, level 46 Mountain Cyclops, level 49 Ravenous Slime, and the level 50 Golem.

Of the four, the hardest to defeat were the Ravenous Slimes and the Golem.

In many of the old-school RPGs of yore, slimes were the weakest of monsters—the starter monster, if you will. That was not the case here.

-100; -100; -100; -100!

Adam grimaced as he attacked the gelatinous body with several [Slash] attacks. He was not used to seeing such small damage numbers, but according to Titania's [Scan], this creature had a 90% resistance to slash and piercing damage. The only physical attack that worked well on it was blunt damage. Too bad he didn't have a blunt weapon he could use. Even if he did have one, he wasn't allowed to use anything except his spear.

Fortunately, there were other ways of dealing with this.

"Fayte!"

"I'm on it! [Wind Hammer]!"

Fayte raised her staff in the air. Wind swirled through the cave from all directions, converging on the staff and creating a tornado-shaped funnel, though it soon shifted into the shape of a hammer. With the staff firmly gripped in both hands, Fayte brought the hammer down.

-49,200!

Wind Hammer was an elemental attack, but it dealt blunt damage as well, meaning the attack was suitable for fighting slimes. Adam felt satisfaction as a large number sign floated over the Ravenous Slime. He also enjoyed the way the monster was squished flat by Fayte's attack.

Sadly, because she did the most damage, Fayte also drew the most agro.

"Retreat for now, Fayte! Aris, Lilith! With me!"

"I'm ready!" Aris shouted.

Lilith said nothing, but she darted forward with the fleet-footed quickness of her class.

Fayte retreated to the back as Adam, Aris, and Lilith attacked the creature as quickly as they could, trying to deal it enough damage to pull its agro so it wouldn't target Fayte. At the same time, Susan and Kureha peppered the monster with attacks of their own. Susan's attacks didn't do any more damage than the rest of the physical attackers. However, Kureha's magic, while not as effective as Fayte's, stole a decent amount of health.

The [Ravenous Slime] eventually stopped targeting Fayte. When that happened, they switched out with her again, let her attack, then had her retreat so they could draw its agro.

Their tactics whittled away the monster's health until it eventually died.

[Congratulations! You have defeated [Ravenous Slime]! [Ravenous Slime] has dropped the item [Slime Core] and 30,000 gold coins. +1,500,240 experience points!]

The amount of experience they earned was nowhere near enough for them to level up. They would need to find over a hundred of those if they wanted to reach the next level. At present, Adam was at level 25, Titania and Kureha were at level 27, and Aris, Fayte, Lilith, and Susan were at level 24. Those levels were the result of hours of grinding in instance dungeons like this one.

"Whew! That's another slime down!" Aris stretched her arms above her head, brought them back down, and grinned at them. "I think we're getting the hang of this."

"Well, we have been fighting [Ravenous Slimes] for quite a while now. This area is filled with them," Fayte said with a wry smile.

"I would prefer it if we fought something else... but there doesn't seem to be any other monsters in this area." Adam ran a hand through his hair.

"This particular area of the instance dungeon appears to be a slime field," Titania said as she floated over to Adam and made herself comfortable on his shoulder. "Sometimes, dungeons that have several levels like this one will only have one type of monster per level. I suspect we'll confront a different monster on the next level."

"Let's hope so. I'm getting tired of fighting slimes," Adam muttered.

"They are very difficult for physical attackers like us," Susan said. "Things would be different if we had someone with a class that let them use a war hammer. All of the DPS fighters here have classes that rely on swords and daggers. N-not that there's anything wrong with that! I didn't mean to make it sound like one of you should have chosen a different class or anything!"

"It's okay, Su. We understand you weren't criticizing us. Don't worry."

"Uuuuuuuuh."

Susan made a strange sound as Adam rubbed the girl's head. He had become much more affectionate with the young woman ever since he rescued her. He had briefly considered backing off, but the last time he tried to put some distance between them, Susan had given him these teary eyes that caused his willpower to crumble.

I feel a little uncomfortable with this, but... well, I suppose it's fine. No one seems to be bothered by it.

Well, Aris had teased him about having a little sister fetish. He wasn't sure he could deny it. Susan did feel like a younger sibling in many ways—at least, he thought she did. He imagined this was how a younger sister would act, but he would confess his idea of sibling relationships stemmed from pop media, and that probably wasn't the best indicator of how true siblings acted.

He eventually stopped rubbing the girl's head, which caused Susan to look into his face. He wasn't wearing his mask anymore. There was no point since everyone already knew what he looked like, and this was an instance dungeon, so it wasn't like anyone else would be coming here.

He looked away.

"How much time has passed?" he asked Fayte.

"Let's see…" Fayte ran some quick math in her head. "It's been about twelve hours since we entered the dungeon, which means it's been about one hour in our world."

Adam nodded. "Then I think we can continue exploring for another two hours. Let's find the entrance to the next level. Then we can take a break before continuing."

"Sounds like a plan," Fayte agreed.

As they were prepared to move out, Kureha tugged on Adam's pant leg. He looked down to find the young fox yokai staring at him with big eyes.

"Big brother, will you carry me on your back?"

"Sure."

"Yay!"

Adam knelt down and let the girl climb onto his back, then hitched his hands underneath her thighs and stood up. Kureha was light. He barely felt her weight on his back as they began traveling.

Sadly, he did have to set her down as they ran into more slimes.

She pouted, but there was nothing he could do.

Fourteen [Ravenous Slimes] and several hours later, they finally located the entrance to the next level.

"Finally… we can take a break. I'm starving!" Aris exclaimed as she dropped to the ground. She looked imploringly at Adam. "Feed me?"

"Hang on. I need to setup the tent. Fayte?"

"I'll get out the food," Fayte said with a soft chuckle.

One of the more interesting facets of the Time Compression System was that players were now required to eat in-game. It was odd. Their game avatars experienced hunger just like their real bodies, but when they logged out, the hunger would vanish. Adam wasn't sure of the mechanics behind this. He wondered if there was a program in the game that caused their avatars to function more realistically.

I suspect they do. Our bodies even need to use the restroom now.

That was one of the downsides to this game. Adam had discovered within the first day of playing that his body now functioned exactly like his real body, right down to how he needed to use the restroom after digesting his food.

They soon set up camp. Adam opened a tent, Fayte brought out the food, and Susan started a fire. As they sat around the fire and ate, Adam decided it was high time to check his stats, something he hadn't done in a long time.

Name: Adam
Lvl: 25
SP: 0
AP: 16,018,700
Experience: 1,126,224,400/5,097,164,800
Fame: 5,752,000

Strength: +2,730
Constitution: +300
Dexterity: +103
Intelligence: +155
Speed: +200
Physical Attack: +13,860
Health: 10,100/10,700
Hit-rate: 1,000%
MP: 1,190/1,190
Movement: +1,606
Comprehension: +2
Defense: +6,260
Magic Defense: +3,000
Dodge Rate: ???
Magic Attack: +610

Resistances:
Fire: 50%
Water: 50%
Earth: 50%
Wind: 50%
Darkness: 50%
Slashing: 50%

Skill Name: Slash
Description: A basic skill where the player swings his or her
sword and attacks the enemy!
Current lvl: 5
AP needed to reach lvl 6: 50,000
Ability: Causes 150% damage to enemy if it hits MP
consumption: 1

Cooldown time: 0 seconds

Skill Name: Thrust
Description: A basic skill where the player thrusts his or
her sword at the enemy! Current lvl: 5

AP needed to reach lvl 6: 50,000
Ability: Causes 160% damage with a 5% chance at getting
a critical hit
MP Consumption: 5
Cooldown time: 1 second

Skill Name: Blood Sacrifice
Description: By sacrificing 50% of your blood (HP), you
have gained the ability to increase the damage you do
Current lvl: 5
MAXED
Ability: causes x3 attack power for 60 seconds. Disregards
skill cooldown times, allowing the user to attack with every skill
MP consumption: 20
Special limit: Drops HP by half.
Cooldown time: 30 seconds

Skill Name: Dance of Sakura Blossoms
Description: A skill only Adam can use. Attacks with
numerous spear thrusts that eventually form the shape of a
sakura blossom.
Current lvl: 10
MAXED
Ability: Release a constant stream of attacks, does x3

damage increase for every hit, and resets when Adam misses an attack.

Hit-Rate: 100%

MP Consumption: 100 MP per use.

Cooldown time: 30 seconds

Skill Name: Energy Sweep

Description: The wielder of Spear God Seven Dances infuses his energy into a sweeping attack that releases a powerful attack that extends past his natural range.

Current level: 10

MAXED

Ability: Attacks every enemy within five yards of the user. Does 300% damage.

MP Consumption: 50

Cooldown Time: 5 Seconds

Skill Name: Energy Thrust

Description: The wielder of the Spear God, Seven Dances infuses his energy into a thrust that can ignore all defenses and armor.

Current level: 8

AP needed to reach level 9: 512,000

Ability: Ignores enemies' defense and armor to deal critical damage

420% damage dealt

MP Consumption: 25

Cooldown Time: 5 Seconds

Skill Name: Double Jump

Description: Allows wearer to jump on air as if they were jumping on the ground.   Current lvl: 1

MAXED

Ability: Jump in the air after activation.

MP Consumption: 25

Cooldown time: 10 seconds

Skill Name: Flight

Description: Gives wearer the ability to fly.

Current lvl: 1

MAXED

Ability: Fly through the air for 60 seconds.

MP Consumption: 50

Cooldown time:

Equipment:

Item name: Goddess of Creation Spear

Level: 21

Experience points needed to level up:

4,235,100,034/5,242,880,000

Item type: Spear

Grade: Divine Use requirements: Can only be equipped by Adam. Cannot be thrown away, cannot be given away, and cannot be unequipped.

Description: This unknown weapon was found by Adam. It has recognized him as its master and cannot be used by anyone else.

Abilities: Physical Attack+210; Strength=210%

Special ability: Sentient Growth

Item name: Goddess of Creation Greaves Item type: Armor

Grade: Divine Use requirements: Can only be equipped by the wielder of the Goddess of Creation's Spear.

Description: These greaves are made from an unknown

material. They were created by the Goddess of Creation and
worn by the wielder of her spear.
Abilities: Defense+200%; Magic Defense+200%;
Constitution+150%; Speed+200%; Movement+100
Special abilities:
Stacked Speed; Flight; Double Jump

Item name: Dragon Bone Cuirass
Item type: Armor
Grade: Elite
Use requirements: Can be equipped by Warriors level 10
and above.
Description: This chest plate was made from the bones of a
powerful dragon. Not only does it look stylish, but it offers solid
defensive abilities and some special stats.   Abilities:
Defense+200; Constitution+100; 40% resistance to slashing
damage; 25% resistance to fire, earth, wind, and darkness
damage.

Item name: Dragon Bone Gauntlets
Item type: Armor
Grade: Elite
Use requirements: Can be equipped by Warriors level 10
and above. Description: These gauntlets are made from the
bones of a powerful dragon. Not only are they stylish, but they
offer solid defensive abilities and resistance to elemental
damage.
Abilities: Defense+50; Constitution+10; 5% resistance to
slashing damage; 10% resistance to fire, earth, wind, and
darkness damage.

Item name: Enchanted Leggings
Item type: Armor
Grade: Medium
Use requirements: can be equipped by adventures of any
class level 5 and above   Description: Leggings that were
enchanted by an unknown mage
Abilities: Defense+10; speed+5

Item name: Brass Ring
Item Type: Ring
Grade: Low
Equipment Requirements: No requirements
Description: A simple ring made of brass. There is nothing
special about it.
Attributes: Speed+1

He didn't have any new skills and his armor was the same, but the amount of damage he did was nearly double what it had been.

And the reason was his spear.

The [Goddess of Creation Spear] had evolved after reaching level 20. The blade was much longer and had wing-like extensions sprouting from the end of the blade. While the handle was gold, the bladed end was a reddish copper color.

More important than its new aesthetic was the spear's increased power. The increased Strength stat had turned into a percentage that increased his Strength by 210% or 2.1.

Adam wondered what would happen when his spear reached level 30. Would his Physical Attack stat also turn into a percentage? He had no idea, but he hoped it would. His power would truly reach a whole different level if that happened.

After they finished eating and resting, the group traveled through the tunnel that would lead them to the next level.

[MECHA GO-LEM]

THEY WERE UNABLE TO REACH THE ENTRANCE TO THE NEXT LEVEL IN THE TWO HOURS THEY HAD LEFT.

The level they were on was swarming with [Elementals]. While they were not as powerful as the other monsters located inside this dungeon, there were so many of them that it was difficult for their group to proceed.

None of them had leveled up despite how much combat they had seen since coming to this level. [Elementals] only gave them +1,500,000 experience points, which sounded like a lot, but Adam and the others needed several billion experience points to level up.

As their name suggested, [Elementals] were monsters made of pure elemental energy. There were many different types of [Elemental]. Fire. Water. Earth. Lightning. Light. Darkness. Ice. Etc. According to Titania, there was an [Elemental] for each element. [Elementals] could be found where an abundance of a specific elemental energy existed.

This dungeon contained two types of [Elementals].

Earth and darkness.

Between the two, the [Earth Elemental] was easier to deal with. Its only power was the ability to shoot stakes from the ground and create quicksand beneath their feet. Adam drew all of its agro and made liberal use of [Double Jump] and [Fly] to avoid the quicksand, while Kureha and Fayte used magic to demolish it.

[Earth Elementals] were weak against water and fire. The water turned the [Elemental's] body into a mud-like sludge that made it hard to hold itself together. Fire baked the elemental until it was hard. They had experimented with the other elements too, but those two worked the best. Their group made quick work of these monsters.

The [Darkness Elemental] was much harder to fight.

While [Earth Elementals] took the shape of a large mole rat, [Darkness Elementals] looked more like wraiths or shadows. They were just a mass of pure darkness aggregated around a nucleus. That nucleus was its core, which all [Elementals] possessed, but the core was protected by the gathered mass of elemental energy. The best way to pierce it was to use the light element, which diametrically opposed darkness on the elemental scale.

Sadly, none of them could use the light element.

"It's firing!" Adam shouted.

Aris, Lilith, and Adam darted away from each other as the [Darkness Elemental] fired a beam of condensed dark energy. This was one of its primary methods of attack. The beam didn't do any damage to their surroundings. Someone who didn't know any better might think that meant it was a weak attack, but their group knew the truth. Adam had already been struck once and it reduced his health by half.

"Aris!"

"Leave this to me!"

As the speediest among them, Aris was the best at dodging, especially since she had improved her ability to change directions without reducing her speed by much.

After reaching level 20, Aris picked up a new ability called [Dancer's Grace]. It was a passive skill that allowed her to utilize her class's incredible speed better. Now she could move all over the place and only receive a 20% reduction in her speed. Adam suspected she could reduce that to 0% if she maxed out this ability's level.

[Double Slash]

-1

[Blade Dance]

-1; -1; -1; -1!

"Ugh… this stupid thing!" Aris complained.

[Elementals] of any kind were highly resistant to physical attacks. The only way to beat them was to have a mage in your party… or, you know, attack 23,600 times since that was how much health they had.

Fortunately, attacking them was enough to pull its agro.

The [Darkness Elemental] turned to Aris and fired off several projectiles from its body. This was called [Darkness Needle]. It was a wide attack that acted similarly to shots fired from a shotgun.

Aris used her insane speed and reflexes to dodge all the needles. She twirled around, spinning, ducking, and weaving through a hailstorm of black needles as naturally as she breathed.

Adam couldn't help but admire her grace and agility. Not even he could pull off something like that.

While Aris drew its agro to her, Fayte and Kureha gathered the fire elemental around their staff and tale respectively. Streams of flames swirled around Fayte's staff. It was so hot Adam could feel it singing his back.

"Aris! Move!" Fayte called out.

"Outta the way, Big Sis!" shouted Kureha.

Aris ran to the side just as the two fired off their respective attacks.

[Fireball]

-24,928!

[Fireball]

-14,175!

Fayte and Kureha unleashed the same attack. Two massive fireballs slammed into the [Darkness Elemental] and erupted. A massive wave of heat washed over us. Adam had to close his eyes and look away to avoid having them burned. The ground beneath them quaked and several chunks fell from the ceiling, forcing Aris, Lilith, and Adam to dodge.

The fire and smoke soon cleared, revealing a large crater in the ground and cracks traveling up the walls. The monster they had been fighting was nowhere in sight.

Because a [Darkness Elemental] only had one elemental weakness, the damage done by every other element was reduced by half. This normally meant Fayte and Kureha would not be able to kill this thing in one hit like they just did, but they had a secret weapon on their side.

Titania.

Titania had been singing [Song of Vigor] in the background to increase their attack power, tripling their already impressive magical attack state, which allowed the pair of magic users to demolish the [Darkness Elemental's] health in a single hit.

[Congratulations! You have defeated [Darkness Elemental]! Items dropped: [Darkness Fragment] and 2,000,000 gold coins. Inventory is full. Items have been sent to guild storage. +1,500,000

experience points!]

Adam only half paid attention to the sign as he turned to Fayte.

"How long has it been since we came to this level?" he asked.

"About two hours," Fayte answered.

"All right. I think we should log off. Dr. Sofocor is coming over today with a team of scientists, and I'd rather not be there when they do."

Call Adam paranoid, but he didn't want anyone to discover that he and Aris lived with Fayte. There was no telling who was working for the Pleonexia Family. It didn't matter if Dr. Sofocor vouched for these people or not. If even one of them was working for or being blackmailed by the Pleonexia Family, it would spell trouble for him and Aris.

He wasn't willing to take that chance.

Adam quickly set up a [Tent] for Kureha and Titania. This would keep the monsters in this area from respawning and allow the two NPCs to rest.

"See you in the real world," said Fayte before logging off.

"Bye, Adam," Susan said as she logged off.

"Master," Lilith said with a nod before she disappeared.

"Yeah. See you," Adam said to the three.

"It's always disconcerting when you people disappear," Titania muttered.

"Kureha thinks it's cool. She wishes she could disappear like that," the little fox yokai said with a pout.

"Maybe you'll be able to someday," Aris mussed Kureha's hair.

"You ready?" asked Adam.

"Of course."

The two of them soon disappeared, leaving Titania and Kureha behind.

***

Fayte sat on the couch with her legs tucked underneath her bottom. She scrolled through the tablet in her hand, which contained all the information on her guild, Destiny's Overture.

A guild's status combined the Fame and Level of every member and averaged it, then added the amount of gold they had accrued. It then assigned them a rank based on these factors.

Right now, Destiny's Overture was ranked #1.

This wasn't nationally either but internationally.

Her guild was the #1 guild in the entire world.

One of the conditions for the bet she made with Levon was that her guild had to rank within the top five guilds in the American Federation. Her guild being ranked #1 in the entire world meant she had more than succeeded with the third condition, which she had honestly thought would be the hardest.

No, I suppose the issue wasn't reaching #1. It's keeping my ranking. I can't grow complacent now.

The reason her guild had reached #1 was simply because they had been able to accomplish far more than the other guilds thus far because they were the first guild to have been created. Their guild was small, which meant they couldn't accomplish as much. The other guilds had more members, which meant they could accomplish more in a short span of time.

"The biggest issue is going to be accruing Fame," Fayte muttered as she tucked a strand of hair behind her ear.

Fame was the accumulation of one's accomplishments in *Age of Gods*. People could acquire it through a number of ways, such as being the first person to accomplish something, defeating a dungeon, acquiring rare items, completing quests, and beating raid bosses.

What made Fame the biggest issue for them was the size of their guild. They would not be able to accomplish as much as the larger guilds with just seven people.

"Should we recruit more members? I would rather not… I don't know if there's anyone out there who I can trust."

With more people, she would be able to accrue Fame much faster, but she also ran the risk of hiring people who were under the Pleonexia Guild's thumb. Even the most thorough background checks weren't foolproof. There was also the possibility of missing something.

There was also a chance Levon would approach one of the newer members and bribe or blackmail them into working for him. The more people who joined her guild, the greater the chances of that happening became. Fayte wanted to avoid that at all costs.

"Haaaaah. That man makes everything I wish to accomplish exceedingly difficult," Fayte sighed.

The doorbell rang moments later. Fayte stood up, made her way to the door, donned her overly baggy overcoat, and pulled the hood up before opening the door.

Dr. Sofocor stood on the other side, blinking with wide eyes as she stared at Fayte. Several people were behind her. They all gawked at her in the same way, but she didn't let that bother her.

"Dr. Sofocor, I'm glad you could make it. Please, come in," she said.

"Right." Dr. Sofocor shook herself out of her daze and smiled as she walked into the apartment. "Thank you for giving us this wonderful opportunity."

"You're welcome," Fayte said as the others entered. She closed the door behind them.

Everyone took off their shoes as instructed before Fayte led them to the room containing the cryostasis pod. Dr. Sofocor and the others sucked in a breath after getting their first glimpse of the capsule that could heal Mortems Disease.

"This is it? This is what you used to cure someone of Mortems Disease?" asked Dr. Sofocor.

"It is," Fayte answered. "Anyway, you may feel free to study the device all you need. I'm going to sit right there."

Susan had done extensive background checks on every person present, but that didn't mean Fayte trusted them. She knew there was plenty of information you couldn't get on someone with a background check.

"Thank you," Dr. Sofocor said softly.

Fayte went over to the only chair in the room, sat down, and began scrolling through her tablet. It was harder to read with the hood over her head. She wished she could lower it, but two of the four doctors present were men. She didn't want to deal with the lecherous looks they would send her.

She quickly sent off a message to Adam, letting him know the doctors had arrived, and she received a response fairly quickly. She smiled when she read the message.

Time passed by as the group studied the capsule. They poured over the data that showed how long it had taken to cure Aris of Mortems Disease, studied the inside of the capsule, and went through several logs on the terminal.

Fayte perused the internet and chatted with Adam, Aris, and Susan in a group chat app. Adam had personally created this app, or so he said. It was supposedly encrypted with a constantly changing code that prevented unauthorized access. The signal was also bounced between several different remote servers to prevent tracing.

Lilith was also part of the app. She never said anything, but Fayte could see that she read every message sent.

"This is incredible! I've never seen anything so advanced

before," one of the scientists suddenly exclaimed.

"Hmmm. This technology is at least a decade ahead of anything at our hospital," another said.

Dr. Sofocor turned to her. "Miss Fayte, where exactly did you find this again?"

Fayte smiled even though she knew they couldn't see it. "My grandfather hired someone named Lucifer to create this for his wife. Sadly, his wife passed away before she could be cured. It was used for the first time just recently, which is how we discovered it works as intended."

"I see," Dr. Sofocor muttered, pursing her lips. "I find it interesting that the man who made this is called Lucifer. That's not a name you hear often."

Fayte shrugged. "It's probably an alias. I heard it's the name of someone from a popular religion that spanned the globe many decades ago."

"Probably," the doctor agreed. "Anyway, do you mind if we take this apart to study its internal workings?"

"Feel free. I have no more use for it."

"Thank you."

Several more hours passed. The group took apart the device. Everything from the capsule to the monitor was reduced to its base components. Fayte listened to the doctors as they discussed what they discovered.

"I recognize some of these components, but there are many that I've never seen before. What do you suppose this is made of? It's not metal, but it has a metallic quality."

"It's a man-made metal. You won't find it on the periodic table. That said…"

"What? What is it?"

"Well… the method to make this metal is only a theory at the moment. It shouldn't be possible to create this yet since no known method exists."

"But it clearly exists right here."

"Yes, and that's worrying. Someone out there has the technology to create a metal that should only exist in theory. I can't understand how we don't know of this person, or why they haven't come forth to present their findings. Whoever made this could have become the richest and most famous person on the entire planet."

Fayte knew they would begin talking about this device's creator eventually. She could not blame them since she had the same questions they did. Who made this device? Why hadn't they come forward? She didn't want to look a gift horse in the mouth, but she could not understand the motives of the person who created this device.

As the scientists continued discussing their findings, Fayte went back to her tablet and waited for the group to finish.

***

The underground dungeon seemed to consist of at least fifteen levels, and while none of the monsters became more powerful, they did begin cropping up in mixed groups. They usually only fought two or three. Sometimes, however, they were forced to fight as many as four. Four seemed to be the maximum number of monsters that would group together.

Fighting a group of monsters was much harder than fighting individual monsters. They needed to be aware of all the monsters' locations and what they were doing at any given time. This meant it was necessary to have someone in the rear acting as their eyes and handing out orders.

That duty had fallen to Susan.

While Fayte would have been a better option because she possessed more confidence and charisma, she lacked the eyesight and spatial awareness that Susan had. Susan's eyesight was the best in the entire group. She could spot objects from kilometers away and even see in the dark.

Titania said this was a passive effect of the Fairy Archer Class. Adam didn't know about that, but he did know Susan's eyesight was even better than his.

Susan hung further back than normal, with Aris acting as her bodyguard in case a monster snuck up behind them, and told their group when a monster was making a move on either Fayte or Kureha. Her job was basically letting Adam and Lilith know which monster they needed to pull agro for.

Thanks to Susan's observation skills, they managed to defeat the enemies they fought and continued traveling down until they reached the fourteenth floor. They had earned 1.5 billion experience points before reaching the end. Aris, Fayte, Lilith, and Susan had all reached level 25.

Adam was still 2.5 billion experience points from reaching level 26.

Everyone aside from Lilith was currently resting in a small, room-like passage. The entrance to the next level sat several meters from them.

Adam leaned against the wall with his arms crossed. Aris, Fayte, Kureha, Susan, and Titania were sitting around a small campfire. They looked like they were enjoying themselves as the warmth and light emitted from the fire banished the surrounding darkness. Adam found himself focusing on their shadows as they danced along the floor and walls.

"How long do you think it will take Lilith to get back?" asked Aris.

Fayte shrugged. "I couldn't say, but you should probably stop asking. Asking over and over again won't make her return any faster."

"Yeah... but I hate waiting. And I'm bored. I wanna do something," Aris complained.

"Kureha understands. Kureha is bored too," the little fox yokai said. She was sitting on Aris's lap, allowing the young woman to stroke her ears, rub her head, and fluff her tails.

Lilith would be jealous if she was here to see this.

"It depends on how big the next level is. Level fourteen was massive and it took Lilith about eight hours to search the entire floor. If level fifteen is even bigger, it will take her much longer," Susan said.

"Uuuuugh. I just want to head out now though," Aris groaned.

Titania fluttered her wings as she munched on a small slice of bread. "It was a good idea to send Lilith ahead. The monsters in this dungeon are dangerous. Knowing where they are, how many they are, and their composition has aided us in all our battles since the fifth floor. It's only thanks to her that we have been able to make it this far."

Lilith had an ability called [Shadow Masking], which allowed her to become completely invisible. Unlike the lesser skill, [Hide], she was able to move while [Shadow Masking] was activated. The skill was currently at level 3, which meant she could hide from enemies thirty levels higher than her.

Just as it looked like Aris was going to complain some more, a shadow appeared before Adam, kneeling on the ground like a knight to her liege.

"M... Adam, I have finished searching the next floor," Lilith said.

Adam blinked. "That was fast. I expected you to take longer."

"There is only one room on the next floor," Lilith explained.

"The boss room?" he asked.

"I believe so."

"Were you able to see what the boss looked like?" asked Fayte as she stood up and dusted herself off. Susan and Aris followed suit, while Titania fluttered over to Adam and sat on his shoulder. Her weight was oddly reassuring at this point.

Lilith nodded. "I was. The boss is a giant golem. It looks very different from the ones we have fought so far. Not only is it much bigger than the ones we have fought, it is also made up of gears and joints… and it was wielding weapons far more advanced than the other ones."

"That sounds like a [Mecha Golem]," said Titania. When Adam and the others looked at her, she continued. "[Mecha Golems] are Dwarven creations. They are incredibly powerful creations that are capable of taking on entire raid teams. It normally requires at least a raid of thirty people to defeat just one of them."

So it was a super powerful monster the likes of which they had never fought before? That got Adam's blood pumping. He really wanted to fight it now, though he reigned his battle lust in.

"What about the room? Was there anything odd about it?" he asked.

Lilith shook her head. "No. The room is circular and has a circumference of maybe fifty meters. The only thing about it that stood out is the door at the end."

"A door, huh?" Adam mumbled.

"[Mecha Golems] were often used by the Dwarves to guard strongholds and treasures. It is possible that the door leads to a Dwarven treasure vault or maybe even the Dwarves' hidden home."

While a treasure vault was enticing, Adam hoped the door led to the Dwarves' home. Dwarves were master craftsmen and blacksmiths. Their creations were coveted the world over. Titania had told him that even the least skilled blacksmith among the Dwarves was ten times better than the most talented human blacksmith. Adam had seen a few weapons forged by Dwarves and had to concur.

After reaching level 20, Adam and the others had gained the ability to accept a secondary class. None of the secondary classes were combat related. Instead, they were crafting classes like armorer, blacksmith, crafter, carpenter, chef, scribe, etc. Adam didn't know how many classes existed, but he assumed there were many he had never heard of.

Their group had at one point gone to Solum and looked at the classes they could learn from the instructors, but none of them were any good. They were all basic classes. What Adam wanted were special classes like the hidden classes they had. He wouldn't be satisfied with a standard class.

He wanted to gain a blacksmith class one could only learn from the Dwarves.

"Let's head down and have Titania look at its stats with [scan]," Adam decided.

No one argued and their group traveled down the stairs, through a tunnel, and only stopped just before reaching the entrance to the room with the golem.

"Woooooah. That's huge," Aris said, gawking.

Susan's eyes were wide as well. "I've never seen anything this big before?"

It stood in the center of the room, a massive construction made of stone gears, gleaming joints, and a visored helm with a single, glowing red eye. It had four arms instead of two. Two of the arms gripped a pair of hammers that were, at a glance, probably bigger than Adam by a good half a meter. Its second left hand held a bow. Again, it was far larger than an average adult human. Strapped across its back was a quiver full of arrows.

Those are more like ballista bolts than arrows though...

"Even the [hydra] was smaller than this," Adam agreed, turning his head to the fairy on his shoulder. "Titania?"

"Give me a moment."

Titania cast [Scan] and Adam studied its stats.

Name: Mecha Golem

Description: A golem created by the Dwarves. The pinnacle of Dwarven mechanics. These golems were created as defenders against human incursion and are used to guard treasure vaults and strongholds. Only the most talented Dwarven engineers can create one.

Class: 3-Stars

Lvl: 60

HP: 30,000,000,000/30,000,000,000

MP: 100,000/100,000

Strength: +8,500

Constitution: +10,600

Dexterity: +500

Intelligence: +10

Speed: +10

Resistances:

Slashing: 50%

Piercing: 50%

Thrusting: 50%

Magic Damage Negation: 50%

Skill List:

Skill Name: Mega Ton Crush

Description: Swings down hammer and crushes enemy into
paste

Attack does 500% physical damage

Has a 75% chance of crushing enemy

Instant death if enemy is crushed

MP Cost: 10,000

Cooldown Time: 20 Seconds

Skill Name: Side Swipe

Description: Swings hammer sideways to knock away
enemies

Attack does 150% physical damage

Always knocks enemy back

MP Cost: 4,600

Cooldown Time: 10 seconds

Skill Name: Stomp

Description: Mecha Golem stomps on the ground

Attack does 300% physical damage if hit directly

Causes shockwave that does 100% physical damage if hit

50% of knocking back enemy

MP Cost: 7,000

Cooldown Time: 30 seconds

Skill Name: Devastating Shot

Description: Mecha Golem can fire its bow to devastating
effect

Has a range of 100 meters

Instant death if hit

Creates shockwave that does 75% physical damage
MP Cost: 12,000
Cooldown Time: 15 seconds
Special Limit: Can only use this skill so long as it has
arrows

Adam felt his stomach drop as he looked at those stats. Its health, in particular, caused him to sweat buckets.

Adam's strongest skill was [Dance of the Sakura Blossoms]. Provided he was being buffed with [Blood Sacrifice] and [Song of Vigor] and he hit his opponent with all five attacks, he could deal about 1.5 billion points of damage. His strength was, to put it mildly, kind of broken.

But not only did the [Mecha Golem] have over 30 billion health, it could negate every form of damage by 50%, meaning Adam would only do about 750,000,000 damage at most.

That was basically a drop in the bucket for this creature.

"Fayte... how many health and MP potions do we have?" asked Adam.

"Each of us is carrying the maximum amount possible, so we have 495 of each," Fayte answered.

"Do you think that's enough to help us beat this thing?"

"That... is a very good question." Fayte pondered for a moment, sighed, and said, "I believe it is possible to defeat this boss, but doing so will be very difficult. Even a single attack is enough to kill one of us. Its skill [Mega Ton Crush], in particular, will kill anyone who gets hit. You have the highest physical defense out of all of us at +6,260, but if you get hit, that's 36,240 points worth of damage. That's about twice the amount of health you possess. It's complete overkill."

"I thought as much," Adam muttered.

"But it's not like we haven't fought monsters that could kill us in one hit before," Aris said.

"That's true. We have done this many times, and I'm not saying we shouldn't attack, but we should be aware of how dangerous going up against this will be. I believe we should come up with an appropriate strategy before we attempt to fight it," Fayte said.

Susan furrowed her brow and bit her thumb for a moment. "I-if we're going to create a strategy to fight this boss, we should fight it to see what kind of attack patterns it has."

"Since it's a golem, it has a very limited intelligence. Its attack patterns won't be too complex, and it is also quite slow." Titania glanced at him. "Adam should be more than capable of dodging it." She shrugged. "The two biggest issues are its area of effect attacks. [Side Swipe] has a very wide reach and [Stomp] hits everything around it without exception."

"So how do we dodge them?" asked Aris.

"We've fought monsters that use [Stomp] before," Adam cupped a hand to his chin. "The best way to avoid a [Stomp] is to not be on the ground. Jumping allows you to avoid its effects. However…"

"This one's attack creates a shockwave," Fayte stated. "I believe that means simply jumping won't be enough to avoid taking damage."

Adam nodded. "Right. So rather than simply jumping, I'm thinking one of us should disrupt its attack. Using [Stomp] requires it to raise its leg. Anything with two legs is vulnerable when it has one leg raised. It should be possible to knock it off balance. If we can send it to the ground, we can attack it until it gets back up, then retreat. So long as we avoid [Mega Ton Crush] and [Side Swipe], I believe we can defeat it."

"What about its bow skill?" asked Susan. "[Devastating Shot] sounds like a powerful technique."

"It is, but I don't think it will use it unless one of you ranged fighters draws its agro. So long as Aris, Lilith, or I keep pulling its agro, it shouldn't attack you, Fayte, or Kureha," Adam explained.

"I should warn you that not every monster is going to work like that," Titania warned.

Adam frowned. "What do you mean?"

"Only living monsters have aggression. Non-living monsters like the golems do not have aggression so you can't draw them to you by attacking it, and while the [Mecha Golem] is lacking intelligence, it does have enough to attack the enemy it deems the greatest threat," Titania patiently explained.

So pulling agro would not work? Now that he thought about it, Adam realized all the [Golems] they had fought in this dungeon worked on the same principle. Most of them had tried to attack Fayte, who did the most damage among their group. The only time they switched targets was when Adam activated [Blood Sacrifice]. Once his physical attack stat was buffed, they switched targets to him even before he attacked, almost like they knew he had suddenly become the biggest threat.

"So long as [Blood Sacrifice] is activated, it should attack me, but my skill only remains active for sixty seconds and has a thirty-second cooldown time, meaning it will probably go after Fayte once my skill is finished. Fayte, you'll probably have to dodge its [Devastating Shot] during this time. It will only be able to launch two shots before my cooldown period ends, but we don't know the range of its area of effect. Think you're up for it?"

Fayte was not wearing her veil right now since there was no need. Her expression was uncertain. She looked at the [Mecha Golem], then back at him, switching back and forth several times as the rest of them remained silent.

Adam was not worried about himself. He was confident in his

ability to dodge any attack this monster could attack him with. Her speed was not as high, and her dodge rate wasn't as good, meaning there was a chance she would get hit if she didn't get out of the way fast. There was a very real chance she would die here.

Several seconds ticked by before Fayte took a deep breath and hardened her expression.

"I'm up for it," she said.

Adam smiled. "Then let's head back to the real world and rest up for a bit. We'll come back here once we're rested and begin studying the [Mecha Golem] to create an attack plan."

DECLARA-
TION OF WAR

THEIR FIRST ATTEMPT ENDED IN FAILURE.

Adam dashed underneath the legs of the [Mecha Golem] and attacked with a combination of [Thrust] and [Slash]. Damage signs floated over the monster's head, but while the number was comparatively high, it was a mere drop in the bucket for this creature.

He wasn't the only one attacking. Aris was a blur of movement as she constantly rushed back and forth. The continuous stream of attacks she unleashed caused dozens of damage signs to appear above the monster in half as many seconds. She was like a bolt of lightning.

Yet the amount of damage she did was even less than what Adam could do. Her strength stat just wasn't high enough to cause a meaningful change in this monster's health.

Unlike him and Aris, Lilith waited silently for her opportunity before striking with her newest skill.

[Silent Assassination] was a skill that could only be activated once per fight, and only when the enemy was unaware of your presence. It dealt ten times the normal amount of damage and had a twenty-five percent chance of instantly killing a target. Sadly, the instant death opportunity did not apply to raid bosses like this.

The [Mecha Golem] swung two of its four arms at him and Aris, trying everything in its power to attack them, but they were far too fast. Adam had his bizarre ability to dodge faster-than-sound attacks at point-blank range, and Aris's speed was simply out of this world. It couldn't even come close to hitting them.

Fayte, Kureha, and Susan stood far back from the action and peppered the creature with attacks. Just like his own attacks, none of theirs dealt enough damage to really injure it. Adam felt the heat from Fayte's [Fireball] wash over him as her attack slammed into their enemy's face and exploded, but the amount of damage it did was barely enough to chip away at its health.

The problem was two-fold.

The [Mecha Golem] had abnormally large reserves of health, more than any other monster he had fought. This meant even his attacks, which would normally deal over one million points worth of damage, would not even drop this thing's health by a percent.

The second issue was its resistance. It was resistant to everything. Slashing, piercing, thrusting, the elements… every form of attack they could do was reduced by half. That meant even [Dance of the Sakura Blossoms], the strongest attack he had, only did about five hundred thousand points of damage.

"It's about to use [Mega Ton Crush]!" Adam called out.

"Got it!"

Aris darted away from the [Mecha Golem], traveling in the opposite direction as Adam. The [Mecha Golem] had locked onto him. He watched as it turned in his direction, raised its left arm, and swung down.

Adam rolled across the floor to dodge. The sound of ground being pounded echoed behind him, and the feeling of the hammer slamming into the earth caused his bones to rattle. Cracks spread from the floor, though the damage done wasn't as extensive as he thought it should have been.

"Aris! It's going for a sideswipe at you!" Adam warned.

"Don't worry! I've got this!"

Immediately after it tried to pound Adam into paste, it turned on Aris and swung its other hammer in a sweep. Aris leapt clear over the attack. The wind from the attack was powerful enough to launch her away, but she flipped through the air, landed on the ground, and went into a series of back handsprings.

Her health gauge remained unchanged.

Adam looked at their opponent's health even as he dodged its [Stomp]. 29,040,056,987/30,000,000,000.

"What's our time?!" shouted Adam.

"One hour!"

So one hour had passed and they had managed to deal - 959,943,013 points of damage. That was actually a lot. At the same time, it was nowhere near enough. This was a monster with thirty billion points of health. A mere nine hundred million wasn't even worth mentioning.

Despite this, they continued to attack it, whittling away its health a little at a time. Perhaps they could win if they turned this into a battle of attrition. That was what Adam thought.

Until its attack pattern changed.

"Susan! Fayte! Kureha! Move! It's targeting you!"

Adam's shouted warning was enough to alert the three to the danger they were in. The [Mecha Golem] was still attacking Adam, Aris, and Lilith, but now the two arms holding the bow and arrows had begun to move.

The second arms were attached to a part of the torso that swiveled. It could rotate a full 360 degrees, meaning it could fire arrows even as it attacked with its two hammers.

And right now, it was pulling back the bowstring in preparation to release it.

The three long-range fighters scattered. Kureha transformed into a fox and bolted. Fayte rushed in the opposite direction. Susan took off running, though oddly enough, she didn't stop aiming her bow. She fired a single shot that struck the [Mecha Golem] in one of its finger joints. The attack barely did any damage, but it did throw off the monster's aim.

The shot went wide and struck a wall. Adam flinched when the giant bolt impaled the wall, causing cracks to spread all the way to the ceiling. Several chunks of rubble fell. They didn't hit anyone, but imagining how much damage they could do if they did was enough to make him wary.

And now they were in trouble. The [Mecha Golem] attacked all of them, firing arrows as it swung both hammers. Fayte, Kureha, and Susan were no longer able to attack as much since they were constantly forced to dodge. This halved the amount of damage they had been doing.

Thus another half an hour passed and they were only able to remove five hundred million points from its health.

"I think we should retreat!" Fayte said.

"You're right! Let's fall back!" Adam agreed.

The long-range fighters made their way back up the stairs that led into this room. Adam, Aris, and Lilith waited until they were gone before retreating as well. They had to dodge its arrows, but they, too, eventually made it back to the fourteenth floor.

"I don't think we're going to be able to beat this thing any time soon," Fayte said.

They were sitting around a campfire and eating a quick meal. It was easy enough to store food in their inventory. Everything that went inside their inventory stayed fresh. Adam wasn't sure if that was just part of the programming, or if this was a special ability that players were given. He wasn't about to question it.

"Yeah... we barely dealt that thing any damage," Aris mumbled as she bit into a chunk of bread. "Adam, can you pass me the butter?"

Adam handed Aris a jar of butter as he said, "It seems to have multiple attack patterns. Once we removed a billion points of its health, it changed how it attacked. I'm assuming that will happen every time we deal that much damage."

"That will make it difficult to plan out a strategy," Fayte murmured.

Lilith wasn't taking part in the conversation. Adam didn't know if that was because she couldn't think of something to add, or because she was busy feeding Kureha. The little fox yokai was sitting in the older woman's lap. She looked quite content being pampered by the quiet assassin.

"We should probably think of this as a long-term battle," Susan said. She blushed when everyone looked at her but continued. "We're not going to defeat this thing right now. We can't deal it enough damage. I think we should only fight it once a week. We can take on quests and grind our levels, then try again. We'll just keep trying until we manage to beat it."

"That is a good idea," Titania said, swinging her legs back and forth from her place on Adam's shoulder.

"I guess that's about all we can do," Adam said with a sigh.

He didn't like the idea of retreating. It felt like he was admitting defeat, and Adam hated to lose, but he wasn't so prideful that he couldn't admit when he was outclassed either. Being beaten like this just made him more motivated to get stronger.

"Guess that means we should head back to our guild headquarters, huh?" asked Aris.

There really was nothing more that they could do. After storing everything back in their inventory, the group left the small room. Adam took one last glance at the entrance to the [Mecha Golem's] lair. He gave it a hard stare before leaving.

Just wait. I'm not going to let you beat me.

***

Someone was waiting for them when they arrived at their guild headquarters. She had long brown hair styled into a neat braid, wide bluish-green eyes, and an attractive face. The guild uniform fit her body like a glove. She cut a very attractive figure, especially since the uniform had a cutout that showcased her cleavage.

Adam suspected guild uniforms were designed this way to appeal to the male gaze. A man was more likely to drop his guard around an attractive woman than he was another man or someone deemed ugly by society's standards.

On that note, men who worked for the Guild Association were similarly attractive.

Adam recognized the woman pacing back and forth in front of their doorway. She was their Guild Association representative.

"Clarise? What are you doing here?" asked Fayte.

"Eeep!"

Startled, Clarise spun around to face them, her eyes wide, hand to her chest as though to still her swiftly beating heart. She calmed down when she realized who had called out to her, though the expression didn't last long.

"Fayte! Where have you been?!"

Fayte paused at the woman's tone. "We've been in a dungeon. Why? Is something the matter?"

"Yes. No. Well, sort of. Something happened. I've been trying to reach you, but you were never here," Clarise said.

Adam raised an eyebrow. She had been trying to reach them? That must mean something important happened while they were down in that dungeon.

"I understand. In that case, why don't you come on in? We can discuss the reason you're here over tea," Fayte suggested.

"Oh. Thank you. That would be lovely," Clarise admitted.

Fayte unlocked the entrance to their guild house and gestured for everyone to enter. They soon found themselves arrayed around the living room. Adam, Aris, and Lilith sat on one couch. Susan and Fayte sat on the other. Clarise sat on an armchair.

Several cups of tea had been placed in front of them, though only Clarise was drinking. She seemed to need something to sip at to calm her nerves.

Adam shifted uncomfortably as he sat between Aris and Lilith. Was it just him, or was Lilith sitting much closer to him than normal? Was he just being self-conscious? No, no, no. He wasn't the self-conscious type. She was definitely sitting closer to him than normal. They were so close their thighs were touching.

I wonder if she's aware of what she's doing? Is she doing this on purpose?

As he tried to think of what reason Lilith could possibly be sitting so close, he saw something out of the corner of his eye and turned his head.

"What's with that smirk?" he asked Aris.

Aris's smug smile widened. "Oh, no reason."

Adam frowned. He was very tempted to ask this girl to explain herself, but Clarise had chosen that moment to place her teacup on the mahogany coffee table.

"Ahem. I'm really glad you showed up when you did. Had you been even a day later, the Guild Association would have been forced to disband Destiny's Overture," Clarise said.

Her words caused a ripple to spread through their group. Disband their guild? What for? To the best of Adam's knowledge, they had not broken any rules, far as he knew.

"May I ask why?" asked Fayte, doing her best to remain calm.

"Of course. I was going to tell you that." Clarise took a moment to compose herself before continuing. "As you know, your guild was given a one-month grace period. For one month after the creation of the second guild, no guild was allowed to declare war on you. Well, that one-month period has ended, and a guild declared war on yours four days ago. All guilds are given a five-day period to respond. If in five days, the guild does not respond to the declaration of war, their rights as a guild are revoked and they are forced to disband."

Adam's eyes widened, as did everyone else's. Fayte stood up and slammed her hands onto the table, startling poor Clarise and causing her to squeak.

"What do you mean our one-month grace period is over?! We should still have—"

Fayte stopped talking and her eyes widened further. She had realized the issue at the same time as Adam.

They had been given a one-month grace period. In normal circumstances, that would mean one month in real time, because real time and time passed in the game were the same.

Such was not the case here. In this world, one hour in real time equaled seven in-game days. They had been playing for about one week in real time, which meant that, technically speaking, way more than a month had passed in *Age of Gods.*

Their grace period had long since run out.

It was not something Adam had thought about. He didn't think Fayte had considered this either. Who could blame them? No other game had a Time Compression System, so it was natural to assume that the one-month grace period was referring to real-time days instead of in-game days.

No announcement of their grace period ending had been made, but it wouldn't be hard to figure out. All anyone would need to do was ask the Guild Association. Their job was to provide information, and they didn't take sides, so if a guild wanted to declare war on another guild, they would of course facilitate it.

Fayte slowly lowered herself back onto the couch, placed her hands on her lap, and took several deep breaths. Susan looked worriedly at her friend. However, neither she nor anyone else said anything.

Finally, Fayte opened her eyes and looked at Clarise.

"I believe I already have an idea of who declared war on my guild, but why don't you tell us?"

"Yes. Of course. The one who declared war on Destiny's Overture was Levon Pleonexia of the Pleonexia Alliance," Clarise said.

Her words echoed through the living room like the tolling of a bell.

PLANNING

THEY HAD ALWAYS KNOWN THIS DAY WOULD COME. Even if they hadn't been the first guild created in *Age of Gods,* Levon Pleonexia would not stand for the woman he was attempting to back into a corner and force into an arranged marriage to build her powerbase. He would do everything he could to squash her resistance flat.

That was just the kind of person he was.

Fayte took several deep breaths, closed her eyes, and seemed to gather herself. She opened them after a moment and fixed Clarise with a gaze.

"You mentioned when I first formed Destiny's Overture that I can name the time, place, and number of members the other team can bring, right?"

Clarise nodded. "That's correct. The Guild Association would normally be the ones to determine when a Guild War happens, where it happens, and how many members each side can bring. We do this because the Guild Association is impartial. However, that's not the case for your guild. You can choose all that so long as you are not abusing the system."

When Adam and Fayte had gone to form the guild, Clarise had mentioned this. She said if they had one hundred members participating, they could not make their opponent bring less than one hundred members. What they *could* do was force the opposing guild to bring members between a certain level. A good example would be if they only allowed the opposing guild to bring members between levels 10 and 15.

Fayte pondered for a moment before saying, "I will accept their Guild War, of course, but can I take some time to consider everything else? This is rather sudden for me, and I haven't had time to properly consider everything."

"You can take your time thinking about where the Guild War will happen and what kind of numbers each side can bring, but I'm afraid you'll need to set a time for it right now. You normally would have a few days to consider that, but unfortunately, those days disappeared while you were in the dungeon. I'm sorry."

Clarise really did look miserable with the way her shoulders slumped. The dejected expression on her face made her look like a puppy whose master wouldn't play with her.

"I see."

Fayte closed her eyes and took another deep breath. She seemed to be concentrating hard.

Adam glanced at the others. Susan was worrying her lower lip. Out of all the people there, she was easily the most concerned for Fayte. Aris and Lilith were paying attention, but neither seemed particularly concerned; Adam was sure the reason for this was because of their faith in him. Lilith's faith was unquestionable, always had been. Aris believed there was nothing he couldn't do. She probably assumed he already had a plan in mind.

The only ones not paying attention were Titania and Kureha. Kureha was utterly blissed out as she sat on Lilith's lap and let the young woman pamper her. The look on her face as Lilith tenderly rubbed the inside of her ears would have been amusing in any other situation. Titania was just munching on a small slice of honey bread. She looked like she didn't have a care in the world.

Fayte finally opened her eyes. "Two weeks. Tell Levon Pleonexia that our Guild War will take place two weeks from now. I will have a time and place chosen in a few days. Is that acceptable?"

"That will work. I'll tell the Guild Association to let Mr. Pleonexia know," Clarise said, standing up. She dusted off her skirt, then gave everyone a smile that was half forlorn and half optimistic. "Well, I should get going. I have a lot of work to do back at the Guild Association. Please, let me know the details of the Guild War once you've come to a decision."

"We will. Take care of yourself," Fayte said.

"You as well."

Fayte stood up and saw Clarise off. Everyone else sat there and listened to the entrance door opening and closing. When Fayte returned, she flopped almost bonelessly onto the couch, leaned her head back, and expelled a long breath.

"Well… this is a situation I didn't want to find myself in. I knew it would happen eventually, but I really thought we had more time," she said.

"There's no way we could have known our one-month grace period was meant for the game world instead of the real world," Adam said as though to reassure her this wasn't her fault. "No game has a Time Compression System like this one. It's only natural to assume the passage of time refers to real-world hours."

"That may be, but it also means we're now in a bind," Fayte said.

"Then let's come up with a plan," exclaimed Aris.

Fayte gave her a look that was somewhat aggrieved. "You say

that as if coming up with a plan to deal with the American Federation's largest guild is easy."

"I think it will be easier than you're making it out to be," Aris rebutted.

"I admire your enthusiasm, but what you're saying is utterly ridiculous—"

"No. Aris might actually be right," the young girl at Fayte's side said. Everyone looked at Susan, who blushed bright red under their scrutiny. She coughed into her hand and looked away but doggedly continued talking. "Um, uh, I know the situation might seem bad, but we actually do have a huge advantage here. N-not only can we choose the time, place, and numbers, but all of us are far stronger than anyone in the Pleonexia Guild. If we wanted to, we could make it so only the Elemental Four fight us. They wouldn't stand a chance."

"Well… that is true," Fayte admitted.

"I don't think we should do that," Adam said.

"Can you explain your reasons?" asked Fayte.

Adam grinned as he removed his mask. "Because your goal is to build your reputation. If you made it so we only fought the Elemental Four, people would assume we're cowards who only bully the weak. It would cause our reputation as a guild to drop. What we need to do is shock and awe everyone like we did during the tournament."

Adam had found a [Guild Creation Token] early in the game and used it as a prize in a tournament hosted by Solum's mayor. During the tournament, all of them had shocked the entire gaming world by fighting against and defeating the American Federation's best players, including the Spear God. What Adam was suggesting was they perform a similar but even more outstanding feat to further bolster their reputation.

"The entire gaming world has set high expectations for us,"

Adam continued. "We've done things others can only dream of. If we fail to meet and exceed their expectations, it will cause our reputation to take a hit. If we can't consistently outdo everyone else, we will eventually be forgotten once the larger guilds are fully operational."

"You do bring up a good point," Fayte admitted. Her smile was quite the sight to behold. Wry as it was, Adam still found it breathtaking. "What do you suggest?"

"If we exclude the branch guilds, the Pleonexia Alliance currently has 10.5 million members. Their levels are between 15 and 17. Levon and Connor reached level 20 just a few days ago. Meanwhile, the Four Elements are all at level 19. I'm sure they'll hit level 20 by the time our Guild War commences."

Thanks to Belphegor infiltrating the Pleonexia Alliance, Adam had all the information he needed to counter any moves Levon could make. He knew the guild's numbers, the levels of each member, what each unit specialized in. Everything.

I'm going to make him regret picking a fight with us.

"You know a lot about the Pleonexia Alliance. Even I don't have that much information," Fayte said, blinking in surprise.

Adam smiled. "Let's just say I have a means of getting insider information."

"With that much info, I'm sure we can come up with a way to defeat the Pleonexia Alliance in this Guild War," Susan said.

"I still do not understand what this Guild War is about. Can someone please explain this to me?" asked Titania. She looked irritated. Adam surmised it was because they were talking about a lot of topics she had no knowledge of. Titania was the type who enjoyed flaunting her knowledge to others and hated it when others had knowledge she lacked.

She was kinda petty like that.

As Susan took the time to explain what a Guild War was, Adam and Fayte continued their conversation.

"I think the first thing we should do is choose a good location for the Guild War to take place in." Adam placed his forearms on his knees and leaned forward. "The location of our battle will determine how well we can fight. We'll want to choose a location that minimizes the number of forces Levon can bring to bear at any given time, while at the same time maximizing how much damage we can do to their forces."

"Do we know of any good locations like that?" asked Fayte.

"No, but we can probably have Clarise get us some maps," Adam suggested.

Fayte hummed as she bit her index finger in thought. "What sort of terrain would you suggest?"

"Something that we can use to our advantage. A mountain pass would work. Aris, Lilith, and I can act as the vanguards and distractions. We'd fight the enemy head-on. Meanwhile, you and Kureha can stand at the top of the pass and bombard enemies with long-range AoE attacks. Susan will be our sniper who takes out important enemies commanding from the back."

"That's a viable plan. What other options do we have?" asked Fayte after a moment. "I want to think of every plan we can before coming to a decision."

Adam nodded. "That's fair. I was going to do that anyway. Our second option is to choose an abandoned castle or fortress. Titania told me once that this continent is littered with old fortresses that were used long ago during the war against the Demon Lord. I'm sure we can choose one of those for our Guild War. We can make ourselves the defenders and the Pleonexia Alliance the invaders."

"So you're suggesting we make our battle a siege warfare?" asked Fayte.

"Yes."

Siege tactics were a crucial part of medieval warfare. Castles and fortified cities offered protection to both the local population and armed forces and presented a wide array of defensive features which, in turn, led to innovations in weapons, siege engine technology, and strategies. A siege war would give them a large advantage. Those who were defending always had an advantage against those who were attacking.

"Won't we be at a disadvantage?" asked Fayte. "I've read about siege tactics. While the defenders *do* have an advantage, it's dependent upon our numbers. Yes, we need fewer numbers to defend a castle than to attack it, but we also need enough people to man the battlements. With only three long-range attackers, I'm afraid we'll be at a disadvantage."

"You're not wrong in most cases, but aren't you forgetting something?" asked Adam.

Fayte furrowed her brow. "What am I forgetting?"

"This world's level of technology might be similar in some ways to the medieval era of our world, but it's still vastly different. This is a world of swords and sorcery. You and Kureha have magic that can wipe out entire swaths of enemies in a single attack. One attack from either of you is equal to ten or even twenty catapults. I'm pretty sure you can wipe out the vast majority of Levon's forces before they even reach our door."

Adam's explanation had Fayte nodding, but she still had some reservations, which she gave voice to.

"But what if they bring out artillery?" asked Fayte.

Adam shrugged. "It takes time to build artillery weapons like catapults, and they don't have any right now. So long as we give Clarise our decision with barely a week to spare, I doubt Levon will be able to build too many siege weapons. At most, he will be able to build maybe ten or twenty, and we can have Aris destroy them before they deal too much damage."

Aris's speed was unmatched, especially when she moved linearly. If Fayte and Kureha carved a path for her with their magic, Aris could travel straight toward a siege weapon and demolish it within seconds. The only issue Adam could foresee was the possibility of her getting surrounded afterward and having to fight her way through a horde of enemies. However, they could mitigate that by utilizing Susan's skills as a Fairy Archer.

Aris thumped her chest. "Leave any artillery to me. I'll demolish them before you can say threesome."

While Adam placed his hands in his face to hide his embarrassment, Susan blushed right down to the roots of her hair and Fayte gained a small twitch in her right eye.

"Why that word in particular...?" asked Fayte.

"No reason," Aris said.

Fayte raised an eyebrow. "No reason?"

Aris nodded. "No reason."

Fayte sighed. "Fine. I guess that's just the kind of girl you are."

"Tee-hee."

They discussed the matter a bit more and eventually came up with a basic working plan. Barely five hours had passed in this world, meaning not even an hour had passed in the real world. It was late in the game, though. The sun had set and Susan leaned against Fayte, beginning to nod off.

"I guess we should all get some rest and continue this discussion tomorrow," Fayte said.

"Good idea. We can't think of a good plan if we're tired," Adam said.

Now that one day in the real world was the same as fourteen in-game days, their avatar bodies experienced exhaustion and needed to sleep in-game. It was an interesting experience. Their group had already slept in the tents several times while attempting to raid the dungeon with the [Mecha Golem].

Fayte picked up Susan like a prince carrying a princess. After wishing everyone a good night, she traveled up the stairs.

Adam stood up, stretched, and turned to Aris.

"You ready to get some sleep?"

Aris smiled but shook her head. "I actually have something important to discuss with Lilith."

He raised an eyebrow. Aris wanted to talk with Lilith? He hadn't realized they'd gotten so close. They didn't have any dislike for the other person, but nothing about their interactions thus far suggested they were familiar or close in any way, shape, or form.

Still, it's good that Aris is making friends... and Lilith is a good person. I'd like it if she could make friends too. Maybe it would help her become less dependent on me.

Adam still felt uncomfortable with the loyalty Lilith showed him. Her deference was something he didn't deserve.

"All right. Try not to stay up too late," Adam said.

"Don't worry. This conversation won't take long," Aris said with a smile.

Adam thought something in that smile of hers was decidedly devious, but Aris was a mischievous girl in general, so he didn't think much about it. Shrugging, he wished her, Lilith, and Titania a good night. He was about to do the same to Kureha, but she hopped off Lilith's lap and grabbed his hand.

"Kureha wants to sleep with you tonight, Big Brother!"

"Well… yeah, sure. Why not."

While Adam felt a bit awkward, he didn't think much of letting

Kureha sleep with him. She was just a kid and probably wanted to feel the comfort of another person. As he wandered up the stairs with Kureha, he wondered where the young fox yokai's mother was.

THREE'S A CROWD

CLARISE'S OFFICE LOOKED THE SAME AS FAYTE REMEMBERED. The spacious interior seemed bigger than it needed to be. While she wore boots, it was still possible to feel the soft carpet because her feet sank into the floor.

Fayte sat on one of two couches. Clarise sat opposite her. Arrayed before them on a long coffee table made of expensive wood were several dozen maps.

"These are all the maps that fit the description you asked for. They are also areas owned by the Guild Association, so you can choose any one of them for your Guild War," Clarise explained.

"Thank you," said Fayte.

Fayte touched the first map in sight and brought it closer to her. It was a map of a castle complete with a moat and battlements. Several handwritten notes lining the page revealed this was an old fortification from the war between beastmen and humans. She grabbed another map. This one showed off a canyon with a narrow pass that, according to more handwritten notes, said it was about five meters across.

"What do you think? Do any of them meet your needs?" asked Clarise as she nervously wrung her hands. She'd been like that for the past several minutes.

Fayte smiled at the woman. "All of them meet our needs perfectly. I just need to figure out which of these to choose."

Adam would have normally been with her, helping her, but she had asked him not to. Fayte wanted his help, but she didn't want to rely entirely on him.

A person who could only rely on someone else to do all the heavy lifting would never succeed in life. If she wanted to remain independent, she needed to do some of the work on her own.

"Ultimately, the question I need to ask myself is which strategy do I want to go with," Fayte mumbled.

"Excuse me?" asked Clarise.

"Apologies, I was merely talking to myself."

They had discussed several strategies for defeating the Pleonexia Alliance during the upcoming Guild War. Each one would work just fine, but they all required different terrain to be effective. Once she chose a location, their strategy would be set in stone.

The pressure she felt to choose the map and strategy that would work best was unbelievable.

She felt like the weight of the world was resting on this decision.

At the very least, the outcome of this battle might determine her fate.

"Are you okay, Lady Fayte? You look a little pale."

Fayte blinked several times as she came to. She pressed a hand to her face as though to hide the sallowness of her cheeks. Making a decision on her own like this made her more keenly aware of how much Adam helped her. She would have never been this nervous if he was by her side.

Stop it, Fayte. You can't think like that. It'll only hurt you if you grow to rely on him too much. After all... he's with Aris.

It took several deep breaths for Fayte to center herself again. Adam had a way of getting in her head that nobody else did. She constantly found herself thinking about him. When she had gone shopping with Aris and Susan, she would look at an outfit and wonder if he'd enjoy seeing her in it.

That was why this hurt so bad.

It hurt to have feelings for someone they wouldn't be returned.

"I'm fine," Fayte smiled.

Clarise didn't look convinced, but she nodded anyway. "If you say so."

"Anyway, I've chosen the map I'd like us to use. It's this one." Fayte pointed at one map in particular.

Clarise looked at it, nodded, and smiled. "That's a good choice. You'll have a large advantage over your attackers."

"Thanks. I think so too."

"Now, how many members is your opposition allowed to bring? Please remember that you can't have them bring any less than you are. Also, do you have a level requirement for them?"

"I do not, please inform Levon that he can bring as many people as he wants and they can be at any level," Fayte said.

Clarise looked flabbergasted. "A-are you sure? I know your guild is strong, but don't you think you're being too rash? The Pleonexia Alliance has over a million members! Meanwhile, your guild only has seven! Power isn't everything. Even the most powerful of people can be overwhelmed by sheer numbers!"

"I am aware of that, but please don't worry. I wouldn't suggest this if I didn't have a plan," Fayte said with what she hoped was a bold smile.

***

Adam was sitting on the couch, thinking about their upcoming Guild War, when Aris entered the living room. He looked up, then sighed.

"Aris… you should put some clothes on."

"Why? It's not like anyone else is here."

"That may be so, but you have no idea when they'll be back."

Susan and Lilith were running errands. Kureha was with Lilith and Titania with Susan.

It was interesting. Titania and Kureha couldn't join anyone's party but his, but that didn't mean they couldn't go wherever they pleased. That was something they had discovered through experimentation.

"It'll be fine. They shouldn't come back for at least another hour." Aris wandered up to him, grabbed his hand, and tugged. "Anyway, Adam, come with me."

Adam allowed himself to be pulled up. "And just where are we going?"

"To our bedroom," Aris replied.

Now that the Time Compression System had been installed, their avatar bodies required sleep and sustenance inside the game. They acted just like their real bodies. Adam and the others had taken to using the bedrooms periodically whenever they weren't on quests or attempting to raid that dungeon they discovered.

"I think I already know what you're after, but why don't you go ahead and answer me anyway. Why are we heading into the bedroom?" asked Adam as Aris led him up the stairs.

Aris turned back and grinned at him. "I want to find out what sex feels like in the game."

"I figured as much," Adam mumbled with an amused smile.

They made it to the bedroom and Adam was directed to the bed. Aris stood before him as he sat down.

Several seconds passed.

"Aris?" Adam asked.

"I wanted to try something new," Aris said. She sounded quite serious.

Adam shrugged. "All right. What are we gonna do?"

"I'd like to tie you up and blindfold you."

Adam blinked. "You, uh, want to…"

"Tie you up and blindfold you."

Aris opened her inventory and pulled out several items. Ropes and a sleep mask. The rope looked like it was made from something other than typical synthetic fibers. It appeared much softer and had a glossy sheen.

"This is definitely different," Adam admitted.

"Do you not want to?"

"I never said that. I just thought you'd want to be the one tied up and blindfolded."

Aris froze for a moment before her face contorted. A struggle took place within her. Adam could almost see her desire rising to the surface as her cheeks took on a bright blush. She licked her lips erotically as though imagining what it would be like if he tied her up.

"That… does sound fun… but I… I want to try tying you up," Aris struggled to get the words out.

While Aris was very forward and enjoyed actively pursuing him, she was more of a sub than a dom. She liked it when he took the lead even when she was the initiator. Even when she was on top, it was his hands controlling her movements.

"Well, I don't mind if you want to tie me up. A change of pace might spice things up a bit," Adam said after a moment. He removed his clothes and lay on the bed. "All right. What do we do now?"

Aris's eyes became vibrant like stars as she hurried over to him. "Just leave everything to me. Tee-hee. I'm gonna tie you up good."

She seems enthusiastic.

Adam didn't do anything as Aris grabbed one of his arms, tied it to the bedpost, then did the same to his other arm. After that, she tied his legs so he was spread eagle. It was… well, it was a little uncomfortable. Adam didn't really enjoy being bound like this, but since Aris wanted to try it, he was willing to go along.

After that, Aris leaned over, covered his face with the sleep mask, and pressed her lips to his. Her soft lips were warm. She pushed his mouth open with her tongue and breached it.

Hands began touching all over his body. His chest, arms, legs, thighs, and stomach, though they avoided his crotch. Adam felt a lot more sensitive to her touch than he normally did. It was like being robbed of his vision had brought attention to his other senses.

Blood rushed to his groin. He could feel his sword rising.

And then the hands abruptly stopped, Aris's lips left his, and he was left wanting.

"I just forgot something, so I'll be right back," Aris said. He turned his head to his left, where the voice had come from.

"You're leaving me like this?"

"I won't be gone long. Promise."

She didn't give Adam a moment to respond before opening the door, then closing it. He grimaced as he was left alone. He was already quite swollen. His hard shaft felt like it was about to burst. To make matters worse, he couldn't do anything about it since his hands were bound.

He tugged on the ropes. Maybe he could break them, but these ropes were supposed to be quite durable. He was more likely to break the bedpost.

Adam sighed and waited.

Footsteps echoed in the distance, growing closer. The sound of a door opening and closing reached his ear. More footsteps.

"I'm back," Aris announced in a loud voice that masked her footsteps. He felt her weight on the bed a moment later.

"Welcome back. Now, could you please not leave me in suspense like this? I feel like I'm about to explode."

"Tee-hee. Sorry about that. I'll take care of you right now," Aris said.

Adam groaned when something warm, soft, and wet pressed against the underside of his cock and was dragged across it all the way to the tip of his head. He'd recognize Aris's tongue anywhere. His body jerked slightly like it had been shocked as she began licking him like a lollipop.

"Mmmm. You taste kinda salty today," Aris mumbled.

"I... didn't think we'd be doing this... hnnn!"

"So you didn't shower?"

"I can if you... oh... I can if you want."

"No. I like your taste, and your scent."

Those words were enough to make his blood boil. He wanted to rip off these bindings and take Aris right then, but he held back. She wanted to try tying him up, after all.

He nearly choked on his own spit when Aris engulfed him with her mouth. The feeling of her mouth and tongue wrapping around him was far more intense than normal. His entire body shuddered. The sound of her nasal exhalations echoed around the room as she sucked him off, and he could only grit his teeth as the tension within his balls continued building.

"Aris… I'm gonna cum!"

"Not yet!"

Aris released his dick, and he almost cried in frustration. He was so close!

"I don't want you to cum in my mouth. Don't worry. I won't leave you like this. Tee-hee. I think you're going to enjoy this."

Adam was already dying with anticipation, so he nearly exploded when Aris climbed onto the bed and straddled his waist. Her nethers were already drenched as she pressed her lips against his cock. The way she ground herself against him was different than usual. A pair of hands landed on his chest. He would have blinked if he wasn't wearing a mask. Something about those hands felt different, stronger, sturdier.

"Aris, are you—?"

A mouth hampered his. Thoughts fled his mind as he recognized Aris's soft lips. He kissed her back. She released a muffled squeal as he pushed his tongue into her mouth, but that didn't stop her from kissing him back.

At the same time, Aris finally lowered herself onto him, fully sheathing him inside of her warm, wet passage. He was already too gone to think about much. He continued kissing Aris with everything he had as she began riding her.

Sweat formed along his skin. He could feel each individual droplet as it ran across his torso. Several drops of water splashed against his chest, the sweat of his companion, who was enthusiastically riding him.

Hands touched him all over. His face, his chest, his arms. It felt like he was being touched in four different places at once. The sensation combined with his lack of vision made him more keenly aware of the feeling.

The loud slapping sound of her hips bumping against his echoed around the room. Loud, seductive moaning made him briefly wonder what was going on, but he was already on the edge. His balls were swelling. He wasn't going to last much longer.

"Aris… I'm…"

"Go ahead. Cum for me," Aris whispered in his ear before nibbling on it.

Something about a girl telling him to cum for her set him off. His vision went white as he released his seed. Another loud moan came from on top of him. A pair of large breasts pressed against his chest. He took several deep breaths as he came down from his orgasmic high.

It was only after he recovered that he realized something.

"Aris… who's on top of me right now?"

He hadn't heard anyone come in, but he now realized that was why Aris had spoken so loudly before. It was to mask the entrance of this woman.

"Tee-hee. I really can't fool you, can I? Hold on. Let me remove that blindfold."

A pair of soft hands reached out and grabbed the mask. These were Aris's hands. Another pair of hands were resting on his chest, along with a body that was far too stacked to be Aris's. He had thought it was odd. Aris's hands were soft and dainty, but these were strong and calloused from years of weapon training.

The sleeping mask was removed, and Adam looked down to find a curtain of black hair surrounding a pair of equally dark eyes set upon a beautiful face. Her snow-white skin was flushed pink. She possessed a small nose and lush pink lips.

If Aris was the cute girl-next-door type, then this woman was the naughty librarian, the type who seemed cold at first glance, only to reveal how passionate she was when you got her in bed.

What's more, he knew this woman very well. He had known her for years. Even longer than he had known Aris.

The woman who was resting against his torso and looking up at him with equal amounts of desire and shame was none other than Lilith.

"Well… this is a situation I never thought I'd find myself in."

Adam was sitting on the edge of the bed, feet planted firmly on the ground, hands on his knees as he leaned forward and pinned the two women with a look.

Aris and Lilith were kneeling on the floor. One of them— Lilith—was kowtowing so low her head was pressed against the carpet. The other—Aris—had an unrepentant look that said she had no intention of apologizing. She probably didn't even feel bad about what she had done.

"Listen, Adam. I…"

Adam held up a hand, stopping Aris before she could continue. "I'm not going to ask why you decided to trick me into having sex with Lilith. I have a pretty good idea anyway."

While he knew he wasn't the smartest guy around, Adam didn't think himself stupid. He was at least observant enough to know when Aris was going behind his back. The reason he hadn't done anything was because he hadn't known what her plans were.

Perhaps he should have realized it sooner.

After all, he and Aris did have that conversation about Fayte joining them.

He looked at the other woman. "Lilith…"

"I'm sorry, Master. I know what I did was impertinent. I know you have Aris, but I… really wanted… to feel your warmth again…"

Adam could only close his eyes at Lilith's heartfelt words. This woman had no idea how much she made his heart flutter. He never slept with her after leaving Eden, but that wasn't because he never wanted to. His guilt kept him from touching her.

While Aris still remained fully clothed, Lilith was as naked as the day she'd been born. Her bear body was a wonder to behold. Her full breasts were squashed between her thighs and chest. The way they spilled over the sides enticed him to look. Her ass wasn't quite as visible, but he could see the beginning peeks of her peach-shaped butt. Black hair normally kept in a ponytail spread across the floor like a curtain of shimmering silk.

"Lilith, stand up," Adam commanded.

"Yes, Master."

Lilith stood up, revealing everything to him. Adam took in her small feet, her shapely calves, toned thighs, and hairless pussy, her large chest and slender shoulders, all the way to her gorgeous face. While her expression remained mostly the same, the fire in her eyes, the passion hidden behind a pair of dark moons, set him aback.

"Can I stand up too? My legs are beginning to fall asleep," Aris said.

"No. You're going to sit there and think about what you've done."

"Whaaaaaat?! Don't be mean…"

"Both of you are going to be punished for going behind my back like this," Adam continued as if he hadn't heard Aris. "Lilith, come over here."

Lilith stepped forward as Adam spread his legs apart. He was already fully erect. Lilith stared at his engorged cock without blinking. Was she trying to sear the sight into her brain or something?

"I want you to use your mouth and breasts to make me cum," he commanded.

Lilith licked her lips. "Yes, Master."

Kneeling between his legs, Lilith took a firm grip of his thighs before lowering her mouth against his head. She kissed the tip, then lowered herself further, taking him in one centimeter at a time.

Adam inhaled deeply as she continued going down. He leaned back when she relaxed her throat and took him all the way. Lilith had trained herself to not have a gag reflex, so unlike poor Aris who always choked when she tried this, the assassin was more than capable of fully sheathing himself inside of her mouth. Her wet tongue pressed against the underside of his shaft, and an electric current of pleasure raced through him as she began bobbing her head.

She didn't give him head for long. Once he was wet, she released him, then sandwiched his erection between her breasts and began moving.

He felt like the pole dancers used to please the crowd. His breathing had grown heavy. He groaned when Lilith, still titty fucking him, took his head into her mouth and swirled her tongue around it.

"Lilith, I'm… gonna…!"

Adam placed his hands on either side of her head. He didn't do anything more. Lilith let go of her breasts, lowered herself until she was deep-throating him, then began drinking his cum as he released it down her throat. There wasn't a single drop on her when she pulled back.

"How… how was that, Master?"

"Mmmm. It was good. I forgot how great you are at giving head."

"I'm happy you're pleased."

Adam was about to command her again when he saw something out of the corner of his eyes. He pointed at Aris.

"Don't even think about it, Aris. You're just going to sit there and watch."

"But that's just cruel! How can you make me watch something so hot and not allow me to relieve myself?!"

Aris's shorts hung down her ankles and she had been in the

process of pushing her panties aside to reach her wet slit, but Adam stopped the young woman in her tracks. The look of indignation on her face really did something for Adam. He had never teased her like this before, but perhaps he should begin doing so more often.

"It wouldn't be punishment if I let you do that, now would it?"

Aris made a strange noise like a growl in the back of her throat, but one look from him caused the woman to huff and pull her shorts back up. She crossed her legs, then her arms, and then glared at him.

He merely smiled before turning his attention back to Lilith.

"Lay down on the bed."

"Yes, Master."

Once Lilith was lying on her back, Adam grabbed her legs and placed them on his shoulders, then leaned down. Her wet snatch was engorged. The lips of her labia spread open before him like a flower in bloom, and the tiny pearl looked like it had already seen a lot of action, removed as it was from the hood that normally hid it.

Her scent was intoxicating. Adam had forgotten how erotic she smelled when she was like this. Her sweat mixed with the scent of her arousal. He leaned down until his nose was almost buried inside of her and took a deep breath.

"M-Master…" Lilith sounded embarrassed.

"You smell good."

"Oh. Um… th-thank yooOOOUUU?!"

Lilith threw her head back when Adam kissed her. Her hips tried to jerk upward as though she'd been electrocuted, but Adam kept a firm grip on them as he began his assault. He licked along her outer labia, then buried his tongue deep inside of her. He didn't tease her for long, though. He took pressed his mouth over the tiny pearl and began lapping at it with his tongue.

"Haaaaah… hmmmmm…. Oh! Master! I! I! Ahhhhh!"

As he continued assaulting her flower, Adam pushed two fingers inside her drenched cunt and curled them. He already knew where her weak spots were. Lilith let out an incoherent scream and her body shook as she came hard.

Adam didn't let him.

He continued punishing her until she'd had one, two, three more orgasms.

By this point in time, Adam's face was drenched in Lilith's fluids. He licked the area around his mouth as he pulled back and studied the woman before him.

Lilith's body glistened with sweat. Her breasts jiggled with every heave of breath she took. She had abs, and her six-pack was twitching with the aftershocks of multiple orgasms.

Lilith's hips were much wider than Aris's. They combined with her full breasts and thin waist to give her a perfect hourglass figure. He took this in, along with her muscular legs, which he knew could crush a man's head like a grape. He'd seen her snap the necks of men with those thighs.

Adam glanced back at Aris. The girl was biting her lip in frustration. Her shoulders and chest were heaving as sweat drenched her clothes, causing them to stick to her skin.

He gave her a brilliant smile.

She pouted at him.

He turned back to Lilith and shifted until his length was resting between the crevice of her lips. Adam placed a hand on either side of her head and pinned the woman with a look.

Lilith stared at him with half-lidded eyes, though they widened in surprise at his words.

"From this moment onward, you're mine. Let me know now if you have a problem with that. You'll never get another chance to complain."

Lilith shook her sweaty face. "I would never complain. You're not telling me anything new. I've always been yours."

"I figured you'd say that."

Lilith had loyally and faithfully followed him ever since their time in Eden. She had never once been with another man. Even during missions where sleeping with her target would have been easier, she refused. It had driven Lucifer up the wall, but he could never complain because she always gave him results.

Adam didn't waste any more time. He lined himself up and, with one quick thrust, was inside Lilith.

"Ooooh! Oh, Master! We're connected now!"

"You say that like we weren't connected just a few minutes ago."

"This is… this is different. What we did was… dishonest. You didn't know it was me."

"Yes, I suppose that's true. Anyway, get ready. This is gonna be your punishment."

"I'm ready, Master!"

Adam grabbed Lilith's firm hips, pulled back until only his head was inside of her, then thrust forward. He did it again. Again. Each thrust caused Lilith's chest to bounce. Her moans filled the room, so loud he thought they were echoing back to him. He really hoped these walls were soundproof. Shit. What if Susan or Fayte came back from their tasks and heard this?

Those thoughts only briefly filled him before he focused entirely on Lilith. She looked at him with a half-lidded gaze. He didn't think she was trying to be seductive, but those eyes were pulling him in.

He leaned down and kissed her. Lilith's eyes widened.

In all the time they had known each other, Adam had never once kissed her. Back in Eden, his first kiss was something he had been reserving for Lexi. After he found out Lexi disappeared, Aris had claimed his first kiss and Lilith had been cast aside.

Lilith's hands came up to cup his face. She leaned up as he plowed into her with strong, powerful thrusts, and kissed him for all she was worth. Her tongue was in his mouth before he could say anything, twirling, hooking, and playing with his.

It was clear from how inexperienced her movements were that she had never done this before, but there was something innately charming about a woman this sexy being inexperienced. It was cute and created a dichotomy that he found endearing.

Adam let her do as she pleased. He continued thrusting his hips, building up momentum. The sound of his balls slapping against her ass was barely heard amidst the gasps, groans, grunts, and moans.

Neither of them was capable of speaking, so when their mutual orgasm arrived, all they did was moan and cling to each other. Lilith pressed her full body against his. The feeling of her chest was something entirely different than what he was used to.

He wondered what her nipples tasted like. He didn't plan on finding out now. He would take his time refamiliarizing himself with her body at a later date.

Adam pulled back and was about to say something, but he paused and gave her a funny look.

"Why are you crying?"

"Am I... crying?" Lilith reached up and wiped her face, fingers coming away wet. She blinked several times. Tears continued to fall no matter how much she tried to stop him. "I'm sorry you have to see something so unsightly. I'm just... so happy that you've finally accepted me."

"I'm sorry it took this long."

"Don't worry. It was worth the wait."

Adam cupped her cheeks and used his thumbs to gently wipe away her tears, though it didn't do much because new tears replaced the old. Lilith grabbed one of his hands and placed it against her mouth. She kissed his palm, then his fingers, then slowly inserted one of them into his mouth.

Adam had only gone slightly flaccid, and feeling her wet mouth close down on his finger made him hard again.

"Adam?"

He was just about to make love to Lilith again when a voice interrupted him. He turned around as Lilith lifted herself up.

Aris looked absolutely miserable as she stared at the two. Even Adam, the one who punished her, felt sorry for the young woman.

"Please don't torture me anymore. I'm sorry, okay? I've reflected on my actions and won't do it again."

"Have you really?"

"...Yes."

"Don't look away when you say that! Look me in the eye and tell me that again!"

"I've reflected properly, okay?! I just... don't regret it!"

"Haaaaah. You're impossible."

Adam didn't know what he was going to do with this girl. He really thought he should not give her anything right now. Yes, the results of her duplicity weren't bad, but that was only because the one she'd convinced into doing this was Lilith. Lord knows what would have happened if she'd somehow conned poor Susan into having sex with him.

But I guess she did do it for my sake...

"Come on."

Aris's eyes widened before she leapt to her feet—and promptly fell back down.

"Ack! M-my legs are asleep!"

Sighing, Adam got off the bed, lifted Aris into a princess carry, and gently laid her down next to Lilith. He looked over and saw the woman was still awake. She stared at him and Aris with an anticipatory gaze.

"You plan on watching?"

"Do you not want me to?"

"I don't mind."

"Then I'd like to watch."

"Suit yourself."

Adam leaned over until he was nose to nose with Aris.

"I hope you don't think making you watch was the end of your punishment. I need to make sure you really understand what you've done."

Aris's eyes widened, but she couldn't say anything when he kissed her. He didn't remain lip-locked for long. He trailed kisses down her chin, her throat, her collarbone. Then he had her remove her clothes. It was as simple as unequipping them. That kind of ruined it for him. He preferred removing the clothes himself, but this was a game world.

Now naked, Adam took only a moment to admire his petite girlfriend before leaning down and licking her breasts.

"Mmmmm."

Aris moaned and ran her fingers through his hair as he worked her chest over. He soon made his way down. He dragged his tongue over her stomach, kissed her belly button, and soon reached her bare crotch.

"Oh! OOOH! MY! GOD!"

While Lilith had been louder, Aris was a lot more… vocal about what she liked. She was more than willing to tell him what she wanted him to do. Adam listened to her commands, bringing her to several orgasms. The way her hips shook as she ground her crotch into his face pleased him to no end.

But this wasn't all he had planned.

Adam pulled back and flipped Aris onto her stomach before she could complain. She squawked as he grabbed her hips and lifted them off the bed. He forced her legs apart and pressed himself against her, though he didn't insert it yet.

"Aris..."

"Yes—ah?!"

Aris squealed when he spanked her. The sound was loud and reverberated around the room.

"Who's a bad girl?"

"... M-me?"

SMACK!

"AHH!"

"That's right. You're a very bad girl, and it's time for your punishment."

Adam smacked her again. The juices from her cunt flowed down her thighs and stained the bed. That was when he thrust himself inside of her.

"Hnn! Ahhh! Ah! Ah!"

Aris's moans were loud and timed to the rhythm of his thrusts and spanks. Each action brought a different reaction. Adam was careful not to use too much force. He didn't know if he could damage her avatar by spanking it, but he didn't want to risk it.

"Adam! Adam! I'm cumming! I'm cumming so muuuuuch!!!"

Aris had already cum twice, but Adam had yet to cum once. He was holding back, waiting until he had exhausted all of her stamina.

It wasn't long before Aris's body had gone slack. The only thing moving was her twitching nethers, still overflowing with her juices.

"Haaaah... Haaaaah... Adam... n-no more... I can't... last much... longer..."

Adam didn't stop thrusting.

"Have you learned your lesson?"

"Y-yes. I have. I… I promise."

"All right. Here it comes."

Adam thrust himself inside of her one last time, pushing as far into her as he could go before releasing whatever he had left inside of her. Aris moaned into her pillow as her butt shook.

Adam pulled himself out and looked at his seed spilling from inside of her.

"I've always found it odd that games like this allow you to have sex."

"Mmmm. So long as it's consensual," Aris mumbled into the pillow. "I think they have an age limit though… like you can't have sex if you're not of legal age. I read an article about a pair of fourteen-year-olds who tried and got banned from playing again."

"Interesting story."

Adam moved until he was lying between Aris and Lilith. He reached over and pulled Lilith into his side, then did the same with Aris. Both of them were exhausted, so they could hardly move.

I wonder if Fayte and Susan have returned?

They would have to get up soon. Whether those two had returned or not, they would eventually, and he didn't want to deal with the awkwardness that would happen if they discovered what he, Aris, and Lilith had been up to.

"Adam?" Aris suddenly called out to him.

"Yes?"

"That was really fun. Can you punish me again?"

Adam paused.

"… Only if you're a good girl from now on."

SEAMLESS INFILTRATION

"IS THAT WOMAN MOCKING US?! JUST WHO DOES SHE THINK SHE IS?!"

Gaia looked like she was about to spit acid as she spoke with rancor so thick it would have sent her subordinates scurrying for the hills. It was rare to see her get this emotional. Levon could count the number of times it happened on one hand and still have fingers left over.

Guess that would make this time number four.

Gaia was a woman with dark skin, dark hair, and eyes blacker than a starless night. Her hair was drawn into a tight ponytail behind her head. She wore an outfit that was very form-fitting. It was made from a temperature-controlled fabric that was designed with maneuverability in mind.

"I've got to admit that woman has quite the pair. Not many people would tell us that we can bring as many guild members as we want to fight in a Guild War. Fayte Dairing has the largest brass balls

I've ever seen," Thor God of Thunder said as he casually leaned back in his chair. He ran a hand over his stubble, chuckling to himself. He looked like a hobo with his five o'clock shadow and unkempt hair.

"Get your feet off the table," Flame Emperor snapped with a scowl.

Thor God of Thunder grunted but removed his feet from the table. They hit the floor with a thunk.

Because time flowed slower within the game, they had decided to hold this meeting at their *Age of Gods* guild headquarters. It was located on the outskirts of Solum. The fortress was large enough to hold several million people.

The room they were in was a meeting room. Unlike the more modern architecture of the real world, this room looked like something straight out of the Renaissance period. The table they sat around was made of fine wood. Their chairs were curved and had soft padding to prevent their backs and bottoms from getting sore. The floor was made of marble tiles that gleamed in the light as though freshly polished.

"At first glance, it seems rather reckless of her, but it was actually a very cunning move on her part," Ymir said. He tapped a finger against the table, eyes narrowed. "By telling us that we can bring as many guild members as we want, she is not only blatantly calling us out, but she's given us a clear challenge we can't possibly refuse. At the same time, she released the news on every social media platform and the *Age of Gods* forum. Every news station is already talking about it."

Levon had received a message from the Guild Association two days ago in-game time that the battlefield and date had been decided, along with the news that Fayte was allowing him to choose as many people as he wanted to fight in the Guild War. On that same day, Fayte had posted the news everywhere, letting the entire world know what was happening.

"The top guilds of other nations are already mocking us, calling us pathetic for picking a fight with a guild that only has seven members, and we received an email from Daren Daggerfall 'wishing us luck' in our upcoming Guild War," Connor added.

"She definitely put us in a difficult position," Levon said with a sigh.

He was surprised by how calm he felt, but maybe that was because he had already expected all this. Fayte was highly intelligent and incredibly motivated. Aside from her beauty, that was one of the many reasons he coveted her. He expected no less from the woman he planned on making his.

"Rather than complaining about our circumstances, I believe we should focus on deciding what we should do about the situation," Flame Emperor began. "We cannot send too many players to fight in the Guild War. Doing so will make it look like a case of the strong bullying the weak… but we also cannot afford to send too few."

Fayte and the members of her guild had already proven their strength during the tournament last year. They had demolished the competition. It hadn't even been a contest.

It was clear now that Fayte had somehow been responsible for that tournament. Levon suspected the entire purpose had been to let Fayte and her guild showcase their strength to the world. He wouldn't have been surprised if the [guild creation token] had already belonged to her, and she merely put it up as the tournament prize in order to bait him and the others into participating.

Adam is the one most likely responsible for that…

The very thought of that man-made Levon's hatred surge like never before. He forced himself to remain calm, but it felt like lava was boiling underneath his skin.

Fayte on her own is dangerous. That's why I did my best to isolate her and make sure she couldn't call on anyone for help. That begs the question: how did she manage to find such a powerful ally?

Levon had done his best to discover Adam's identity, but every avenue he'd tried had turned to naught. There was nothing. The man was a ghost. Not even going through the government's database had done him any good.

It's like someone is blocking my attempts to find out anything about him. Could it be... Susan Forebear?

While meek and lacking in confidence, Susan was one of the best hackers Levon knew of. She wasn't one to brag. However, hacking into government databases and changing or erasing information was well within her capabilities.

There's just too much I don't know...

Levon shook his head. There was a lot that he remained unaware of, and sadly, there was nothing he could do about that. For now, all he could do was focus on the task at hand.

"The location of our Guild War has already been determined. Connor?" Levon looked at his second-in-command.

"Right."

Connor removed a map from his item box and placed it on the table they sat around. The aged parchment was yellow and wrinkled, but it still clearly showed a fortress built into a mountain. Several lines and notes denoted information like size, distance, and the number of levels the fortress had. Just by looking at the map, Levon could tell the fortress had been designed to withstand sieges.

"This is going to be the location of our Guild War," Connor began. "According to the information provided by the Guild Association, it was a fortress that stood strong against an army of one hundred thousand for two months during the war against the Demon King. As you can see, our only method of attack is a frontal assault."

"A frontal assault sounds like suicide. Fayte Dairing has those AoE spells of hers. You all saw what she did during her fight against Flame Emperor. Are there no secret passages we can use to sneak in?" asked Thor God of Thunder, ignoring the scowl on Flame Emperor's face.

"There is one, but Fayte will already be aware of it. She has the same map we do, and I'm certain she's thoroughly explored the fortress or will if she hasn't already," answered Connor.

Everyone looked at Levon, who had remained silent for the most part. He was busy thinking about the upcoming battle. His subordinates knew better than to interrupt him, so they remained silent as he thought.

"Since we can't bring too many people without putting our reputation at risk, we'll have one hundred thousand take part in this operation. Each of you will take command of twenty thousand people," Levon said.

"What about you?" asked Thor God of Thunder.

"I'm going to take a squadron of our best members and sneak in through the secret passage. Fayte definitely knows about it, but she won't be able to do anything if we can pressure her. I'll wait until you've broken into the fortress through the front. Then I'll sneak in after you've engaged the members of Destiny's Overture. You'll wear their group down. Even if they manage to finish everyone in our forces off, they'll be too exhausted to deal with us. We can take them out with a surprise attack from behind."

It wasn't a bad plan, but Levon knew better than to assume they would be victorious. This was the only plan they could feasibly come up with. Anything less would result in failure. What's more, the avenues they could attack from were limited. Was there anything else he could use to further guarantee their victory?

"How many siege weapons have we been able to produce?" asked Levon.

"Not many," Gaia admitted. "We've hired out several blacksmiths from Solum, but even with all of them working, we've only made five siege towers and one battering ram. We should have at least ten siege towers and maybe one dozen trebuchets by the time we're ready for the Guild War, but that won't be enough to turn the tide of battle."

Levon grunted. He never expected to be forced into a battle where he needed to seize a castle, so they had only started producing weapons a few days ago. Fayte had predicted this and made sure not to give them enough time to build a significant amount of weapons meant for breaching fortifications.

"We'll make what we can, but we won't rely on our siege weapons then," said Levon. "That said, I'll leave the siege weapons under your command, Thor. You know more about siege warfare than anyone else."

Thor God of Thunder was an avid fan of siege warfare games. He still played many old-school console games. His favorite was called Simulation Siege, in which the main purpose of the game was to either defend or attack a fortress. He ranked number one in that game out of the two hundred thousand hardcore players who continued to play even though console games were obsolete.

"Leave it to me," Thor God of Thunder said, thumping his chest.

"Connor, get me a list of all our members. Since we're only bringing one hundred thousand, we'll want to hand-select only the best," said Levon.

"Sir," Connor said before searching through his inventory for the list.

Levon crossed his arms and leaned back. The pressure he felt right now was immense, but the dice had been cast, and all he could do was figure out a workaround to his current problems.

***

Belphegor had seamlessly inserted himself into the Pleonexia Alliance's forces. His high level, excellent deduction skills, and ability to work as part of a team had earned him a reputation among not only the new recruits, but the senior members as well. Everyone respected him. And many captains wanted him on their teams.

Because of his talent, he tended to work with a bunch of different squads, including the squadrons led by the Four Elements, which allowed him to accomplish his goal of keeping an eye on any potential threats. He'd already sent off a document containing all the information he had on Gaia, Ymir, Flame Emperor, and Thor God of Thunder.

At present, he was not working with the Four Elements. They had stopped raiding dungeons and were currently going over the groundwork for the upcoming Guild War with Destiny's Overture.

"Good work today. I really don't know what we would have done without you," said an older man with graying hair. His name was Rykard. He had led today's dungeon raid.

"Thank you, sir," Belphegor said with a bow.

"You were pretty awesome out there!" A younger man with a cheerful grin slapped Belphegor on the back. Matthew was his name. Matthew Bellows. He was just a normal member of the Pleonexia Alliance.

"Thank you very much for saving me," said the last member of their squadron, one Susan Maan. She was a pretty woman with red hair and green eyes. Her skin was tan and she had freckles dotting her cheeks.

"There's no need for thanks. It's only natural to protect one's squad mates," said Belphegor.

"Hah! Look at you, Mr. Smooth Operator," Matthew chuckled as Susan blushed.

"All right. That's enough. Get some rest, all of you. I have no doubt you'll be called upon soon."

"Yes, sir."

Belphegor parted ways with everyone else and began walking through the wide hallway of the Pleonexia Alliance's guild headquarters. It was a large compound with three hundred buildings that ranged in size. The barracks were four-story buildings large enough to fit ten thousand people inside. This place was almost the same size as Solum itself.

As he wandered through the hall, a man of average height but an extraordinary appearance. His eyebrows were sharp like swords. The arrogance in his gaze was really something else. Belphegor wondered how this man fit his head through the door, such was his ego. While his smile looked lazy for all intents and purposes, he knew better than to underestimate this man.

"Axel Rose, I assume?" Connor asked.

Axel Rose, one of many names registered in the American Federation's database that he and the other members of the Grim Reapers used. They had over ten thousand on file. This was the first time it had been used.

"Yessir." Belphegor stopped walking and stood at attention.

Connor nodded in approval. "Come with me. Levon would like to speak with you."

The man turned around and walked away without another word, forcing Belphegor to start walking again to catch up. Given that Levon wanted to speak with him personally, he could only assume the man planned on asking him to join the upcoming Guild War.

That was perfect. He would be able to acquire all the information he needed on Levon's plans and send them to Belial. He wondered what sort of face the man would make if he knew there was a venomous snake in their midst.

PREPARA-TION

THERE WERE A LOT OF THINGS ADAM AND THE OTHERS NEEDED TO prepare for the upcoming Guild War. They had spoken of these matters at length and decided the most important matter was checking out the location where the Guild War was going to take place.

Fayte, Lilith, and Aris were already at the location. Adam, Susan, Titania, and Kureha would be joining them soon, but there was something Adam wanted to do before they met up with the others.

"Adam! Good to see you!" Bromley Paxton, the Mayor of Solum, greeted Adam with a wide smile as he and his companions entered the man's office.

Bromley Paxton was a dignified man. He wore an elegant doublet crafted from fine cotton. His pants and long-sleeved shirt, made from glimmering silk, sparkled in the light as he enthusiastically shook Adam's hand. The finely-crafted fencing sword strapped to his belt shook as he moved.

"I cannot thank you enough for taking on all of these dangerous quests. My people have suffered far fewer casualties thanks to you," he continued.

Adam gave the man a diplomatic smile. "I'm pleased to know that I have been of some use to you."

"Come now. There's no need to be so humble. You've taken on more than your fair share of dangerous quests. My soldiers have even started talking about how you're like the heroes from yore. They tell tales about the indomitable man in the mask and his fairy and fox companions."

Adam could only smile. He had no idea NPCs were now talking about him—or was this just part of the story? VRMMOs often have a story that was woven into the gameplay.

"Now, what can I do for you? I imagine you're not here just to chat with this old man, not with your upcoming Guild War," Bromley Paxton said.

"You're right. I'm not here for idle chitchat."

Susan squeaked as Adam took her hand and pulled her forward. The girl was dressed in green clothing and silver armor. Her doe-like brown eyes stood out on her pale face. If she'd had pointed ears, someone might have mistaken the adorable girl for an elf.

"This is Susan. She's the Fairy Archer Class," he introduced.

Bromley Paxton cupped his chin. "Aaaah. So this is the young lass you gave the [Fairy Archer Class Scroll] to. Is she your…?"

"She's my companion."

"Very well. Let's leave it at that." Bromley Paxton paused long enough to study Susan, who squirmed uncomfortably as she bore the man's scrutiny. "If you're introducing me to her, I can only assume you want something from my vault. The [Bow of Prosperity]?"

Adam nodded. "I was hoping you would let me buy it from you."

"Hmmm…"

Bromley Paxton didn't say anything at first. Adam let the man think as he turned to look at Susan.

While Susan had a great class, her equipment was lacking. Everyone else in their party had equipment that enhanced their already impressive strength. Susan was the only one who lacked such equipment. Her bow and clothing were still the same beginner-level equipment she had been wearing since the game started.

There were two important factors that gamers could use to increase their prowess: their stats and their equipment. Stats increased a person's base powers. Someone with a high Strength stat would do more damage than someone with a low Strength stat. On the other hand, equipment could be used to increase anything from a person's base stats to the amount of damage they did.

Adam's spear was the perfect example. It increased his Strength by 210% and his Physical Attack by another 210, making it easily the most powerful physical weapon currently in the game. The [Alexandra's Staff] that Fayte had equipped was another weapon that gave her a massive buff.

"I suppose… I could sell the bow to you," Bromley Paxton said at last. He stroked his beard. "Truth be told, I have a firm belief that weapons are meant to be used. A weapon that just sits in a vault, collecting dust, is a sad weapon indeed. I would even be willing to give the little lady some Fairy Armor I have."

"You have Fairy Armor?!" Titania suddenly asked. She shot off Adam's shoulder and flew to Bromley Paxton's face. "Where is it?! What kind of armor is it?!"

"Ah…" Bromley Paxton backed off in shock at the little fairy's sudden intensity. He cleared his throat. "It's called [Fae Guardian Armor]. I found it long ago when I was much younger. I was full of vigor and vim back then, and I loved to go exploring against my father's wishes. The armor was something I discovered in an old, underground ruin on the northeastern side of the Sun Continent."

"Were these ruins located on a peninsula?" asked Titania.

"Yes... but how did you know?" asked the shocked mayor.

Titania swallowed heavily. "I'll tell you... if you allow me to see them."

Bromley Paxton looked hesitant for a moment, but he eventually capitulated. This man was full of curiosity. It was clear that, while he may have settled down after growing older, he still longed for adventure.

Adam, Susan, Titania, and Kureha in her human form followed Bromley Paxton as he led them to the vault. Adam kept a firm grip on Kureha's hand so she wouldn't run off.

The vault was being guarded by the same two people as last time. Adam remembered their faces. The vault itself was huge, towering over him like a goliath. It was made from a type of gleaming alloy and reminded Adam of the high-security vaults used by nobles in the real world. The guards snapped off a salute to the mayor before inserting a pair of keys into two keyholes, which unlocked the mechanism keeping the vault shut.

Bromley Paxton led the four inside as the guards opened the door. He wove through the neat and orderly rows of shelves, eventually reaching a mannequin that stood in a corner of the room.

The mannequin had clothing and armor adorning it. A green gown that trailed around the ankles served as the undergarment to prevent the armor itself from rubbing against one's skin. Gleaming silver pauldrons sat on the shoulders, a chestplate made from overlapping metal plates resembling leaves adorned the torso, and wrist guards of the same design were strapped across the forearms with leather bands. The faulds also looked like leaves as they rested upon the hips. Wrapped around the waist was a thick golden sash made of an unknown material that shimmered like liquid gold.

"Oh…" Titania breathed, bringing a hand to her mouth as tears gathered in her eyes.

Bromley Paxton had been observing Titania. "Do you… know who this armor belonged to?"

"I do." Titania closed her eyes and took a shuddering breath. "It belonged to… my older sister."

"Y-you have a sister?!" Susan asked in shock.

"I *had* a sister, yes. She's not here anymore."

"O-oh… I'm so sorry."

"It is fine. She died a very long time ago." Titania pursed her lips as she stared at the armor. Her eyes became distant as though she was lost in the past, and her lips moved slowly as she began to speak once more. "My sister was a prodigy among the Fairy Clan. She could do anything she set her mind to. I always looked up to her, and I relied on her for everything. It was actually her death that caused the Fairy Clan to decide to seal themselves off. The war between humans and beastmen had grown more violent. The number of atrocities both sides committed was beyond recompense. The Fairy Council refused to let me go, saying it was too dangerous to get involved, so I asked my sister… to try and mediate… to stop the fight from growing worse. She did as I commanded without hesitation. The last I saw of her was the day she left for the Sunset Peninsula. I later learned that she had died trying to stop the fighting…"

Adam reached out and placed his palms underneath the little fairy so she could land on them. Her legs wobbled before she collapsed as if all the strength in them had gone out. She cupped her hands to her face and cried.

"If I hadn't been selfish and asked her to stop the fighting, I'm sure she would still be with me."

No one said anything as Titania cried. Susan had tears in her eyes and Kureha was sniffling as she cried. Adam didn't think the little fox yokai understood what they were talking about, but she was empathic enough to know her friend was in pain. Bromley Paxton was silent, eyes closed, lips drawn into a tight line.

"I had no idea this armor had that kind of history. It may not mean much, but on behalf of the human race, I deeply apologize for the atrocities that were committed during that senseless war," he said.

Titania shook her head as she wiped her eyes, now rimmed red. "It is not something you should apologize for. Blaming the child for the sins of the parent is a fallacy. So long as you do not repeat the mistakes made by your ancestors and renew that horrible war, there is no need to apologize.

"I can't speak for anyone else, but I can assure you that Solum will never take part in a war like that," Bromley Paxton said, thumping his chest. He then glanced at the armor. "In either event, now that I know this armor once belonged to your relative, it would be dishonorable of me to sell it to you. I'll give you the armor. It belongs to you anyway. The bow, however, I will have to sell. That was given to my ancestors by the Fairy Clan long ago and parting with it will be hard."

"Thank you," Titania muttered.

She flew off Adam's hand, fluttered over to the armor, and pressed her hands and forehead against it. Silence reigned as the fairy took a moment to bask in the armor's presence. She then turned around to face Susan and smiled.

"Su… please wear this armor."

"A-are you sure it's okay for me to wear it? That's your sister's armor…"

"I am sure. My sister loved humanity as much as I did, and among the humans I have met, you are one of the kindest. She would be honored to know you're putting her armor to good use."

Susan still looked uncertain, but Adam, Titania, and even Bromley Paxton gave the young girl a push. She eventually reached out and stored the armor in her inventory. Then equipped it.

The armor certainly gave Susan a very different aesthetic than her previous outfit. She looked down at herself. Raising her hands, now covered in a pair of thin archery gloves that only covered the thumb and index finger. She clenched and unclenched her fingers, then looked at Adam with a soft pink hue lighting up her cheeks.

"H-how do I look?"

"Like a true Fairy Archer," Titania said.

"You look kind of like an elf," Adam confessed.

"What's an elf?" asked a confused Titania.

"…A creature from our world."

Susan giggled into her hand at their byplay.

"You look marvelous, young lass. Now… the [Bow of Prosperity] will cost you one hundred million gold coins. It is not something I can just give away on a whim," Bromley Paxton said.

One hundred million gold coins was a lot, but they, fortunately, had the money. Adam agreed immediately.

Bromley led them to the bow, took it from its stand, then reluctantly handed it to Susan. The bow also came with a quiver and two dozen arrows. They were different from your standard arrows, however. The tips were made of mythril and had a sleeker design.

Something strange occurred when the bow was placed in her hand. It began glowing. Then a screen appeared before the young woman. Susan blinked several times before turning to Adam.

"Adam… I just received an announcement saying I've become the owner of the [Bow of Prosperity]."

"Something similar happened to me when I became the owner

of this spear," Adam admitted as he tapped the spear strapped to his back.

"It seems the bow has recognized you as its owner," Bromley Paxton said. "That's quite a significant feat. My family has tried to use this bow for generations, but only the one who received it was ever able to wield it. Congratulations, young lass."

As Susan was happily checking out her new bow and armor, Adam decided to look at the young lady's stats.

Name: Little_Su
Class: Fairy Archer
Lvl: 25
SP: 10
AP: 429,150
Experience: 1,250,188,000/5,097,164,800
Fame: 2,945,000
Strength: +765
Constitution: +100
Dexterity: +100
Intelligence: +100
Speed: +100
Physical Attack: +15,100
Health: 4,020/4,020
Hit-rate: 400%
MP: 1,110/1,110
Movement: +400
Luck: +1
Physical Defense: +1,645
Magical Defense: +1,075
Dodge Rate: 150%
Magic Attack: +500

Resistances:
95% Poison
95% Death
95% Blindness
95% Confusion
95% Sleep
95% Paralysis
95% Burn
95% Shock
50% Fire
50% Earth
50% Water
50% Wind
50% Lightning
50% Light
50% Darkness

Skill List:
Skill Name: Deadeye
Description: Archers can increase their hit-rate and critical hit-rate by increasing their perceptions through the Deadeye skill.
Current lvl: 5
AP Needed to Reach Next lvl: 30,000
Ability: Increases Hit-rate to 110%
Deals x2 critical damage
MP consumption: 5
Cooldown time: 5 seconds

Skill Name: Rain of Arrows
Description: Archers who learn this skill can fire a
hailstorm of arrows that deals damage to multiple enemies.
Current lvl: 5
AP Needed to Reach Next lvl: 35,000
Ability: Causes 150% damage to all enemies within 15
yards of targeted enemy
MP Consumption: 5
Cooldown time: 10 seconds

Skill Name: Fairy Shot
Description: A skill that can only be used by someone of the
Fairy Archer Class.
Current lvl: 5
AP Needed to Reach Next lvl: 50,000
Ability: Increases accuracy by 100%
If enemy is hit, x5 critical damage is dealt
MP Consumption: 10
Cooldown time: 10 seconds

Skill Name: Light Arrow
Description: A skill used by the Fairy Archer Class. Infuses
arrow with the power of light.   Current lvl: 5
AP Needed to Reach Next lvl: 45,000
Ability: Deals 700% damage to undead and enemies of the
darkness element.
MP Consumption: 20
Cooldown time: 10 seconds

Skill Name: Nature Arrow
Description: A skill used by someone with the Fairy Archer

Class. Infuses the power of nature into the arrow.

Current lvl: 5

AP Needed to Reach Next lvl: 60,000

Ability: When an enemy is struck by a Nature Arrow, they become entrapped in vines for 120 seconds.

MP Consumption: 30

Cooldown time: 10 seconds

Skill Name: Rapid Fire

Description: Fairy Archers can fire a continuous stream of arrows until they run out in exchange for dealing less damage than normal.

Current lvl: 1

AP Needed to Reach Next lvl: 50,000

Ability: Damage = 50% of Physical Attack

Continuous fire until out of arrows

MP Consumption: 100 MP for every arrow fired

Cooldown Time: 60 seconds

Skill Name: Long Shot

Description: Fairy Archers have the longest range of any archer class. With the use of [Long Shot], they can fire accurately hit a target over five hundred meters away.

Current lvl: 1

AP Needed to Reach Next lvl: 60,000

Ability: Accurately hit target 500 meters away

Damage = Physical Attack

MP Consumption: 150

Cooldown Time: 5 seconds

Skill Name: Farsight
Description: Fairies are well-known for their incredible
vision. They can see for several dozen kilometers in the clearest
detail. As a Fairy Archer, you also have this ability.
Current lvl: 1
MAXED
Ability: See precisely 24 kilometers out
MP Consumption: None
Cooldown Time: None
Passive Skill

Skill Name: Bow Blocking
Description: Use your bow to block close-range attacks.
This skill was developed by the Fairy Clan to defend oneself
when close combat is unavoidable.
Current lvl: 1
AP Needed to Reach Next lvl: 55,000
Ability: Negates 50% damage
MP Consumption: 200
Cooldown Time: 0 seconds

Equipment:
Name: Bow of Prosperity
Item type: Bow
Grade: 3-Star
Use requirements: Can only be equipped by Archers level
40 and above or someone with the Fairy Archer Class.
Description: The Bow of Prosperity was given to the
Paxton Family by the Fairy Clan before they disappeared. It is
one of the highest classes of bow in existence.

Abilities: Physical Attack+400%; Hit-Rate+200%;
Luck+40

Name: Fairy Guardian Armor
Item type: Armor
Grade: 4-Star
Use requirements: Can only be equipped by someone with
a Fairy Class.
Description: This armor was once worn by Mab, elder
sister of Titania. This is the best armor crafted by the Fairy
Clan. Its defensive capabilities rival even armor made by the
Dwarves.
Abilities: Physical Defense+500; Magical Defense+500;
75% Resistance Against All Status Ailments; 50% Resistance
Against All Elements

Name: Fairy Boots
Item type: Footwear
Grade: 4-Star
Use requirements: Can only be worn by someone with a
Fairy Class.
Description: Boots worn by Mab. They are woven from
strands of the Life Tree. They offer solid defense and boost the
wearer's speed.
Abilities: Physical Defense+50; Magical Defense+50;
Speed+150%

Name: Fairy Grieves
Item type: Armor
Grade: 4-Star

Use requirements: Can only be equipped by someone with a Fairy Class.

Description: These protective grieves are part of the Fairy Guardian Mab's armor set. They boost the wearer's defense and resistance to status ailments.

Abilities: Physical Defense+25; Magical Defense+25; 20% Resistance to Status Ailments

Item name: Ring of Earthly Protection
Item type: Ring
Grade: Lord

Use requirements: Can be used by any class of any level.

Description: This ring was born from the earth and offers incredible protection against physical attacks plus a passive regeneration ability.

Abilities: Physical Defense+500; Recovers +1 HP every 1 second

THE DAY BE-
FORE

FAYTE STOOD INSIDE THE STRONGHOLD THEY WOULD BE USING FOR the Guild War. Known as Iron Fortress, it was a fortified gorge with a narrow path and cliffs on either side, heightening its northernmost point, where Iron Fortress lay.

Iron Fortress was built upon a great spur of rock, which extended from the gorge's southern cliff, and from the fortress to the northern cliff, was a massive wall at least one dozen meters in height if not taller. The wall was the first line of defense and spanned the width of the entire gorge.

There was no wind in this gorge, for the tall cliffs prevented it. This entire fortress felt stifling.

"This is an amazing fortress," Aris said in awe. "It's so big."

"It is quite massive, yes. I do worry about whether we will be able to defend this fortress with just the seven of us," Fayte said.

She and Kureha did have some rather powerful AoE spells that dealt massive amounts of damage to a large number of individuals, but the gorge must have been at least several dozen meters across. None of their attacks were large enough to cover that broad an area.

She, Aris, and the silent Lilith traveled up a set of winding steps and made it to the front of the fortress battlements. There, she stared at the long causeway that wound up to the great gate meant to keep intruders out. The gate was made from thick iron and could only be opened using several levers. It was so big, Fayte wondered how the people who built this fortress ever managed to put it in place.

"Look! I see Adam and Susan!" Aris pointed at something in the distance.

Fayte narrowed her eyes as a speck appeared in her vision. The speck eventually gained shape. It was Adam and Susan, riding a white horse. Titania and Kureha were with them.

Fayte smiled. "Let's go greet them, shall we?"

"Mhmm!"

The trio left the battlement and traveled to the door. The narrow hallway was only big enough for six people to stand abreast. It was designed to prevent an army from utilizing its overwhelming numbers to simply sweep over the defenders. Adam, Aris, and Lilith would likely be stationed here during the assault.

Aris rushed over to the door and pulled a lever, which activated the mechanism needed to open the door. A low groan of rusted hinges echoed around them as the door slowly opened. Adam arrived on his white horse with Susan holding him tight soon after.

"I'm back, and look at what we managed to get!" Adam said. He looked happier than he normally did. His bright smile was... well, it made Fayte feel a flutter in her chest. She tried to will the butterflies to leave by focusing on Susan.

"Oh, my. You do look magnificent in that outfit," Fayte complimented.

"D-dank you," Susan said, bumbling over her words.

So cute.

Susan did look a lot better with her new outfit and bow. She reminded Fayte of the elven warriors from old movies and fantasy games. If she could have just acted a bit more elegant, she would have been a picture-perfect elf.

But then she wouldn't be so cute.

Adam climbed off the horse, then helped Susan down as well. While Lilith grabbed the horse's reins to lead it away, Aris flung her arms around Adam and kissed him. Fayte looked away and Susan blushed. But even though she wasn't looking, the sound of smacking lips made her distinctly aware of the two.

"If you're quite finished, perhaps I can start by showing you around?" Fayte said.

"Yes, please," Adam said.

"Yeah. I guess we're done… for now," Aris added.

"That 'for now' was completely uncalled for," Fayte mumbled, but then she sighed and began showing Adam and Susan around. They had yet to see the fortress and would need to know the layout if they wanted to properly defend it.

Iron Fortress had three courtyards. If enemy troops ever breached the walls, the narrow passages, with their high walls that were too high and impossible to climb, would funnel them into one of these courtyards, which could be used as excellent ambush points. When Adam saw these courtyards, he narrowed his eyes in thought.

"Do you think we can pack these courtyards with explosives?" he asked.

Fayte blinked. "You want to blow the courtyards up?"

He shook his head. "The material used in the construction of this fortress is durable enough to withstand an explosion. I was thinking we could pack it with boxes filled with gunpowder. Then, when Levon's men entered the courtyard, we'd blow them up."

"Oh. That could work," Fayte muttered.

"I'll go into Solum tomorrow and see if we can buy any explosives," said Aris. She was the fastest among them. It would take her less than an hour to reach Solum by running at full speed.

They continued the tour. Fayte showed him to the kitchens, the barracks, the armory… a lot of this place was empty. This fortress had been abandoned centuries ago, so all of the equipment that had been stored inside was long gone. The last place Fayte showed Adam was the hold.

"This is pretty spacious. It looks almost like a throne room," Adam said as he turned his head left, then right, studying the columns that stood tall on either side of a red carpet. The carpet led to a dais near the back. There was no chair, but it was clear that was where the leader relayed their orders.

"Long ago, the Sun Continent was divided into many different kingdoms. Keeps like this were created to house the kings and queens of their respective countries, so the hold was designed with comfort in mind. These holds were also used as a last stand. Should the fortress ever be overrun, the remaining defenders could hole themselves inside here and prepare for the final battle," Titania explained.

"Makes sense," Adam said.

"The secret passage leading out of the keep is located over there, through that door. There is a statue of Stella the Sun Goddess that can be moved via a lever to reveal the passage." Fayte pointed at the door.

"Can it be opened from the other side?" asked Adam.

Fayte shook her head. "Not to my knowledge, but that doesn't mean it can't be blasted through with overwhelming firepower."

Adam stroked his chin. "Should the situation not go well for him, I suspect Levon will take an elite unit of men and attempt to break in through the passage."

"I thought so too. That poses a problem since we already have so few people here to defend the front," Fayte muttered, biting her lip.

"Don't worry about that. I've already got a plan," said Adam.

Fayte stared in delighted surprise. "You do? Well, let's hear it."

"In a bit. We need to wait before I can fully unveil my plan to you," said Adam with a mysterious grin.

Fayte wanted to pout, but the air of mystery and intrigue Adam exuded left her momentarily stunned. She needed to take several deep breaths to regain her sense of self-control.

Adam, Aris, Fayte, Kureha, Lilith, Susan, and Titania went into the kitchens and pulled enough food for a feast from their inventory. They all chatted as they ate, but the topics of their conversation were nothing of consequence. It was just a relaxing lunch filled with laughter and light-heartedness.

"How many days have we been in *Age of Gods* now?" asked Susan.

"Three days, which means about five hours have passed in our world," Fayte answered.

"It feels so weird to think about how little time passes outside," Susan said. She paused long enough to take a bite of her salad, then added. "I remember a time when Time Compression was nothing more than a concept from the realm of fiction. Now it's a reality."

"Whoever made *Age of Gods* was a genius for being able to create something like this," Fayte added.

"I really hate it when you all talk about things I'm unfamiliar with," Titania groused. She pouted as she ladled her tiny spoon with some soup. The tableware she used to eat with was something Adam bought from a toy store in Solum. He figured she'd want to eat using something Titania-sized.

Adam also thought about the Time Compression System. It really was a marvel, and yet for some reason, it made him shudder in dread. How many people were intelligent enough to create and implement something like this? He'd wager not many. The fact that he had no information on the creator of *Age of Gods* further instilled a sense of dread inside of him.

A *ping* echoed around him as a screen suddenly appeared before his eyes, diverting his attention. He looked at the screen, which contained a simple message, and grinned.

He stood up.

"Adam?" asked Fayte.

"Come on, everyone. We need to head over to the front gate," he said.

"And why must we do that?" asked Fayte.

Wearing a grin, Adam said, "Because our reinforcements have arrived."

***

The time before the Guild War passed swiftly, and it was soon the eve before the big event.

Adam lay on the bed inside his bedroom. This was not his bedroom in the real world but the one inside the guild house. Sweat caused his skin to take on a sheen in the low lighting of a magical lamp, which sat on the nightstand to his left.

He wasn't alone. Resting on his left, naked and covered in sweat, was Aris. Lilith lay on his right. She, like him and Aris, was also coated in a shiny layer of sweat.

Lilith rubbed his leg against him as she rested her head on his shoulder. Her actions reminded him of a kitten. Aris drew circles on his chest as she lay on her side, her body propped up on her elbow.

"Tomorrow is the big day," she said.

"It is," Adam agreed.

"Do you think we'll win?" asked Aris.

"Of course. Levon is strong and has a lot of members, but he can't bring them all to this fight, or it will make him look weak. We'll be more than capable of demolishing whoever he brings," Adam said.

"Plus, we have backup," Lilith added softly.

"I'm a little surprised, Aris admitted. "I didn't think you'd want them to associate with us since it means cutting off a large source of your income."

Adam hummed as Lilith's leg bumped against his groin. "It's true that we won't be able to make money off them once everyone realizes they're our allies, but I've deemed it more necessary to let everyone know whose side they are on. Besides, their purpose was never to make money. It was to acquire information, and they've been doing that for years. We have more than enough information on every noble family in the American Federation to blackmail them into silence should that be needed."

"That's true. I guess they aren't really needed anymore," Aris said, shifting underneath the covers.

Adam twitched when five soft digits wrapped around him. The warm hand stroked his quickly growing erection, causing him to bite his lip.

Aris grinned. "Hmmm. Seems someone is ready to go again. I wonder… should I do the honors, or would you like to go a second round with him, Lilith?"

Lilith hesitated, then shook her head. "I don't mind being second. You should have your second round before me."

As Aris mounted him, Adam thought about their situation. Tomorrow was the day of their Guild War, and they really should have been sleeping, but here they were having sex. Susan. Fayte, Kureha, and Titania were also sleeping in the next room over. He was worried they might hear.

Those thoughts left him as he slid inside Aris. He grabbed her hips as the woman began bouncing up and down. Lilith came up behind Aris and cupped her chest from behind as the more petite woman rode him. As Lilith began suckling on Aris's neck, bringing forth a lurid moan from the younger woman's lips, Adam decided to forget his worries and focus on the matter at hand.

It would take all his concentration to please the two women in his bed, after all.

THE OPENING
SALVO

EVERY SOCIAL MEDIA PLATFORM AND ONLINE FORUM EXPLODED WITH excitement from the moment it was announced that the Pleonexia Alliance had challenged Destiny's Overture to a Guild War. People had been eagerly counting down the days until this event. It wasn't just the average citizen who was anticipating the Guild War either.

Many of the foremost guilds in not only the American Federation but the entire world had their eyes on what was happening. The guilds in the Eurasian Federation, Japan, and the European Union were all waiting to see what would happen when the American Federation's largest guild clashed with the guild everyone else currently had their eyes on.

The event was going to be broadcast using a larger version of the magic stones that had been used to project the tournament onto a screen so viewers could watch. They were called "All-Seeing Stones." Adam still didn't understand how they worked, but he chalked it up to video game logic and decided not to question it.

In either event, this battle would be broadcast to everyone in the entire world. It was a big event. The first Guild War to ever take place. Clarise had secretly confessed the Guild Association had created a gambling pool for people who wanted to place bets on who would win.

Adam had bet on Destiny's Overture, of course.

At the moment, Adam stood on the parapet that overlooked Ironwrought Gorge. Levon's army was already present. It was like staring into a sea of bobbing heads that spanned the gorge's entire length. There must have been at least a hundred thousand people.

Standing at the front were Levon and his five most powerful fighters: Connor Sword, Flame Emperor, Thor God of Thunder, Gaia, and Ymir.

Siege towers dotted the landscape, and several siege weapons like ballistae and catapults sat behind enemy lines. Adam knew Levon would bring those to bare. He wasn't too worried. He had a plan to deal with them.

"Th-there are so many people... can we really fight off an army this big?" asked Susan.

Adam glanced down and to his left. Susan stood beside him, tightly gripping her bow. He placed a hand on her shoulder.

"We can. Don't worry. Fayte and Kureha will destroy most of the enemies from the front. Aris, Lilith, and I will defeat any that manage to breach our walls. I'll be counting on you to snipe the commanders and captains giving orders."

"I-I'll do my beck! O-owie... my tongue..."

He smiled and began rubbing Susan's head as the girl looked at him with tears in her eyes. He hoped she never changed.

Footsteps came from behind him. Adam and Susan turned around as Fayte walked over, the ends of her elemental master robes billowing.

"Everything is ready. All we need to do now is wait," she said.

"I guess we should just relax in the meantime," Adam said. "Where are Aris and Lilith?"

"Last I saw of them, they were playing a game of Knucklebones."

Knucklebones went by many names: scatter jacks, snobs, astragalus, tali, dibs… it was a game of dexterity played with a number of small objects that were thrown up, caught, and manipulated in various manners.

Adam had no idea where the game originated from, but the name "knucklebones" was derived from the Ancient Greek version of the game, which used the astragalus of a sheep.

"Those two have been getting along very well lately," Fayte said with a smile. "I'm a little envious."

Adam's smile was awkward. Her feelings might change if she knew the reason those two were getting along so well.

At that moment, a dot appeared on the horizon. Susan noticed it first. She pointed it out to Adam and Fayte, who looked at it with squinted eyes. Adam had to channel energy into his eyes to see what the object was.

"Isn't that Sandra Rowland?" asked Adam.

"It is. I recognize her from the tournament," Susan said.

Sandra Rowland was a cute girl with a bubbly personality. She played host during the tournament Adam had used as a means of showcasing their strength to the world. As always, she wore skimpy clothes that showed off quite a bit. Adam was almost certain he would be able to see up her skirt if she wasn't so far away.

A massive screen suddenly appeared overhead, projected by the All-Seeing Stone, revealing the image of Sandra's face up close. She was grinning from ear to ear as she held something akin to a microphone in her hand.

"Good morning, ladies and gentlemen across the world! I hope you're all excited for what's about to happen! Today, the first Guild War in the history of our world will happen! This battle will take place between the two guilds, Destiny's Overture and the Pleonexia Alliance! I'm Sandra Rowland, and it is with great honor that I'll be your host for this event!"

"She hasn't changed much since we last saw her," Adam said with a wry smile.

Fayte smiled back while Susan giggled.

"Now, please allow me to explain more about the Guild War. The two guilds shall be taking part in a siege battle. Destiny's Overture are the defenders. Their goal is to defend Iron Fortress. They will win if they can defend it for two days, or if they defeat every member of the enemy's forces. The Pleonexia Alliance are the attackers. Their goal is to storm Iron Fortress and lay waste to the defenders. If they can defeat all the defenders or make the defenders raise the white flag, then they win."

Aris and Lilith appeared as Sandra explained the rules of engagement to everyone. Aris was bouncing on the balls of her feet. She looked like a loaded gun ready to be fired.

"Excited?" Adam asked.

"You know it! I am so pumped!" Aris shouted jubilantly.

"Don't get so excited you lose yourself," Adam warned.

"I know that. Don't worry. I won't let what happened last time happen again."

Aris was referring to when they were having their guild house built. She had gotten so lost in the excitement of battle that she stopped protecting their long-range fighters. If it wasn't for Lilith stopping her, they might have lost.

Sandra continued talking. "There are a few rules that both sides must abide by. First, no one can leave this gorge. If any member of either guild leaves, that guild will be disqualified and victory will go to the opposing guild. Second, you can only use members of your guild. You cannot have any outside help. Finally, this is not a rule and more of a warning, but death is very real here. Otherworlders might not die permanently, but you will lose a level if you are killed during the Guild War. Please keep that in mind and try your best not to die. Now, are both guilds ready? Then let the Guild War begin!!"

***

The Spear God stood on a ledge overlooking Ironwrought Gorge. They watched as the battle started. Levon's armies were on the move. Several dozen people pushed the siege towers forward while the rest swarmed toward the castle like ants.

"This is quite the sight," someone said on her left. It was Daren Daggerfall. He stood with one leg bent forward, a hand on his knee, as he looked at the battle beginning below. "It's been a very long time since I've seen someone use an army of this size for a Guild War."

While they were called Guild Wars, the battles that took place were often much smaller in scale. Larger armies tended to hinder instead of help in many cases. A good example was Capture the Flag. When someone proposed that as a Guild War, both sides would never bring more than twelve people—six to guard the flag and six to try and take the enemy flag.

"I still can't believe Levon brought so many people for this. Isn't he worried about his reputation?" asked Skyrim.

"I'm sure he is, but he has little choice in the matter. You all saw how powerful Destiny's Overture is. If they bring any less than a full army, they're doomed to lose," said Morrowind.

Skyrim grimaced. "Well… I suppose so. Still, I'd be embarrassed if I brought an army of a hundred thousand to fight against a mere seven people."

"Seven? I'm guessing you haven't looked at Destiny Overture's lineup yet," Daren said.

"What?" Skyrim looked confused.

"I wasn't able to see their roster, but it seems they have expanded their members. They now have thirty members."

"Meaning they added twenty-three more people before the Guild War began. Who could they have added?" Oblivion mumbled.

"That's the question, isn't it?" asked Daren. "Either way, I've placed my bets on Destiny's Overture winning. Ga ha ha ha ha! I'm gonna be raking in the cash soon enough!"

The Spear God remained silent as the four brothers conversed, eyes fixated on a single figure standing on the parapet of Iron Fortress.

***

Adam nodded as the Pleonexia Alliance's army raced toward them. Everything was ready.

"Fayte, why don't you start us off? Take out those siege weapons. That should serve as a good warning."

"All right."

Fayte stepped forward and raised her staff into the air. A strange chill ran down Adam's spine as the woman began waving her staff. It felt like an electric current had washed over them.

"Here it comes…" Aris muttered with bright eyes and a wide grin.

Clouds gathered overhead, darkening the sky. The air became cold as clouds blotted out the Sun.

The Pleonexia Alliance's army stopped and looked up. That was a mistake.

Something burst through the clouds, a massive body of rock plummeting toward the ground at speeds so fast no one could dodge it. None in the army had time to so much as blink before it slammed into the ground where the siege weapons were arrayed.

The first thing to happen after the meteor struck the earth was an explosion. Flames and smoke erupted from the ground and rose into the air.

Then came the shockwave. It was so strong Adam felt it wash over him from where he stood. Those below the fortress wall suffered even more. They were knocked over like bowling pins. Even some of the siege towers toppled over, crushing who knew how many people underneath them.

Lastly came the ash, which descended upon the battlefield near the back, covering several people in the searing hot remains of ground and meteor fragments. Those unfortunate souls were lit on fire. They screamed in horror and rolled on the ground as their HP quickly dropped to zero.

This was Fayte's newest spell.

[Meteor]

Fayte had spent almost all of her AP on acquiring this spell after reaching level 20. It was easily the most powerful spell in her arsenal, an attack so powerful that it could destroy entire armies. The spell did 1,500% damage to any enemy unfortunate enough to be hit, and it had an area of effect of about thirty meters, not including the shockwave, which swept out for about one hundred meters.

In short, it was the most powerful attack their guild possessed.

But it was not without its drawbacks. It had a twenty-four-hour cooldown time. Since she could only fire it off once a day, its viability in combat was limited to the start of a battle. She could not use it underground… unless she wanted to commit suicide, at least. It was also the only spell Adam knew of that did not discriminate between allies and enemies.

Basically, its use was limited to large-scale conflicts like the one they were in right now, and she couldn't use it once the enemy got too close or she risked killing her allies.

That was another reason he had her aim for the siege weapons in the back. He didn't want them to get caught up in the attack.

Ding!

[Congratulations! Fayte has defeated 5,000 enemy players, 15 ballistae, and 10 catapults! No items gained. +160,556,250 experience points!]

Adam only gave the announcement a cursory glance. It looked like they didn't gain any items from killing fellow players. The experience points were nice, but they needed more than a billion just to level up.

He wondered if they would gain another level after destroying this army. With one hundred thousand players to kill, surely, they would gain enough to level up at least once, right?

Aris whistled. "I knew that attack was powerful, but wow, I didn't think it would be that impressive."

"It's an incredible attack to start off with. The Pleonexia Alliance army is frozen in shock," Lilith added.

"Sh-should we begin attacking while they're too stunned to move?" asked Susan.

Adam slowly shook his head. "I would suggest that if our goal was merely to win, but we also want to deliver a message. It doesn't matter how prepared you are, or how many people you bring against us. We'll always win no matter what. Also, letting our enemies regain their wits is an insult. It shows we don't consider them a threat."

Susan needed to think about that for a moment, but then she nodded. "I understand your reasoning… but it seems a little cruel."

Adam shrugged. "It might be cruel, but it's also necessary."

Adam was determined to make their guild untouchable. By not only defeating but also humiliating the Pleonexia Alliance, they would gain a reputation as a powerful and merciless guild that could and would destroy anyone who fought against them. A reputation like that would act as a huge deterrent.

No guild would want to challenge them after today.

"Anyway, let's wait until our enemies regain their wits before beginning the second phase of our plan," Adam said.

The battle had only just started, but they had already struck fear into the hearts of their enemies.

***

The entire battlefield had gone silent. No one moved. A few even stopped breathing. That was how shocked they were.

Levon felt like he was falling into a deep, dark hole, one which he couldn't crawl out of. He wondered if he was hallucinating. Maybe this whole situation was just a bad dream.

But no.

It wasn't a dream.

It was a nightmare.

"What… the hell… was that?!" Levon shouted. No one answered him. "What the fucking hell was that?! Fayte just summoned down a meteor?! No way! No fucking way!"

Connor sword awkwardly glanced away from Levon as he ranted, but the man in question was too frenzied to pay any attention.

A glance toward the back of their formation revealed that all of the siege weapons they had made specifically for this battle were gone.

All of them. Destroyed in a single attack.

Levon wanted to tear his hair out.

"… Lord Levon," Gaia began cautiously. "I understand your… frustration, but we are still in the middle of a Guild War. We can ill afford to just stand here, lest we give our enemies more time to attack."

"She's right, man. What happened sucked, but we gotta keep pressing forward." Connor placed a hand on Levon's shoulder.

Levon took several deep breaths. He needed to calm down. He breathed in, held it, then breathed out.

"You're right. Let's focus on the battle."

Everyone looked relieved to see Levon regain his wits, but they were still in a dire situation, and they needed to think fast. There was no telling how many times Fayte could launch that attack. Maybe she could only do it once, but they had no way of knowing for sure, and even if she could only use it this one time, she still had other AoE attacks that could wipe out hundreds of their men in the blink of an eye.

Finally, Levon looked at the others and gave his orders. "Connor, I want you to lead things up front. Divide our forces into five and launch an attack on Iron Fortress. Use the siege towers. Gaia, I want you to hit the front gates. Use your earth magic to destroy it. You have that new technique, right?"

"Yes, sir."

"Use that." Levon took a deep breath. "In the meantime, I'm going to travel through the secret passage with a squad of elites and attack them from behind."

"Sounds like a plan," Connor said.

"If possible, I would like to fight Fayte," Flame Emperor said.

Thor God of Thunder raised an eyebrow. "You wanna fight her after how handily she beat you in that tournament?"

Flame Emperor scowled but still responded. "That is precisely why I wish to fight her. I need to regain the honor I lost in that shameful bout."

"All right. I won't stop you from fighting her if you reach her first, but remember where your priorities lay. This isn't a one-on-one duel. It's a Guild War," Levon said.

"I understand."

"Good. Then I'll take Alpha and Delta squad with me."

Alpha and Delta were their strongest squads, filled with members who had reached level 20. There were only about one dozen in each squad. Leveling up was difficult in this game, and so the ones who could reach such a high level were easily the best and brightest amongst their guilds. They had all been placed in a single squad for this Guild War to be used for the most dangerous missions.

"Good luck," Connor said.

"Right back at you," replied Levon before he went off to gather the two squads.

As he moved, Levon gritted his teeth in frustration. This Guild War was already off to a humiliating start.

***

Skyrim whistled. "Daaaaaaamn. Would you look at that? I don't think I've ever seen an attack with that much destructive power before."

He had a good reason to be impressed. It was hard to see if you were standing at ground level, but with the bird's eye view they had, spotting the massive crater was child's play.

It was big.

Daren had never seen a crater that large before outside of the Barringer Crater in Arizona. That monster had a diameter of about fifty meters. The one down below looked comparable in size and depth.

"The fact that a single person could cause such destruction is impressive… and worrying. Destiny's Overture might not have the size of a large guild, but they have the power of one. Each member is a monster in human guise," Morrowind mumbled.

"You got that right. Seriously. I wouldn't want to mess with them," said Skyrim.

Daren didn't say anything as he watched the battle begin anew. Levon had taken a group of about twenty or thirty and was heading off toward the cliff opposite them. What was that man doing? He put Levon out of his mind to focus on the battle.

The massive army opposing Destiny's Overture was rushing toward the wall. They pushed their siege towers forward. It looked like four of the five squads were acting as a distraction by attacking the wall, while Gaia's squad traveled toward the fortress door. He didn't think such a tactic would work, but to his surprise, no one seemed to contest her.

Just then, a massive firestorm swept over the attacking units, demolishing them in a single hit. Daren didn't even need to see the number signs floating above to know they had been killed by that one attack.

The fire attack was followed by a bolt of lightning, which struck one attacker, then another, another, another, and another. It hit about ten enemies. They, too, were killed by that one attack.

A second firestorm soon swept out from a different place on the wall. It didn't seem as strong as the first, but it still killed every enemy it touched. Those not outright annihilated were lit ablaze like a bonfire. They ran around as burn damage accumulated until their health reached zero and they died.

"Fayte's guild is really giving it to them. The Pleonexia Alliance hasn't even been able to use their siege towers," said Morrowind.

"Most are being destroyed by Fayte or that other mage... I wonder who it is? I didn't have a chance to look at their guild roster, but I don't believe there was another mage in their group," said Oblivion.

"It's the little fox yokai," Daren said.

His brothers turned to him.

"You mean, that little fox we saw with them at the tournament?" asked Skyrim.

"That's right. I did some research after the tournament and discovered there exists a race of powerful beings known as yokai. They're different from beastmen and monsters. According to the lore, fox yokai are a race created to serve the Moon Goddess. The little fox had two tails, so she should still be quite young. It's incredible that she can wield this much power," Daren explained.

"Well... damn. So they have a fox yokai and a fairy on their side," Skyrim mumbled. "Now I really don't want to mess with them."

"You and me both."

***

Susan used [Farsight] to look at the people down below. There were a lot, and they were moving fast. She normally would never be able to see individuals with any clarity in such a crowd, but [Farsight] granted her not only the ability to see objects from far away, but it also let her see those objects with perfect clarity. Everything was brought into sharp focus when using this skill.

Thanks to that, she was able to see the people giving orders.

[Deadeye]

Susan took aim, notched back her arrow, and let it fly.

-90,600!

Her arrow punched straight through her target's head. The damage dealt was so massive that he was instantly killed. He hit the ground with a thud and his body burst into particles of light. He would be resurrected at the church in Solum.

Several enemies were getting close to the wall. It looked like they had grappling hooks. Their intentions were to no doubt secure the hooks on the parapets so they could ascend the wall.

Not on my watch!

[Rain of Arrows]

Susan fired off a volley of arrows faster than the eye could blink. The hailstorm pelted the ground like rain, piercing her enemies so many times that their bodies looked like pin cushions.

-67,950; -67,950; -67,950; -67,950; -67,950; -67,950; -67,950; -67,950; -67,950; -67,950; -67,950; -67,950; -67,950; -67,950; -67,950; -67,950; -67,950; -67,950; -67,950!

Every attack was a one-hit kill. Susan could only marvel at how powerful her bow was.

Until now, she had the lowest attack power because her equipment was nowhere near as powerful as everyone else's. Minus Kureha and Titania, exceptions to the rule, the other members of her party had powerful weapons that increased the damage they could do, but not her, not until this moment. Now she finally had a powerful weapon of her own.

She felt strong.

In the real world, Susan was meek, deferential, and had trouble speaking her mind. She was getting better, but she suspected it would be a long time before she could truly be strong in real life.

That was not the case in the game world.

Here, Susan could be strong. Here, Susan could be at least

somewhat confident in her abilities. She might not be able to change who she was, but she could acquire powers she would never attain in the real world.

That was why Susan liked video games so much. They gave her the chance to be someone she was not. Someone strong, confident, and able to make her own choices in life.

Someone like Fayte.

[Deadeye]

-90,600!

Another captain was pierced through the head with her arrow. It was easy to tell who was in charge. The Pleonexia Alliance was a guild that believed in conformity. All members wore the same type of armor. Higher-ranked members had better armor.

Captains wore a form of silver platemail, including breastplate, helmet, greaves, gauntlets, and pauldrons. They looked like knights spoken of in tails of yore.

Above the captains were the Elemental Four and Connor Sword, whose equipment was custom. They were the only ones allowed to distinguish themselves by wearing unique armor that didn't conform.

Speaking of...

Susan finally found one of the Elemental Four. It was the man with a feminine face and cold demeanor. The icy blue robes he wore billowed as he raced between his allies, using their bodies as shields to move closer. He was quick. Gripped within his hand was a silver staff that glowing blue lines flowing over it like water, or ice. It was definitely a staff that enhanced his ice magic.

Susan was tempted to ask Titania to use [Scan] on him, but she was busy singing [Song of Vigor] to increase their attack power. She also didn't think his stats mattered. The power she and her companions wielded right now was beyond anything their enemies could defend against.

She took aim, held her breath, and let loose an arrow.

[Rapid Fire]

Susan used one of her new skills, firing off arrow after arrow in quick succession to create a near-continuous stream of attacks. It was almost like machine gun fire.

While some of her shots missed, more than half her attacks hit.

-22,650; -22,650; -22,650; -22,650; -22,650; -22,650; -22,650; -22,650; -22,650; -22,650; -22,650; -22,650; -22,650; -22,650; -22,650; -22,650; -22,650; -22,650!

[Rapid Fire] decreased the power of her arrows in exchange for a higher fire rate. All of her attacks did fifty percent of their normal damage. This would normally mean her attacks only did around -7,000, but thanks to Titania, each shot did upwards of -22,000, meaning each arrow fired was still enough to kill a single person in one hit.

Ymir didn't stand a chance.

As he fell to the ground, already dead, and burst into light particles, Susan continued firing shot after shot into the crowd, demolishing them almost as quickly as Fayte and Kureha with their AoE skills. She soon ran out of MP, but she just downed a [medium-grade magic potion] to restore what she had lost and kept attacking.

The battle had just begun and already more than half of the Pleonexia Alliance's forces were gone.

CRY HAVOC

GAIA STOOD BEFORE THE MASSIVE PORTCULLIS THAT KEPT INTRUDERS out of Iron Fortress. She looked up to see no one standing on the parapet. Fayte, Susan, and Kureha—Destiny's Overture's three long-range attackers—were situated on the wall far to her left. They were in the process of destroying the last of the Pleonexia Alliance's siege towers.

Why did they leave this gate unguarded? Are they foolish, or do they have such confidence in the gate's defensive properties that they felt no need to defend it?

Everything from the environment to objects was destructible in *Age of Gods.* Their destructibility was marked by invisible stats to avoid letting players know how close they were to destroying them. The only way to tell was signified by the damage a player could visibly see.

For example, when you heat metal in this game, it turned red. If you slashed at a tree with your sword, slash marks would gouge out the bark. In some cases, a player might cut right through the three and it would topple.

Those were just examples, but they served to highlight an important aspect of *Age of Gods* that Gaia planned to capitalize on.

"All of you, get back. I need you to retreat by at least ten meters."

The members of her battalion backed off. Taking a deep breath, Gaia held her staff aloft, then slammed it into the gate.

[Earth Shatter]

This was the latest spell she had learned. It was normally used to create earthquakes, which not only caused damage but disrupted a person's balance. She had learned this technique to counter people like Mist. Even now that humiliating defeat during the tournament served to motivate her into acquiring more power and spells.

One day, I will make that man pay for humiliating me in front of Levon!

Gaia watched in grim silence as the gate and surrounding wall shook fiercely. Cracks soon formed on the surrounding walls, but the gate remained intact.

She frowned.

While steel and metal were susceptible to warping and denting, the overall continuity and consistency of metal protected it from breaking apart. The malleability of steel also let it absorb seismic shocks without passing on the reverberating damage.

"I see. So this attack is no good."

Gaia took a deep breath, then raised her staff again.

[Stone Sphere]

The ground around the gate was ripped apart, chunks of earth traveling toward the tip of her staff, where it all agglomerated together as though attracted by a gravity well. A massive ball of stone formed above her. It glowed a bright green.

This was the second attack she had learned after the tournament.

"HAAAAAAAAAAA!"

With a piercing, elongated scream of effort, Gaia swung her staff and lobbed the stone sphere at the gate. The cacophonous sound of stone meeting metal nearly made her go deaf. Several people covered their ears. Gaia wished she could do the same, but she was still holding her staff with both hands to maintain the [Stone Sphere].

The gate warped inward under the strain of her assault. The stone keeping it intact broke. With a groan, the gate fell inward, clattering against the ground with a loud noise that echoed across the battlefield.

"All forces! Head inside the fortress!" Gaia commanded.

With a shout, she and her force of twenty-five thousand rushed into Iron Fortress—only to find it empty?

She and her forces stopped when they noticed the eerie silence that descended upon them. Gaia had expected Adam to be standing by the gate, waiting for it to come down so he could fight them. Her plan had been to overwhelm him with sheer numbers. But he wasn't here. No one was here.

What's going on?

"Ma'am, your orders?" one of her men asked.

"Let's keep moving, but do so cautiously. I'm sure they've set up traps somewhere."

They all moved forward, soon coming upon a T-junction, where she had her forces split up. She took the left. The sound of hers and her force's footsteps echoed along the walls.

Something wasn't right.

It took Gaia several minutes to figure out what was bothering her, but a cold sweat formed on her brow when she did.

The sound of explosions, which had been a near-constant companion, had stopped. Up to this point, Fayte and Kureha had been bombarding their forces with magic. Gaia had been able to constantly hear the sound of their spells going off. Now all noise had ceased. It was as if she had entered a vacuum.

What did that mean?

Just as her nerves were beginning to fray, a whizzing sound zipped past her ear, followed by a scream. She turned just her head to see the man who'd been walking beside her fall backward. An arrow was pierced through his head.

Her eyes widened as he burst into light particles.

"We're being attacked!"

At that moment, several hundred more arrows rained down from the sky. Gaia grimaced as she raised her staff and activated the spell [Earthen Wall] to protect her forces from the onslaught. It created a wall that could be formed anywhere. It didn't have to remain on the ground. She could create it in the air and it would hover there, protecting them from attacks overhead.

Yet the moment she did that, a loud roaring sound echoed behind her.

She turned her head, eyes widening in horror. A rushing wall of flames burst through the hallway and washed over the men and women under her command. A shudder ran through her as screams of agony echoed from those who were consumed.

As if that wasn't enough, bolts of lightning rained down from the sky, killing even more of her forces. They slammed into the ground, exploded in a shower of sparks, and took out several of her men with ease. Each bolt also released a shockwave that knocked several people from at least two meters out to the ground. Those people were then picked off by arrows.

Gaia looked up and searched everywhere. She soon found the attackers. Fayte, Susan, Kureha, and that tiny fairy stood on one of the walls, launching attacks at them from above.

She was about to order an attack on them, but then the group vanished. The attacks stopped. It was so abrupt that many of her forces were still screaming in horror as if they hadn't realized it.

"Everyone! Keep moving! Move quickly! We need to get out of this hallway!"

Gaia now realized why no one had been at the front gate. The interior of this fortress was a killing field. The halls were wide enough for several people to stand shoulder to shoulder, but that was all. Anyone with a powerful AoE skill could launch attacks from above and kill them by the dozens.

It wasn't until she began rushing through this fortress that she realized how big it was. There were numerous passages they could take. Some of them led to dead ends, which resulted in her forces being led into traps.

Men and women were killed in droves as Fayte, Susan, and Kureha launched attacks from above. They never remained for long. After their initial assault, the trio would retreat and attack from somewhere else. The walkways seemed to be connected from above, allowing them to traverse across the parapet without being spotted.

They didn't always launch attacks at Gaia. Sometimes, she would hear explosions and thunder in the distance. It was clear to her that Fayte's group was whittling away at their forces both physically and mentally. She was playing mind games to cause panic among Gaia's forces.

Damn it! Damn it! Damn it!

Gaia swore as she continued to race through the fortress. Her troops followed behind her. She didn't know how many were left, but there had to be at least more than half her original force. She'd started this Guild War with twenty-five thousand. Even if Fayte and the others had AoE attacks that could kill several dozen people in one hit, they couldn't reduce her entire force to nothing in so short a time.

Not that it mattered.

She glanced at the man on her left. His face was pale, eyes shifty. He was on the verge of panic. She turned her head. The woman on her right was crying as she ran. She was actually bawling and mumbling something under her breath as she clutched a spear in her hands.

My forces are broken.

The mental strain of knowing they could be attacked at any moment but not when had taken its toll on them. Knowing that Fayte could literally wipe them out by the dozens with a single spell further enhanced the terror they felt.

Gaia eventually burst out of the narrow hall and found herself standing in a courtyard. She blinked several times. There was nothing... no, wait. There was something there.

A single woman stood before an iron gate. She had brown hair, doe-like blue eyes, and fair skin. Her outfit barely covered anything. It looked like a bikini top and bottom. The green armor held a metallic sheen and the small skirt shimmered like silk as it split around her hips. She wore sandals with shin guards and fingerless gloves that went up to her forearms. Held in her hands were a pair of scimitars.

Oddly enough, the most covered part of her was her face. She wore a veil that covered the entire lower portion of her face, from her nose to her jaw.

"Welcome. Tee-hee. I've been waiting for you," the girl said. She sounded young and vibrant. The tone of her voice was at odds with the sharp weapons in her grip.

"You are... Aris," Gaia said.

"That's right."

Her in-game name was Aris Lancer. She was sure the name was an alias. No one would be stupid enough to use their real name.

Aris raised her left hand and pointed the sword at her. "You don't know how long I've been waiting for this. Do you realize how bored

I've been? Fayte and Susan have been hogging all the fun to themselves. It's not fair."

Gaia felt uncomfortable at the young woman's words. She shifted on her feet, tempted to step back but knowing she could not.

She did feel reassurance as her forces began pouring into the courtyard. With them at her back, filling most of the space, she walked forward until she was just a few meters from Aris.

"Why are you alone? Do you really think you can fight us all on your own?"

Aris's grin unnerved her. "Who said I'm alone?"

"What?"

Gaia didn't have even a moment to ponder those words. Loud screams erupted from her left. She swiveled around to see a handful of her men dying at the hands of several shadowing figures who dropped from the wall. There was no blood as the men and women were impaled through the skull with sharp knives, but that just made their deaths more unnerving.

The figures stood to their feet. Each one was covered in black clothes reminiscent of a ninja. Black pants, long-sleeved shirts, and full facemasks hid all but their eyes. They wore shin guards and vambraces as well. Each one carried a knife, which gleamed in the light.

Their forces were all uniform.

In fact, she recognized these people.

"The Grim Reapers?! What?! How?!" she gasped.

The Grim Reapers was a guild made entirely of assassins that had formed several years ago during the last major VRMMO. They quickly gained notoriety for accepting almost any job from anyone so long as they were willing to pay. The Pleonexia Alliance had used them several times for jobs in the past.

But they had never been used like this.

What was going on?!

"You shouldn't turn your back on your opponent," a singsong voice said in her ear.

Gaia turned around just in time to see bright blue eyes hidden behind a veil.

There was a flash of steel. A sharp burst of pain. Then Gaia's head was removed from her shoulders.

***

Adam stood in the middle of the hold. It really did look like a throne room. The rolled-out carpet beneath his feet was a dark red. The columns on either side were the ostentatious kind expected from manors belonging to the nobility. He glanced at the throne near the end, which was something only a king should have possessed.

This place is as good as any for a battlefield.

Adam didn't know how the battle outside was going, but he wasn't worried. The members of their guild were few but powerful. He didn't doubt they were currently decimating the enemy forces with overwhelming firepower.

I can easily imagine Aris grinning from ear to ear as she hacks everyone to pieces.

He chuckled. Just a little. The image of Aris happily slaughtering their enemies was both pleasant and unnerving. It was a good thing this was all just a game, or he would have had a psychopathic murderer on his hands.

His attention was torn from his musings when the door leading to the secret passage opened and almost two dozen people emerged.

Levon was in the lead.

He struck quite the imposing image in his armor.

The armor had something of a gothic aesthetic. His breastplate had a narrow profile that thinned into a V-shape before shifting into a pair of full-leg greaves that were connected to the breastplate by golden circlets. Two massive pauldrons clacked against the chest armor as they sat on his shoulder. They possessed lance slides that were on the larger side. He supposed they would do a decent job of stopping a weapon from decapitating Levon if this were real life.

Levon did not wear a helmet. That meant Adam could see the displeased expression on his face.

"I've been waiting for you," Adam began as he twirled his spear around before setting the butt on the ground. "Welcome, Levon. Welcome... to your demise."

MEETING AGAIN ON THE FIELD OF BATTLE

CONNOR HAD RUSHED INTO THE FORTRESS SHORTLY AFTER GAIA opened the path. They had taken separate paths. Connor and his group rushed through the narrow passages, wary of attacks from above.

"Arrows!"

A shout went up. Several people with shields moved to intercept the arrows.

This game had a very high level of realism, so even if the arrows did a lot of damage, that was only if they hit. Blocking them with shields prevented their group from taking any damage.

They could do nothing about the magic, however.

"AAAAAHHHHH!!!"

"IT BURNS!"

"HELP! HELP!"

"WE NEED A MEDIC!!"

A wave of flames swept through the hall and demolished many of his forces. Connor could do nothing for these people except keep running. The moment those flames caught up to him, it would all be over.

Dammit! Dammit! Dammit! Why are all the members of this small guild so overpowered?!

Connor couldn't figure out how Fayte and her guild had been able to gather so much power unto themselves. It was inconceivable that a tiny group could get all these hidden classes, find all these powerful weapons, and level up so quickly. They had to be doing something. There had to be some secret to their incredible strength.

Unfortunately, Connor couldn't even imagine what that secret might be.

The heat from the flames nipped at his heels, but Connor ran for all he was worth alongside several dozen others and soon burst into a courtyard.

A lone figure stood in the courtyard.

Even though he was wary, Connor could not help but admire the glorious curves on this generously proportioned woman. Her wide hips, large tits, and tiny waist made her look like an hourglass. He couldn't see her face, but the cold eyes that were like icy tundra was enough to give him chills.

His—former—fiancée, Susan Forebear, was a cutie. He would love to break her. However, this woman was a conquest. He wanted to make her submit to him.

"You're Lilith, right?" asked Connor.

Lilith didn't say anything but instead removed the two daggers from a pair of sheaths behind her back. She slid her left foot forward, bent her knee, and adopted a stance that he did not recognize.

Dagger-wielding was not something a noble would ever do.

Daggers were seen by the nobility as a coward's weapon.

Daggers were short, stubby, and lacked elegance. They were only good for stabbing people in the back. When a noble fought, he did so from the front, attacking in a straightforward and elegant manner befitting his noble stature. No noble worth his weight in gold would deign to use such an inelegant weapon.

"Do you really want to fight me?" asked Connor, smirking. "Very well. Let me show you why I'm called the Sword King. Men, stay out of this fight. She's mine."

The men and women who had made it out of that death trap behind them backed off, giving them room for their duel.

Connor walked forward slowly as he twirled the sword in his hand. He adopted the fighting stance his family was known for.

The Eight-Headed Serpent Style of swordsmanship was a Japanese style that the first to take on the Sword family name learned from a master during his trip to Japan. That was before World War III decimated the entire world.

This style had eight stances that could be used to maximize a certain physical attribute. Connor had mastered the Speed Stance and Counter Stance. He had gone with them first because the ability to outpace and counter your opponent was more beneficial than any of the other stances. They were also harder to master.

Connor had been highly competitive for as long as he had been alive. He hated it when others were better at him than something.

That was why he trained so hard. Connor wanted to be the best, the greatest. He wanted everyone to know that he was the most powerful person in the entire world. His greatest dream was to gain recognition by defeating the current strongest—Lin Akamine.

Of course, before he did that, he would need to defeat the second strongest, the Spear God. But that would come with time. Connor was not resting on his laurels. Whenever he wasn't working for the guild or bedding women, he was training.

He would defeat the God of Flash, the Spear God, and this woman. Then he would defeat Adam as well.

"I warn you now, you might be strong, but you cannot beat me," Connor said.

Lilith tilted her head, then finally spoke. Her voice was as cold as the look in her eyes.

"Who said I was going to fight you?"

"Wha—gack!"

Connor's eyes went wide as pain pierced his throat. This awful feeling lasted for only a second before he fell to the floor and his body burst into particles of light.

***

The moment the arrow pierced through Connor's throat, Lilith bolted forward like a leopard pouncing on pray. There were about twenty people in the courtyard. None of them were moving. They stared at the place where Connor had been killed as if expecting him to appear again.

She reached her first victim and swung the dagger in her left hand.

[Slash]

-30,393!

Her first attack tore through a young woman's throat. She died instantly.

Twirling on the balls of her feet, she managed to kill her second enemy using [Blade Extension] to increase the length of her weapon.

The Pleonexia Alliance members finally snapped out of their shock and attacked her, though it was clear from their sluggish movements that their morale was at an all-time low. Every step contained uncertainty and fear. Lilith could practically smell it.

"You damn bitch! Take this!"

An older man swung his sword at her to activate the [Slash] skill, but Lilith timed his attack perfectly and used [Counter].

-101,310!

Her attack tore through the man like he was made of paper. Her attack did so much damage that the others stopped before they could reach her.

"W-what the hell?!"

"How can anyone do so much damage?!"

"She's a monster! A monster!"

Lilith was not bothered by their words. She pushed off the ground, twirled through the air, and used [Slash] to slice open someone's neck. They died instantly. Then she landed on the ground and activated [Shadow Masking].

"What the—where did she go?!"

"She's completely disappeared!"

"Dammit! Dammit!"

[Shadow Masking] was the greatest skill in her arsenal. It was perfect for an assassin like her, allowing her to remain completely invisible to anyone sixty levels higher even while moving.

She used this skill to sneak up behind one of her enemies and activate [Throat Slit].

-81,048!

Another person died to her blade.

"Oh, shit! She just killed Kenney!"

"That bitch!"

Still unseen thanks to [Shadow Masking], Lilith moved into the middle of her enemies' formation and activated two more skills in quick succession.

[Blade Extension]

[Dimension Cutter]

Her most recent skill was her strongest attack skill. [Dimension Cutter] gave Lilith the ability to cut through the third dimension. She didn't understand what that meant, but she did know it did either 350% if her enemies knew she was there, or 700% if they were unaware of her presence. While she would always believe [Shadow Masking] was her greatest skill, this one was definitely her most powerful.

-70,917; -70,917; -70,917; -70,917; -70,917; -70,917; -70,917; -70,917; -70,917; -70,917!

The remaining enemies in the courtyard were cut in twain. The two halves of their bodies fell to the floor with thumps, then burst into light and disappeared.

As Lilith deactivated [Shadow Masking] and [Blade Extension], Susan jumped down from where she'd been hiding on the parapet. She walked over to Lilith and smiled uncertainly.

"You beat them. You made it look so easy. That was really incredible."

"Thank you, but those people were not worth mentioning. You could have also defeated them on your own."

"I-I don't know about that…"

Susan looked down at her boots and scuffed them against the floor. Lilith felt a jolt run through her. She reached out before being conscious of her own actions and placed a hand on Susan's head, rubbing the younger woman's hair.

"Hwa?! L-Lilith?!"

I think I understand why Master feels such a strong desire to protect her. She's truly adorable.

Lilith loved cute things. She had for as long as she could remember, though even she didn't understand why. This love for cute things had persisted even during the harshest times of her life.

Susan was cuteness incarnate. She was small, petite, and had big eyes. Every inch of her screamed innocent.

She was basically Lilith's ideal.

"Um… uh… shouldn't you be going to aid Adam now?" asked Susan after several seconds of silence had passed.

"Hmmm. You're right."

Lilith reluctantly removed her hand from the blushing Susan's head. This girl had such adorable reactions to gestures of affection, but she didn't seem to dislike it. Lilith would have to see if Susan would be okay with more head petting after this Guild War was over.

If I could pet both her and Kureha, I might die from cuteness overload.

"I'll go and find Master. He should be in the hold. I imagine Levon has already arrived, so he might be in combat."

"Good luck, Lilith."

"Thank you."

Lilith bent her knees before dashing through the entrance she had been guarding. She took one last look behind her to see Susan turning around just as several more men and women emerge from the other passage.

Good luck to you too, Su.

***

Aris was enjoying herself as she used her incredible speed to slice through enemies left, right, and center. She felt unstoppable. This was the second greatest feeling in her life.

The first was whenever Adam made her orgasm.

-8,004; -8,004; -8,004; -8,004; -8,004; -8,004; -8,004; -8,004; -

8,004; -8,004; -8,004; -8,004; -8,004; -8,004; -8,004!

She danced across the battlefield, slicing and dicing as she used the skill, [Dancing Swords] to decimate her enemies. She didn't know how many she had killed. It had to be in the thousands by this point, though.

Clang!

"Whoa, now. That was pretty dangerous!"

It happened while she was kicking ass and taking names. The sword in her left hand struck something hard after she swung it.

Leaping back, Aris looked at the man now standing before her. She wrinkled her nose.

He looked like a slob. A five o'clock shadow covered his jaw, dirty blond hair hung down his face in thick curls, and his clothing seemed more rumpled compared to the other Elemental Four members she had seen. He looked like a slovenly playboy.

But the worst thing about this man was not his appearance.

She knew him.

"It's you!"

"Huh? Me?"

Thor God of Thunder pointed to himself as Aris jabbed a sword in his direction as if accusing him.

"I remember you! You're that annoying pervert who hit on me when I was in the Village of Beginnings!"

Thor God of Thunder blinked several times, then smacked his left fist into the palm of his right hand. "Oh! I remember you! You're that cute girl I saw coming out of the church! How've you been? You look... a lot hotter than before. I like your outfit."

"Hmph! Your compliment doesn't make me happy at all, but thanks anyway. I know I'm hot."

"Shame you decided to cover your face though."

"Fuck you."

Thor God of Thunder chuckled. "You've got a pretty foul mouth, huh? I kinda like that."

"Whether you like it or not means nothing to me. The only person whose opinion I care about is Adam's." She paused. "And Fayte's, too, I guess."

"Adam's that guy Levon's got a rage boner for, yeah? What's he to you?"

"He's my soul mate, obviously."

"That so? That explains why you weren't receptive to my advances. Well, shoot. I'm not the type of guy to hit on a taken woman, so it's a real shame. You're exactly my type."

"Whatever. Are we gonna do this or not? I'd like to kill you quickly."

"What? You don't even want some pre-battle banter?"

"We've done enough of that. Hurry up and die."

"Whoa!"

Thor God of Thunder leapt back as Aris appeared before him like a ghost and slashed at him with her sword. He backpedaled, though only enough to avoid her attack, then swung his own weapon, which crackled with lightning.

Unlike all the other members of the Elemental Four, Thor God of Thunder used a massive war hammer. It was a very unwieldy weapon, but he swung it like it weighed less than a feather.

Aris used her speed to dodge. She leapt back, darted left, then came at him from his blind spot.

[Lightning Shield]

-165!

"Nnng!"

Aris clenched her teeth as a jolt raced through her body, shocking her. She retreated and shook out her hand.

The lightning shield that had sprung up around Thor God of Thunder, which looked like a dome of sparks, vanished. The man himself turned to face her. She wanted to wipe that stupid smirk from his face.

"You're really fast, but I'm afraid being fast doesn't mean much if your opponent can predict what you're going to do. Didn't you learn that from your fight against Daren?"

Daren Daggerfall was the man she had fought during the tournament to obtain the [Guild Token]. She had managed to come close to beating him, but he had used his wealth of experience to defeat her.

"Don't worry. I'm not the same woman I was back then. I'll show you how much better I've gotten since that shameful fight."

Aris hadn't been resting on her laurels. After realizing how her recklessness was a weakness, she had been working hard with Adam and Lilith to fix it. They had been training her in combat.

Though it seems I still slip up occasionally... I need to be more mindful.

Aris dashed forward. Thor God of Thunder raised his hammer. Sparks crackled along the surface as he brought it down, unleashing a wave of lighting that would have swept over Aris had she not jumped.

She soared above the man's head, landed on the ground, and attacked from behind--or so it seemed.

[Lightning Shield]

Aris had predicted he would activate his defensive spell again, so she backed off after making it look like she would attack. She counted down the seconds until the shield disappeared. Thirty. The shield lasted for thirty seconds.

Racing forward again, Aris attacked with [Double Slash].

-1,180!

[Double Slash] was a skill that dealt twice the damage of a normal [Slash], but that was only on the presupposition that both sword slashes hit.

Thor God of Thunder used his war hammer to block one slash, meaning only one got through. Even so, she expected her attack to kill him, so she was surprised when he leapt back, still alive.

"Whew. You really are impressive. That would have killed me if I was anyone else."

Thor God of Thunder quickly downed a [health potion] to restore the damage she had done. She frowned at him.

"How did you survive that?"

"You wanna know? Heh heh. I guess I can tell you." Thor God of Thunder puffed out his chest. "You know how most mage classes are all glass canons, right? They have incredibly destructive firepower but very little health or defense? Well, I'm a frontline fighter. I like fighting my opponents up close, so I created my build around the idea of close-range magic combat. My equipment, my skills, and my stats are all geared toward buffing my defense, physical attack, and magic attack power."

So this guy was actually, like, pretty good at combat then? Aris was surprised. He didn't strike her as the type of person who was intelligent enough to create a unique build that suited his play style, but she supposed she should have. He *was* one of the Elemental Four. You didn't rise to the top like he had by being stupid.

"It seems I've been taking you lightly. No offense, but your personality doesn't really make you seem all that formidable," Aris said.

Thor God of Thunder shrugged. "None taken. Even my own comrades think the same way you do."

"But you should know, now that I know how strong you are, I'm going to take you completely seriously."

"You mean you weren't already taking this seriously?"

Aris said nothing as she took a deep breath, spread her legs apart, and focused her mind on the task at hand. She was not going to let someone else beat her like Daren had. She would not drag Adam and Fayte down.

Here and now, Aris was going to prove that she was worthy of standing beside those two.

She would never allow herself to be weak again.

DOG OF THE PLEONEXIA ALLI-ANCE

FAYTE FIRED DOWN SPELL AFTER SPELL FROM HER PLACE ON THE parapet. Fire exploded against the ground and engulfed her foes. Lightning tore them asunder. Bullets of water shot forward so fast they penetrated armor with ease. Fayte didn't even bother paying attention to the damage signs that appeared nonstop. Every hit was a one-hit kill.

Susan was gone, having left to help Lilith confront Connor Sword. She wished her friend luck--not that she needed it.

Su has become so strong, Fayte thought with a smile. Her best friend was becoming stronger every day, and she didn't just mean that physically. Susan had become emotionally stronger as well. *It's almost unfair. She's changed so much, but I wonder if I've changed at all.*

All the people around her seemed to be changing. Adam was becoming even kinder and more open, Aris was learning prudence and not to be so reckless… even Lilith had come out of her shell lately. But what about her? Had she changed at all? It oftentimes felt like she was standing still.

I can't think like that. All I can do is keep moving forward.

Fayte shook her head and got back to the task at hand--namely, killing enemies. It was a somewhat monotonous task at this point. That was why it was so easy to get distracted.

"There sure are a lot of bad guys," a voice said to her left.

The one who had spoken was Kureha, the little fox yokai who launched fire, lightning, and water in a near-continuous stream that decimated the people down below. Her expression was bored. She didn't look at all bothered by the slaughter they were committing.

It was a little unnerving to see such a cute little girl killing people with such ease.

Even if this was just a game.

"Yeah. The Pleonexia Alliance brought one hundred thousand players to this Guild War. That's certainly a lot. I wonder how many enemies are left," Fayte said.

"We have already killed about seventy thousand," Titania informed her.

"So roughly twenty-five thousand," Fayte murmured.

That was still a lot of enemies, but they would easily be able to defeat that many. None of them were at a high enough level to contest Fayte and her guild. Even Levon's best players, the Elemental Four, did not have the levels or skills required to defeat them.

"FAAAAYYYYTTTTTEEEE!"

A shout from behind alerted Fayte to the danger. She turned to find Flame Emperor charging at her, a vicious snarl causing his features to twist his normally handsome face into something ugly.

Magical Defense: +620
Dodge Rate: 5%
Magical Attack: +200

Skill List:
Skill Name: Energy Bolt
Description: A mage aims their staff and calls the name
[Energy Bolt] to release a bolt of magical energy at enemies.
Current lvl: 5
AP Needed to Reach Next Lvl: 100,000
Ability: Deals 200% non-elemental damage to enemies.
MP consumption: 10
Cooldown time: 0 seconds

Skill Name: Energy Blast
Description: An area of effect attack that targets multiple
enemies and fires a beam that sweeps across the battlefield.
Current lvl: 5
Ability: Causes 150% non-elemental damage to multiple
targets.
MP Consumption: 25
Cooldown time: 5 seconds

Skill Name: Scorching Blaze
Description: The mage casts a spell on a single target,
creating a fire tornado to surround and damage the enemy.
Current lvl: 5
AP Needed to Reach Next Lvl: 80,000
Ability: Creates a fire tornado that lasts for 30 seconds and
does -200 damage every second.
MP Consumption: 200

Cooldown time: 60 seconds

Skill Name: Fire Spear
Description: Launches a spear of fire at the enemy.
Current lvl: 5
AP Needed to Reach Next Lvl: 120,000
Ability: Does 200% damage and has a 50% chance of
causing the burn status effect.   MP Consumption: 250
Cooldown time: 60 seconds

Skill Name: Firestorm
Description: User creates a powerful storm of fire that
sweeps over enemies within a fifteen-yard radius.
Current lvl: 4
AP needed to reach lvl 5: 30,000
Ability: Does 140% damage to enemies
Has a 20% chance of burning enemies
MP Consumption: 100
Cooldown time: 30 seconds

Skill Name: Rend
Description: A barbarian skill that combines the player's
strength with that of gravity to unleash an incredibly powerful
downward slash.
Current lvl: 5
AP Needed to Reach Next Lvl: 65,000
Ability: 250% damage scaled to strength
MP Consumption: 25
Cooldown Time: 5 seconds
Skill Name: Slash

Description: A basic skill where the player swings his or her sword and attacks the enemy!
Current lvl: 5
AP Needed to Reach Next Lvl: 55,000
Ability: Causes 150% damage to enemy if it hits
MP consumption: 1
Cooldown time: 0 seconds

Skill Name: Thrust
Description: A basic skill where the player thrusts his or her sword at the enemy! Current lvl: 5
AP Needed to Reach Next Lvl: 60,000
Ability: Causes 160% damage with a 10% chance at getting a critical hit
MP Consumption: 5
Cooldown time: 1 second

Fayte read the stats with a cool gaze. She wasn't surprised by them, though she hadn't known about his stats beforehand. Levon had been keeping his member's levels and stats a closely guarded secret ever since declaring Guild War on them.

"I see you've reached level 20. Congratulations."

"Don't you dare be condescending to me, you unfilial brat!"

With a war cry, Flame Emperor swung his sword again, but Fayte dodged deftly to the side, shuffling across the ground on light feet. The sound of his sword striking the ground echoed around them once more.

"I did not realize you could add a combat class as your secondary class," Fayte said calmly as if Flame Emperor was trying to cleave her head from her shoulders.

"It's normally not. I'm the exception," Flame Emperor declared with pride.

"I see. So you have an item that gives you a second combat class. Your sword, perhaps," Fayte mumbled.

The sword in question was much larger than a standard broadsword. Its length was comparable to Fayte's own not-inconsiderable height. Not only was it long, but it was thick as well and the blade had jagged edges like a saw. Flame Emperor gripped it firmly with both hands as he held it aloft.

"Titania?" Fayte asked again.

"All right. Give me just a—"

"As if I'd let you do that again!"

Flame Emperor launched a [Fireball] at Titania. Left with no choice but to dodge, Titania canceled her spell and flitted high above the attack.

As the flames passed beneath her, Flame Emperor launched himself at Fayte and began swinging his weapon with even greater ferocity. It soon became clear that he was doing this to make it impossible for her to analyze his weapon.

So I was right. That weapon is what gives him a second combat class. That must mean there are more weapons like it, though I imagine a weapon like that is quite rare.

Fayte didn't let her thoughts show as she dodged Flame Emperor's attack, then swung her staff. The [Energy Bolt] she unleashed almost slammed into Flame Emperor's chest. He dodged at the last second.

Flame Emperor tried to attack once more, but Fayte slammed her staff into the ground, which turned into a quagmire before her. While he tried to dodge, the ground under his feet had already turned into quicksand. Flame Emperor sank into the ground up to his knees.

"Looks like you lose," Fayte said coldly.

Flame Emperor glared at her with such hatred that only Fayte's indomitable will kept her from flinching.

"Damn you! How dare you do this to me! You're not even a true member of the Dairing Family! You're just the daughter of some slut who spread her legs for someone other than her husband!"

Fayte closed her eyes as the vicious words spoken drove stakes into her heart. The pain was almost enough to make her double over.

She opened her eyes once more, and her expression was impassive, as though her face was composed of solid ice.

"Goodbye, brother."

"Don't call me that!"

[Fireball]

-39,125!

Fayte's spell struck Flame Emperor. The man was turned into cinders before he could even shout. Her eyes remained locked on where her brother had been even after he vanished.

As thoughts and unwanted emotions whirled through her mind, someone tugged on her robes. She looked down.

"Are you okay, Big Sister?" asked Kureha.

Gently smiling, Fayte knelt down and began stroking the young yokai's head. "Yes, I am fine. Thank you for your concern."

Titania fluttered down to them and crossed her arms. "That man is most unpleasant. Are you two truly related? I can't see it."

Fayte's smile became brittle. "I wonder… anyway, let's finish off the rest of these men. Adam said he wanted everyone in the Pleonexia Alliance defeated before he kills Levon."

With a tired sigh that contained more than simple exhaustion, Fayte turned back to the enemies still streaming in down below and began blasting them apart with magic.

***

He wished he didn't have to wear this mask. Adam wanted Levon to see the smile on his face. Enemies were often angered or unnerved by his smile.

"You knew I would try to use the secret passage," Levon said in a dark voice.

Adam shrugged. "Obviously. We were given the same schematics as you. Anyone would be smart enough to figure out you'd attempt to sneak in and attack us from behind."

"I figured you would, but so what? I'll admit you're strong. I wouldn't stand a chance in a normal duel against you. But even you can't defeat so many of us at the same time." Levon lifted his spear to point it at Adam. "And once I've dealt with you, I'll finish off the rest of your guild's members."

Adam watched, uncaring as the people who'd come with Levon surrounded him. His eyes caught those of Belphegor, but he said nothing and simply swept his gaze past the man. Only after they had him completely boxed in did he act, twirling the spear in his grip and adopting a stance quite similar to the one of his enemy.

"If you think you and your men have what it takes to beat me, then come. I'll even give you a handicap by not attacking for ten minutes."

"I'll make you eat those words," Levon gritted his teeth.

On Levon's signal, his men attacked Adam, unleashing war cries as they came in with weapons swinging.

One-on-many battles were interesting. The group certainly had the advantage of numbers on their side, but it wasn't like that gave them a clear advantage, especially not against someone trained to fight multiple opponents.

Adam spun around on the balls of his feet and used his spear to redirect several weapons, doing so in such a way that his enemies' weapons obstructed the movement of their allies instead. One man nearly found himself impaled upon his comrade's spear. Another almost lost his head when Adam ducked underneath a swing.

One of the reasons Adam preferred spears over other weapons was because of both its range and also its ability to deal with multiple enemies. A sword could only be used against one enemy at a time. While a spear couldn't attack at a certain range, it was easy to deflect multiple attacks at the same time using both ends.

Adam soon broke the encirclement and maneuvered around one of the columns. A loud clang echoed around him as someone accidentally struck the column with their sword. Two men came in from the left and right, but Adam shuffled against the floor until only one of them could attack without the risk of injuring his ally.

"Dammit! What are you people doing?! It's just one man!" shouted Levon.

"I-I'm sorry, sir! He's… really good!"

"I can't seem to attack him without hitting my allies!"

Thanks to his combat training, Adam was adept at predicting his opponents and maneuvering in such a way that only one or two of them could attack at any given time. The rest were forced to back off lest they attack their own allies. In this way, a battle of many-on-one became a battle of two-on-one, which was a much easier fight.

Adam was not relying on his skills to fight these men. He simply moved and defended. Thanks to the realistic combat system, he would not be injured so long as he successfully defended against their attacks.

"Shit! Shit, shit, shit, shit, shit!"

Levon swore as Adam continued to trip up his opponents and rushed in to attack as well. Adam sensed him coming in from behind, spun around, and thrust out his spear.

[Thrust]

Clang!

The tip of his spear struck the tip of Levon's, but because Adam had a higher Strength stat, Levon was the one forced back despite attacking first. He stumbled and Adam used that chance to slam a high kick into the man's face.

"Lord Levon!"

"How dare you!"

"Bastard!"

Levon's men attacked with renewed ferocity, for all the good it did. They were becoming even more predictable. Adam wove through their attacks like he was taking a stroll through the park.

Adam didn't know how long the battle continued, but a scream soon alerted him to a shift in the atmosphere. One of Levon's men disappeared in a burst of particles. Behind the man, wielding two daggers, was Lilith.

"Oh, Lilith. I didn't see you come in."

"I snuck in."

"Does that mean the battle outside is over?"

"Yes, all of Levon's men have been defeated."

"Nice. Okay then. I guess we can wrap things up here."

The short conversation ended and the two went on the attack. It barely took ten seconds to kill everyone inside the hall, sans Levon, who stood a few meters away with a look of horror etched on his face.

"No! Why?! Why are you so much stronger than me?! Why are you better than me?! Don't you know who I am?! I'm fucking Levon Pleonexia! I... I should be the greatest... the most powerful person here!"

Adam couldn't remember a time when he'd seen Levon this unhinged, but then again, this was probably the first time he had been driven so far into a corner. It was only natural for a man this entitled to act like this when faced with such an insurmountable wall.

"Ha. The best. Give me a break. The Pleonexia Alliance might be the strongest guild in the American Federation, but you're on the lower end of the International Power Rankings." Levon gnashed his teeth in anger, but he could say nothing in the face of truth. "Anyway, I don't feel like dealing with you anymore. Go ahead and die for me."

"Wait! Just answer one question!"

"Nope."

"Dammit! Just… where did you learn to wield a—"

Levon's words were cut off when Adam unleashed [Energy Sweep].

-21,251!

Ding!

[The Guild War is over. The winner is Destiny's Overture!]

Adam looked up as the announcement appeared before him.

[Congratulations on winning your first Guild War. As a reward for being the first guild to ever win a Guild War, Destiny's Overture is being given 1,000,000,000 gold coins. Your Fame has also increased by 5,000,000.]

Ding!

[We have tallied the total number of kills from each side. The Pleonexia Alliance has killed 0 opponents. Destiny's Overture has killed 100,000 opponents. Every member of the Pleonexia Alliance was defeated. As a result, Destiny's Overture will gain a special bonus to the experience they earned. The amount of experience earned is 10,000,000,000 for each player.]

Ding!

[Congratulations! You have leveled up! You are now at level 26! +1,500 health! +400 MP! +5 SP! +10,000,000 AP!]

Ding!

Several more announcements were made as all the members of his party except, sadly, Kureha, leveled up. He didn't pay too much attention.

"We did it. We won," Adam said.

"Yes, Master. We did."

He couldn't see her face behind that mask, but Adam thought Lilith was smiling.

"Let's go see how the others are doing. I'm sure they're excited."

"Yes, Master."

Turning around together, the pair left the now empty hold behind.

A SMALL
BREAK

ADAM CRACKED A COUPLE OF EGGS AND ADDED THEM INTO A BOWL already filled with all-purpose flour. He whisked the two ingredients, gradually adding milk and water, then adding salt and butter after all the ingredients were properly mixed together. Once the batter was smooth, he added it to a lightly oiled frying pan set over medium-high heat.

The key to cooking a crêpe was to not let either side cook for too long. After adding the batter, he smoothed it out so it lay evenly over the entire pan, let it cook, then tossed it when the edges started to crisp. The half-cooked crêpe flipped through the air and landed back on the pan.

"You're pretty good at that," someone said.

Adam smiled at Fayte as she walked into the kitchen. "I've had a lot of practice."

"You flip crêpes often?"

"I used to."

Fayte went over to the coffee machine, made three cups, and added a ton of sugar and milk to one of them.

"Maybe you should open a crêpe stall somewhere. I hear those are becoming popular again."

"Did you? Maybe I will then. I bet I could make some world-famous crêpes if I did. Speaking of, what would you like in yours?"

"Cream cheese and fruit, please."

"Got it. Aris! What would you like in your crêpes?" Adam called out.

Aris was practicing yoga in the living room. She was on a mat and performing the bakasana, or crow pose, which involved planting one's hands on the floor, resting your shins upon your upper arms, and lifting your feet off the ground. It was a combination of chaturanga and plank pose.

She's getting much stronger.

It hadn't been that long since Aris woke up from cryostasis, and yet her physical strength already exceeded what it had been before she had gotten Mortems Disease. She would have never been able to do poses like that several years ago.

"I'd like Nutella, please!" Aris called back. She did not disrupt her pose. Instead, she moved her legs out until they were parallel to the floor, then lifted them and tilted her torso until she was performing a handstand.

Adam made about one dozen crêpes total. Two were for Aris, another two for Fayte, and Adam was eating eight. He spread Nutella on the ones for Aris. Then he spread cream cheese across the two for Fayte and added some diced strawberries, bananas, and blueberries. He wrapped the crêpes up, set them on a plate, and served them to the two women.

"Breakfast is served."

"Thanks, Adam," Aris said as she bounded to the couch and plopped down beside him.

"Yes. Thank you. This looks delicious," Fayte added from where she sat.

"It was my pleasure."

Adam cut into his own crêpes, which were stuffed with a light whipped cream and powdered sugar. He wasn't often one for sweets, but they had just defeated the Pleonexia Alliance in a Guild War a few days ago. It put him in an indulgent mood.

"What do the forums look like?" asked Adam as he cut a slice of his food.

"They're still exploding with news about the Guild War." Fayte paused to take another bite of her crêpe. The look of bliss on her face told Adam he'd done a good job. "The Guild War was recorded. Several people put up video files of the Guild War. Our reputation has climbed higher than ever thanks to this… and the addition of the Grim Reapers has only added to our reputation."

Adam smiled before taking a sip of his coffee, then said, "Nice. I'd say we did a good job."

Not even a day after the Guild War ended, the Grim Reapers made a public announcement that they were officially joining Destiny's Overture. This news rocked the world. Every media outlet across the world had broadcast the announcement that the infamous assassins guild, known for taking on any job for the right price, had finally sworn allegiance to one guild.

Many of the larger guilds were not happy.

Because the Grim Reapers were given a lot of jobs from a variety of sources, they had a lot of dirt on various powerful figures and guilds. It went without saying that the Grim Reapers could blackmail anyone they wanted.

There were a few reasons they hadn't been destroyed despite knowing so much.

The first was because they were simply too good at what they did. Every guild wanted to utilize their services. Not only were they the only all-assassin guild, but they were also the only guild that could assassinate powerful figures without getting caught. Even if someone knew they were the ones responsible, they never left any evidence that it was them.

The second reason was because of their connections. Nearly every guild on the planet had utilized their services at least once. This wasn't just the powerful guilds. Even smaller guilds hired them. They had a lot of powerful backers. With so many people who desired their services, someone could not risk trying to annihilate them without invoking the wrath of the other guilds who hired them.

And the last reason was because they were simply too powerful. A few guilds had tried to destroy them when they were first establishing themselves. Those guilds were made an example of. It only took one night to completely wipe out each guild from the face of the map, and the Grim Reapers had let the world know who had done the deed. Those acts further served as a deterrent.

No one wanted to get on their bad side.

It helped that the Grim Reapers never pledged allegiance to anyone. The various guilds who hired them had felt secure in the knowledge that this group of powerful assassins had no master.

Except now they did have a master.

They had sworn allegiance to Fayte.

Adam planned to use the information that the Grim Reapers had acquired to keep everyone else in check. He was already in the process of sorting through all the info they had on various guilds, independent players, and other powerful figures. His plan was to make contact with several of these people and blackmail them into supporting Fayte.

While individual power was important, it was not the only kind of power, nor was it even the most important kind. The strength of a single individual could only take you so far.

That was why it was important to have connections.

There were several types of power in this world.

Legitimate power, in which a person in a higher position has control over people in a lower position within an organization. Coercive power, where a person leads via threats and force. Informational power, where a person possesses needed or wanted information. Reward power--the power to motivate others with the promise of a reward. Connection power, where a person attained influence by gaining favor or becoming acquainted with powerful individuals. And referent power, which was the ability to convey a sense of personal acceptance or approval.

That last power was not something that could be attained but something people had to possess naturally. It was the power of charisma. Someone with positive qualities and a high level of integrity possessed this type of power.

Fayte was fortunately one of those people.

Adam was currently working on getting Fayte the power of connections. That was what she needed right now. Once she gained the favor of various influential figures, she would be able to build an even stronger powerbase, which would become a shield against Levon Pleonexia's and the Dairing Family's influence.

"Are you sure it was a good idea to have them swear their allegiance to me? I thought you would want to keep using them as assassins," Fayte said carefully.

"It's fine. The Grim Reapers have served their purpose. It was time for them to move on anyway."

"Well, so long as you're sure."

Fayte already knew about most of Adam's history. He had decided to come clean after the Guild War was announced. She knew that he was an assassin, that the Grim Reapers were secretly under his command, and that they had been operating in secret for years now.

He had told her all this not only because he planned to use the Grim Reapers for her benefit but also because he didn't want to keep secrets from her anymore. Fayte had been good to him and Aris. Adam always repaid his debts.

"But what are we going to do now?" asked Aris. She'd already cleaned off her plate and was leaning against Adam's shoulder. "I mean... how much more work do we need to do before Fayte wins her bet?"

Adam placed a hand on Aris's thigh, almost out of habit. "I'm pretty sure Fayte could win her bet right now if she wanted, but there's no telling whether Levon will uphold the bet since it was just a verbal agreement."

"I did secretly record the bet we made," Fayte said. Then she smiled wryly. "But I doubt that will be enough to stop Levon from doing what he wants."

Adam agreed. "He might publicly declare his intentions, but he still has numerous avenues he can use to get at you. It's safer in the long run to not declare you've won the bet until after you're untouchable."

"I agree."

Aris looked back and forth between the two of them and grinned like a cat that ate the canary. "You two always seem so close when you talk like this. It's like you're on the same wavelength."

"Well... that's... it's just because we both have similar knowledge about this subject. It's easy to be on the same page when you both know enough about something," Fayte defended herself.

"Aris, no teasing Fayte," Adam said, a warning in his tone.

"Tee-hee. Okay. I'll stop… for now."

"Please spare me any further embarrassment," Fayte said dryly.

As the two girls bantered, Adam thought about the situation Fayte was in.

The problem with verbal agreements like the bet between Fayte and Levon was that, barring when it was overheard by a great many people to act as witnesses, anyone who didn't want to uphold the agreement could simply say it never happened. When that happened, the one who people believed would be the person in the stronger position.

Fayte's reputation might be soaring, but Levon still held the stronger position.

The Pleonexia Family's influence went far beyond that of individual power. They had connections to other powerful families and even the government. They were also rich enough to make any problem disappear by throwing money at it. The Grim Reapers had even reported that the Pleonexia Family owned a private militia.

With the complete ban on war and violence in the real world, anyone caught with a private army faced harsh punishment. Most would have all their assets seized and be sentenced to a life of indentured servitude. The fact that this had not happened to the Pleonexia Alliance was proof of their influence and power.

Aris suddenly coughed into her hand. "Anyway, what should we do today? It's our day off, right?"

Fayte tapped an index finger against her lips. "I suppose we could go out somewhere."

"Yes! I like that idea! I want to go somewhere fun! We could even invite Su and Lilith to come with us!" Aris clapped her hands excitedly.

"If you ladies are going out, I'll go with you," Adam declared.

"Really? I thought you wanted to keep our relationship a secret?" Fayte said.

"I do, but I also don't want a repeat of what happened last time."

The last time Adam had let them all go off on their own, Susan was kidnapped and almost smuggled out of the state. Adam had rescued her. However, whoever had done the kidnapping had erased all their tracks, and so he'd been unable to discover the one responsible.

"Yeah... I don't want a repeat of what happened either," Fayte added with a grimace.

"Anyway, to avoid letting people know about us, we won't go anywhere with public security cameras.

"Do you want to go back to that outlet we went to before?" asked Aris.

"There are other places we can go. I was actually thinking of going on a picnic," Adam suggested.

Fayte clasped her hands together. "That sounds lovely. I even know the perfect spot. It doesn't have any public security cameras."

"Where is that?" asked Adam.

"The Forebear Estate."

"Ah. Of course."

While all politicians and public figures had security cameras installed in their homes, none of them were connected to the public security camera system, which was a government-controlled monitoring system to prevent crimes. Of course, the Forebear Estate would be no exception.

"Will that work?" asked Fayte.

Adam shrugged. "Works for me."

"Me too," added Aris.

Fayte smiled. "In that case, I'll call up Su and ask her if we can come over."

"And I'll call Lilith," Aris said.

With their plans set, the group got to work, and Adam decided to head back into the kitchen. They would need food for a picnic, after all.

ANOTHER ATTEMPT

THE RUMBLING OF FOOTSTEPS ECHOED AROUND THE CHAMBER AS THE massive golem tried to fight against Adam, Aris, Lilith, and the former members of the Grim Reapers.

"It's going to fire its bow! Stagger it!" Susan shouted.

Adam twirled the spear in his hands. "On it! Asmodeus!"

"I'm with you, Master!"

Like every member of the Grim Reapers, Asmodeus was an assassin, so his main weapon of choice was a dagger. He held the thin, black dagger in a reverse grip as he charged the golem behind Adam.

Adam didn't activate [Blood Sacrifice] yet as he slammed into the [Mecha Golem], attacking its legs with a combination of [Energy Sweep], [Energy Thrust], [Slash], and [Thrust] in quick succession.

Asmodeus attacked the same leg, but while Adam attacked the Achilles heel, he stabbed at the joints. His [Pinpoint Strike] penetrated deeply into the golem's mechanic joints. Sparks flew out from where he struck and a loud grinding sound echoed around them.

The attack caused the [Mecha Golem] to wobble and Adam swung his spear once more. This caused the [Mecha Golem] to stagger back, which prevented it from firing its bow at Susan, Fayte, and Kureha.

"Keep it distracted while we aim for its weak point!" Susan continued to command.

"I've got this! Lilith, let's kick its butt!" Aris said.

Lilith responded with a solemn nod. "I shall assist you."

Aris reached the [Mecha Golem] first thanks to her incredible speed. She ran up its leg, swinging her swords, sparks flashing as the loud clang of metal on metal resounded.

Lilith followed. She leapt onto an arm on its other side, ran toward its elbow joint, and stabbed one of her two daggers deeply into it. The grinding sound that came forth was like nails on a chalkboard, but it served to stall whatever gears were used to help it move.

While they were keeping it distracted, Susan took to a knee, notched back an arrow, and released it.

[Long Shot]

-90,600!

While [Long Shot] was technically not a skill meant to be used in enclosed spaces like this and more of a sniper attack, it could be used to great effect due to the amount of damage it did. Susan had also upgraded the skill to level 4, increasing both its range and power.

The arrow she fired penetrated the core located near the golem's chest. Sadly, while the attack was aimed perfectly, a barrier around the core prevented it from penetrating. This [Mecha Golem] seemed to have some kind of magic field that protected its weak point from all forms of attack.

"Fayte! Kureha!" Susan commanded.

"Right!"

"Kureha's got this!"

[Overflowing Cascade]

[Thunder Bolt]

The first attack that struck was Kureha's [Overflowing Cascade]. A massive tidal wave of water appeared out of nowhere and swept over the [Mecha Golem]. It would have taken Adam and the other vanguard with it, but they were warned ahead of time and leapt out of the way. The ferocious attack did an impressive -94,500 points of damage, but more than that, it staggered the [Mecha Golem] once more, disrupting its attack pattern.

That was when Fayte's attack slammed into it.

A bolt of lightning flashed through the cavern and struck the [Mecha Golem] right in the core. An attack like that would have normally done an already impressive -201,096 points of damage, but because the [Mecha Golem] was both wet and a mechanical contraption, it did -603,288 instead.

The attack was so impressive that the [Mecha Golem] came crashing to the ground with a loud rumble. It tried to get back up, but lightning cascaded over its body, a sign of paralysis.

"My turn," Adam mumbled.

[Blood Sacrifice]

[Dance of the Sakura Blossoms]

Adam dashed forward and used his two greatest abilities in conjunction with each other. [Blood Sacrifice], which increased his attack power by three in exchange for halving his health, and [Dance of the Sakura Blossoms], which stacked the damage he did by three for every hit he landed.

-270,270; -810,810; 2,432,430; -7,297,290; MISS!

Adam clicked his tongue when his last attack missed. He backed off as a massive hand came down, crashing into the ground where he'd been standing. Such was the force behind the attack that a gale wind slammed into Adam and sent him stumbling back. He turned his stagger into a roll and came back on his feet, but the [Mecha Golem] used that time to stand back up as well.

"Titania, how's its health?!" asked Adam.

"It's down to half health," Titania called back after casting [Scan].

Now that their numbers have swelled thanks to the Grim Reapers joining Destiny's Overture, they had decided to tackle the [Mecha Golem] again with a raid party.

A raid party was made up of up to eight parties consisting of five players each. They had about thirty-six people, so their raid party only consisted of eight parties.

In the case of most VRMMOs, each party would have a number of different classes, including a tank, healer, DPS, and a long-range attacker like a mage or archer. The Grim Reapers couldn't do that. Their entire guild was made of assassins. This put them at a disadvantage when they did PvE, though they excelled at PvP.

"It's getting ready to attack again," warned Susan. "Adam, draw its agro!"

"Right!"

Adam raced forward and began attacking once more, whittling away at its health. The damage he did would have been considerable against anyone else, but against a monster that had thirty-billion health, it was just a drop in the bucket.

Once the [Mecha Golem] locked onto him, Susan directed Aris and Lilith to back him up. Then she had Asmodeus and his party go around and attack from behind. Once both groups attacked, she further directed the remaining parties to hang back and heal up before joining the fray again.

The [Mecha Golem] did not know what to do after being

attacked from two sides. It only became more confused when Susan, Fayte, and Kureha launched a long-range assault. It tried to fire its bow, but Susan paid careful attention and would direct the two attacking groups to stagger it whenever that happened.

Just like before, they brought the [Mecha Golem] to the ground, and Adam attacked with his two most powerful skills.

-270,270; -810,810; 2,432,430; -7,297,290; -21,891,870!

"We almost have it! Let's keep fighting!" Aris cheered as she went on the attack.

"Do not get overconfident," Lilith warned.

"I know. I know. Don't worry. I'm being careful."

Because the [Mecha Golem] had so much health, Adam and Asmodeus's parties were forced to swap out with the others several times and rest up. The battle had been going on for well over twelve hours.

Adam watched the battle during one of his moments of rest. The other two parties could not deal the kind of damage his party could, but that was to be expected. Every member of the Grim Reapers had a standard assassin class. Those might deal the most damage among the starter classes, but they couldn't hold a candle to the special classes.

"Su is doing a really good job directing us," Aris interrupted his musings.

"Hmm? Oh, yeah. Su has an incredible sense of spatial awareness and a really good head on her shoulders. She's also well-versed in strategy. And thanks to her Fairy Archer Class, she can survey the entire battlefield much more easily than anyone else," Adam explained.

"Is that why you recommended she lead us?"

"Yes."

Adam and Aris stood side-by-side. They had already downed their MP and HP potions to restore what they had lost, so now they were just resting to recover from the mental strain of fighting for several hours.

"Su is pretty cute, isn't she?" Aris suddenly asked.

Adam skewed a glance at Aris from his peripheral. "I guess. Where are you going with this?"

Aris gave a mischievous smile. "I'm not going anywhere. It was just an observation."

"Riiiiiight."

"Adam! Asmodeus! Swap back in," Susan ordered.

Adam wrapped his fingers around his spear, embedded into the ground, and pulled it out.

"Well, time to get back out there."

"Right! Let's do this!" Aris cheered, thrusting one scimitar into the air.

***

-270,270; -810,810; 2,432,430; -7,297,290; -21,891,870!

Adam backpedaled after finishing his latest attack, then watched silently as the [Mecha Golem] toppled over and didn't get back up.

Ding!

[Congratulations! You have defeated [Mecha Golem]! Items dropped: [High-Class Magic Core], [Golem's Bow], [Golem's Great Hammer], [Golem's Greataxe], 10 [Mythril Ingots], 10 [Mythril Gears], and 20,000,000 gold coins! +1,500,000,000 experience points! +150,000,000 ability points!]

Ding!

[Congratulations! Kureha has leveled up! She is now at level 28! +740 HP! + 3,820 MP! +10 SP!]

Ding!

[Congratulations! Asmodeus has leveled up!]

Ding!

[Congratulations! Beelzebub has leveled up!

Ding!

A number of notifications popped up to show that almost everyone within the Grim Reapers had gained at least one level. They were all around level 20 and 21, so that made sense. Only Kureha leveled up among Adam's party. He put all ten of her skill points into Intelligence to bring up her magical attack, defense, and MP.

"Oh, man! That was rough," Aris said as she stretched.

"Good job, Su. You were great at directing us," Fayte said with a smile.

Susan blushed but smiled back. "Th-thank you. I was a little worried, to be honest. I was afraid I would let everyone down."

"Well, I had complete faith in you."

While Fayte was complementing Susan, Kureha walked over to Adam and tugged on his pant leg.

"Big brother! Big brother! Did Kureha do a good job?! Tell her she did a good job!"

The little fox yokai looked at him with such big, innocent eyes that Adam had no choice but to kneel and rub the girl's head. Kureha's fox ears twitched happily as she leaned into his hand and began rubbing herself against it like a cat seeking affection.

"You were great."

"Hehe."

"I want you to rub my head, too," Aris said with a pout.

"Maybe later," replied Adam.

While everyone else congratulated themselves on a job well done, Titania flew over to the massive door and studied it. Adam only noticed after several minutes when he didn't feel her familiar weight appear on his shoulder.

He walked up to her. "You wanna see what's on the other side?"

"Of course," Titania responded immediately. "Are you not also curious? The Dwarves would never have such a strong [Mecha Golem] guarding any old treasure vault. There must be something of incredible value on the other side. I have no doubt that whatever it is, it will help increase our strength."

"I don't doubt that you're right… but how do we open this door?" asked Adam.

"Now that the [Mecha Golem] is beaten, it should open on its own."

"… But it isn't."

"I… I'm sure it will open in time."

Adam and Titania stood and waited to see if the door would open. The others, curious to see what they were doing, also came over. Several minutes passed and yet the door remained closed.

"This is so strange… the door should be opening," Titania murmured.

A closer inspection of the door revealed several indents. They were small circular depressions with a number of grooves inside that looked to be in the shape of gears.

An idea formed in Adam's mind, and he retrieved the [Mechanical Gears] from his inventory, inserting five of the ten into the door. The gears spun. Loud clicks echoed around them as mechanisms inside the door began unlocking one by one. There was a soft creak, followed by the cranking of gears before the door slowly opened.

"Nice thinking, Adam," Aris said.

"I figured there was some trick to opening the door," Adam replied with a shrug.

"Hmph. I would have figured that out sooner or later," Titania muttered with a huff as she landed on Adam's shoulder.

"Shall we see what's on the other side?" asked Fayte.

"I am curious," Susan added.

"Master, I doubt you need us for anything else, so I think our groups should head back up while you check out whatever is in there. We shall return to the guild," Asmodeus said.

"All right. Contact us if anything happens," Adam said.

"Yes, Master."

The seven parties that made up the Grim Reapers traveled back the way they had originally come. Adam, Aris, Fayte, Susan, Lilith, and Kureha turned back toward the now-open door, their hearts hammering with anticipation as they took their first steps through.

UNDER THE MOUNTAIN

THE FIRST THING ADAM FELT UPON STEPPING THROUGH THE DOORWAY was sweltering heat. The first thing he saw was a waterfall made of lava.

"What is this place?" Aris asked as she looked around with inquisitive eyes.

"Some kind of city?" theorized Fayte.

They were inside what appeared to be a volcano, or perhaps an underground riverbed of lava. Red hot magma flowed from an area above into a pool down below. The walkway they stood on was maybe halfway between the top and bottom.

But it wasn't just a pool of lava they found. Sitting on shelves against the mountain's interior were several domiciles that reminded Adam of adobe huts. They were made of thick granite and cobblestone. Adam counted at least two hundred located on various levels. Now that he was studying the area in depth, he could see the walkway they were on traveled around the interior like a spiral.

"Hey! There are people over there!" pointed Susan.

Adam and the others turned toward the direction Susan pointed and found several people running over to them. All of them were armed with axes and hammers of massive proportions. They wore armor made of gleaming metal. Their thick beards were the kind that would have made performers like ZZ Top mad with envy.

They were also short.

Really short.

Really *really* short.

"Are those Dwarves?" wondered Adam.

"Looks like it," said Fayte.

"I've never seen a Dwarf before!" Aris exclaimed.

"They're so short! They're even shorter than Kureha," the little fox yokai said excitedly.

"Halt, intruders! Don't take a single step! Stay right where ye are, or yer gonna regret it!"

The one standing at the forefront of this group was a Dwarf with red hair like a lion's mane, a beard to match, and beady black eyes. Like all members of his race, he was quite stout. He possessed a stocky build, thick arms, a barrel chest, and was diminutive enough that he didn't even come up to Adam's waist.

His armor was more decorative than the other Dwarves. It was made of a golden material, though he didn't think it was made from gold. Gold alloys were far too soft to be practical. Etched into the armor was a majestic lion roaring. It was intricately detailed beyond anything he'd seen a human create.

"Are you the leader of these Dwarves?" Adam stepped forward.

"I said don't take another step!" warned the Dwarf.

Adam stopped moving and held up his hands. He didn't want to start a battle right now.

"Who are ye people? How did ye get in here?" asked the Dwarf.

Adam shared a look with Fayte. He gestured toward the Dwarf with his head, indicating she should do the talking.

Fayte looked at the Dwarf, careful not to move from where she stood. "Hello. I am Fayte. My party and I were exploring the dungeon above when we found the [Mecha Golem]. We were able to get here because we defeated it and unlocked the door."

"Ya beat [Mecha Golem]?!" the Dwarf was shocked.

It wasn't just him. The other Dwarves began whispering in hushed tones of surprise as well. Adam couldn't hear what was being said. He wondered what they were talking about. Their expressions were an odd mix of fear and hope that he couldn't make heads or tails of.

"We did," Fayte confirmed.

"Aye cannae believe it. Someone actually managed to beat that monstrosity," the Dwarf murmured. He was so shocked that he dropped the halberd he had been holding. Like the rest of his equipment, that halberd was something special.

"Does that mean we're free?" asked another Dwarf.

"It's been so long since we've been outside!" cried one.

"Maybe I'll finally be able to smell something other than brimstone!"

They seem rather excited all of a sudden.

"Quiet, the lot of ya! No one will be going outside! Don't forget why we sealed ourselves here in the first place!" After quieting down the Dwarves, the leader turned back to them. "Ye must be rather strong if ya defeat [Mecha Golem]. That monster was made by the best craftsmen of the Dwarves. We've tried many times to beat it ourselves, but it defeated us every time," said the Dwarf.

"Wait a moment. You were trying to beat it? Why? Aren't you

its creators?" asked Fayte.

The Dwarf shook his head. "Everyone played a part in makin' it, but the one who created the core went mad after being locked inside here for so long. He tried gettin' out, and when the rest o' us tried to stop him, he commanded [Mecha Golem] to attack. Unfortunately, he died before we could make him command it to stop, so it went on o' rampage. Took everythin' we had just to lock it outside."

Adam was beginning to understand what happened. The Dwarves sealed themselves away during the war between humans and beastmen and created the [Mecha Golem] to protect themselves. Thousands of years passed, however, and the Dwarves began going crazy from being stuck in one place this entire time. One of them tried to break out. When the others tried to stop him, he set the [Mecha Golem] loose. It was probably a case of very bad luck that the one who went mad just happened to be the same person who created the core, which Adam guessed was like a command console.

Fayte opened her mouth to speak again, but Titania flitted forward and captured everyone's attention. The Dwarves stared at her with uncomprehending eyes. It was like they couldn't figure out what they were looking at.

"It's been a long time, Thohkum Boulderblade," Titania said.

"Ee gads! Titania?! Is that you?! Why are ye so tiny?!"

Titania's face went bright red.

"Excuse you! How dare you call me tiny, you hairy midget!"

"Gya ha ha ha! By the Sun Goddess, it really is you! Yer the only one who would ever insult me, the leader of the Dwarves, like that!"

Aris placed her hands behind her back and leaned over. "Do you know him, Titania?"

Titania clicked her tongue, but then sighed and gestured toward the Dwarf. "Everyone, this is Thohkum Boulderblade. He's the leader of the Dwarves and someone I'm unfortunate enough to know very well."

"Don't be like that, Titania. Didnae we create many great memories after forming a party together?" asked Thohkum. He didn't seem particularly hurt even though her words were quite harsh. He actually seemed rather pleased.

It turned out, the Dwarf known as Thohkum had been one of four other people who formed a party with Titania several thousand years ago, which would make him really old. He didn't know Dwarves could live for so long. In either event, it was clear that Titania didn't really like him. She hurtled insults like it was going out of style and always had a harsh quip for anything and everything he said.

Just what kind of relationship do these two have? Why does Titania seem to hate him so much?

Adam wanted to know, but now wasn't the time. He would ask later.

"Since yer friends with Titania, I won't kill ye, but don't think that means I trust ye either. We Dwarves still remember how you humans captured and enslaved our people and forced them to work in yer mines and smithies. We also cannae let ye leave. The last thing we need is fer the humans and beastfolk ter find us again," said Thohkum.

"I'm sorry, but did you just say you won't let us leave?" asked Aris.

"That's right. Now that yer here, yer stuck here for life," said Thohkum.

"Now, wait just a minute. We can't remain here. We have many things we need to do up on the surface," said Fayte.

Thohkum shrugged. "That's not my problem. Yer the ones who barged in here. It's not like ye can even leave anyway. The gate's been shut and it's locked from the outside. Ain't no gettin' out that way.

Anyway, yer free to explore our city. Just don't cause any trouble."

Thohkum and the other Dwarves slowly left one by one, though not before casting them curious glances. They hadn't seen a human in a very long time. Of course, they would be curious. However, Adam was in no mood to pay attention to them.

He turned toward the door. It was shut just like Thohkum had said. He tried to open it, but it didn't budge. There was also no unlocking mechanism or keyhole on this side.

"It's not good. This door won't open." Adam turned around and shook his head at the others.

"Then what are we supposed to do?" asked Susan.

"Let's look around the city first," suggested Fayte. "There may be a clue about how to leave this place. We might find a way to open this door, or even discover another way out."

Everyone agreed with her suggestion, and they set off to explore the city.

The Dwarven City, which they learned was called Karak Verum, was bigger than it first appeared. Only a small portion of the buildings was visible from the outside. Each building was anywhere from ten to fifty times larger on the inside. The Dwarves had carved out these buildings into the mountain itself, and they all had anywhere from ten to one hundred rooms connected via hallways and stairs.

They entered one such building. Pillars hewn from stone stood on either side, lined up in two neat rows as they held up a ceiling. The pillars led to a majestic staircase that went both up and down.

The hall was not empty. Several Dwarves traveled up or down the stairs, or through doorways on either side of the room.

This building turned out to be a smithy; there were several rooms that contained a variety of different ores, rooms with nothing but already forged weapons and armor, and several forges.

The forges ranged in size. Some were massive and used by

multiple Dwarves at once, but others were small and seemed to be for personal use. Adam couldn't figure out what they were used for, and when he tried asking, the Dwarves would snub him.

"Yer free to explore, but we were ordered not to talk to ye," they would say.

"Pleasant bunch, aren't they?" asked Adam with a tired sigh.

"I can't believe they won't even answer a simple question. Do they really hate humans that much?" muttered Fayte.

"It's far more complex than something simple like hatred," Titania said. "You have to understand that what they feel for you humans is a combination of hatred and fear. They loathe how humans treated them during the war, but they also fear what you can do to them. Dwarves are strong and great blacksmiths, but their strength is not so great that they can fight against a species with superior numbers."

None of them said anything. They couldn't understand how the Dwarves felt. It was difficult to place yourselves in the shoes of someone else when you had never experienced what they did.

Matters were only made more complicated because this was just a game. *Age of Gods* might have deep lore and feel so realistic it was sometimes hard to remember this was all virtual reality, but it didn't change the fact that this was just a game.

The group wandered around some more, watched a few Dwarves as they forged items like weapons and hammers, and even looked at some of their creations. Adam wondered why they were forging so much equipment when it didn't even have someone to sell it to.

"Dwarves love forging items," Titania answered his unspoken question. "It's as natural to them as breathing."

"Why is that?" asked Aris.

"It probably has something to do with their greed." When Titania only got confused expressions in return, she sighed and said, "Dwarves are a very greedy race. They love rare and valuable materials like gold, silver, mythril, and adamantine. I believe their avarice has taken the form of a desire to forge these materials into items. This is why they continue crafting items even though they have no one to sell them to."

"That's odd, but I suppose it makes a kind of sense," Fayte said with a nod.

"Anyway, it looks like we aren't going to find a way out for now. Why don't we log out, get something to eat, and come back in a few hours?" suggested Adam.

"That's a good idea," Fayte agreed.

The group opened their screens to log out, but a problem occurred during their attempt.

Ding!

[Cannot log out while enemies are nearby.]

GARYCK
IRONHAND

"LOOK, I DONNAE KNOW ANYTHIN'! STOP BOTHERIN' ME!"

Adam grimaced as the Dwarf he tried speaking with walked away. This response was one he had gotten several times now. It seemed like every Dwarf in this mountain was extremely grouchy.

"Well… that was a bust," Titania said with a sigh.

"Yeah. Something tells me, we're not going to get anything out of talking to these people," Adam agreed.

He thought about trying to pry the information he wanted from the Dwarf through interrogation, but he thought better of it. There was a chance this Dwarf really didn't have the information he sought. Even if he did, torturing a Dwarf while inside a Dwarven stronghold sounded like a stupid idea, especially since they couldn't get out.

Adam pondered what he should do as he began walking once more. It didn't look like talking to the Dwarves would avail him anything. Should he explore the area some more in the hopes of finding a secret passage or some way to open the door? He didn't think that option would meet with much success, but it also wasn't like he had a choice.

"W-w-what do ye think yer doin'?! Unhand me this instant!"

"All I want is information. Just give me what I want, and no one has to get hurt."

"Hiiiiiiii! What are ye doin' with that knife?! Keep it away from me!!!!"

Someone tugged on his pant leg. It was Kureha. She had been quietly following him up until now, so her suddenly speaking caught him by surprise.

"Big Brother! Big Brother, look over there!"

A loud ruckus caught Kureha's attention. Adam turned in the direction she pointed to find Lilith pinning a Dwarf against the wall, holding a knife to his throat as she glared down at him with a menacing expression. She looked ten seconds away from spilling his blood all over the floor.

Adam sighed and walked over to them. "Stand down, Lilith."

"Master?" Lilith turned, surprise on her face.

"Stand down," Adam repeated. "And let the Dwarf go."

"Yes, Master."

Lilith re-sheathed her knife and stepped away from the Dwarf, who breathed a sigh of relief and touched his throat as though to check for injuries.

"Sorry about my friend. She's anxious because we really want to get out of here," Adam apologized.

"Hmph. You and me both. Listen here, you lot. We donnae want no trouble. I recommend ye stop doin' what yer doin'. There ain't no gettin' outta here. Yer stuck, just like we are."

With that warning hanging ominously in the air, the Dwarf left them, grumbling about pushy outsiders who couldn't mind their own business.

"Are you sure that was wise, Master?" asked Lilith.

"I doubt he knows anything. He said it himself, didn't he? He'd like to get out of here as well. Anyway, let's meet up with the others. We all promised to meet at the tavern."

"Yes, Master."

There were several taverns located inside this mountain stronghold. The one they were heading to was on this level.

"You are awfully quick to violence," Titania said to Lilith.

"Violence is often the quickest and easiest solution to our problems," Lilith said.

"I think the fact that you believe this is a problem in and of itself."

Adam looked at the top of the mountain's interior as they walked. The spiral ramp ended with a large palace surrounded by thick walls and columns more majestic than anything he'd seen in real life. It was hard to judge the type of architecture used in its construction. He would have said it resembled the sort of palace where a sultan lived, but it was so much bigger, and there were many architectural choices that reminded him of the Renaissance era.

In the end, he simply decided the building had a very fantasy feel and left it at that.

The tavern was much larger than Adam would have expected, given the size of its occupants. He walked into the sprawling space, Lilith at his side, and searched the numerous tables spread across the floor.

Most of them were already packed full of drunk Dwarves happily chugging away at frothing mugs of amber ale. The raucous energy and laughter stopped, however, when Adam and Lilith entered. It was a silence so profound it was rattling. Never mind hearing a pin drop. Adam could even hear the bubbling magma outside.

They walked toward a dark corner of the tavern. Aris, Fayte, and Susan were already there, sitting quietly as they nursed drinks.

"Aaaaaaah! That hits the spot! Nothing like a stiff drink after a long day of work!"

Well, Fayte and Susan were quiet. Aris was enjoying herself.

Adam chuckled as he sat down. "Having fun?"

"You bet! I've always wanted to say that! Tee-hee, being inside a game is the best! There's no legal drinking age, so I can have as much booze as I want."

Kureha looked at Adam with raised hands. He got the hint, lifted the girl up, and set her on his lap. The little fox yokai hummed happily, ears twitching as she looked at the plates of meat.

"Can I?" she asked.

"Go ahead," Adam said.

"Yay!"

"I'm glad someone is having fun," Fayte said with a sigh as Aris guzzled down more ale.

Several plates of food sat on the table. They looked like mostly meat dishes. Fayte picked at them periodically, but she didn't seem to have much of an appetite. Susan was also nibbling on what appeared to be a kebob.

"I'm guessing none of you found anything?" Adam asked.

"Correct," Fayte sighed. "I tried questioning more Dwarves, but none of them answered me. Then I tried exploring the area, but there's nothing here that stood out. If there is a secret passage that leads out of this mountain, then it's probably inside the palace, and that's the one place we're not allowed to enter."

The palace was guarded by a pair of [Dwarven Warriors] who were at level 60. They possessed incredible stats. While Adam was certain their party could defeat them since they weren't stronger than the [Mecha Golem], he didn't want to push his luck. There was a good chance there were more than just those two.

The last thing they needed was to have an angry horde of Dwarves after them.

"What should we do?" asked Susan.

"I think the more important question is what *can* we do?" Adam began rubbing Kureha's head. It was oddly soothing and served to help him think. "The door won't open again, there are no secrets to be found here, and the only place where we might find a way out is guarded by very strong NPCs. I would normally suggest we sneak in, but the only person with any stealth skills is Lilith."

Everyone looked at Lilith. The woman had been glaring enviously at Adam, but she looked up after feeling everyone's eyes on her.

"I can slip inside and do reconnaissance," she suggested.

"I think that's what we'll have you do. I'm sure there's something in that palace that can help us leave this place," Adam said.

"So it's true. I didnae believe it when I heard the rumor about outsiders bein' here, but seein' is believin', as they say," a voice said from behind.

Adam and the others turned to find a Dwarf with oddly neat and tidy red hair. His hair was shorter than any other Dwarf he had seen so far, with a brushed-up hairstyle. Likewise, his beard was not long and thick but trimmed into a classic goatee. He looked so different from what Adam thought of as the standard Dwarf that all he could do was stare.

"You're... a Dwarf, right?" Aris asked.

The Dwarf guffawed. "Course I'm a Dwarf. Do I look like a human to ye?"

"Well... no. It's just you don't look much like a Dwarf either."

"Well, I s'pose I cannae blame ye for thinking that way, lass. I guess ye could say I'm something of an oddball, what with me hair and everything," the Dwarf said. Then he sat down at their table. "Me name's Garyck Ironhand. I couldnae help but overhear yer conversation and figured I'd offer ye me help."

Up to this point, none of the Dwarves had been helpful. All of them had refused to answer any of their questions, so to have one come up to them with an offer of aid made them understandably suspicious.

Adam subtly held up his hand in a gesture only Lilith could see. She didn't nod, but she did discreetly slip her hand behind her back, fingers grasping the hilt of her dagger.

"No one offers their help for free," Adam stated with narrowed eyes. "I'm assuming you would like something in return. What is it?"

The Dwarf didn't speak at first. A stout Dwarf woman in thick coveralls had come by and Garyck ordered an ale. Adam didn't miss the look of disgust on the woman's face as she accepted his order.

"Yer damn right I'd like something in return. I want ye to get me outta this hellhole. I'm sick of being stuck in this mountain, of seein' the same damn rocks every frickin' day. I wanna see something new. You lot are trying to get back to where yer from, yeah? I figured you'd let me come with if I help ye escape. Ye know how it goes. I scratch yer back, you scratch mine. Isn't that what you humans say?"

The woman came back and slammed a frothing mug of amber liquid in front of Garyck.

"Enjoy yer drink, ye damn schwule."

"Such a pleasant woman, she is," Garyck mumbled as he gripped his ale and took a hearty swig.

Fayte leaned over the table, carefully watching the Dwarf even as she kept up her polite, politician's façade. "Let's say that we agree to let you come with us. How can you help us escape from this place?"

"Not here. The walls have ears. Let's finish eating, then head back to my place."

Garyck finished his ale. Adam and the others polished off whatever was left on their plates, then stood up and followed Garyck out of the tavern. He was not unaware of the eyes staring holes into their backs as they left.

They're even warier than before. Is it because of Garyck?

Garyck owned a little hut not quite near the bottom of the spiral ramp but close enough that it felt a lot hotter. Far more minuscule than any other building present, it resembled something... much more normal than most Dwarven buildings.

"Come on in. Donnae mind the mess," Garyck opened the door and gestured for them to head inside.

This hut only had one room. It reminded Adam of a studio apartment--except no studio apartment he knew of had a forge. There was a bed, a dresser, and a forge in one corner of the room. Half-finished swords and armor pieces lay strewn across the floor and workstation. All of them looked quite intricately detailed for unfinished projects.

Garyck sat down on his bed while everyone else found a place to stand. Adam leaned against the table and crossed his arms.

"So, how can you help us escape?" asked Adam.

Garyck raised a hand to forestall further conversation. "Before I get into that, I want yer word that ye'll take me with ye."

Adam looked at Fayte, who pondered the request for a moment before nodding.

"You have our word. We will take you with us when we leave."

"Good. Ye should know, we Dwarves take our word seriously. If ye try to double-cross me, I won't hesitate to crush yer face in with me hammer." No one responded to that ominous threat with words, but Lilith looked like she was about to slit Garyick's throat, not that he seemed to notice as he continued talking. "Now, then, ye wanted to know how to get outta here. There is a way. In fact, Thohkum uses this method quite often to leave the mountain."

Aris perked up. "Really? But I thought he said there was no way out."

"That was obviously a lie," Titania said, gritting her teeth. "I knew he was lying when he told us there wasn't a way out. That damn, no good, lying, cheating scumbag. I expected this. He was never one to tell the truth, but I still hoped he would know better than to lie to me."

"Oh, boy. Looks like someone is mad," Aris said.

Titania scowled. "You would be too if you found out a former member of your party lied to you."

Garyck nodded. "Thohkum likes power. He wants to hold power over us. That's why only he and a few others know about the hidden passage outta here. Thanks to that, Thohkum controls everything in this mountain. He determines how much food we get, what kind o' ores we can smith... we're basically his slaves."

"And let me guess, no one does anything because they're too afraid of Thohkum to go against him," Adam said.

"There is that, but much as many o' us would like to leave, we Dwarves are also afraid of the outside world. Thohkum has brainwashed our people with horror stories about the outside. Says any Dwarf who goes outside will be enslaved by humans and forced to work until we drop dead. Hmph. Not like we're not doin' the same thing here," Garyck snorted derisively. He seemed to have an intense dislike of his leader, not that Adam couldn't see why.

"Back to the matter at hand, how do we get out of here?" asked Adam.

"I was just gettin' to that." Garyck placed his hands on his knees and leaned forward. "There's a mine down near the bottom o' this ledge. Only a select few are allowed to mine the ore inside. Thohkum personally selects who gets to mine the ore. Anyhoo, not even those people know about the secret passage outside. It's sealed tight with a magic emblem."

"I'm guessing the one who has the emblem is Thohkum?" asked Fayte.

Garyck nodded. "Aye. The emblem is a necklace Thohkum always wears. Only time he takes it off is when he goes to sleep."

Adam took a deep breath as he realized what this meant. "In other words, in order to get outside of this mountain, we'll have to infiltrate his palace, steal the emblem while he's asleep, then head into the mine and use the secret passage before he realizes what's happened."

"Aye. Pretty much," Garyck said.

Adam wondered if it was a good thing he wasn't wearing his mask right now. It was impossible to hide his smile as blood began pumping through his veins.

"Well, it looks like you're in luck," he said, his smile growing. "We have two people here who are well-versed in infiltration missions. We'll get that emblem before Thohkum can say 'Thorin Oakenshield.'"

"Eh? Who's that?" asked Garyck, but Adam didn't pay attention. He was already thinking about the best way to infiltrate Thohkum's palace.

INFILTRA-
TION

FOUR BROTHERS SAT AROUND A CIRCULAR TABLE. Daren Daggerfall looked at his three brothers. Skyrim looked serious, Morrowind appeared bored, and Oblivion was simply staring at him.

Standing behind Daren was the Spear God. They were like a statue.

Because of how the Time Compression System worked, the four brothers had opted to remain inside the game for as long as humanly possible. The only time they logged off was to eat, exercise, sleep, and use the toilet. They didn't take any breaks. They didn't go out in public. Even now, they had changed their meeting place from their home in Sacramento to their guild house in the game.

"I trust there are no objections to this plan?" asked Daren.

"None from me," said Skyrim.

Oblivion shook his head. "I also don't have any objections."

"I don't have any objections, but I do have a question,"

Morrowind raised his hand.

Daren looked at him. "What is it?"

Morrowind placed his elbows on the table and leaned forward. "Are we sure Destiny's Overture will even agree to forming an alliance? From what I've seen, they seem like the type who prefer going their own way."

Daren tapped his index finger against the table. The thumping sound was timed to the rhythm of his heartbeat.

"That's why the alliance isn't going to be your typical one. In most cases, a small guild like theirs would become a subsidiary branch of Daggerfall Dynasty, but not only are they not the sort to let themselves be subordinate to anyone, they have the power to contend with even large guilds."

Daren still felt a chill when he remembered how handily Destiny's Overture had defeated the Pleonexia Alliance. They might not have fought against the entire guild, but it had been barely fifty people against an army of one hundred thousand. Not only had they won, but they had done so without a single casualty.

Daren knew that he and his brothers could not replicate that feat- -not even with the Spear God in their corner.

"This will be an alliance of equals. It will offer them far more benefits than any alliance we have ever formed. I am even willing to give our own guild a disadvantage if need be to get them on our side," Daren continued.

"Those guys really left an impression on you, huh?" said Skyrim.

"Are you saying they didn't leave an impression on you?" asked Daren.

Skyrim shrugged. "I didn't say that."

"Since the moment they appeared, Destiny's Overture has been at the top of the food chain despite their small size. They also have Adam on their side. That man has been making waves ever since *Age of Gods* began. I don't doubt that he is the single greatest player this game will ever see, so I want him on our side, and I'm willing to do whatever I have to in order to make that happen."

His brothers didn't say anything. They didn't need to. Even if they refused to admit it, Daren knew that Adam, Fayte, and the other members of Destiny's Overture had left a deep impression on them as well.

He turned to the Spear God. "I take it you don't have a problem with this arrangement?"

The Spear God shook their head.

"Good." Daren turned back to his brothers. "Skyrim, I want you to send a letter to the Guild Association asking them to set up a meeting with Destiny's Overture. The sooner we talk to them, the better."

***

It had been a very long time since Lilith had been given an infiltration mission. When was the last mission? It had been before she, Adam, and the others had escaped from Eden. Was it during their mission to assassinate a member of the European Union, or was it perhaps when they were sent to the Eurasian Federation? That felt like a lifetime ago.

Lilith easily slipped past the guards at the front gate with [Shadow Masking], climbed over the gate, and walked toward the mansion. The front door was locked. Even if it wasn't, going in through the front was a bad idea. Anyone on the other side would become suspicious if they suddenly saw a door open and close on its own.

She looked around for a moment. There were several windows

high overhead, but they were not easily accessed. The walls were perfectly smooth, which made climbing them hard.

Another moment passed as Lilith observed her surroundings, seeking out a path she could follow to ascend up to one of those windows. It looked like she could make use of the flying buttresses. They had bits she could use to pull herself up.

Lilith took a deep breath before bursting into action. She ran forward, leapt onto the nearest flying buttress, and raced up the wall until she reached the first ledge, which she grabbed onto. Her biceps flexed as she pulled herself up.

This ledge was small. She could only remain on it by standing on her toes and grabbing either side of the buttress. Someone less nimble and strong would never be able to remain there.

She didn't stay there long, however, and quickly began ascending. She leapt up to the next grabbable protrusion, swung her feet, and used the resulting momentum to flip onto it. Then she jumped again. Her jump created a long arc that took her another flying buttress, which she grabbed hold of and hauled herself up.

Lilith continued to climb until she eventually reached the window. Unlike most human windows, this one didn't have a glass panel, so she was able to easily slip inside. She wondered about that. Did the Dwarves not make glass? She dismissed the thought a moment later after setting her feet on the floor.

The area she found herself in was a hallway much bigger than your typical one found in a noble's mansion. It could easily fit ten people standing shoulder to shoulder and the ceiling was at least five meters above her head.

Her MP was getting low, so Lilith consumed a [Mid-level Magic Potion] to restore what her skill had taken, then set off again.

Garyck had said that the key they needed would be located inside a vault in Thohkum's room. That was where Thohkum put it every night. His room was located on the first floor, which meant she needed to go down a level.

I need to find the stairs.

The hallways she traveled through were eerily empty. There didn't seem to be anyone present--not at first.

Lilith froze after traveling down one hall and nearly running into a golem. This one was much smaller than the [Mecha Golem] they had fought, but it was still quite a bit taller than her. Its design was a bit more streamlined as well. Perhaps the biggest difference was the single red eye located on its head.

The golem turned to her, and for a moment, she thought it had seen her somehow. She held her breath. Then the creature turned back and began lumbering away. Lilith waited until it was gone before breathing a sigh of relief.

That... was too close.

These golems made her wary. She didn't know what sort of abilities they had. [Shadow Masking] should allow her to remain invisible to any enemy up to sixty levels higher than her, but that didn't mean some enemies couldn't see her. She was sure there were enemies that had unique skills to detect people using stealth skills. That single red eye made her feel like these golems might be one of them.

Yet that didn't happen, and Lilith continued unimpeded as she found a set of stairs and traveled down it.

Finding Thohkum's room was a little more difficult than she first assumed it would be. All the doors looked the exact same. They were big, imposing, and had ornate carvings drawn on them. She had never seen anything quite like it. To make matters worse, they made noise when she opened them.

How am I supposed to open these without alerting the entire mansion? Thohkum's gonna wake up if I open a door like this and he's on the other side.

Lilith wondered if there was another method she could use to enter Thohkum's bedroom. A secret passage perhaps? She didn't have time to search for one of those.

If only I had spent my skill points on [Instant Teleportation], perhaps I could have used that to enter his bedroom unnoticed.

There was a skill in the Demon Knight Assassin's class called [Instant Teleportation], which did exactly what it sounded like. It was a short-range teleportation technique that allowed the user to instantly teleport to any location they could see with their eyes. She had opted not to acquire that one in favor of [Dimension Cutter] because she wanted more firepower at the time.

Now she was regretting her decision.

There's no medicine for regret, Lilith thought as she closed her eyes and sighed. *I suppose I'll just have to hope for the best.*

Lilith continued her search. Once again, there were no guards. Just golems. Thohkum either really liked his privacy, or he had something to hide. That was the conclusion Lilith came to as she wandered down hallways and checked out doors.

Many of the rooms looked like workshops, armories, or storage rooms. The amount of equipment located in the armories was impressive. There were more weapons and armor than Lilith had ever seen. It made her wonder what all of this was for. Was Thohkum planning to start a war with someone?

After what felt like hours of searching, Lilith came upon the last door on the first floor. It was no different than the others. However, as this was the last door, Thohkum's bedroom had to be behind it.

Lilith took a deep breath. She placed her hand on the door. Then she slowly pushed, wincing at the noise it made as it opened.

The room on the other side was definitely a bedroom. There was a bed so massive it took up nearly a fourth of the entire room in the center. It was the kind she would have expected to see in the room of royalty, with dark red sheets and an intricate canopy of elegant design. What the heck did a Dwarf need such a massive bed for? They were tiny!

Thohkum was lying on the bed, sound asleep. She could hear his loud snoring echoing around the room. Perhaps the reason he hadn't heard her come in was because of the noise he was making? The thought amused her.

It did not take long to find the vault Garyck told her about. In fact, that was the second thing she saw after the bed.

The vault was located on the other side of the room and so massive that it took up the entire wall. The door was round and embedded into an archway. On either side of the archway as though standing guard were two statues of Dwarves wielding battleaxes.

First things first.

Lilith went over to Thohkum, removed a vial from her inventory, and climbed onto the bed. Thanks to her training, she was able to climb on without disturbing the bed. Once beside Thohkum, she opened the vial.

Glittering dust poured out of the vial. It was called [Sleep Dust] and the name made its effects self-explanatory. She gently blew the dust in Thohkum's face. He snorted several times, but his body soon relaxed. He entered such a deep sleep that his snoring even stopped.

[Sleep Dust] had the effect of putting someone to sleep for exactly one hour. That meant she had one hour to open the vault, find the key, and exit the mansion. He would wake up after that.

She would have preferred not to use [Sleep Dust] since it would cause him to wake once the effects wore off, but it was better for him to wake up after she left than while she was trying to enter his vault.

She walked over to the vault and looked at the keyhole in the very center. It was much bigger than your typical one. She would not be able to pick this lock, but fortunately, Garyck had given her an item to open it.

Lilith took the [Imitation Key] out of her inventory. It looked like a massive key made of gears. She inserted it, then twisted. The sound of gears grinding together echoed around her. Several loud thumping noises from inside the vault door accompanied the grinding. The vault soon opened with a creak that would have definitely woken Thohkum. Her decision had been a sound one.

Downing another [Mid-Rank Magic Potion], Lilith entered the room and became flabbergasted.

She had expected to see mountains of gold and treasure. That was what people typically thought to find in a Dwarven vault. But that was not what this vault contained. In fact, this vault only had one item.

It sat on a pedestal in the center of the room, a small necklace with an emblem attached to it. Lilith walked over and picked it up. No sirens went off. Not that she had expected it to. Thohkum was obviously confident no one could get this far.

The necklace was called [Emblem Key]. She stashed it in her inventory, left the vault, and closed the door behind her. Then she began making her way out of Thohkum's mansion.

She had accomplished her mission, and now they were on the clock to escape.

***

Adam sat inside Garyck's small hut with the others as they waited for Lilith to return. Aris sat right next to him, their thighs touching. She seemed to be the only one aside from him who wasn't worried.

Garyck was pacing back and forth across the room, muttering nervously under his breath as he ran a hand through his hair. Fayte and Susan remained motionless as they sat at a small table. Titania was perched on his shoulder, per usual.

And Kureha was sitting on his lap.

Adam had noticed it a lot more, especially recently, but Kureha was a very affectionate child and seemed to have no compunctions about showing it. Whether it was him or Lilith, she was always having someone pamper her. Even now, Adam was rubbing the little fox yokai's head, causing the girl to release a pleasant hum as her tails brushed against his chest.

"Tee-hee, you two look a lot like a father and his daughter," Aris said with a teasing smile.

"You think so?" asked Adam, not really paying attention.

"I do."

Kureha twisted her torso to look up at him with inquisitive eyes. "Does that mean I should call you papa?"

"Please don't."

Adam was an assassin, and before that, he was a parentless orphan living on the streets. He didn't think he would ever be ready to raise a child.

Aris tapped her lower lip and look toward the ceiling. Her curious expression masked her devious intentions.

"Maybe I should call you papa too?"

Adam twitched.

"Why would you call him papa, Big Sis Aris?" asked Kureha.

Aris grinned. "Well, you see…"

"Just what sort of filth are you trying to poison this poor girl's mind with?" asked Adam as he covered Kureha's ears so she couldn't hear anything. The little yokai pouted at him, but he wasn't about to let her listen to Aris explain what they did in bed.

"You two seem awfully relaxed, considerin' yer friend is currently tryin' te sneak into the most secure mansion in te world," Garyck grumbled.

"Lilith is a Demon Knight Assassin and has a plethora of skills designed for stealth. I have complete confidence that she'll come back soon with the key in hand," Adam said.

"Truly?" asked Garyck.

"It's still quite terrifying to think about how that little girl has such an evil class," Titania mumbled.

Adam shook his head. "No class is truly evil. Even the so-called righteous classes can be used for evil purposes if they fall into the wrong hands. Similarly, classes like Demon Knight Assassin can be used for good if the person using it is good."

Titania crossed her arms. "I have heard that argument before, and I don't buy it. You don't understand the corrupting influence evil classes can have on a person. I sometimes worry that Lilith will eventually turn to the path of evil eventually."

"I doubt that would ever happen," Adam said.

Titania might have been about to say something, but the door opened that moment and Lilith walked in. Everyone turned to the masked woman with expectation in their cases.

"Welcome back. Did you get the key?" asked Adam.

"I did." Lilith removed a necklace with an emblem from her inventory. "I believe this is it."

Adam studied the necklace details and saw that Garyck really had been right.

Item Name: Thohkum's Emblem
Item Type: Key
Grade: 2-Star

Use Requirements: Can be used by anyone.
Description: A necklace forged by the Dwarf, Thohkum.
This necklace has an emblem that can be used to unlock the
secret passage leading out of the Dwarven Stronghold.
Abilities: None

If Adam hadn't believed Garyck before, then he had no choice but to believe him now.

He set Kureha on the floor and stood up. Aris and the others also stood.

"Excellent job, Lilith. It seems you were the right woman for the job."

"Thank you, Ma… Adam," Lilith said. He thought she might be blushing.

"Since Lilith has the key, there's no reason for us to remain here," Fayte spoke up for the first time in a while. "I think we should head out before Thohkum wakes up. I don't want to have a bunch of Dwarves chasing after us."

"You're right. Let's go," Adam agreed.

They left Garyck's house and followed after the Dwarf in question as he led them even deeper into the Dwarven City. A small area at the bottom of this spiral ramp marked the entrance to the mines. Two Dwarves guarded it.

"I donnae wanna kill 'em. Let's knock em out quick," Garyck said.

No one acknowledged his request with words, but Lilith suddenly disappeared from their side. The guards finally noticed them and pointed. They quickly readied their polearms, which were nearly two times longer than they were tall.

"Halt! Yer not allowed to come down this way!" one of the

Dwarves shouted.

That was all he could say before Lilith appeared behind him. She didn't have her daggers in hand. Sliding her feet apart, she slammed both hands into his temples.

Hitting someone in the temple like that was an easy way to knock them unconscious. If you could apply enough force, it would rattle the brain. Unlike the jaw, which was quite sturdy, the temple was vulnerable due to the relative thinness of the bone located there. Whenever he wanted to knock someone out, this was where he often hit them.

Adam didn't think this attack would work in *Age of Gods*, so he was surprised when the Dwarf dropped like a sack of bricks.

"What the--"

The other Dwarf turned around after realizing what happened to his friend, but he was too slow. Lilith was already inside his defenses. Her strike was a powerful palm thrust to the underside of his jaw. The attack was so strong that the Dwarf was lifted off his feet and hit the ground with a loud clatter.

He was out like a light.

Garyck whistled. "Damn. That girl is good."

"Of course. She is a member of our party, after all," Fayte said.

"Let's keep moving," Adam instructed.

There was a ladder just inside the entrance, which the group descended. It was much longer than Adam initially thought it would be. He couldn't even see the bottom.

He made sure to go down before Susan. He wanted to be able to catch her if she fell.

Kureha wasn't climbing at all. She transformed back into a fox and clung to his back.

He didn't know how long they spent climbing, but they eventually reached the bottom, which was a wide tunnel with magic lamps lining the walls every several meters. A track traveled through the tunnel. There was a cart attached to it. It was currently empty, but he imagined it was normally full of the ore they mined down here.

There were no monsters down in this mine. Perhaps they had all been killed by the Dwarves. Whatever the case, it made traversing the tunnels much easier. The only issue they ran into was when the path split off several ways.

"Do you know which way to go?" Fayte asked Garyck.

The Dwarf shook his head. "I donnae ever been down here. Thohkum didnae trust me enough te let me do any minin'."

"Then let's pick a path at random. Standing around won't get us anywhere," Adam said.

They chose the rightmost path, which turned out to be a dead end. Traversing back the way they had come, they traveled down the second path, and fortunately, that led to a much wide mineshaft.

Adam walked over to the ledge they stood on and looked down. Nothing but darkness greeted him. A little ways over was a rickety-looking rope bridge, which led to another ledge several meters away.

"Ooooh... I-I'm not sure I like this," Susan muttered.

"It'll be okay, Su," Fayte placed a reassuring hand on her friend's shoulder.

"Su, hold my hand while we cross," Adam reached out his hand to the girl. Susan's cheeks burned scarlet as she reached out and gripped his hand.

"I wanna hold your hand too," Aris said.

Adam shook his head. "I need at least one hand free to keep my balance. Besides, you'll be fine."

"Oh, poo."

"You two must have balls o' steel to be jokin' at a time like this," Garyck shook his head in exasperation.

"Cracking jokes to lighten the mood is what I do best," Aris puffed up her chest. "Well, that and sucking Adam's--"

Whack!

"Ouch!"

"That's enough out of you."

After Adam chopped Aris over the head, the group began moving across the bridge. Aris went first, followed by Lilith (with Kureha), Garyck, Fayte, and then Adam and Susan.

Susan squealed in fright when the bridge swayed and creaked under their feet. Her breathing had grown heavy as they moved. She slipped several times and might have fallen if Adam wasn't holding her hand.

"Take a deep breath, Su. You've got this. Just don't look down."

"R-right…"

Susan kept her eyes on Adam's back as they walked across the bridge, eventually reaching the other side. The poor girl nearly collapsed. She leaned against Adam and took several shuddering breaths.

"Not a fan of heights?" asked Adam.

"I don't mind when I'm in a plane… but no, I really don't like them. I remember one time when I had to walk across a tall bridge in California. I made the mistake of looking down and got so dizzy I nearly fell over. I've been afraid of heights ever since," Susan confessed.

"We'll try to avoid high places if we can," Adam assured.

There was another tunnel here, so they traveled through it. The tunnel eventually opened into a large mineral deposit. There were no lodes to be found. It looked like this area had already been picked clean.

It felt like they spent hours exploring this mineshaft. They walked through long tunnels, traveled down fissures that split the ground like a god had slashed the earth with a sword, and walked across more bridges than he cared to count. This place was a maze. Their only blessing in all this was the lack of monsters. It would have taken them a lot more time to traverse this place if they had to stop and fight every few minutes.

"How much longer do you think it will take to fight the exit?" asked Aris.

Adam shrugged. "Who knows."

"I'm getting bored."

"Please don't do anything rash to quell your boredom."

"I think I see something up ahead!" Fayte shouted, interrupting their banter.

A light brighter than anything they had seen lay at the end of the tunnel. The group picked up the pace and emerged into a wide, open space. Several other tunnels fed into this area. There must have been multiple ways to get here. On the other side of the space was a massive door that looked similar to the one Adam's party had traveled through to reach the Dwarven City.

And standing before it was Thohkum and almost a dozen Dwarves. They were all decked in armor and wielded a variety of weapons, from axes to polearms to hammers.

Thohkum must have realized what happened after waking up and raced down here. He knows this place better than anyone else. He probably used a shorter path than the one we took to head us off. Damn. We were careless.

"Our friendship be damned, if I knew ye would steal me emblem and attempt te escape, I would have done away with the lot of ye. I'm especially disappointed in ye, Garyck. I didn't raise ye to be so rebellious," Thohkum said as he readied the massive axe gripped firmly in both hands.

Garyck clenched his hands before reaching behind him and pulling a large hammer from his back. It was not a tool meant for war. This hammer was obviously one used to forge weapons and armor, but the young Dwarf didn't appear to have anything else with which he could defend himself.

"Ye never did much raisin'. Yer a sorry excuse for a father."

"I feel like Garyck just said something plot-twisty here," Aris muttered.

"Shhh," Adam shushed her.

Titania fluttered off Adam's shoulder and shouted at the man. "Why?! Why can't you just let us leave?! All we want to do is get back to where we came from!"

"Ye know too much. I cannae let ye leave here and risk the humans finding out about us. I'll not let my people be enslaved ever again," Thohkum stated.

"They're already enslaved! By you!" Garyck shouted with vitriol. "Ye don't let us leave, ye don't let us mine, ye don't let us do anythin'. We dinnae have no freedom down here! Yer no better than the humans who enslaved us before!"

"Don't ye talk to me like that. I do what I do for the good of our people. Yer too young to understand the horrors we went through back then."

Thohkum raised his axe and slammed the butt into the ground. A mighty crash echoed around them as cracks spread from the point of impact. That axe must have weighed a ton.

"The time fer talk is over. I'm gonna kill these intruders. Then I'm gonna punish ye for tryin' to run away. I won't let anyone destroy the security of ma people."

Adam, Aris, Lilith, and Garyck stepped forward as Fayte, Kureha, Titania, and Susan stepped back. Tension filled the room, thick and cloying, as the two sides eyed each other.

It looked like a battle was inevitable now.

BATTLE UNDER-NEATH THE MOUN-TAIN

TITANIA CAST [SCAN] BEFORE THE FIRST BLOW WAS STRUCK. The Dwarves, known as [Dwarven Battlehands], were all at level 50 and had +100,500 health. Their Strength stat was +2,600 and their Constitution +500. They were weak against magic, but the armor they wore had a 75% resistance to all forms of damage.

The strongest among them was Thohkum.

Name: Thohkum, Lord of the Dwarves
Description: Thohkum is the ruling monarch of the Dwarves. Long ago, he decided to seal himself and his people away in the mountains, isolating himself from the outside world. He is also an old acquaintance of Titania's, having been in a party with her before becoming king.

Class: 2-Stars
Lvl: 60
HP: 300,000/300,000
MP: 10,000/10,000
Strength: +500
Constitution: +10,600
Dexterity: +60
Intelligence: +1,600
Speed: +30

Resistances:
Slashing: 75%
Piercing: 75%
Thrusting: 75%
Magic Damage Negation: 75%

Skill List:
Skill Name: Bisection
Description: Thohkum swings his hammer in a horizontal slash
Attack does 250% physical damage
Has a 75% chance of causing [Instant Death]
MP Cost: 500
Cooldown Time: 30 Seconds

Skill Name: Overhand Slice
Description: Thohkum uses his physical strength and gravity to swing his axe down
Attack does 400% physical damage
75% chance of causing [Instant Death]
MP Cost: 650

Cooldown Time: 40 seconds

Skill Name: Slash
Description: Thohkum swings his or her sword and attacks
the enemy!
Ability: Causes 150% damage to enemy if it hits
MP consumption: 1
Cooldown time: 0 seconds

Skill Name: Enrage
Description: All enemies within a 15-meter radius are
drawn to attack Thohkum
Abilities: Prevents enemies from attacking other members
of Thohkum's party
MP Cost: 2,000
Cooldown Time: 60 seconds
Skill Name: Earthen Defense
Description: Thohkum's skin turns to stone
Abilities: Negates all forms of damage
Duration: 60 seconds
Limitations: Thohkum cannot move while skill is active
MP Cost: 4,000
Cooldown Time: 120 seconds

Thohkum was the first Tank that Adam had seen.

Tanks in MMORPGs were characters whose primary role was to absorb damage and prevent others from being attacked. One might even call them meat shields. They put themselves between the mobs and their more vulnerable party members.

A Tank's role was very important. They had an extremely high defense and health, which allowed them to protect the damage dealers. Adam had been hoping they would eventually find someone who could play the role of Tank in their party. All their current frontline fighters were DPS classes right now.

"It looks like Thohkum is a tank. We'll need to be wary of his [Enrage] skill. If possible, I'd like you to leave attacking him to the long-range attackers. We'll keep out of range of his [Enrage] and pepper him from a distance," Susan began directing them. "Garyck, can you also take on the role of a tank?"

"Aye." Garyck hefted his hammer over his shoulder. "I've the skills ye be needin' fer a tank... though I'm not as strong as Thohkum. I'll be needin' a healer to keep me goin', but I should be able to keep him occupied while ye take out the others. Jus'... dinnae kill them, okay? We may be at odds now, but ther still me kin."

"That's a tall order, but we'll see what we can do," Adam said.

Even with their incredible defenses and health, Adam was positive he could kill every enemy here easily, but trying to fight while also not striking the killing blow was going to be hard. He wouldn't be able to use [Blood Sacrifice] or [Dance of the Sakura Blossoms] since they dealt too much damage. Those were his go-to skills. Not using them was akin to crippling himself.

But we need Garyck. Having a skilled blacksmith and someone who can act as a tank will be a huge boon to our guild. It's a pain in the ass, but we'll have to do this the hard way.

"Titania, use [Song of Refreshing Rain]," Susan instructed.

"Very well," Titania said before she began to sing.

[Song of Refreshing Rain] was one of Titania's many buffs. It restored +30 health to all members of their party for as long as she was singing. It did consume 50 MP every second, but Titania's reserves of magic were monstrous. She could sing this without worry for around an hour if not longer.

The moment Titania began to sing, Adam, Aris, Lilith, and Garyck split up. They planned to go around Thohkum and attack his allies.

"Do ye think I'll let ye sneak around me?!" Thohkum shouted as he raised his battleaxe.

In the next moment, Adam felt an inexplicable pull on his gut. It was like a force beyond him was forcing him to turn toward Thohkum. This must have been the [Enrage] skill.

This shouldn't affect me, should it? I'm more than fifteen meters away!

Adam wondered if perhaps Thohkum was wearing an accessory that increased the distance his skill worked. It was the only thing that made sense. And Titania's [Scan] could not show what sort of equipment their opponent was wearing. It was the limitation of her skills.

Adam wasn't the only one affected. Aris, Garyck, and Lilith were also drawn to Thohkum. They attacked him at the same time Adam did.

Sadly, it was for naught.

Thohkum activated [Earthen Defense]. Their weapons glanced off the Dwarf's hardened body, which had taken the same gray quality as stone. Nothing happened no matter how much they attacked. Large -0 signs floated above Thohkum's head to indicate their inability to damage him.

The Dwarves under Thohkum's command rushed forward to attack them in turn. Fortunately, Fayte, Kureha, and Susan were not affected by [Enrage].

Susan fired off [Rain of Arrows]. Her target was the [Dwarven Battlehand] in the center of the rushing formation.

Hundreds of arrows rained down on the Dwarves, who were

forced to hide behind their giant axes. The axes were so big they could second as a shield. This prevented the arrows from dealing any damage.

But that was when Fayte and Kureha acted.

Kureha's second tail writhed as blue arcs of electricity skittered across it. Dark clouds gathered near the ceiling. Distant rumbling echoed around the room, causing the Dwarves to stop for a moment and look up. That was when lightning came crashing down. Numerous bolts slammed into the Dwarves and lit them up like fireworks at New York Town Square on New Year's Day.

-9,168; -9,168; -9,168; -9,168; -9,168; -9,168; -9,168; -9,168; -9,168; -9,168; -9,168; -9,168; -9,168; -9,168; -9,168!

Kureha's attack didn't deal as much damage as it normally would thanks to the armor those [Dwarven Battlehands] were wearing, but it was still far in excess of what a normal player could do.

Fayte's attack came seconds after Kureha's. Lightning gathered on her staff. She thrust the weapon forward and a bolt of bright blue lightning shot out, slammed into a [Dwarven Battlehand], then traveled from one enemy to the next, creating a chain that connected them all together.

-50,274; -50,274; -50,274; -50,274; -50,274; -50,274; -50,274; -50,274; -50,274; -50,274; -50,274; -50,274; -50,274; -50,274; -50,274; -50,274!

Once again, the damage she did wasn't what she normally did, but she seemed to have gotten lucky. None of the [Dwarven Battlehands] could move after her attack ended. Small currents of lightning skittered across their bodies and bound them like chains. They had been successfully stunned.

That was the moment Thohkum's two skills ended. His skin returned to normal and Adam felt the pull on his body disappear.

He thought beating Thohkum and his group would be easy now

that Thohkum's two skills had entered a cooldown time.

He had never been more wrong.

-14,085; +15,000; -14,085; +15,000; -14,085; +15,000!

"What the hell is this?!" asked Adam in shock.

He had attacked one of the [Dwarven Battlehands] with [Slash], but for every attack he landed, his opponent kept healing. The healing effect didn't just negate the damage he did but also heal the damage done by Kureha and Fayte.

"It's a special passive skill granted to them by their armor!" Titania suddenly shouted. "[Physical Damage Regeneration]! It heals damage done by physical attacks!"

"Dammit! Why can't we see this skill?!"

Adam leapt back as he realized his attacks were useless. He adopted the [Form Five] stance to increase his defense. [Form Five] was the fifth stance in the Pleonexia Family's spearmanship. In *Age of Gods,* it granted Adam a 450% buff to his defense. It was only at level 1 right now. He wondered how great his defenses would be once he MAXED this skill out.

-1,600; -1,600!

Adam grinned viciously as he saw his health drop. Pain stuck his chest after two [Dwarven Battlehands] swung their axes. He had not been able to dodge because [Form Five] required him to remain standing in one place. Perhaps dodging would have been a better option, but he also didn't have much room to maneuver since he was surrounded.

+30; +30; +30; +30; +30; +30; +30; +30; +30; +30; +30; +30!

Even with Titania's [Song of Refreshing Rain] healing him, Adam still found himself hard-pressed. This was his first time in a while that he had found himself at a disadvantage.

A [Dwarven Battlehand] charged him from the front. He raised his axe and brought it down.

Adam decided not to block. He shuffled to the left. While the attack missed, one of the other [Dwarven Battlehands] was already attacking him.

Gritting his teeth as he thrust out his spear, Adam was able to use [Thrust] to perfectly parry the spear away. A loud clang echoed around them as the axe went wide and struck the ground. Adam wasted no time in using [Energy Sweep] to attack all the [Dwarven Battlehands] surrounding him.

-14,085; -14,085; -14,085; -14,085; -14,085; -14,085; -14,085; -14,085; -14,085; -14,085!

+15,000; +15,000; +15,000; +15,000; +15,000; +15,000; +15,000; +15,000; +15,000; +15,000!

Adam could only feel dismayed as all his damage was negated by the passive restoration ability, but he wasn't one to give up. His competitive spirit was also soaring. His blood was pounding in his ears. He had always enjoyed pushing his limits, and was this not the perfect opportunity to do just that?

"Bring it on! I'll take on every single one of you!" Adam roared as he mentally said "fuck it" and activated [Blood Sacrifice]. So what if this would increase his damage severalfold? He was sure these Dwarves could take it.

Probably.

***

While Adam was surrounded on all sides, Aris was completely free to do what she wanted. Her speed was such that none of the enemies attacking could pin her down.

She blitzed back and forth across the battlefield like a bolt of lightning. Her methods were simple. She ran in a straight line from one side of the cavern to the other, attacking anything and everything that was in her path.

-812; -1,624; -3,248; -6,496!

Aris raced through a throng of [Dwarven Battlehands]. Her blades sang as she swung them around in graceful arcs. She could feel the resistance of her enemies' armor. Sparks flew as her swords dug furrows in the gleaming metal surface.

+15,000; +15,000; +15,000; +15,000!

The damage she did was negligible and the Dwarves had that passive skill that let them regenerate lost health. All of the damage she did was negated thanks to that.

But Aris didn't care.

She was having the time of her life.

"Let's see you take this!"

Aris danced into the center of the Dwarven formation and spun around like a ballerina. [Spirited Twirl] was one of her AoE attacks. Once more she felt the resistance of their armor. Was it because their armor was resistant to slashing damage? Well. Whatever. She didn't care about that.

-435; -435; -435; -435; -435; -435; -435; -435; -435; -435; -435; -435; -435; -435; -435; -435; -435; -435; -435; -435!

Aris didn't stop attacking. Immediately after using [Spirited Twirl], she swung both her weapons down on a single [Dwarven Battlehand]. [Double Slash] was an attack that did twice the damage as a normal [Slash].

In this case, all her attack did was a measly -1,870, but she did not let this stop her.

She raced out of the enemy formation, stopped on the other side of the caver, spun around, bent her knees, and blasted off again.

Several [Dwarven Battlehands] had slammed their axes into the ground and were using them as shields. Even with her speed, she would not survive ramming headfirst into those undamaged. She leapt at the very last second, jumping over her enemies' heads.

"Now, Lilith!"

-54,032!

Lilith appeared behind one of the [Dwarven Battlehands], grabbed them by the head, and slid her dagger across his throat. The amount of damage she did was incredible. Even the +15,000 regeneration passive skill was only able to heal a little bit of the damage done.

Before her enemies could notice her, Lilith vanished again. Aris could only shake her head. That [Shadow Masking] skill really was incredible.

"Where did that bleedin' woman go?!"

"I can't see her!"

"Dammit! She's like a ghost!"

While Adam fought alone, Aris and Lilith had teamed up to take on the majority of the enemies. They weren't aiming to win. All they wanted to do was prevent them from attacking their long-range fighters.

Before the Dwarves could try and locate Lilith—not that it was possible—Aris dashed back into their formation and began attacking once more. She avoided attacking the enemies Lilith attacked. That passive ability these [Dwarven Battlehands] had seemed to only activate when they received physical damage. She didn't want to negate all of Lilith's hard work.

And while she, Lilith, Adam, and Garyck continued defending the front line, Fayte and Kureha peppered the enemy from the back.

Susan was not attacking them. Just like Aris, she must have realized her arrows would not do any good here. She studied the enemy with a keen eye as Fayte launched one [Energy Bolt] after another into the group of [Dwarven Battlehands]. While the attacks didn't do much damage on their own, they did stack up, and their enemies' passive regeneration skill didn't activate since it was a magical attack.

Kureha did not have [Energy Bolt], but she was able to launch a continuous stream of magical attacks by using her skills one after another in two-second intervals. Fire exploded against their enemies. Lightning jolted the Dwarves. Spears of water slammed into armored chests. She was like a walking, talking storm.

Yet even though Fayte and Kureha were attacking with everything they had, the [Dwarven Battlehands] refused to back down. They fought back with equal tenacity.

And in the center of this maelstrom of combat, Garyck continued to fight against Thohkum.

The battle was at a stalemate. This had become a war of attrition. And the one to claim victory would be the one who outlasted the other.

Aris licked her lips as dove once more into the fray.

***

[Energy Sweep]

Adam swung his spear as he rotated a full 360 degrees. A blue wave of energy erupted from his weapon and flew out in a wide circle that sliced into the [Dwarven Battlehands] surrounding him.

-4,695; -4,695; -4,695; -4,695; -4,695; -4,695; -4,695; -4,695; -4,695; -4,695; -4,695; -4,695; -4,695; -4,695; -4,695; -4,695; -4,695!

+15,000; +15,000; +15,000; +15,000; +15,000; +15,000; +15,000; +15,000; +15,000; +15,000; +15,000; +15,000; +15,000!

While the amount of damage he did was negligible, his attack caused the enemies around him to stagger. Adam used that moment to break through their guard. He thrust his spear at one [Dwarven Battlehand]. The loud clang of metal against metal echoed around him. His enemy wasn't too injured, but the attack sent him flying.

Adam broke the enemy formation and met up with Aris.

"How are you doing?" he asked.

"Not… not bad…"

"You're getting tired."

"We've been fighting for so long. Of course, I'm tired."

Aris looked pretty exhausted now. She no longer had a vibrant smile on her face as she fended off several enemies, and she wasn't using her speed anymore.

This battle had been going on for far longer than it should have. Adam calculated the passage of at least several hours.

A [Dwarven Battlehand] with red hair and a thick beard charged him, but Adam adopted the [Form Five] stance and spun his spear around to create a shield. The [Dwarven Battlehand] plowed right into it and was knocked back.

Adam didn't bother attacking since he would just regenerate.

We can't keep this up. We need a decisive means of victory.

Adam looked around. He and Aris were keeping the enemy from attacking Fayte, Kureha, and Susan. Garyck was fighting Thohkum and pulling agro with his tank skills. Lilith was using [Shadow Masking] in conjunction with her numerous other assassin class skills to wreak havoc on the enemy. Each of them was doing their best.

But it was still all for naught.

The biggest problem was the armor their enemies were wearing. It not only granted them a 75% reduction to all forms of damage, but it had a passive regeneration skill that let them heal every time they received a physical attack.

Maybe if they could kill these bastards, they would win, but Garyck had requested they not kill anyone. That made this whole thing infinitely harder.

"Garyck! Use your skills again!" Susan called out. "Adam! Activated [Blood Sacrifice] and use [Dance of the Sakura Blossoms] on Thohkum!"

Adam was confused. She wanted him to use his two most powerful skills? They could probably win, but he would end up killing Thohkum. Had she decided it was better to kill him? No. Susan wasn't that kind of woman, so why was she asking him to use those two skills, unless…

I think I see what's going on here. I know what she wants me to do.

"Aris, Lilith, clear a path for me."

"Yes, Master."

"Don't worry, Adam. I've got this!"

Lilith appeared beside Aris and the two raced straight through the enemy formation. Garyck had activated [Anchor]. It was a tank skill, but very different from Thohkum's [Enrage]. While the latter drew enemies in by pulling agro, the former pinned enemies in place, keeping them from moving.

All the enemies stopped moving. Aris and Lilith didn't bother attacking. They instead used their physical stats to simply shove the [Dwarven Battlehands] out of the way.

Adam raced through the breach, activated [Blood Sacrifice], and used [Dance of the Sakura Blossoms]. At the same time, Titania switched from [Song of Refreshing Rain] to [Song of Vigor].

-14,088; +15,000; -42,264; +15,000; 126,792; +15,000!

Adam stopped attacking. Their goal wasn't to kill Thohkum.

He grabbed Garyck and leapt back.

Fayte and Kureha both released their respective attacks. Lightning gathered around Fayte's staff. As she swung it, a powerful bolt of crackling blue lightning surged forward and struck the still-pinned Thohkum. The attack lit him like a fireworks display.

-50,274!

Thanks to the seventy-five percent magic reduction skill on that armor, Fayte's attack didn't do nearly as much damage as it could, but it was still enough to drop Thohkum's health into the red.

Kureha had also unleashed a [Thunder Bolt] of her own. It struck Thohkum a mere second or so after Fayte's attack.

-18,909!

Once again, very little damage was done compared to what it should have been, but it was enough to drop Thohkum's health so much that a single attack would now kill him.

"Lilith!" Susan shouted.

"Right!"

Lilith appeared behind Thohkum before the Dwarf could recover and pressed a blade against his throat. Thohkum froze as he was halfway through the process of getting up. He eyed the obsidian blade warily.

"Do not move. Even with your regeneration, you won't be able to survive my next attack."

"What are ye plannin'?"

"Order your men to stand down."

Thohkum hesitated, which caused Lilith to press the blade further against his throat. He sighed, coughed a little, then shouted.

"Oi! Everyone, stand down! No more fightin'!"

The [Dwarven Battlehands] who had recovered from Garyck's [Anchor] skill and reengaged in combat with Aris and Adam ceased what they were doing. They all turned toward Thohkum.

"My lord!" they shouted as they realized he was in danger.

"I highly recommend none of you move," Lilith commanded in a cold tone. "Take one step, and I'll slit his throat."

The [Dwarven Battlehands] glared at Lilith as they backed down. A tense silence filled the air. No one moved for a while until Susan commanded everyone to set up a perimeter around Lilith and Thohkum.

"What are ye gonna do now?" Thohkum sounded resigned as he spoke.

"Why ask a question when you already know the answer?" Adam shrugged when Thohkum glared at him. "We're going to use you as a hostage to get out of this mountain. We don't want to stay here. After that, you can return to your mountain. We don't care. We just want to leave."

"Haaaaah. I should have killed ye when I had the chance."

"If that's how you're going to be, then maybe we should kill you now to avoid letting a potential enemy live?"

Thohkum went silent.

With the [Dwarven Battlehands] following close behind, their group, led by Susan, went over to the door. Lilith was in charge of holding the key. She removed the emblem from her inventory and placed it inside a small indentation.

This door was very similar to the one they had come through. The intricate mechanisms inside created loud cranking sounds that reverberated around the cavern. Soon, those noises stopped, then a much louder noise echoed around them as the door split open down the middle. Both sides disappeared into the wall, revealing a passageway.

"Do not follow us," Susan said to the [Dwarven Battlehands] before they could make a move. "We'll let your leader go, but I can't guarantee his safety if you follow us."

The [Dwarven Battlehands] glared reluctantly at her, making it clear they had no desire to follow that order, but they also didn't want their leader to die. It seemed this old Dwarf was quite charismatic. Even though he had all but locked these people inside a mountain, all of them remained loyal.

"Dinnae follow us," Thohkum ordered. "I'll be back."

The order from their leader seemed to settle the group. The [Dwarven Battlehands] stood still as Adam and the others went up the passage, which turned into a staircase.

Blue skies and a brilliant sun greeted them as they emerged from the staircase. Adam glanced around. They were in a forest, but he didn't know which one. It had to be close to where they had first discovered the location of this dungeon, so it shouldn't be too hard to orient themselves and return home.

"There. Yer outside. Now let me go," Thohkum commanded.

"You're free to go, as promised," Susan said.

Lilith released the old Dwarf, who huffed as he dusted himself off. He didn't attack them. Smart man. He knew what would happen if he tried. Now that his health was so low and he didn't have his comrades to fight beside him, there was nothing he could do to them.

He turned around and began stalking back into the mountain entrance, but he paused just before entering and turned around to glare at Garyck.

"Do ye really want this? Ye really want to leave the sanctity o' this mountain?"

Garyck puffed out his chest. "Course I do! I hate livin' all cooped up in that blasted place. I hate not bein' able to craft whatever I want. More than anythin', I hate the fact that ye can't seem to accept me. Yer a terrible father."

"Everythin' I did was fer yer own good. You'll see that eventually. I just hope it's not too late by then."

Thohkum didn't say anything else as he turned around and stalked back down the stairs. Garyck growled and shook an angry fist at his old man's departing back.

"I'll never regret my decision! Do ye 'ear me?!"

Adam and the others remained silent for a moment as Garyck huffed and puffed. It seemed he had a lot of pent-up emotions. However, they couldn't remain this way forever.

"Garyck, what are you planning to do now?" asked Fayte.

"I haven't thought much about it. All I wanted was ter escape from that place." Garyck stroked his beard in thoughtful contemplation, having calmed down.

"Then would you like to come with us?" asked Fayte with a smile. "We could use a skilled blacksmith."

"Aye. That sounds like a good idea. I got nothin' better to do and don't know me way around, so goin' with ye sounds like me best option."

A screen suddenly appeared in front of Fayte. Adam knew what this was. It was an announcement stating Garyck wanted to join their party and asking Fayte if she would accept him. Fayte pressed "yes."

"Welcome to our guild, Garyck," Fayte said as she held out a hand.

"Pleasure to be workin' with ye," Garyck returned as he clasped her hand in a firm shake.

With Garyck now a permanent member of their party, the group first got their bearings. They seemed to be east of the original entrance. To return to the original entrance, they had to travel southwest, around the mountain.

It would take several days, unfortunately. They didn't have any horses to travel more quickly.

Garyck didn't seem to mind. He asked Fayte all kinds of questions about the world outside, from the infrastructure of human cities to the duties of their guild and even what kind of weapons and armor they wanted him to make. He seemed pretty enthusiastic.

"I don't know too much about other cities since I've only been to Solum, but it's very different from your mountain. We don't have a king. Each city is run by a mayor. Solum's mayor is in control of this region of the Sun Continent. I don't know too much else," Fayte was explaining.

"What about the armor and weapons? How does human-made equipment compare to what we Dwarves can make?" asked Garyck.

"It can't," Fayte said. "Having faced off against those [Dwarven Battlehands], I can tell you that nothing a human creates will ever be as good."

Garyck looked confused. "What about the equipment ye all are wieldin'? Is that not made with human hands? It's quite good."

"Our equipment was not crafted by humans, to my knowledge. At the very least, I know Lilith's and Susan's were not made by humans."

"I see."

Garyck was a curious Dwarf. Titania had told him that Dwarves were a greedy race that cared little for anything but gold. Perhaps Garyck was cut from a different cloth. He didn't display any of the arrogance or greed his kind was known for. He seemed more like an inquisitive scholar than anything.

They eventually reached the dungeon entrance, which meant they could easily reach their home within a day or two of travel. It was late, however, and so they decided to set up camp.

Adam was in charge of the cooking.

Cooking in *Age of Gods* was just like cooking in real life. You couldn't just magic food into existence by combining several ingredients and pressing a button. You actually had to use your hands and perform all the steps necessary to cook the food.

The only real difference between cooking in-game and cooking in real life was that the recipes Adam used in-game were all recipes implanted inside of his head via [Recipe Scrolls], which he had bought from the general store in Solum.

Adam made a luxurious pottage called mortrew made with pork, chicken, chicken liver, gode brother, eggs, and various other ingredients—all of which were stored inside of his inventory. He used a big pot to cook the food, then served them up in several wooden bowls.

"Mmmmmm! This food is delicious!" Aris squealed in delight.

"It seems even your cooking in-game is excellent," Fayte complimented.

"Master's cooking…" Lilith murmured as she slowly sipped her soup.

"I didn't realize you were such a good cook. I'm… a little jealous of Fayte and Aris," Susan admitted.

"Then why don't you come over?" asked Aris.

"What? Me? Come over?" Susan's eyes widened.

"Yeah! You can come over in the real world and try some of Adam's cooking," Aris said.

"Oh… I don't know if that would be appropriate…"

They were all sitting around a campfire, sharing the meal. Garyck was mostly quiet… if you didn't count the loud noises he made while eating. Aris and Susan were chatting the most, though it seemed more like Aris was talking and Susan was listening.

Adam was silent as he watched all this with a smile. His good mood was interrupted, however, when a loud ringing alerted him to someone in his friend's list calling.

It was Asmodeus.

"Master? Thank goodness. I'm glad my call finally got through."

"Sorry about that. We were trapped inside a location that didn't allow us to log out or contact the outside world. Has something happened?"

Yeah. Something big has happened." Adam waited for Asmodeus to continue, but the man's next words were so unexpected that not even he could keep the shock from his face. *"Daggerfall Dynasty contacted the Guild Association several days ago, asking to set up a meeting between you and them. I believe they want to form an alliance with us. "*

A MEETING WITH DAREN DAGGER-FALL

AFTER LEARNING THAT DAGGERFALL DYNASTY WANTED TO SET UP A meeting with Destiny's Overture, Fayte decided to forego resting at their guild house and instead went straight to the Guild Association branch in Solum.

The members of Daggerfall Dynasty weren't there, of course, but Fayte spoke with Clarise about setting up an appointment for the two guilds to meet.

All interactions between guilds needed to be approved by the Guild Association. Violations were met with harsh penalties. Adam didn't know how the Guild Association could find out when someone had violated this rule, but since this was a video game, there had to be some kind of programming that alerted the Guild Association when someone broke it. That was his assumption anyway.

A meeting was quickly set to take place two days after they emerged from the Dwarven city. Garyck became an official member of their guild. Clarise had been quite shocked when she discovered a Dwarf wanted to join Destiny's Overture.

Not only did they now have an able tank, but Garyck was also a talented blacksmith. They didn't have a forge at their guild house yet. However, Fayte had requested Clarise to help her find several carpenters and stonesmiths to help build a forge for him. It would take around five days before they could come out.

It was also going to cost a pretty penny.

"Are you sure this is what you want, Garyck?" Fayte asked.

The meeting between Destiny's Overture and Daggerfall Dynasty was set to take place in several hours. Fayte and Adam would be the only ones attending. Adam was merely going as a bodyguard. Guild Association rules stated that guild masters could only take one person with them during a meeting with another guild. The others would remain in the guild house to wait for the news.

At present, Adam and the others were sitting around the living room, drinking tea or coffee. Or sleeping. Aris and Kureha were both out like lights. While the little fox yokai slept curled up on Lilith's lap, Aris was sprawled out on the couch and using Adam's lap as a pillow.

"Course I'm sure," Garyck said. "I've thought about it a lot, and I dinnae 'bout you, but I'm well aware that Dwarves can't move about freely in human cities. That's just asking to be enslaved. Belonging to a guild will help protect me."

"Just so long as you're sure. I know I'm the one who suggested it, but I don't want to restrict your freedom," Fayte said.

Garyck grinned. "Yer a kind lass. So long as I have a roof over me head, a forge to make weapons, good food, and good drink, I'm fine."

"What kind of items do you make?" asked the ever-timid Susan.

Garyck stroked his chin. "I mostly craft swords and armor, but I can also make some accessories. All of ye already have some amazin' equipment. I don't think there's I can make armor or weapons better than what ye have, so I'll start by making some accessories that provide unique buffs to yer stats."

"That would be amazing," Fayte said.

"It would, wouldn't it?" Garyck grinned, then furrowed his brow. "That said, ye'll need to get the parts necessary for me to craft the accessories. I'll need lots o' ore and monster parts. Craftin' requires a lot o' material, and different materials create different effects when combined."

The crafting system in *Age of Gods* seemed similar in some ways to the systems of other games, but only insomuch as it required collecting materials to make items. Everything else was completely different.

The biggest difference was that you couldn't just select materials and automatically make items appear as if by magic. Just like cooking in this world, to make an item, you had to actually forge it by hand. Adam assumed every crafting class was like this.

The addition of Garyck was a welcome one. They finally had a tank to help them absorb enemy damage. Thus far, Adam, Aris, and Lilith had been required to simply avoid damage as much as possible, which put a lot of stress on them. Having Garyck on their team would help lessen the mental burden required of them during combat.

Name: Garyck Ironhand
Class: Dwarven Blacksmith
Subclass: Warsmith
Lvl: 30

SP: 0

AP 0

Experience: 0/107,374,182,400

Fame: 0

Strength: +300

Constitution: +1,500

Dexterity: +300

Intelligence: +350

Speed: +10

Physical Attack: +2,700

Health: 15,000/15,000

Hit-rate: 15%

MP: 2,000/2,000

Movement: +10

Physical Defense: +6,000

Magical Defense: +6,000

Dodge Rate: 15%

Magic Attack: +700

Resistances:

75% Poison

75% Death

75% Blindness

75% Confusion

75% Sleep

75% Paralysis

75% Burn

75% Shock

75% Fire

75% Earth

75% Water

75% Wind

75% Lightning

75% Light

75% Darkness

Skill List:

Skill Name: Bash

Description: Swings warhammer down on enemy.

Current lvl: MAXED

Ability: Causes 250% damage

MP Consumption: 1

Cooldown Time: 0 Seconds

Skill Name: Heavy Bash

Description: An upgraded version of the [Bash] skill

Current lvl: 5

AP Needed to Reach Next Lvl: 400,000

Ability: 500% damage

Generates a shockwave that staggers enemies within a 15-meter radius

MP Consumption: 5

Cooldown Time: 5 Seconds

Skill Name: Anchor

Description: Paralyzes every enemy within its area of effect.

Current Lvl: MAXED

Ability: Prevents enemies up to 20 levels higher than user from moving for 60 seconds

Has an area of effect of up to 20 meters

MP Consumption: 100
Cooldown Time: 60 Seconds

Skill Name: Pile Bunker
Description: User uses the tip of weapon to pierce through
armor
Current lvl: 6
AP Needed to Reach Next Lvl: 1,500,000
Ability: Deals 1,000% damage
Ignores armor

Skill Name: Earthen Defense
Description: Turns skin as solid as the earth to increase
user's defensive power
Current Lvl: 4
AP Needed to Reach Next Lvl: 240,000
Ability: Increases Physical and Magical Defense by 250%
Lasts 60 seconds
MP Consumption: 500
Cooldown Time: 120 Seconds

Skill Name: Weapons Crafting
Description: Grants the ability to forge weapons
Current Lvl: MAXED
Ability: Can forge weapons up to 3-Stars
MP Consumption: 0
Cooldown Time: 0 Seconds
Passive Skill

Skill Name: Armorer
Description: Grants the ability to forge armor

Current Lvl: MAXED
Ability: Can forge weapons up to 3-Stars
MP Consumption: 0
Cooldown Time: 0 Seconds
Passive Skill

Skill Name: Jeweler
Description: Grants the ability to forge accessories
Current Lvl: MAXED
Ability: Can Forge accessories up to 3-Stars
MP Consumption: 0
Cooldown Time: 0 Seconds
Passive Skill

Skill Name: Dwarven Hands
Description: Boosts crafting skills
Current Lvl: MAXED
Ability: Allows crafter to create items one star above their natural abilities
MP Consumption: 0
Cooldown Time: 0
Passive Skill

Equipment:
Name: Garyck's Forging Hammer
Item Type: Crafting Tool
Grade: 3-Star
User Requirements: Can only be used by the Dwarf, Garyck
Description: This forging hammer was crafted by

Thohkum for Garyck during his coming-of-age ceremony.
Abilities: Decreases crafting time by 50%; Strength+300%;

Name: Leather Dwarven Armor Set
Item Type: Armor
Grade: 2-Star
Use Requirements: Can only be worn by Dwarves
**Description: Armor made by Garyck. Made from hard
leather. Solid defense.**
**Abilities: Physical Defense+500%; Magical Defense+500%;
75% resistance to all status ailments and damage types**

Garyck's stats were all excellent and the armor he wore was incredible despite its 2-Star rating. It was clear the materials Garyck used when creating this armor were also of subpar quality. Adam wondered what kind of armor he could create with better materials.

Perhaps the most unusual aspect of Garyck's stats was the fact that his main class was Dwarven Blacksmith and his subclass Warsmith. Was this because he was a Dwarf?

In every story and game Adam had played, Dwarves were considered the best craftsmen of all time, but their primary class would still always be a combat class. It was interesting to see how different things were in this game.

"Hey, Garyck, I have a question for you," Adam suddenly said.

Garyck looked at him curiously. "Ask away?"

"Have you ever considered taking on an apprentice?"

"An apprentice? Me? Why do ye ask?"

Adam leaned forward, then remembered there was a girl using him as a lap pillow and stopped. He sighed and began stroking Aris's hair. The girl shifted a little and mumbled something about pancakes under her breath before going silent.

"I have the ability to add a secondary class. I've been thinking about what secondary class I should have. I don't want something ordinary. I'd like a class that can really help increase Destiny's Overture's fighting overall prowess. I think having a Blacksmith class would really help with that, and what better person to teach me than a Dwarf?"

"Adam, you've been thinking about that this whole time?" asked Fayte, a hand to her mouth.

Adam nodded. "Of course."

"Are ye tryin' to replace me already?" asked Garyck.

Adam shook his head. "Not at all. I doubt I could ever be as good as you anyway, but it would be beneficial to have a helper, wouldn't it? Plus, it would be a good idea to have at least two people who can help maintain our armor and weapons. We could even make blacksmithing a business and sell high-quality weapons to shops or create custom weapons for individuals who are willing to pay more money."

Money was still something Fayte needed in abundance to win her bet. The more money they had, the better off she would be. Adam didn't just want her to win the bet either. He wanted her to smash Levon's expectations to pieces.

"Hmmm." Garyck rubbed his chin. It was still weird seeing a Dwarf without a thick beard. "I suppose I could teach ye a few things, but I'm not much of a teacher meself. I'll have to warn ye in advance that I don't know the first thing about teachin' others. Whether or not you can actually become a blacksmith will depend entirely on yer own aptitude."

"I understand," Adam said.

"Then we'll get started after ye get back from yer meetin' with that other guild. Daggerfall Whatserhoosit."

"Daggerfall Dynasty," Susan corrected softly.

"Right. Them," Garyck nodded.

"Speaking of, it's about time for us to leave," Fayte said, standing up.

Adam woke up Aris and, after giving the girl a kiss goodbye, left with Fayte. They used the [Warp Pad] to arrive inside the Guild Association's Solum Branch.

Clarise was waiting for them. She was an attractive woman with a thin waist, wide hips, and a modest chest dressed in something that looked like an attendant uniform. It was a pleated skirt and long-sleeved shirt combo with a vest thrown over it.

"I'm glad you two could make it. Daren Daggerfall and Spear God are already waiting in the meeting room," the woman greeted.

A jolt raced through Adam's spine the moment he heard the woman say, "Spear God." He tried hard not to let the wave of emotions inundating him affect how he acted as he followed Fayte and Clarise out of the warp room.

"We're not late, are we?" asked Fayte.

Clarise shook her head. "No. You're just in time. Daren Daggerfall arrived an hour early. He seems quite eager to meet with you. Not that I blame him, of course. You're strong, pretty, intelligent—not to mention beautiful."

"I think pretty and beautiful mean the same thing," Adam muttered.

Fayte and Adam were currently wearing their mask and veil respectively. Since they were meeting someone who wasn't part of their guild--and was an important figure to boot--they had decided to keep their appearances a secret.

They soon reached a door with a number marked on it. Number 011. That was their personal meeting room and the office Clarise used when doing work for the Guild Association.

Adam bit his lip as he stared at the door. Beyond it was the Spear God. The person he had been thinking about non-stop for so long now. Was that person really Lexi? He both longed to find out and was also terrified of the answer. What if they were Lexi? What would he do? What if they weren't her? Could he handle the disappointment?

Clarise opened the door and gestured for them to precede her. Fayte did just that. However, she turned around and stared at him when he didn't move.

"Adam?" Fayte called to him.

He blinked several times and shook his head. "Sorry. I got distracted."

With hesitant steps, Adam entered the room, where two people were waiting for them.

LEXI

DARREN DAGGERFALL'S BROTHERS WERE NOT IN THE ROOM. It was unusual but not unheard of. Fayte had heard through the rumor mill that, while Darren and his brothers were almost inseparable, he would occasionally act alone if he deemed it necessary.

The man in question sat on one of two couches. He stood up when Fayte and Adam entered the room and smiled cordially.

"Good of you to make it. Thank you for agreeing to this meeting," he said.

"I should be the one thanking you for the invitation," Fayte returned as she walked to the other side of the couch and sat down.

Adam stood behind the couch, just like the figure standing silently behind the one Darren was using. Fayte eyed the Spear God for a moment. She could see nothing, however. Covered from head to toe in a cloak, bandages, and concealing their face with a mask, it was impossible to tell anything about them. She couldn't even figure out if they were a man or a woman.

"I would like to congratulate you on your victory against Levon in the Guild War," Darren continued. "Watching you demolish his entire force was inspiring."

"Oh, did you see it?" Fayte inquired with a raised eyebrow.

"Gya ha ha ha! I had front row seats."

Front row seats, meaning he had been present during the battle, watching from afar. Fayte did not delude herself into thinking he was the only one. Her Guild War might have been broadcast live, but that didn't mean some adventurous spirits wouldn't try to see it in person.

"I appreciate the sentiment, but to be honest, Levon's forces didn't amount to much," Fayte said.

"Gya ha ha ha! I'm sure! You pulverized him like it was as natural as breathing! To top it off, you even convinced the Grim Reapers to join you! They've always been an independent guild and never taken sides before. I was quite surprised."

Fayte briefly reviewed what she knew of Darren from the intelligence she had Susan gather.

Darren Daggerfall was a straightforward man. He did not use subterfuge to get his way. He was earnest, but he also had a stubborn streak and would relentlessly pursue his goal until he got his way. That stubbornness of his was what led to his Daggerfall Dynasty becoming the second most powerful guild in the American Federation.

Clarise served them some tea, and Fayte used the time it took to finish her drink making small talk.

"I heard you recently managed to reach level 24. That's very impressive."

"Not nearly as impressive as your group, I'm afraid."

"Well, we've had many fortuitous encounters while playing."

Flattery played an important role in political discourse. It was merely the act of providing excessive praise to ingratiate oneself with another. By flattering someone, you provided them with an ego boost, and while this could be dangerous since some people had an ego that was far too big for their station, it was often used during many political discussions and even friendly gatherings between nobles.

Of course, it didn't always work. Some people had an intense dislike of flattery and preferred you speak frankly. Darren was in the latter group, which was why Fayte kept her flattery to a minimum.

Setting her teacup down, Fayte leaned back, crossed her left leg over her right, and looked at the man with a calm expression.

"Asmodeus mentioned in your message that you would like to form an alliance with Destiny's Overture. Can I ask what this alliance will entail?"

"Of course." Darren leaned forward and rested his forearms against his knees. "We of Daggerfall Dynasty wish to work with your Destiny's Overture for mutual benefit. Your guild will remain fully autonomous. I'm not stupid enough to think my guild can even control yours. What I want is your help in certain matters and the promise of aid should I need it. In exchange, we will keep guilds like the Pleonexia Alliance off your back, provide resources that you might need, and help you in other ways should you need it."

"It sounds like you're offering us an equal partnership," Fayte said carefully.

"That is exactly what I'm offering," Darren said seriously.

Daggerfall Dynasty was second only to the Pleonexia Alliance, and the only reason they were second was because they lacked the accrued wealth and manpower of the latter. In terms of strength, they were about equal. Daggerfall Dynasty might even have the upper hand since they had the Spear God--currently the second strongest player on the Power Charts.

That he was offering her such lucrative terms for an alliance was a testament to how much he valued her guild.

But it wasn't like his offer was without merit either. They had just demolished one hundred thousand members of the Pleonexia

Alliance's elites in a Guild War not long ago. They also had Adam, a player who had beaten the Spear God in single combat. And finally, the Grim Reapers had joined Destiny's Overture.

That last fact must have been the main reason for the terms Darren was offering. The Grim Reapers were a well-known assassination guild that had been around for several years. They were the best at what they did. No one knew who they were in real life despite numerous people trying, and all those people who attempted to discover them not only failed but were silenced.

Though none of them were actually killed...

Fayte didn't let the shiver that wanted to run down her spine show as she pretended to consider the proposal. She had already discussed this matter with everyone else, and in truth, she already knew what she wanted to do.

"I am not against forming an alliance. However, I do have one request. Don't worry. It's not something you can't do or even something that will require you to exert any effort," Fayte said when she saw the way Darren furrowed his brow.

"What is your request?" Caution plagued Darren's voice.

"My friend here would like to speak with the Spear God in private," Fayte said, gesturing toward Adam, who had been silently staring at the Spear God through his mask.

Darren seemed bemused like he couldn't understand why Adam would even want to speak with the Spear God, but then he looked at the cloaked figure behind him. Several silent seconds passed. Then the Spear God nodded once. Darren turned back to Fayte.

"So, as long as Adam can speak with the Spear God privately, you'll agree to form an alliance?" he asked.

Fayte smiled behind her veil. "Correct."

Darren slapped his knee. "Gya ha ha ha! Then the answer is easy! Why don't we leave this two alone and discuss the particulars of the alliance outside?"

"I am amenable to that," Fayte said.

She and Darren stood up and left the room alongside Clarise who had been presiding over the meeting. Fayte only looked back once before the door shut.

I hope that person is the one you've been looking for, she prayed to herself.

***

Adam's chest felt painfully tight and his knees weak as he stared at the person on the other side of the room. He had wanted to speak with this person, but now that the opportunity had finally presented itself, he didn't know what to say. What if this person wasn't Lexi? What if it was? He didn't know what he would do regardless of what he found out.

Come on, Adam! Get it together! This isn't like you! Just... just go for it. You can deal with the consequences later.

Taking a slow, shuddering breath, Adam finally opened his mouth.

"Lexi?"

There was no response, but the cloaked figure shifted.

"Are you... Alexis Pleonexia?" he asked cautiously.

Once again, no response.

Maybe this isn't Lexi, but then, how do they know our stance?

Adam finally reached up and placed a hand on his mask. He hesitated for a moment before removing it. Perhaps it was his imagination, but he thought the figure before him had sucked in a breath.

"Lexi... it's me... it's Adam... if that's you... please tell me."

Nothing happened for nearly a full minute, and Adam wondered if maybe his hopes would be dashed once more, but then the Spear God reached up.

Long hair the color of midnight spilled from the hood as it was lowered. Each strand seemed to glimmer as though catching starlight. And with the removal of the hood, Adam was finally able to make out this person's eyes.

Her right eye... it's blind.

The Spear God next removed the bandages, unwinding them at a steady pace that was far too slow for his liking. Seconds ticked by as pale skin revealed itself. Most of it was unblemished like fresh snow after a winter storm. Only the scar traveling down the right side of her face marred her otherwise perfect features. It traveled from several centimeters above her eye, straight through it, all the way down to the middle of her cheek. Cataracts had formed on the iris to give it a milky hue.

As the bandage at last came undone, Adam fell to his knees, no longer possessing the strength to stand.

"It's... really you... you're really alive."

Adam's eyes felt hot. He couldn't contain his tears nor his emotions even if he tried. He stared at the woman through blurry eyes.

"I searched for you... for so long... I... I'm so sorry, Lexi. I couldn't do anything for you. You gave me so much, and I gave you nothing but pain in return..."

Perhaps it was because his tears were blurring his vision, or maybe it was because he was too emotional to see, but he didn't see Lexi walk over to him until a soft hand rested on his head. He looked up. Lexi was looking down at him with a smile on her face. She looked older now, more mature, more elegant, and more beautiful, but that smile was the same as he remembered.

"Lexi, I... um..."

Lexi knelt down, grabbed his shoulders, and pulled him into a hug.

Adam broke. It was like something inside of him snapped. Hot tears stung his eyes as he rested his chin on Lexi's shoulder and hugged her. All the emotions he had long kept buried surfaced and swept over him like a tidal wave.

Something wet hit his neck, and he realized with a start that Lexi was crying too. Perhaps she had also been searching for him all this time. Maybe she, too, had despaired when no news of him appeared. Whatever the case, it only made him hold her tighter as the two of them cried in each other's embrace.

"I'm so glad that you're alive," Adam whispered with a voice full of emotion. "After I returned to the American Federation, I went to infiltrate the Pleonexia Alliance and heard you had gone missing. I looked for you, but it was like you had vanished. I couldn't find you no matter how much I looked."

His words caused Lexi to hug him tighter. He ran a hand down her back, cursing her thick cloak for getting in the way.

"What have you been up to?" he asked after several seconds of silence.

"…"

"Lexi?"

A breathy sigh echoed in his ear. Adam became confused when Lexi pushed him away until he was at about arm's length. She then lowered her cloak, revealing an ugly scar that went from one side of her throat to the other.

He sucked in a breath.

The avatars in *Age of Gods* were perfect representations of the person using them. If Lexi's avatar had a scar, then it meant her real body had a similar scar.

"You… lost your voice?" he asked, unable to quite believe it. Lexi nodded. "When?" Lexi held up both hands, showed ten fingers, then clenched her left hand. "When you were fifteen?" Another nod. "I see."

Adam reached out and gently brushed his fingers over the scar. Lexi closed her eyes. The scar tissue was such a vivid red it was like it was still fresh.

There had been many advancements in medical technology, but even now, some wounds were still too dire to repair. Whatever damage she had received to destroy her vocal cords was likely one such injury.

"You have suffered a lot," Adam murmured. Lexi reached out to cup his face. He stared into her eyes, then smiled. "Yes, I suppose you're not the only one. Would you… like me to tell you about it?"

Lexi nodded.

"All right. Let's sit down then. This is going to be a long story."

Adam grabbed Lexi's hands, stood up, and pulled her over to the couch, where he began telling her about everything that happened to him from the time the Pleonexia Family dumped his broken body into the river to now.

It truly was a long story.

ALLIANCE

FORGED

FAYTE WAITED ALONGSIDE DAREN DAGGERFALL IN THE HALLWAY. Time passed. The silence was oppressive. She felt like she should say something, but she didn't have the slightest clue as to what she should say.

"You have an impressive ability to bring in amazing talent," Daren said at last.

"Excuse me?" Fayte asked.

"That man you have at your side… Adam, right? He's the same person who destroyed the top-rank players several years ago if I'm not mistaken."

Fayte wasn't too shocked that Daren had discovered Adam's identity. They never said anything, but it wasn't like they tried to keep it a secret either.

"How did you figure it out?"

"You mean aside from his name?" Daren shrugged. "He has the

same fighting style as the Adam who took part in the tournament several years ago. I'm sure you remember it."

Fayte hadn't considered someone else might be able to recognize his fighting style. It was true. Adam hadn't changed the way he fought, but only someone with the same observational skills as her would be able to notice. Most people did not pay enough attention to figure out how someone moved when they fought.

The door to the meeting room opened before Fayte could respond and revealed Adam and the Spear God. Fayte could immediately tell that something was different. Adam stood strangely close to the cloaked figure. Most people probably would have missed it—Daren didn't seem to notice—but Fayte did not.

"All finished talking?" asked Daren.

"We are," Adam said. "I appreciate you letting me talk to your bodyguard."

"It's no trouble. Anyway, let's continue our discussion." Daren waved off the thanks as though it was no big deal.

"Of course," said Fayte.

Fayte and Daren sat back down on the couches, and Adam and the Spear God stood behind them once more. Nothing seemed out of place. Everything looked normal at a glance.

And yet Fayte could tell something was different. Maybe she was imagining things, but it felt like the Spear God was staring at Adam with more intensity than before. She was probably seeing things. After all, it was impossible to even see what the Spear God was looking at thanks to all those bandages covering their face.

I need to pay more attention to my discussion with Daren.

"One thing I would like is to have Adam come over and train the members of my guild," Daren stated. "I have several companies of spearmen that I use primarily for anti-calvary and defensive formations, but it would be nice if they could expand their repertoire of strategies." Fayte raised an eyebrow and briefly glanced at the Spear God, causing Daren to chuckle. "I know what you're thinking, but the Spear God is... well, let's just say he's not the best person when it comes to teaching others."

The sound of rustling clothes behind Fayte let her know that Adam was shifting. She wanted to turn around and look, but she kept her eyes focused on Daren.

"I have no problem with this. We can lend Adam for a month in-game and let him train your forces at some point in the future. In exchange, I would like your help establishing a number of storefronts," Fayte said.

Daren raised an eyebrow. "Storefronts? Are you looking to sell stuff?"

"I have a lot of powerful and rare items stored in the guild treasury right now but nowhere to sell them. I don't want to simply sell them to a general store. I won't make much money that way. It would be better to open my own shop and sell them. However, stores require you to purchase land and find people who can run your shop. I'm not hurting for money, but I don't have that many personnel, and I'd rather use the members of my guild to find more items to sell."

Daren didn't speak for several seconds to ponder her request, then nodded. "I don't mind sending some people to help man your store. I have many non-combat personnel who usually manage shops and accounting in-game. But if I'm going to lend out my own personnel to you, I want a cut of the profit."

"That's a reasonable request."

The conversation went back and forth like this as Fayte and Daren worked out the details of the alliance.

Most alliances were formed out of convenience or because someone had something the other person wanted and they were too powerful to simply take it from.

Fayte's guild was small, but it had already proven itself to be powerful by taking on a force much larger than itself. The Guild War with the Pleonexia Alliance had proven the value of Destiny's Overture.

Daren wanted that power on his side. He wanted the power that a small group who could decimate an army of one hundred thousand could bring him. Since the power of Fayte's guild lay in her people, the only thing he could do was forge an alliance.

Fayte needed manpower. Her guild was small. Even if you added the Grim Reapers, there were still fewer than forty members.

Both sides had something the other wanted.

"I think that concludes our discussion for now," Daren said after another moment.

"I agree. Clarise, you were taking notes during this, right? Can we get you to write up a contract that includes everything we agreed upon?" asked Fayte.

Clarise had been standing off to the side this entire time. She had left the room when Adam and the Spear God had their conversation and came back in. She was so unobtrusive that Fayte might have mistaken her for background decoration if she hadn't kept an eye on the woman.

"Of course. Give me just a moment. I'll be right back," Clarise said with a bow.

She left the room. Fayte and Daren decided to make small talk while they waited, but most of it was just pointless and served no purpose other than to distract them.

Clarise came back several minutes later with a rolled-up sheet of parchment in hand, a bottle of ink, and a quill. She unrolled the parchment and set it, along with the ink and quill, in front of Fayte.

Fayte read the parchment, which was a treatise regarding the alliance between their two guilds. She made sure every point on the treatise was present, then took the quill, dipped it in ink, and signed it. She passed it over to Daren after that, who did the same thing.

"And with that, our alliance has been formalized. I'll announce that we have become an alliance once I leave here. I also believe we should celebrate with a small party. I'll send you invitations within the next month if you'd like," Daren said.

"Of course. We would be happy to attend," Fayte replied with a smile.

With that, the meeting concluded and the alliance between the Daggerfall Dynasty and Destiny's Overture became finalized.

***

The days following the announcement of an alliance between Destiny's Overture and Daggerfall Dynasty did not bring about any monumental changes--on the surface, at least.

A lot of people spoke of the alliance, of course. It was the hottest topic right now. All the forums related to *Age of Gods* had exploded with comments and discussions. Everyone seemed to have an opinion about this, even though most of those opinions were way off the mark.

The funniest one to Adam was the theory that proposed Daren had fallen in love with Fayte and that's why he asked for an alliance.

In either event, everyone shared at least one opinion that was true.

The Pleonexia Alliance was no longer the top guild.

They might still have the number one ranking in the American Federation, but with their loss in the Guild War and the alliance between Fayte and Daren, it was a ball toss as to whether or not they could keep that ranking. Their loss during the Guild War had seriously damaged their reputation. Meanwhile, Daggerfall Dynasty had acquired an alliance with the same guild that demolished their force of one hundred thousand members with just over thirty people.

Currently, the Pleonexia Alliance was scrambling to increase their fighting power. Whether or not they could was up in the air.

Adam woke up two days after the alliance was announced to find his bed empty. The fact that Aris woke up before him was surprising. She was the type to sleep in and complain when he tried to get her out of bed.

I wonder where she could have gone off to...

Adam shrugged after a moment and got up. He took a quick rinse, put on his clothes, then entered the living room.

He stopped in his tracks.

"Good morning, Adam," Aris greeted him.

"Good... morning... what exactly is going on here?" asked Adam.

"Can't you figure it out? I'm preparing you breakfast."

Aris's words seemed incongruous with her actions. She was not in the kitchen cooking. She stood in the middle of the living room, naked as the day she was born--if one didn't count the whipped cream and chocolate covering her naughty bits.

Adam glanced at her crotch, which had been liberally covered in whipped cream. He moved his gaze upward, following the contours of her flat stomach. Her small breasts were painted over with dark chocolate. He absently wondered how the two cherries were able to stay attached without falling off, but most of his blood flow had traveled south, so his brain wasn't firing on all cylinders.

"Uh-huh. So... where's breakfast?" asked Adam in a daze.

Aris looked at him with smoldering eyes. "Can't you tell? I'm breakfast."

There was nothing Adam could think to say, so he didn't bother.

He walked over to the young woman and scooped her into his arms. He was careful not to let the whipped cream or chocolate get wiped away as he set Aris on the table.

"Are you hungry, Adam?" asked Aris with hooded eyes.

"I am famished."

Aris smiled as she held out her arms as though to hug him. "Then eat up."

Adam did just that. The first thing he did was attack her breasts. He licked the chocolate that had spilled down her stomach and the sides of her torso, then traveled inward. The chocolate hadn't dried so it was easy to lick up. Aris moaned and squealed as he used his tongue and mouth to clean her off.

Chocolate was pretty sticky and couldn't be removed just by licking it. Streaks appeared on her skin, and Adam had to work extra hard to clean them all off. The strange blend of chocolate and Aris's natural taste tantalized his tongue as he worked his way in a spiral up her breasts.

Adam soon reached the first cherry and slurped it into his mouth. He ate it quickly because he could see her nipple underneath. It was already stiff and pointed. Taking the stiff point into his mouth, he swirled his tongue around it, then took it between his teeth and tugged.

"Oooh! Mmm! Adam, you're so rough!"

"Should I be gentler?"

"Of course not!"

It felt like the room was growing hotter, or maybe Aris's body was what had become hotter. Sweat broke out on her skin as the chocolate began melting. He had cleaned off one boob, but the other was starting to drip, so he hurriedly switched targets. He licked, slurped, and sucked the chocolate off her tit. The cherry fell to the floor before he could grab it, but that was okay. There was another cherry ripe for plucking, and it wouldn't fall like the other one.

"Mmmm! Aaaaahn! Haaaaah! Ooooh! Adam!"

Adam eventually finished licking the chocolate and sweat off her chest, but then he trailed down her body, licking her stomach until it was coated in his saliva. He eventually reached her crotch. Her legs were already spread. Some of the whipped cream was smeared since he'd not been careful. He could see her hairless mound.

"Mmmmmmm! Fuck!"

Aris squealed when Adam went down on her. He first licked around her inner thighs, enjoying the salty sweat combination of sweat and whipped cream. Then he attacked her snatch with his tongue. He probed her outer labia before latching onto the small pearl that was already standing out from behind its hood. As he worked over her clit, he inserted a finger into her tight passage and found the spot inside that drove her crazy.

"Fuck! Fuck! Haaah! Hrrrn! Adam! I'm!"

Aris's hips jerked off the table and slammed back down. The sound was so loud Adam worried someone might have heard it. This didn't stop him. The whipped cream was gone, so all that was left was Aris's natural flavor and the juices leaking from her.

It didn't take long before Aris was a quivering mess. Her orgasm was particularly spectacular this time. She squirted her fluids all over his face. He wiped his face as the woman on the table slackened. She was breathing like she'd run a marathon.

Adam positioned himself over her, placed his hands on either side of her head, and watched as her eyes fluttered.

"You're not finished, are you?" he asked.

"Hmph. Who do you think you're talking to? I'm nowhere near tired."

Aris wrapped her legs around Adam's hips and locked her heels against the small of his back. She didn't even wait for him. She just pulled him inside of her.

"Hmmmm. You always make me feel… so full… Adam. Pound me. Fuck me so hard this table breaks."

"I'm pretty sure Fayte would be upset if we broke her table," Adam said dryly—not that this stopped him from setting a hard, fast pace.

The sound of Aris's ass slapping against both the table and his balls echoed around them and mixed with Aris's ragged gasps and his grunts. The scent of sweat hung heavy in the air. Adam thrust his hips quickly and relentlessly, giving Aris the pounding she asked for.

The way her pussy stretched obscenely around his cock drove him forward.

The sensation of her tight passage rubbing against him drove him mad.

He wanted to mark this woman in such a way that everyone would realize she belonged to him.

As Adam staved off his own orgasm for as long as he could, long enough that Aris came first, then removed his cock and stroked it a few times. Several shots of white semen splashed against Aris's chest, covering her in much the same way the chocolate had. The exhausted Aris looked at the spunk now coating her chest and stomach, then looked up at him.

There was a glint in her eyes.

"Is this my breakfast?"

"Figured you could use some protein," Adam said with a shrug.

BACK TO THE MAGIC ACADEMY

ADAM SAT WITH ARIS AND LILITH ON THE COUCH IN THE GUILD HOUSE of Destiny's Overture. Kureha and Titania were also with them, but Kureha had curled up into a ball on Lilith's lap while Titania was floating in front of him with a cross look. Fayte and Susan were also present, sitting on the opposite couch.

"You seem to be in an awfully good mood lately," Titania said.

"Do I?"

"You do. Did something happen?"

Adam gave her a vague smile. "Something may have happened."

Titania crossed her arms. "Are you not going to tell me what that something is?"

"Why would I ruin such a good surprise?"

"Hmph! Surprises are all well and good, but I really wish you'd wipe that disgusting smirk off your face. Anyway, why are we just sitting around here? Shouldn't we be doing our best to level up?" she asked.

"Oi, lass. Ye need to calm down. I'm sure they have a reason for not heading out right away," Garyck said as he entered the room, wiping grease from his hands with a wet rag.

Titania frowned at him. "Where have you been?"

"Smithing, of course." Garyck sat down on a chair and puffed out his chest. "That new workshop ye made me is great. It's unfortunate we dinnae have the power of the mountain to heat up the forge, but all the equipment was made to me exact specifications."

"I'm glad you like it. While we're waiting here, why don't you show us what you made?" asked Fayte.

"Aye."

Garyck removed several items from his inventory. Most of it was weapons, swords and such, but there were also several sets of armor. Each item was a work of art. The way they gleamed with fresh polish, the incredible attention to detail, and the stats Adam could see when he studied them showcased the natural talent of a Dwarf.

"This 'ere is called Dragon Slayer. Great name, ain't it? I made it from the [Bone Dragon Rib] ye had in storage. Dragon bones are sturdier than most metals and make excellent weapons. Ya see this pair o' knives? I call 'em Pincushion Knives. They're made from the smelted needles of a level 60 [Needler]. Not only can they punch through most armor, but they also accumulated bleed damage."

Bleed damage was what happened when someone received a wound that "bled." It basically caused someone's health to periodically drop and also made them slow down as though they were tiring.

Adam and the others were astonished as they listened to Garyck explain the specifics of each item. None of them were as powerful as the weapons they wielded, but they were still better than perhaps ninety percent of the weapons currently being used by players right now.

"Did you make the spear I requested?" Adam asked suddenly.

"Aye, I did. Yer lucky you had the materials I need. I remember ye requested some armor a while back, but ye dinnae have the materials necessary fer me to forge it. Anyway, take a look at this and see what ye think."

Garyck took another weapon out of his inventory. While the others gasped in Astonishment, Adam grabbed the weapon and placed it on his lap. He was unable to equip it, but just studying it was fine.

The spear was both beautiful and deadly. Gleaming with an otherworldly light, the blade was made from a purple crystal called [Nightshade Crystal], while the handle had been crafted from [Black Mythril]. Different from the standard [Mythril], this was completely obsidian and stronger than the standard crafting material.

Looking at the spear's stats, Adam could see that it was quite powerful.

Item Name: Nightshade Spear
Item Type: Polearm
Grade: 3-Star
Use Requirements: Can only be equipped by someone with a class that specializes in the use of polearms.
Description: This spear was made by Garyck. It offers an abundance of buffs that raise a person's Strength, Dexterity, Physical Attack, and Magical Attack.
Abilities: Strength+400%; Physical Attack+400%; Magical Attack+200; Dexterity+100; has 25% chance of casting random debuff
Special Abilities: Nihility

While the [Goddess of Creating Spear] was still a better weapon, that was only by virtue of its ability to level up. This weapon currently did more damage than his.

"This is an amazing spear," Adam said in awe.

"Right?" Garyck puffed out his chest. The look on his face was the kind Adam might expect from a dog who wanted to be praised.

"But… why do you need another spear? Isn't the one you have already great?" asked Susan with a curious tilt of her head.

"It's not for me," Adam confessed.

Susan looked like she was about to ask about who it was for, but a knock from the entrance hall door caused Adam to stand up.

"It looks like they're here. I'll introduce you to our newest party member."

Adam left the room and opened the entrance hall door, smiling when he saw the cloaked and masked figure on the other side. Their outfit hadn't changed at all since the last time he saw them.

I wish she didn't have to wear that bulky cloak…

"I'm glad you could make it," he greeted.

The Spear God nodded.

At that moment, the door to the living room opened and Aris, Fayte, Garyck, Lilith, Kureha, Susan, and Titania peeked out from the other side. Susan gasped when she spotted the person whom Adam had come to greet.

"What?! Why is he here?!"

Adam turned around and beamed at the group.

"I'd like to introduce to you the newest member of our party, though I'm sure you already know them."

"The Spear God is joining us?" asked a shocked Susan.

"That's right," Adam said.

"How did you manage that?"

"Let's just say I can be very persuasive."

Having the Spear God join their party was not something that had been in the original alliance treatise, but something Adam and the Spear God had requested themselves. It had taken both Daren and Fayte aback.

Daren had refused to part with the Spear God at first. He didn't want his strongest player joining Fayte's party since they were already so strong. It had taken Adam several days to convince the man that this would actually be a boon for him.

His first step had been telling Daren about their new Dwarf companion and claiming that Garyck would make the Spear God a weapon and armor that was far superior to what she had now. That still hadn't been enough to convince him, but then Adam told him that he could help the Spear God level up even more. He also said the Spear God wouldn't be joining Destiny's Overture. She would still be part of Daggerfall Dynasty. She was just joining Fayte's party temporarily. That, along with the Spear God requesting to join Adam, had been the deciding factors.

"Now that the Spear God has arrived, we can finally get going," Fayte said.

"Where are we going?" asked Aris.

Fayte smiled eerily. "We're going to finally clear the magic academy ruins."

***

With the addition of Garyck and the Spear God, they now had nine people, which meant they had to split up into two parties--one party of five and one of four.

Party One consisted of Adam, Lilith, Kureha, and Titania. Party Two consisted of Aris, Fayte, Susan, Lilith, and the Spear God.

Adam had actually wanted the Spear God in his party, but that would have made their parties unbalanced. He was currently the strongest member of the group, and the Spear God, with her new weapon in hand, was also quite the powerhouse.

Name: Spear God
Class: Spear Dancer
Lvl: 23
SP: 0
AP: 65,000
Experience: 101,050/1,274,291,2000
Strength: +621
Constitution: +100
Dexterity: +105
Intelligence: +5
Speed: +5
Physical Attack: +9,925
Health: 3,320/3,320
Hit-rate: ???
MP: 520/520
Movement: +15
Defense: +2,860
Magic Defense: +2,400
Dodge Rate: 50%
Magic Attack: +205

Resistances:
50% Slashing
50% Piercing
50% Blunt
50% Magic
50% Bleed

Skill Name: Slash
Description: A basic skill where the player swings his or her sword and attacks the enemy!
Current lvl: 10
MAXED
Ability: Causes 300% damage to enemy if it hits
MP consumption: 1
Cooldown time: 0 seconds

Skill Name: Thrust
Description: A basic skill where the player thrusts his or her sword at the enemy! Current lvl: 10
MAXED
Ability: Causes 320% damage with a 10% chance at getting a critical hit
MP Consumption: 5
Cooldown time: 0 second

Skill Name: Dance of the Spider
Description: Much like a spider weaves its webs, the user of this skill will create numerous flashes of light with their spear intent to weave an impenetrable offense that entraps opponents, making it impossible for them to escape.
Current lvl: 6
AP needed to reach lvl 5: 240,000
Ability: Each flash of spear intent combines to create a web-like barrier of spear light. Enemies who fall into this barrier receive 400% damage for every spear light they hit.
MP Consumption: 100

Cooldown time: 30 seconds

Skill Name: Dance of the Serpent
Description: This dance is one that requires the spearman to lunge forward with quick and powerful movements just like a serpent. The attack happens so far most people cannot even see the spearman move.
Current lvl: 5
AP needed to reach lvl 6: 160,000
Ability: Lunges forward six times to do x7 damage.
MP Consumption: 100
Cooldown time: 30 seconds

Skill Name: Self Sacrifice
Description: A kamikaze skill that sacrifices oneself to damage their enemy.
Current lvl: 5
AP needed to reach lvl 6: 100,000
Ability: Sacrifices 50% HP to do 50% damage to selected enemy
MP Consumption: 500
Cooldown time: 120 seconds

Skill Name: Dance of the Cherry Blossoms
Description: A skill that only the Spear God can use. A dance that allows the user five consecutive attacks as they dance around their opponent. When all the attacks are completed, an outline will form on the ground in the shape of a cherry blossom.
Current lvl: 5
MAXED
Ability: Release a constant stream of attacks, does x3

damage increase for every hit, and resets when the Spear God
misses an attack.

Hit-Rate: 100%

MP Consumption: 50 MP per attack

Cooldown time: 30 seconds

Skill Name: Nihility

Description: This skill causes a player's weapon to
transform into a spirit weapon that can pass through all forms
of defense and attack the spirit and restore the vitality of the
user.

Current lvl: 1

MAXED

Ability: Drains Vitality=100% Physical Attack

Restores 50% of Damage dealt

Passive Skill

Skill Name: EXP Gain

Description: A passive skill that increases the amount of
experience gained.

Current lvl: 1

MAXED

Ability: Increase EXP gain by 150%

Passive Skill

With her new weapon in hand and some armor crafted by
Garyck, the Spear God was a powerhouse who could contend with
Adam on even footing. Her spearwork was also flawless. Even Adam
was no match for her when it came to sheer talent with a spear.

Which made sense.

Everything he had learned he learned from her.

Now that they had two parties, fighting their way through the Magic Academy Ruins was much easier. It helped that they had all leveled up a great deal since the last time they had been here.

After reaching the floor where they fought against Alexandra Mystique, they continued climbing. A variety of monsters attacked them, mostly ghost types and enchanted armors, but they defeated them all.

Thanks to an item Garyck had crafted called the [Necklace of Wisdom], the experience they gained by killing enemies had also increased. The necklace was an accessory that granted them the skill [EXP Gain]. With it, they were all able to earn +1,000,000,000 experience points before reaching the last floor. Adam finally reached level 28 and the Spear God was now level 23.

It still took several days to reach the top. There were one hundred floors in this dungeon. But reach the top they did.

The door that led into what Adam assumed was the boss room was inconspicuous. It was just a normal wooden door with a copper knob. A plaque hung on it that read "Dean's Office" in elegant cursive.

"I guess this is it," Adam murmured.

"I can't imagine what we'll find on the other side, but we should be prepared," Fayte said.

"Right."

Adam took a deep breath and grasped the handle. He looked at the others to make sure everyone was ready, then counted to three in his head before opening the door.

The room on the other side was small and resembled the kind of appearance Adam might have expected from the principal of a school--if one didn't include the wide array of magical implements. All the devices looked broken. However, even he could tell these contraptions had once been magnificent magical devices, though just what they did was beyond him.

At the very end of the room was an ornately furnished desk, worn down from age and disuse. The last vestiges of elegance it contained were fading. Nothing, it seemed, could escape the vicissitudes of time.

Behind the desk was a skeleton.

Adam could tell at a glance that this skeleton belonged to the woman they fought on floor 50. She wore the same robes that Alexandra Mystique had worn, though these were ratty and faded like everything else. The skeleton sat straight and had its hands placed elegantly on the desk. It looked like it was waiting for something.

"What's this? Is there no boss to fight?" asked Susan.

"Dinnae look like it," Garyck said.

"Let's go further in, but remain cautious," Adam warned.

Everyone heeded his advice, and together, they cautiously began walking into the room. Nothing happened. As they approached the desk, Adam glanced around. There really didn't seem to be anything here.

"Look at the skeleton's right hand," Aris pointed out.

On the skeleton's ring finger was a ring. It shone brightly in the light that filtered in through the windows. Strange sigils were engraved on its surface. How he missed this was something he couldn't fathom.

It was called [The Dean's Ring].

"Looks like a magic ring," Garyck said.

"Fayte, I think you should have it," said Adam.

"You sure?" she asked.

Adam nodded. "Your outfit is the same one Alexandra wore. And this ring also belongs to her. I feel like the ring is meant to complete your clothes."

"All right."

Fayte walked over, carefully slid the ring off the skeleton's finger, and placed it on her own. The moment she did, the ring glowed brightly before resizing to fit her finger. At the same time, the floor beneath their feet glowed as well. A massive magic circle appeared underneath their feet.

"This is a teleportation circle!" Titania shouted in shock.

Adam didn't need to ask to know what this thing was. The name was self-explanatory. Before he could tell everyone to get off the circle, a bright life engulfed the room, forcing him to close his eyes. He felt a moment of weightlessness, and then the world around him changed.

BECAUSE YOU'RE A PERVERT

DAREN DAGGERFALL WAS GOING OVER SOME LOGISTICS DOCUMENTS in his office when Skyrim entered. He could tell from the look on his brother's face that this conversation was going to be annoying. With a sigh, he stopped working and looked at the younger man marching up to his desk.

"You look like you've got something you want to say. Well? Let's hear it?"

Skyrim pressed his hands on the desk. "Don't act so blaze with me! Why did you let the Spear God go with Fayte and her guild? He's our trump card! We need him here!"

"And normally, I would agree with you," Daren admitted. "But

I've come to believe letting him go with Adam and the others will be a good experience. Do not forget which players among the top-ranking guilds have the highest levels."

There was no disputing his point. Even now, all a person needed to do was look at the ranking charts and they would know that Destiny's Overture had the highest levels of anyone playing *Age of Gods.*

"My hope is that by letting the Spear God join Fayte's party, he can level up even faster. If he can, then we'll be able to stand above the Pleonexia Alliance even if we don't have as many members."

The Pleonexia Alliance was the number one guild in the American Federation specifically because of how many members it had and their levels. They also had many subsidiary guilds that paid tribute to them, which further increased their power.

That was something Daren didn't do. He disliked having subsidiaries because they weren't loyal. They would abandon ship the moment someone made them a better offer.

"I get that you want him to level up quickly, but was this really necessary?" asked Skyrim.

"It was." Daren paused for a moment, debating whether or not he should say anything, but then he shrugged. "Also, the Spear God requested this himself."

"The Spear God… requested it?" Skyrim looked stupefied.

Daren nodded. He wore a wry grin. "That's right. He requested that I allow him to team up with Adam. It was the first time he's ever made a request of me before. How could I refuse?"

He had been shocked when the Spear God made this request. Not only had the Spear God never once requested anything from him, but he never seemed to care about people or worldly affairs. For the longest time, Daren had wondered if maybe the Spear God was a robot.

Which was impossible, of course. Robots couldn't play VRMMOs, but the thought had occurred to him several times.

"I guess… if he made the request himself… it would be hard to refuse," Skyrim murmured.

"Very hard."

The Spear God was their ace in the hole, the strongest card they had to play. Many a time, the Spear God had turned the tides in their favor and brought them out of a hopeless situation. The biggest reason Daren and his brothers had been able to find the success they had despite their modest background was his contribution to their cause.

Daren owed the Spear God.

How could he refuse his first request?

"Did the Spear God actually join their party?" asked Skyrim.

Daren nodded once. "He did. I was very surprised. Whenever the Spear God plays with us, he never joins our party as an official member." Daren leaned back and crossed his arms. "It's always been obvious that he's been hiding something. I never bothered to ask about it since I know he won't answer me. We all have skeletons in our closet, after all."

"Do you not think it's suspicious that sh… he joined their party?" Skyrim inquired.

"I won't lie and say I don't, but I already have a hunch as to why the Spear God was willing to join Fayte's party but not ours," Daren paused, then shrugged. "In the end, so long as this benefits Daggerfall Dynasty, I'm not going to make a big deal out of it. Do you have any more complaints?"

"No… I don't," Skyrim seemed sulky for some reason, but he didn't let that bother him.

"All right. Then why don't you go see to our members' training?"

"Sure…"

Daren looked up as Skyrim walked out of the room with a heavy gait. He furrowed his brow, wondering why his brother was so upset, but he couldn't think of the reason, so he shrugged and went back to work.

***

Skyrim grimaced as he stomped down the hall. People made way for him, but he ignored everyone as he turned a corner.

He didn't like the idea of the Spear God working with Destiny's Overture, but it wasn't for the reasons his oldest brother probably imagined. In truth, Skyrim couldn't care less about how the Spear God's absence would impact their ranking or power. He just used those as an excuse because he wanted to keep the Spear God in their guild.

Skyrim soon reached a hallway with a single door. It was unobtrusive and had no markings to denote what was on the other side, but everyone knew who this room belonged to. He pressed his hand to the door.

"She's in there right now..."

One of the Spear God's conditions when she first joined was that she would get her own room and no one would be allowed to enter without her permission. Daren thought the Spear God just liked her privacy, but Skyrim knew the real reason.

He could still remember the one time he had seen the Spear God without that cloak and ski mask she always wore. It had been a mystical moment. No one could have imagined that the second strongest person was a woman of such beauty. Everyone thought the Spear God was a man. Only he knew the truth.

"Could Adam know as well...?"

It was absurd to think about, but it also made sense. Skyrim had heard that Adam and the Spear God had spoken with each other in private during the talks of allying themselves. It had been done at Adam's request too.

What if the reason he had done so was because he knew the Spear God's identity? What if those two had some shared history?

It didn't escape Skyrim's notice that Adam and the Spear God had a nearly identical combat style. Even their most powerful attacks had been the same. Daren thought it a coincidence, but Skyrim had to wonder if that was really the case.

"Dammit…"

Muttering softly, Skyrim left the hall to do his job as a member of the Daggerfall Dynasty.

Even if Adam knew the Spear God's real identity, it didn't matter. Skyrim would not let anyone else have her.

***

Adam opened his eyes when the bright light vanished. The feeling of weightlessness had also left. He studied his new surroundings, blinking several times. He, Aris, Fayte, Garyck, Lexi, Lilith, Susan, Titania, and Kureha had been transported together. It was good to see that everyone was safe. More importantly, however, was where they had been transported to.

"This is… amazing! Look at all this treasure!" Garyck exclaimed.

The area they had been transported to was a vault. It reminded Adam of the classic treasure vaults he used to see in movies and video games. Piles of gold lay scattered along the walls. Numerous artifacts sat on pedestals. There were weapons, armor, and a variety of jeweled artifacts like rings and necklaces.

"So pretty. So shiny," Kureha's eyes sparkled as she gazed at the mountains of gold.

"I've never seen so much gold," Fayte confessed.

"Me neither," said Susan. "I wonder how much gold there is here."

"I wanna swim it," declared Aris. Everyone looked at her. "What? You can't tell me none of you were thinking about doing that."

"I'm pretty sure you're the only one who did," Adam retorted dryly. He looked around the room and nodded. "It looks like this is the magic academy's treasure vault. I guess that ring and Fayte's outfit were the keys to unlocking it. Basically, only someone who had acquired Alexandra Mystique's approval could get here."

"I think you are correct," Titania said.

Ding!

[Congratulations! You have conquered the unique dungeon: Alexandra's Magic Academy! Rewards are as follows: 10,000,000,000 experience points. 5,000,000 reputation!]

Ding!

[Congratulations! Titania has leveled up! She is now at level 28! +400 HP! +10,820 MP. +2 SP!]

Ding!

[Congratulations! Lilith has leveled up! She is now at level 26! +1,200 HP! +440 MP! +2 SP!]

Ding!

Congratulations! Changing_Fayte has leveled up! She is now at level 26! +1,600 HP! +856 MP! +1 SP!]

Ding!

[Congratulations! Little_Su has leveled up! She is now at level 26! +500 HP! +200 MP! +1 SP!]

Ding!

[Congratulations! Aris_Lancer has leveled up! She is now at

level 26! +400 HP! +80 MP! +1 SP!]

Ding!

[Congratulations! Spear_God has leveled up! She is now at level 25! +1,600 HP! +21 MP! +4 SP!]

Several announcement screens appeared, though Fayte and the others were too busy staring at all the treasures to pay attention. Only Aris, Lilith, and Titania actually looked at the screens. Titania did a double-take when she saw the Spear God's announcement. She soon turned to stare at the person in question, who stood next to Adam, seemingly ignoring her.

Fayte bit her finger for a moment, then said, "There's a lot here. I doubt we have enough room in our inventory, so let's stash it in our guild storage. We can sort it out when we get back."

Their inventory had a space limit of 100 different items, and you could have 100 of each item, meaning you could potentially store 10,000 items in your inventory. Even if they filled up every item slot in their inventory, it still wouldn't be enough to put even a dent in this."

Because Fayte was the Guild Master of Destiny's Overture, she was also the one who could store it all in their guild's storage. It was very strange watching all the treasure disappear.

"Let's head back to the guild," Fayte said.

Getting back to the guild was easier than Adam thought it would be. According to Fayte, she was now the dungeon master of the magic academy, which was her reward for defeating the dungeon. Adam had never heard of a reward like this. He wondered if this dungeon was maybe special due to its history.

In either event, now that she was the dungeon master, Fayte could connect their guild house to the magic academy via a warp gate. She installed the warp gate in the vault. Then they all teleported back to the guild house, where they immediately began sorting through the items they had acquired.

Money would never be an issue again. The amount in that vault had been a grand total of 62,000,000,000 gold coins. If they were to convert that into real-world currency, then it would be more than triple or even quadruple what the Dairing Family made in a year.

More important than the money were the items they had gained. Some of them were useful to their guild and they decided to keep them, but there were a lot of items they would never use. They needed to figure out what to do with them.

"There are three options for us here." Fayte held up a hand and extended a single finger. "One, we can sell these at an in-game auction house for gold. There's an auction house in Solum that we can use." She held up a second finger. "Two, we can sell these at an online auction for real-world currency. The government has already set up in auction for this purpose." She held up a third finger. "Three, we can give the items we don't want to the Daggerfall Dynasty. This would help increase their power, and it would also leave them in our debt. They'll owe us big time and do everything in their power to repay us."

They were standing in the guild house's storage room, which looked bigger than it had before. Adam had learned recently that these storage rooms contained a kind of magic that could change the size of the storage space to accommodate their items. Unlike the vault at Alexandra's Magic Academy, their storage room was neat and orderly. The money went in chests, the accessories and consumables on shelves, and the weapons and armor on display stands and racks.

Aris thrust a hand in the air. "I say we sell them! Let's make even more money!"

"We don't really need more money, though," Susan murmured. "We're already wealthy."

"Tsk, tsk, tsk. You can never have enough money," Aris wagged her finger at Susan.

"While you are correct in some ways, I believe we can put these items to better use by gifting them to the Daggerfall Dynasty," Fayte said. "I would like to cement our alliance with them. I want them to see us as too valuable to ever consider betraying."

Money was important, but so were favors. Daggerfall Dynasty was the second most powerful guild in the American Federation. There were a lot of things they could do that Fayte could not. This didn't just include things in *Age of Gods* but also things in real life. Adam suspected she wanted to use their manpower for something in the real world as opposed to something in the game.

"Why don't we auction half the items and give the rest to Daren?" suggested Adam.

"Oooh! I like that idea," Aris said.

Everyone ignored her.

"It's not a bad idea. I suppose having more money would indeed benefit us in the long run. I'm planning to make several upgrades to our guild house, and they are expensive," Fayte admitted. She nodded once. "Very well. That's what we'll do. All of you should also grab any items that you think would be beneficial to you."

Since that was settled, the group began going through the items once more to see if there was anything they might want.

Adam went through the list again and quickly found the item he wanted.

Item Name: Goddess of Creation Gauntlets
Item Type: Armor
Grade 4-Star
Use Requirements: Can only be equipped by the wielder of the Goddess of Creation's Spear.

**Description: Gauntlets made from an unknown material.
They were created by the Goddess of Creation and worn by the
wielder of her spear.
Abilities: Physical Defense+100%; Magical Defense+100%;
Constitution+50%
Special Abilities: Heaven's Might**

While these gauntlets lowered his resistance to various types of physical and elemental damage, they raised his Physical and Magical Defense by so much that it didn't even matter.

This was the only item he really wanted, though he also grabbed the [Ring of Regeneration], which let him regenerate +10 health every one second.

He looked at the others to see they were still looking through their storage inventory. Even Lexi seemed to be keenly invested in seeing what kind of item she wanted.

The only one who wasn't looking through the items was Titania. Instead, she was staring at Lexi with sharp eyes.

"Something on your mind?" he asked.

Titania pursed her lips, then asked, "Did you know that the Spear God is a woman?"

"I did."

"I see."

"That a problem?"

"No. I just now understand why you allowed her to join us."

Adam raised an eyebrow. "And why is that?"

"Because you're a pervert, of course. Don't think I don't know what you, Aris, and Lilith have been up to in your room. You might have been able to keep it from Fayte, Susan, and Kureha, but I've heard you through the walls," Titania glared at Adam.

"You really shouldn't spy on people," Adam said in a deadpan voice.

"I'm not spying on anyone! You're just too loud!" Titania snapped, causing everyone to turn in their direction.

Adam sighed at this troublesome fairy and her big mouth.

TRAINING

ADAM SOON ARRIVED AT THE DAGGERFALL DYNASTY GUILD headquarters. He wasn't alone. Kureha, Titania, and Lexi were with him.

While Destiny's Overture's guild house was small and cozy, the guild headquarters for Daggerfall Dynasty was a study in contrast. Imposing was the word he would have used to describe it.

The massive structure was a giant castle. It had three layers. Guild members patrolled the outer wall, which was connected by several drum towers, their forms visible behind the parapet. Behind the first defensive wall was a series of courtyards that contained the barracks for standard guild members.

Large guilds like this one had its members play in shifts so as to assure their operations ran twenty-four-seven. Members used the barracks during their stay here. Fayte had told him that most members would stay for seven in-game days total.

They reached the first gate. A pair of members dressed in the red and gold uniform of the Daggerfall Dynasty saluted when they saw who was walking up.

"Spear God, sir! It's good to have you back!" one of them said.

"I'd heard you were partying with the famous Adam and his group, but I didn't realize it was true!" the second one added. Adam thought he could see stars in the man's eyes, and it kind of creeped him out.

Lexi nodded and gestured toward the gate.

"Of course! We'll have this open right away!" said the first guard.

The gate wasn't quite as medieval as the rest of the castle. The guards pressed their hands against two red gems set along either side of the wall, which glowed brightly before the gate slowly opened. They saluted Lexi once more. She seemingly ignored them as she walked through the portcullis.

"Do you ever feel the desire to correct everyone about your gender?" asked Adam.

Lexi stopped walking for a moment, her hood shifting as she looked at him. She shook her head once and began walking again.

"I guess it is easier to hide your identity if no one knows your gender, but I think people would figure out who you're related to based on your fighting style. It's very distinctive."

"..."

"You really think the Pleonexia Family won't realize who you are?"

"..."

"Well, I suppose they haven't done anything in the last several years."

"..."

"Yes, that's true. They do teach their spearmanship to others outside of the family. I guess I didn't consider that."

Titania and Kureha watched the conversation between Adam and Lexi, the former with a frown and the latter with wide eyes.

Kureha eventually tugged on his sleeve.

"Big brother, how can you understand what this big sister is saying?"

Adam tilted his head and pondered how to answer. He eventually shrugged and said, "Intuition, I guess." Then he paused after realizing something. "Wait. How did you know she's a girl?"

"Um. 'Cause she smells like one," Kureha said.

Adam stared at her for a second, then glanced at Lexi. She met his stare, though it was hard to tell.

"Do you mind if I smell you?" he asked seriously.

Lexi shoved his face away when he tried to get close and sniff her. He grinned at her, then turned to Kureha.

"Kureha, while we're here, make sure you address this nice lady as 'Big Brother.' She's trying to hide her gender."

Kureha tilted her head to the side. "Why is that?"

"Because… she wants to pull a prank on everyone."

The little fox girl's eyes lit up. "Kureha likes pranks!"

"I figured you would," Adam rubbed Kureha's head, causing the kid to rub herself against his hand.

There were a lot of guild members stationed inside the outer bailey, and they all turned their heads to stare as Adam and Lexi walked past them.

Like the first rampart, there was another massive wall between the outer and inner bailey. Larger than the first, Adam glanced up at the watchtowers where guild members stood to keep watch. He wondered if that was necessary. There were rules in *Age of Gods* that couldn't be broken, and one of those rules was other guilds couldn't attack unless they declared a Guild War.

Well, he supposed they could technically attack, but there were consequences for it. The Guild Association would get involved since everything relating to guilds needed to be processed through them, and that would just cause one helluva mess.

They entered the inner bailey after the guards in the gatehouse opened the gate. The space passed the outer bailey was much more open. There was a great hall, a stable, and a keep, which looked like the kind of castles that dotted the countryside of the European Union, with glimmering towers and flying buttresses.

Several open areas were dedicated to training. Quite a few guild members were sparring with each other and others were practicing group maneuvers. All of them stopped when Adam, Lexi, Titania, and Kureha appeared before them.

Among the group of onlookers were two individuals Adam recognized. They both had the same dark skin and features, marking them as brothers. The taller one saw them and began walking over. The shorter one, who looked a few years younger, didn't respond at first, but he eventually noticed them and raced to catch up with his brother.

"Spear God, we're glad to have you back. Adam, thank you for coming on our request. We appreciate the aid," Skyrim said.

"It's no problem. We're allies, after all," Adam said.

As part of their alliance, Daren Daggerfall had asked Adam to come in and teach his spearmen how to properly wield a spear. Lexi had apparently tried to teach them herself, but not only was she unable to speak, her ability to teach was hampered by her outfit. Her guildmates couldn't even copy her movements because those robes covered everything.

"Daren isn't in-game right now. He had to deal with some business in the real world, so I'll be supervising your training. I hope you don't mind if I watch?"

Something about the way Skyrim spoke made Adam wary. His tone wasn't hostile, but it wasn't friendly either. He shrugged and decided not to worry. If Skyrim tried to do something, he would deal with it then.

"Feel free."

"I can't believe you're really here," the younger Daggerfall brother exclaimed. Adam thought his name was Oblivion. "Mr. Adam, I have been a huge fan of yours ever since the tournament! Can I shake your hand?!"

"Uh…"

Adam felt his smile become fixed as the man thrust out his hand and bowed like a young boy seeing his favorite pop idol at an event for the first time. It was disconcerting, especially for someone like Adam, who had never enjoyed being the center of attention.

"Yeah. Sure."

Adam eventually extended his hand and shook Oblivion's. The other young man became so happy that it was kind of disturbing. The way he blushed to the tips of his ears might have been considered cute by women, but Adam just found himself mildly repulsed.

"I can't believe I got to shake THE Adam's hand. I'm never washing this hand again," Oblivion said.

"Please wash your hands regularly. It's unsanitary to not wash them," Skyrim sighed as he turned to Adam. "I apologize for my youngest brother's actions. He's always been easily star-struck by impressive people."

"It's fine," Adam said. "Anyway, since I'm here, I might as well get started on the training. Which group do you want me to train?"

"That one, right over there," said Skyrim.

The group in question stood on an open training field made of dirt, spears held firmly in their hands as they practiced the standard thrust that was the most basic attack of all spearmen. It looked like they had the basics down, at least, which meant he wouldn't need to teach them something any spear user should already know.

Adam walked over with his group, now with two extra individuals. The spearmen all stopped what they were doing and watched with anticipation clear in their eyes.

"I'm sure you all know who I am, but for the sake of niceties, I'll introduce myself. My name is Adam. Thanks to the alliance between Destiny's Overture and Daggerfall Dynasty, I have been asked to teach all of you how to wield a spear. I noticed that you all have the basics down already. That's good. It means we can begin with more advanced stances and forms."

Excited murmurs broke out among the spearmen. Adam could hear some of what was being said, but he chose not to pay attention. His actions also caused people from other groups to look over. He ignored them too.

"Since I'm not very good at oral instructions, what I'm going to do is have Le... the Spear God and myself give you a live demonstration of the forms we use. I want all of you to copy what we do."

"Yes, sir!" The men and women in the spearmen group shouted at the same time.

"The style I use has seven forms. We're going to start with Form I today. All of you, copy me."

Adam twirled the spear in his hand, then began shifting on his feet. He skittered across the ground as though he had eight legs instead of two. Web-like patterns of light formed in the air as he thrust out his spear with quick, successive movements. The whistling sound as he cut through the air echoed around them.

"This is form one. It relies on deceptive, erratic movements, along with a combination of thrusts and slashes to entrap an enemy."

The Seven Phoenix Forms were created based on nature. Form I had been inspired by arachnids. Spiders created webs to entrap their prey, and so spearmen swung and thrust their spears so fast that it formed a web with their spear intent.

"The key to using this ability is to infuse your spear intent into your spear. It doesn't matter if you get the movements down. If you can't use spear intent, you won't be able to use this skill. For the moment, however, all I want you to do is get the movements down. We can work on spear intent at a later date."

Spear intent was simply the ability to infuse chi and killing intent into a spear. Not everyone could even use chi, which was an esper power, but he was certain everyone here had been selected for this training course because they could. Daren Daggerfall did not strike him as the kind of man who would waste Adam's time training someone who couldn't learn his skills.

Adam paid attention to the man in front, who kept tripping over his own two feet when he tried to move like Adam had. To his left was a young woman who had the foot movements down but couldn't include the spear attacks. Everyone else seemed to be somewhere between these two.

"I'm not going to lie. This form is difficult to master. It requires you to split your attention two ways. You need to pay attention to the movement of your feet, and also the way you use your spear. I find that it helps if you only focus on the feet first. Burn the foot movements into muscle memory. Once you can move your feet without conscious thought, add in the spear movements," Adam instructed.

The guild members had an easier time of it after they followed his advice. Most of them got the foot movements down within an hour, but they still had issues when it came to adding spear movements. It was because the foot movements weren't ingrained into their muscle memory yet. Just getting the movements down didn't mean someone

could move without conscious thought. They would need at least one
month of practice before he would deem them even close to being
ready to add the spear movements.

Lexi moved close to Adam as he watched the Daggerfall
Dynasty guild members work hard.

"..."

"It'll definitely be a while before they master this form."

"..."

"No, I don't plan on teaching them another form until this we
get this down."

"..."

"Isn't it obvious? Because that's how you taught me."

Lexi's clothing shifted. It was hard to see what she was doing.
Adam wished she wouldn't wear that baggy cloak of hers.

"You seem to be quite well-versed in understanding the Spear
God," Skyrim said with a fixed smile.

*Oops. I completely forgot about him. Come to think of it, most
people wouldn't be able to understand Lexi like this. Even Daren can't
seem to understand her right away.*

"The Spear God and I are both warriors of the spear, so we
naturally can understand one another," Adam bullshitted.

"Is that how it is?"

"It is."

"I guess I chose the wrong class, then." Skyrim had an
easygoing smile that hid something behind it. "I might not be able to
become a spearman since I'm a mage, but would you mind if we had
a spar? I'd like to experience what it's like fighting a warrior of your
caliber."

"If you wish to experience my spearmanship firsthand, who am
I to stop you? All right. Let's clear some space. I'll fight with you,"
Adam said.

"Great," Skyrim clapped his hands.

They soon cleared out a large space for their duel. A screen popped up before Adam.

Ding!

[Skyrim has challenged you to a duel! Do you accept? Yes or no?]

Adam selected "yes."

Duels in *Age of Gods* were simple affairs. Anyone could challenge someone to a duel, and the rules were straightforward. The winner was decided when someone either forfeited or their health reached 1. It was impossible to kill someone in a duel. Once the health reached 1, the duel would end, and you couldn't force their health down.

That was a good thing since a single attack from Adam was enough to kill any player.

"Do you want me to use [Scan]?" asked Titania.

"No need," Adam shook his head. It didn't matter what level Skryim was at. He would lose either way.

The battle started off and Skyrim immediately cast [Earth Bullet] followed by [Wind Blade]. Adam used the fifth form, adopting a wide stance as he spun the spear in his grip, which created an impenetrable shield that both the bullets and blade crashed against.

Even before his attacks had dissipated, Skyrim slammed his staff into the ground. The earth swelled and rose. A hand formed and slammed on the ground, followed by another hand. Then a head appeared before the body followed. It was like a living creature rising from the earth's surface.

"[Earth Golem], huh?" Adam muttered.

The [Earth Golem] lumbered toward Adam as Skyrim cast a wide array of spells, though most of them were [Energy Bolt] and

[Energy Blast] due to their low MP consumption and quick cooldown times.

Adam darted forward, zigzagging left and right to avoid Skyrim's attacks, closed the distance between him and the [Earth Golem], then attacked with [Dance of the Sakura Blossoms].

-31,420; -62,840; -125,680!

That was enough damage to destroy the [Earth Golem], so Adam rolled across the ground to halt his attack. He skipped back to his feet and raced toward Skyrim. His opponent panicked and began casting various AoE attacks to try and pin him down. Adam slashed through the man's [Fire Blast], leapt over his [Shockwave], and took his [Lightning Wall] head-on. It didn't even damage him thanks to his magical defense.

Adam was soon standing over Skyrim, who had fallen onto his backside, warily eyeing the spear pointed at his neck.

"This victory belongs to me," Adam said.

"So it does," Skyrim admitted with a sigh, though there was a hard look in his eyes. "I might have lost here, but I won't lose to you in anything else."

Adam had the distinct feeling this man wasn't referring to combat, but he couldn't for the life of him figure out what Skyrim was talking about.

AUCTION

FAYTE STEPPED OUT OF HER CAR AS A MIDDLE-AGED MAN HELD THE door open for her. She thanked him, but all he did was nod. She was positive this man dressed in the garb of a butler was wondering why someone with such a dinghy vehicle was allowed to visit the Forebear Estate.

Another pair of butlers opened the door. Fayte was greeted by a rapidly approaching blur.

"Fayte!!"

Susan crashed into Fayte, wrapping her arms around the older woman, who returned the hug with a smile.

"Su... are you that excited to see me? We see each other every day, you know."

Susan shook her head against Fayte's chest. "Seeing you in the game isn't the same as seeing you in real life."

"I understand how you feel. There is something special about being able to touch the real you. Anyway, is everything ready?"

"Yes! Come on. I'll take you to my room."

Susan grabbed Fayte's hand and pulled her into an adjoining

hallway. Fayte merely smiled as she allowed the girl to pull her along.

The reason for Fayte's visit was the online auction they would be doing with the many items they acquired after conquering Alexandra's Magic Academy. She had decided to do a real-world auction in exchange for real currency instead of in-game currency. Since the bet she made with Levon required real-world money, she believed this was the best way to accomplish the task rather than exchanging the money they already had.

She also didn't like the conversion rate or the fact that the government would take a percentage of the money for itself.

"Adam and Aris didn't come, I see," Susan said as they turned a corner.

Fayte tried hard not to smile at the disappointment in her friend's voice. "Are you disappointed that you didn't get to see your savior in real life again?"

"Wha... n-no! Of course not! I was just curious!"

"Do you really think you can hide your crush from me? I've been your friend for years now, Su. I can tell when you like someone."

Susan's ears turned bright pink. "D-don't tell Adam, please? I don't want to be a bother to him."

"I don't think he would see it that way, but I won't tell him."

Chances are good that he already knows.

Adam was a pretty self-aware guy. He didn't strike her as the type to not notice someone else's feelings. He just... ignored them.

Fayte felt a surge of anger at that. Adam obviously knew how she felt about him, but he wouldn't do anything about it. She understood that was because he had Aris. If he had started hitting on her, Fayte would have been disappointed in him for his lack of integrity, and yet she couldn't lie and say that she wasn't angry that he wasn't at least acknowledging her feelings.

Then again, it's not like I know what I even want him to do. What would I even say if he did acknowledge my feelings and confronted me about it?

Her feelings toward Adam were a mess, and she didn't even understand them half the time.

They soon reached Susan's bedroom. Her computer was already set up. It was one of the higher-end gaming computers that cost upwards of ten thousand credits to buy and had all the gadgets and doodads a gamer girl could want. Susan had built this computer herself, though her father had bought the parts.

Susan sat down on the chair, the latest model of gaming chair. Unlike the models of old, which featured unusual designs that were said to be ergonomic and good for your posture, her chair was more like a couch. It was soft and comfy, had a retractable footrest, and everything was automated. Her keyboard was also connected to her chair. With a simple push of a button, the keyboard located on the side moved up and positioned itself in front of her.

Fayte shook her head. She loved video games, but Susan took her gaming to an entirely different level.

After booting up her computer, Susan went straight to the website where the auction would be held.

"I've already supplied a list of the items we plan to sell via the auction house. The American Federation was very accommodating. They said they would only take a ten percent cut of the profits from the items auctioned," Susan said as she tapped away at her keyboard, bringing up the auction page. This was a real-time view of the auction. Right now, the item being auctioned wasn't one of theirs but a weapon that someone had found in a dungeon. The current bid price was $120,000.

"That's probably because of the quality and quantity of items we have for sale," Fayte determined.

They had a lot of items to sell, and many of those items were 3 to 4-Star equipment.

At this stage in the game, most people were still using 1 to 2-Star equipment. That was the current standard. Only a few people from large guilds like the Pleonexia Alliance, Daggerfall Dynasty, and the big international guilds had better equipment.

"How much do you think we'll make?" asked Susan.

"A lot," was Fayte's immediate answer. "I can't even estimate how much our items will sell for, but the auction house has been advertising them for a while. A lot of people on the forums were very excited when they saw some of the items on sale. I can't see us making any less than a few billion credits."

"Do you think you'll make enough to win the first stage of your bet?"

"I believe so. I hope so."

Several items were auctioned before one of their items appeared. It was called the Staff of Everlasting Peace and was a healer-specific magic staff. It not only provided a fifty percent boost to all buffing spells, but it also gave a one hundred and twenty percent boost to healing spells like Cure, Cure All, Heal, and Heal All.

Fayte placed a hand on Susan's chair and leaned forward to watch as the item was auctioned. The starting price was $1,000,000, but it quickly went up $1,500,000, then $2,000,000. She narrowed her eyes as the price continued to rise.

"It's already up to ten million! That's unbelievable!" Susan exclaimed.

But Fayte shook her head. "It's not that big. I've seen some items get auctioned for several billion before. This is a good item, but since it is specific to healers, I can't imagine too many people are interested."

Healers played an important role in gaming, but *Age of Gods* did not have a lot of good healer classes. So far, there was Medic, Healer, and Doctor. Each class had its own unique healing skill set and buffs, but they were very basic classes and didn't offer that many benefits. A lot of people were waiting for a specialized healer class to appear.

The Staff of Everlasting Peace sold for $50,000,000 in the end, which was good, but it wasn't near enough to win her bet.

The next item was called Robes of the Forlorn Mage. It was a robe set that could be worn by any class and provided a massive boost to every magic-related stat as well as resistance to status effects. If Fayte didn't have her Elemental Sorcerer Robes, she would have worn this.

Unlike the healer staff, this one went for 3.5 billion credits, which was about what she had expected.

"S-so much money…" Susan mumbled.

"You say that like you don't have enough to buy that," Fayte said.

"I mean… we do, but it just seems so wasteful. Father would never spend that much on an in-game item."

Eugine Forebear was not a gamer. He was one of the ten percent of the population who had never touched a VRMMORPG. His life was firmly planted in the real world, helping the citizens of the American Federation live better lives. Fayte had a lot of respect for him.

Another item was soon placed in the auction. Fayte and Susan turned their attention back to the screen and watched as the price climbed higher and higher.

***

Aris was bored.

She was so bored.

Fayte was visiting Susan to watch the auctioning of their items, Adam was currently inside *Age of Gods*, teaching spearmanship to the members of Daggerfall Dynasty, and Aris? She was lying on the couch in Fayte's living room, bored out of her mind.

"There's nothing to do in *Age of Gods* right now. There's not even much point in playing if Adam isn't with me. Haaaaaaaah."

Aris had tried playing on her own for a while, but she had quickly grown weary. She was a social creature. Aris liked spending time with others and hated being by herself. She was like this even before getting Mortems Disease.

"Hmmmm. What should I do? I don't want to just sit around here."

Now that she was able to move freely again, Aris wanted to explore her newfound freedom by doing all the things she couldn't do when she was bedridden.

"I want to go out, but I don't want to go alone. And I don't want Adam to worry. It would be bad if he logged off and found out I wasn't here."

Adam was a worrywart, but she didn't think he worried without reason. She knew that he was just concerned for her safety. He had been looking after her for many years now, and acting like a mother hen was just ingrained into him by this point.

"Hmmm."

Aris got off the couch and wandered into the bedroom she and Adam shared. He was lying on the bed, seemingly comatose. She knelt beside the bed and reached out to poke his face. His brow furrowed.

"You realize it's all your fault that I'm bored right now, right? How are you going to take responsibility if all you do is teach a bunch of nobodies which end of a spear you're supposed to stab someone with, huh?"

Her poking soon turned into stroking as she ran her fingers along Adam's strong jawline, then his collarbone. He wasn't wearing a shirt, so she had full access to his torso, and what a magnificent torso it was. Adam wasn't big, but he was defined. Every muscle on his body had the kind of hard definition that made them visible even without a strong light source.

Aris leaned down and began kissing Adam's stomach. She enjoyed the way it twitched underneath her lips. He was definitely feeling this. She giggled at the thought of him suddenly feeling horny while teaching those spearman how to fight. The thought tickled her funny bone.

Her hands weren't idle either. While she branded Adam's abs with her mouth, she mapped out his chest and sides with her hands. The muscles of his body were like mountains and grooves, and she was the cartographer mapping it all out. If people had classes in real life, she was certain hers would be something like Explorer.

After several minutes of kissing and touching Adam, Aris noticed the pitched tent his boxers were making. She reached over and was about to stick her hand inside when another idea occurred to her.

"Having sex is fun... but wouldn't it be more fun if there were more of us?"

Ever since their seduction of him, Lilith had been joining them in bed, but it was only in the game world. Adam had yet to sleep with her in real life. Aris wondered why that was. Could it be that a part of him was still hesitant to accept Lilith? She pouted at the thought. That just would not do.

Aris grabbed Adam's phone from the charging stand and quickly dialed up Lilith.

"What do you need from me, Master?"

"Sorry, but I'm not your master."

"... Mistress?"

"Oooh! I do like the sound of that. I definitely don't mind you calling me 'Mistress' from now on. Anyway, are you free right now?"

"I am. Did you need something from me?"

"Yes! Please come over, pronto!"

"Very well. I will be over soon."

Aris placed the phone back on the charge and thought about what she should do while waiting. She glanced at Adam's face. He wasn't really sleeping, but he looked so vulnerable just like someone who was sleeping.

"You're so defenseless right now. It really makes me want to play with you."

Aris pressed her fingers against her crotch. She was only wearing one of Adam's shirts and white lace panties, so she had easy access. She bit her lip to contain her moan as she rubbed herself over her undergarments. What she wouldn't give to push this fabric aside and play with herself directly... but no. She couldn't do that yet. She had to wait until Lilith got here at least.

Ugh... I'm so horny right now.

Aris reluctantly stopped what she was doing and told herself to be a good girl and wait for Lilith. She sat silently. She glanced at the clock. It was only 8:30 in the morning. She looked away. Several minutes seemed to pass before she glanced at the clock.

It was 8:31.

"Are you kidding me," Aris complained. "Why does time only go slowly like this when I'm waiting for something? Unbelievable. Dammit, Lilith. You had better get here soon or I really will start without you."

Fortunately for Aris's sanity, the doorbell chose that moment to ring.

Aris bolted out of the bedroom and headed for the door. Lilith stood on the other side.

"Come on," Aris didn't even give the woman a chance to say hello before she was dragging her to the bedroom.

CAUGHT IN
THE ACT

ARIS DRAGGED LILITH OFF TO THE BEDROOM, where Adam was still lying on the bed, eyes closed. Lilith furrowed her brow as the younger woman dragged her over.

"What are we doing?" asked Lilith.

Aris turned to her with a shit-eating grin. "Hee-hee. We're going to have some fun with Adam."

"I… am not sure that's a good idea," Lilith tried to say.

Aris waved her off. "It'll be fine. I do this all the time. Come on. Just follow my lead."

Lilith hesitated as Aris crawled onto the bed, but she eventually followed her master's woman. She slipped off her shoes because Aris had dragged her off before she had the chance to remove them. Then she delicately climbed onto the bed.

Aris was already touching Adam's chest by the time Lilith was on all fours. Her mouth went dry at the sight. Lilith had seen Adam's chest many times in the past, and she'd even seen it up close, but she had never just touched him like that. Jealousy welled up inside of her.

"Come over here, Lilith."

Lilith shunted aside those emotions. How could she think this way about her master's woman? She crawled over on all fours, careful not to step on Adam. She reached Aris and sat on her thighs as though waiting for the other woman to tell her what to do.

"Have you ever wanted to kiss Adam's body?" asked Aris.

"Well..."

"Now's your chance."

Lilith didn't know if this was appropriate, and yet, as she stared at Adam, she felt an inexplicable urge to worship his body. She reached out and placed a hand on his chest. His skin was warm, the muscles hard. Taking a shaky breath, she moved her hand across his chest, mapping out the contours of his torso.

Aris grinned. "He's got a nice body, right?"

"Mmmm." Lilith nodded.

"Why don't you stop using your hand and start using your mouth?"

"I... what?" Lilith looked startled.

"Come on. Kiss him. You're already his. He's had sex with you several times now, so it's fine."

It was true they'd had sex a number of times since she and Aris had seduced Adam, but it was always in the game. She was still worried about overstepping her boundaries. That was why she had avoided Adam in real life.

Aris continued to goad her, and Lilith eventually capitulated. She gave into her desire and pressed her lips to Adam's chest. A jolt passed through her lips and traveled straight to her brain. Once she began kissing him, Lilith found herself unable to stop; even the idea of stopping didn't occur to her.

A pair of breasts pressed against her back. Lilith went ramrod straight when Aris cupped her wet sex through her pants and whispered alluringly in her ear. "Use your tongue."

Lilith shuddered but did as commanded, sticking out her tongue and dragging it across Adam's skin. He tasted a little salty. She didn't mind that at all.

While Lilith busied herself licking Adam's chest and stomach, Aris went behind her. She grabbed the hem of her pants, then pulled them and her underwear down, until her wet snatch was exposed to the cool air. Lilith shivered, but then she moaned when a small tongue licked her outer labia.

"I've never tasted another girl before," Aris said in between licks. "But I've always wanted to." Another lick. "Hmmm. You don't taste as good as Adam." This time, her lick was long and slow, and caused Lilith to moan loudly. "But I could get used to this."

Lilith couldn't think of anything to say, so she said nothing and continued servicing Adam as Aris ate her out. The girl was good. Lilith wasn't what one might call experienced. Not only had she never been with a man besides Adam, but she didn't play with herself like Aris. Even so, she felt like Aris was very talented at pleasing people. It did not take long before Lilith's body was shuddering from head to toe with an orgasm.

"How was that?" asked Aris as she wiped her mouth.

"M-Master is better," Lilith said.

"I'd be worried if Adam wasn't better. Anyway, let's get on to the main prize."

"What?"

"Come on. Help me get Adam's boxers off."

"Oh. Um. Okay?"

Lilith felt like she was being swept up in a whirlwind of carnal lust. Aris enthusiastically directed her to help lift Adam's hips so she could remove his boxers.

Lilith felt her throat grow dry at the sight of her master's cock. It looked big, had several veins passing through it, and the head was shaped like a mushroom. She reached out and grabbed it with both hands. A startled gasp escaped her when it twitched.

"It's been so long since I saw the real thing," she muttered. "Has it gotten bigger?"

"What are you doing? Stop holding it like a joystick. This isn't a game. We've got work to do," Aris said.

"What... are we doing?" asked Lilith as she reluctantly removed her hands.

Aris went over to Adam's other side. She removed her shirt, shucked off her pants, and discarded her socks, then leaned down, until she was rubbing her cheek against his erection. Lilith swallowed as the woman stared at her with a predatory gleam in her eyes.

"You and I are gonna give Adam the best wake-up of his life," she declared.

***

Adam was giving a demonstration of how to fight off multiple opponents when surrounded when a strange sensation caused his entire body to shudder. The Spear God looked at him curiously. She was part of this demonstration, but he just smiled and continued on as though nothing had happened.

Since time in the game world was longer than the real world, Adam had to deal with the distractingly pleasant sensations for much longer than he would have liked. He had to quickly say goodbye to the Spear God before logging off without warning.

The moment he opened his eyes, Adam felt himself being

bombarded with the feeling of two soft, warm, and wet tongues lapping at his dick like a lollipop. He raised his head to look down at Aris and Lilith. Both women were naked as they licked his shaft from either side. Aris fondled his balls as she dragged her tongue from the base, then sucked on his head as though to milk him dry.

"You two…"

"Good morning, Adam," Aris grinned as she released his head with a pop. Lilith took her place. "Were you enjoying your time with Lexi?"

"I was… until someone interrupted me… ah…"

Adam wasn't sure how long these two had been at it, but his end approached quite quickly. Aris pushed Lilith back just before Adam shot his load. Thick strands of white fluid splashed against the two girls. It got on their shoulders, chest, stomach, and thighs. While Lilith's eyes were wide, Aris's were narrowed like a cat's.

"You're all dirty, Lilith. Here, let me help you."

"Wha… oh…"

Adam sat up as Aris began licking his milk off Lilith's chest. The older but much less experienced woman leaned back and moaned as Aris swirled her tongue around her nipple.

"Haaah… ahhhhh… mmmm…"

Aris made sure to put on a show for Adam's sake, keeping her mouth wide open so he could see the way her tongue flicked across Lilith's nipple. She only closed her mouth to give it a gentle tug.

While Lilith allowed herself to be pleasured, she eventually took some initiative and began cleaning Aris as well. The sight of two women licking each other clean was mesmerizing. Adam was already hard, but this would have made his soldier stiffer than a musket if it wasn't.

Aris soon pushed Lilith down. She straddled the older woman, pressing her thighs against Lilith's so the older woman's feet were in the air. Adam had a perfect sight of their exposed nethers pressing together. Aris's clit was already exposed, proof that she had been masturbating while she sucked him off.

The invitation was quite clear, so Adam didn't hesitate to crawl forward, until he was right in front of the two girls. Since Aris had been playing with herself, Adam decided to ignore her snatch. He pressed his cock against Lilith's entrance, then slowly thrust his hips forward. The way her pussy stretched obscenely around his dick made him want to cum. Lilith's moan was muffled as Aris pressed their lips together.

Adam stared at the two as he retracted his hips. He wished he could see more. He was sure Aris was taking complete advantage of Lilith to push her tongue into the other woman's mouth and explore her depths. The girl had an insatiable sexual appetite. She was oddly well-matched with him, now that he thought about it.

He thrust his hips forward, and a loud but muffled moan echoed from where Lilith's head was. The sound was mixed with the noises of lips smacking together and heavy breathing.

As he continued to plow Lilith, he noticed her toes spasming. He grabbed her legs and increased his pace. Her toes went ballistic. It was fascinating to watch. He could actually tell what was doing it for her based on their reaction.

Just as it seemed like Lilith was about to cum, Adam removed his dick. He ignored her moan of complaint as he pressed his head against Aris's soaking genitals. Her lips were puffy with arousal. He didn't move slowly and instead thrust himself inside of her with one, quick action.

Aris's muffled scream as he began plowing her from behind told him all he needed to know. He set a heavy pace. The sound of his balls slapping against hers and Lilith's ass cheeks echoed around the room.

Unlike Lilith, Aris only clenched her toes as Adam fucked her from behind, though she did arch her back like a cat when it stretched.

And just like with Lilith, Adam retracted his cock before she came.

"Adam! What the hell?! Why did you stop?" Aris finally stopped kissing Lilith to complain.

Adam grinned. "This is punishment for playing with me while I was working."

"But that's… mmm… that's not fair…" Aris muttered, breathing hitched as Lilith, lost in the throes of rapture, began kissing her neck.

"Life's not fair. Lilith?"

Aris looked like she wanted to say more, but Lilith grabbed her face and began kissing her again. Maybe she was just following Adam's unspoken orders. Maybe she was simply horny. Either way, Adam appreciated the sight.

He quickly thrust himself back inside Lilith. He didn't remain there for long and switched back to Aris soon after before once more switching again. He constantly teased the two, bringing them to the edge, then pulling back.

"Adam… please… I'm sorry… haaaah… mmmm… I'll… I'll be a good girl, so just give it to me."

"Master… I… I… aaaah… I can't take much more…"

Minutes passed. Aris and Lilith were covered in sweat and drool. Aris was resting her head against Lilith's chest, shuddering as Adam teased her. Lilith was almost completely limp by this point. She couldn't even lift her hands.

"Have you both learned your lesson?"

"Yes!"

"Okay then. Here you go."

Since he started with her, Adam thrust himself back inside Lilith. The woman was already so worked up that her body seized up with an orgasm not long after he entered her. As her toes spasmed like she was being electrocuted, Adam shoved himself inside of Aris, whose back arched as she released a loud wail. He would have thought she was dying if it wasn't for the way her pussy clenched around him.

Adam was also close to cumming, but he wouldn't be able to cum more than once, so he stuck his cock between the two, sandwiching himself with their cunts and ejaculating. His sperm splattered against their stomachs, then drizzled over Lilith's dripping vagina.

As the two girls panted and shuddered, Adam leaned back and decided to get some rest, but he was tempted to see if they wanted to go another round afterward.

"Are you three done now?"

Yet just before he could, a voice spoke up from the doorway.

***

Fayte had returned home in high spirits. The auction had gone even better than expected. She had acquired 65.7 billion dollars—far more than she had expected. It seemed powerful items for *Age of Gods* were something everyone wanted right now, and she supposed it made sense. This was the game that, as of now, would be used to determine the course of world politics. Everyone wanted to have the most powerful items they could in order to get ahead.

She removed her jacket, then her shoes, and finally stepped into the living room.

"I'm home," she called out, but she got no response. "Adam? Aris?"

She wondered if the two were still gaming, but today was

supposed to be their rest day. Aris should have at least been out here in the living room.

Walking toward the hallway, Fayte soon stopped when a sound reached her ears. Loud moaning. She closed her eyes and bit her lip. It seemed Aris and Adam were at it again. They normally tried to stay quiet, but perhaps they decided not to hold back, assuming they'd be done before she got home.

She decided to ignore them and went to take a shower. Yet she couldn't concentrate. Even though her shower was located further away from Adam's bedroom, their loud moans reached her ears. She gritted her teeth and tried to ignore them, but it was impossible.

After getting dressed in a bathrobe, Fayte found herself standing just outside their bedroom door. She debated what to do. Should she knock and tell them not to be so loud? That seemed like the most appropriate thing to do, though she also felt like it was kind of rude. They didn't know she had come home. At the same time, this was her house. She had the right to tell them to quiet down, didn't she?

As Fayte struggled with herself, a second moan echoed from the bedroom. She froze. This was not Aris's voice. It wasn't Adam's either. The pitch was deeper than Aris's, huskier. It was such a wanton, lustful sound that it took her a moment to recognize who that voice belonged to, but once she did, Fayte set her lips into a thin line as anger permeated her.

She opened the door.

Adam was having sex with Aris… and Lilith.

Fayte struggled to keep her emotions in check, but it was hard. Seeing Adam having sex with two women hurt more than she thought possible. Red slowly seeped into her vision as she watched them. Her emotions felt like a balloon being filled with too much air, waiting to pop.

"Are you three done now?" she asked after Adam finished cumming on Aris and Lilith. Adam froze when he saw her standing in the doorway. She tried to mask the hurt she felt as guilt flashed through his eyes. In the coldest voice she could muster, she said, "take a shower, get dressed, and meet me in the living room. We need to talk."

She turned around and left the three to scramble out of bed. Her day had been going so well, but now it felt like someone had cast a cloud over it.

SEPARATION

FAYTE PACED BACK AND FORTH AS ADAM, Aris, and Lilith sat on the couch before her. Aris turned her head left and right to track the woman's movements, but Adam and Lilith remained staring straight ahead.

Finally, she stopped and turned to face them.

She was glaring at Adam.

"I want an explanation for what I saw."

"Fayte, this was all my fault. I'm the one who--"

Aris started to defend Adam, but Fayte held up a hand. The glare she turned on the younger woman was enough to chill a person's blood. Aris froze like she was back in that cryopod.

"I wasn't asking you." Aris bit her lip. Fayte turned back to Adam. "Well?"

"I have no justification to give that would make you feel better," Adam said with a sigh. "Lilith has devoted herself wholeheartedly to me for many years, and I have neglected her feelings all this time. Yet she has not once shown disloyalty. I just couldn't continue letting her watch me from the shadows without reciprocating her feelings."

Fayte felt her face twisting into something unpleasant, so she took several deep breaths. She knew of Lilith's relationship with Adam because she had overheard Adam telling Aris about it. Fayte had always felt bad for the woman who Adam had ignored in favor of others. In some ways, this was a good thing. Lilith must certainly be happier now than she was before.

And yet…

Why… why does this hurt so much?

"I see. So you've decided to take responsibility for Lilith's feelings toward you. I suppose congratulations are in order." Fayte smiled at Lilith, but it was so fixed that the woman it was directed at, someone who could mercilessly kill without batting an eye, flinched. "Congratulations, Lilith. I'm sure Adam will make you very happy."

"… Thank you."

"And you, Aris, congratulations. I'm sure you're very happy that Lilith has joined you in Adam's bed. You're one step closer to your goal of creating a harem."

"Uh… Fayte, listen. I—"

"I don't want to hear it," Fayte snapped. She only realized what she'd done when Aris flinched. She took several more breaths, shoulders visibly heaving. "I understand your reasonings, and they are actually quite sound. I don't fault you for them, nor is it my place to tell any of you how to live your lives, but I…"

I don't want this…

"…I can't be a part of this."

I wanted Adam to myself.

"So, Adam, Aris, Lilith… I think it would be best if you three leave now. Aris is cured, so there's no reason to stay here."

I don't want this. I want Adam to stay. I want him to choose me over everyone else. I don't want him to look at other women.

Fayte let none of her thoughts show on her face, but she was almost positive Adam had seen them. He stared into her eyes like he was staring straight into her soul. She was forced to look away, to avoid drowning in those dark eyes that seemed to want nothing more than comfort her. Fayte worried that she might lose her nerve if she looked at him any longer.

"I understand," Adam placed his hands on his knees and stood up. "It seems we have troubled you for a bit too long. Aris and I will pack our belongings. We'll get out of your hair."

"..."

Fayte said nothing, but her lips trembled.

Under Adam's directions, he, Aris, and Lilith quickly packed all the items they had brought to Fayte's apartment. It wasn't long before they were all packed and standing at the front door.

Aris looked miserable, like she might cry any second. Fayte ignored her. She didn't want to see that look on the girl's face. It would break her heart even more.

"Fayte, thank you for everything you've done for us," Adam said.

Don't say that to me...

"We might not be living together, but our deal isn't over. I'm going to continue helping you win your bet against Levon as a member of your guild."

Don't look at me with that smile while saying something so beautiful.

Fayte kept her political façade up as she smiled. "I would appreciate that. Thank you for your help. I'll be relying on you."

After what just happened, Fayte didn't know if she really wanted Adam's help. Her emotions were in shambles. Yet beyond her pain, beyond the heartache, lay the same fierce determination to not be Levon's bride. That was the one thing motivating her now. She refused to belong to someone who only saw her as an object.

Adam gave her one last smile before opening the door and walking out. He held the door open for Lilith and Aris. While the quiet woman followed Adam without a backward glance, Aris stole several looks at Fayte. She opened her mouth several times as though to speak, then closed it and continued walking, shoulders slumped in abject dejection.

I'm sorry, Aris... but I just can't do what you want. I don't want to be someone else's mistress on the side. I want to be the only person my husband ever looks at.

The door soon closed behind the trio. Fayte remained standing in place for several minutes. She eventually turned, ready to begin all the tasks she had set for herself that day, but the strength in her legs gave out. She stumbled back, bumped against the door, and slid down until she was sitting on the floor.

Why did things have to be this way?

It had never been her intention to fall in love with Adam. She knew going in that he was already in a relationship with Aris, and so she had believed herself safe. Fayte was not the kind of woman who would steal another person's man.

And yet...

Why couldn't you have loved me instead?

Fayte buried her face between her legs, wrapped her arms around them, and wept bitter tears.

***

Adam heard Fayte's crying as he stood on the other side of the door. Her sobs were filled with a pain that he wished he could banish. He wanted to take her pain onto his shoulders, so she wouldn't have to deal with it, but he knew that was impossible.

After all, he was the cause of her pain.

I'm sorry, Fayte.

Aris and Lilith looked back at him when they noticed he wasn't following. He sighed and walked silently to catch up. He didn't want Fayte to realize he'd heard her cries. That would just make her feel worse.

"Let's go," he said softly.

Aris looked like she wanted to say something, but Adam walked past her. She and Lilith were left with no choice but to follow.

The trip to the parking garage was made in complete silence. Lilith was always quiet, but it was rare for Aris to not chat up a storm. Her predilection to create a constant stream of conversation was something Adam had grown used to over the years.

Adam's car was parked right next to Fayte's. They couldn't have looked more different. While Adam's vehicle was long, sleek, and looked like something more suited to air travel than ground transportation, Fayte's was old and battered. He had once asked why she didn't get a better car now that she had money, but she told him she had grown attached to her little car.

Adam pressed a button to automatically open the doors, which revealed a chair that was fully reclined. Another button caused the chair to go back to normal.

He looked at Aris and Lilith. "You two will have to share a seat."

"Master, the vehicle I used to get here is over there. Perhaps it would be better if I drove myself?" suggested Lilith.

Adam thought on that for a moment, then shook his head. "No… I'd rather you stay with me. I'll call Asmodeus and have him get someone to pick it up."

Lilith merely nodded.

Aris and Lilith slid into the passenger seat. Being the smaller of the two, Aris sat between Lilith's legs. Adam meanwhile sat in the driver's side and started up the car, which emitted a low hum. This car ran on solar power and a miniature pulse reactor. It was nearly silent as he put it in reverse and pulled out.

"Adam—" Aris started, but Adam held out a hand. She flinched, but he smiled at her to try to allay her fears.

He pressed a button on his steering wheel. The sound of ringing soon echoed throughout the car. It only lasted for a second before it was picked up.

"Master, what are your orders?" asked Asmodeus.

"I would like you to station two squads around Fayte from now on. Eliminate any threats to her well-being. If you're not sure something is a threat, report back to me immediately," said Adam.

"Yes, Master."

"Also, one of our vehicles is in Fayte's parking garage. Have someone pick it up."

"It shall be as you command."

"Sorry," Adam said as the call ended. "Since I'm no longer able to protect Fayte, I need to make sure we have people around her at all times. I don't doubt Levon will try something once it becomes clear Fayte will win their bet. He's not the type who can suffer any form of humiliation."

Aris just nodded.

"What was it you wanted to say?"

"I… I'm… sorry," Aris mumbled, then she spoke in a louder voice. "I'm so sorry! I'm sorry I acted without thinking! I'm sorry my actions put us in this situation! I always thought everything would be okay so long as I was by your side. I thought things would always work themselves out somehow, but I was wrong! And now my recklessness has caused a rift to open between us and Fayte! I… I hurt someone I really care about! I love Fayte so much, and I hurt her! I promise to never do something like this again! I'll think before I act from now on! I won't be so reckless! Adam... I'm so sorry!"

As Aris cried out all her grievances, Adam glanced at Lilith. She saw his look and wrapped her arms around the young woman as she cried. Adam couldn't do much while driving, so she acted in his place.

Aris's sobs didn't quiet down until they were halfway to their old apartment. After that, she just sniffled several times. Adam reached out a few times to pat her on the thigh, but he otherwise kept his eyes on the road.

Adam eventually pulled into their parking lot. He shut the vehicle down, then got out and walked around to the other side. The door was already open, so he just scooped Aris into his arms like she was a princess. The girl didn't hesitate to bury her face in his neck. She shuddered several times like she might start crying again.

Lilith stepped outside and closed the doors. Adam smiled at her, which caused the woman's face to turn red.

"Let's head inside and have a warm meal."

"Yes, Master."

Adam's apartment was quite clean. Someone from the Grim Reapers must have been coming every day to clean the place. He made a mental note to find out who had been doing that and thank them.

He set Aris on the couch, then went into the kitchen and set about preparing some food. They were fortunate his fridge was so advanced. It kept things in stasis rather than freezing them. "Fridge" wasn't even an appropriate word for what he had, but companies continued to call it that. Old habits die hard.

Adam prepared simple burritos with rice, beans, lettuce, and cheese. It wasn't his best meal, but he wasn't in the mood to cook right now.

The three of them ate in silence. Lilith took away and cleaned the dishes when they were done.

"Come on, Aris. Let's get ready for bed."

"…Okay."

"Master, what should I do?"

"You're sleeping with us, so get ready for bed too."

"Yes, Master."

All three of them took turns in the shower, brushed their teeth, and got dressed in nightwear. Lilith didn't have anything to wear since she had come over unprepared, but Adam gave her one of his large shirts. It looked good on her. Really good. Adam could admit, if only to himself, that he could get used to the sight.

Adam slept in the middle. Lilith lay on her side, facing him. She wasn't close enough for them to be touching, but she had grabbed onto his hand and held it tightly as though afraid he would disappear. Aris slept the same way she always did. Directly on top of him.

"Adam?" she asked in a whisper.

"Yes?"

"Do you think… Fayte hates me now?"

"No. She's definitely upset with you—and me—but I know she doesn't hate you. She's just hurt."

"I feel really guilty."

"That's good. You should feel guilty, but that's a good thing." Aris looked up at him. He smiled back. "If you felt no guilt over what happened… well, I don't know what I would think. The fact that you feel this way shows you're a good person. Remember what this feels like. Don't forget, lest you make the same mistake a second time."

"Mmm. I'll never forget how horrible this feels." Aris tilted her face down and pressed her lips to his bare chest, then turned her head to press her ear against it. "I love you, Adam. Thanks for always being with me even though I'm such a mess."

"I love you too." He turned his head to look at the other woman sharing their bed. "I also love you, Lilith."

Lilith didn't say anything.

But she did squeeze his hand a little tighter.

IDENTITY DISCOVERED

LEVON WAS NOT PLAYING *AGE OF GODS* AT THE MOMENT. He would have liked to since that was what most of his holdings were now invested in, but there was a far more pressing matter that he was dealing with.

"I see. So you were unable to find any information on the player, Adam."

"Correct. If we had more information to go on, we might be able to discover his identity, but without so much as an image of his face, I'm afraid there's nothing we can do. We even checked to see if there was anyone named Adam who had been taught the Seven Phoenix Forms and came up empty."

"I see. Well, I appreciate you trying."

The call ended. Levon leaned back in his chair, closed his eyes, and pinched the bridge of his nose.

He had been putting more effort into discovering Adam's identity ever since the Guild War. That man was a menace. All of his plans felt like they were on the brink of being ruined thanks to him.

He also stole Fayte from me...

Levon had Fayte in the palm of his hand. He had set up everything perfectly, bribing her father to disown her, alienating her from everyone who could possibly help her--well, almost everyone-- and coming to her with that bet just as she was on the verge of despair. She had accepted it without much thought. He believed it would only be a matter of time after that before she lost and became his.

And yet that blasted man somehow arrived on the scene like a knight in shining armor and took her away from me.

There was nothing Levon hated more than someone taking what was rightfully his. Adam needed to pay for what he had done. More than that, however, Levon needed to restore his shattered reputation, and the only way to do that would be to deal with Adam.

Levon once more pulled up all the images he had of Adam and his party. Minus Susan, the fairy, and the little fox girl, everyone wore a mask. He assumed it was so no one could find them in the real world. The game avatars in *Age of Gods* were built on a person's exact specifications and could not be changed, which meant it was easier to find someone IRL in this game than others.

"A man who uses my family's style is humiliating my family. The irony's not lost on me. Since we couldn't find anyone named Adam who was registered with the family, it means Adam is either an alias or he was taught in secret..."

The Seven Phoenix Forms was an old style the Pleonexia Family had cultivated for many generations, long before they settled down in the American Federation. His family had existed for thousands of years. Each generation of his family was built upon the foundations of previous generations. And the Seven Phoenix Forms was as old as the family itself.

"The Spear God also seems to know a variation of the Seven

Phoenix Forms. He might be even better than Adam…"

Levon remembered the battle between Adam and the Spear God. He had never noticed it before because all of the Spear God's battles ended so quickly, but he now recognized that many of that man's stances were similar to the Seven Phoenix Forms. Did that mean he had also been taught in secret? Just who was he?

"Let's focus on Adam for now."

The Spear God was a nuisance, but he was not a threat like Adam.

Someone knocked on the door.

"Come in," Levon commanded.

The door opened. Levon looked up, then raised an eyebrow when he saw who had entered.

"What are you doing here, Thor? I thought you were doing a raid."

Thor God of Thunder shrugged as he closed the door behind him. His clothing was so much more casual than Levon's that the disparity was not lost on him, but this man's slovenly appearance belied his skills. He was too good at what he did for Levon to decry his lack of decorum and fashion… much.

"We just finished. I heard you weren't appearing in the game as much. Figured I'd come by."

"Unfortunately, I've been busy with more pressing matters."

"More pressing than running the guild?"

"Yes."

Thor raised an eyebrow, then moved behind the desk to stand by Levon, who felt his right eye twitch. This was the only person brazen enough to get in his personal space like this. Even Connor Sword, known for his arrogance, would not do this. What made it worse was that Thor didn't even realize he was doing something he shouldn't.

He just had no sense of propriety.

"Oh! I see you're looking at Fayte's guild!" Thor exclaimed.

"I've been trying to figure out Adam's identity, though I've had little success," Levon admitted.

"Ah. Well, if he's been wearing a mask this whole time, I doubt you'll find anything about him," Thor mumbled.

Levon glanced at the man to see that he wasn't staring at Adam at all, but at the lithe young woman dual-wielding scimitars. A veil covered her face, so he couldn't make out her more prominent features, but even Levon would admit she was a beauty.

"Is that your type?" asked Levon.

"You know I don't have a type. I love all women equally," Thor said. Levon snorted, but Thor ignored that as he stroked his stubble. "I was just thinking about what a waste it is that she decided to put on a veil. She's got such a cute face."

Levon felt like someone had dunked his mind in liquid nitrogen. He slowly cranked his neck to look at Thor, who seemed to feel the sudden intensity in his gaze. Of course, Thor being Thor merely tilted his head.

"Something wrong, Boss?"

"You know what this woman looks like?"

"Yeah. That's what I just said, isn't it?"

Levon took a deep breath to avoid shouting. Thor wasn't the type to think most things through, so there was no way he would have considered the importance of telling Levon this long before now. He needed to stay focused.

"Tell me what she looks like. Describe her in as much detail as possible."

"Er... all right. Wait. You're not interested in her, are you? 'Cause if so, I hate to break it to you but--"

"Just tell me!"

"Okay! Okay! Yeesh. Gimme a second here…"

Thor quickly described what Aris looked like. Levon made sure to memorize everything that was said, then sent Thor out of the room.

He once more made a call to his contact within the government, explained that he wanted to find someone, and gave him the description of Aris. It wasn't long before they had a match. The contact sent several files over, which Levon wasted no time digging into.

"Aris Purity. Seventeen years old. She has Mortems Disease… hmm… relatives dead. Has one adopted older brother… Adam… Lancer…"

Levon read through her files quickly, but began pulling up every image of Aris that had been captured on the security cameras. All of them contained two people. One of them was Aris, no doubt, but the other was a man. Levon felt a moment of competitiveness when he realized how handsome this Adam Lancer was, but beyond that, he felt elation.

"This is him. This must be him. Adam Lancer… so you were using your real name this whole time."

Now that he knew Adam's identity in the real world, he began making phone calls. It was time to finally remove the thorn in his side.

***

With the money Fayte made from auctioning off the items they got from clearing Alexandra's Magic Academy, she had cleared the first goal of her bet with Levon. And thanks to her recent fame from winning the tournament and defeating the Pleonexia Alliance during the Guild War, she was well on her way to completing the second goal of her bet.

The current least powerful family among the top ten was the Peking Family. They were a family of Chinese immigrants who had settled in the American Federation due to some friction between them and the current largest guild in the Eurasian Continent. What made them so famous was their medicines, which were able to stall the progression of Mortems Disease if not halt it entirely.

Once Dr. Sofocor was able to replicate the device used to cure Aris, goal two would be resolved.

The last goal was that she needed to create a guild in *Age of Gods* that ranked among the top five guilds. Adam figured they had more or less completed this already. They had demolished the Pleonexia Alliance in a Guild War and everyone saw it. No one could contest were among the strongest guilds in the game.

That didn't mean they could rest on their laurels, however.

Adam, Aris, Fayte, Garyck, Kureha, Lilith, Susan, and Titania had set about completing tasks other than leveling up.

Garyck spent most of his time in the forge, smithing weapons and armor that they would sell at the auction house. Several of his items had already sold for over a hundred million gold coins, which was about a billion dollars in American Federation credits. Dwarf-made items were a hot commodity, and they made sure to advertise them as such to make sure everyone knew their value.

Adam had also decided to add [Blacksmith] as his secondary class skill. His current class was technically [Blacksmith Apprentice] because he was apprenticed under Garyck, but that was neither here nor there. He was already well on his way to learning how to forge swords under Garyck's tutelage, though right now, all he did was help the Dwarf.

Aris had also chosen a secondary class, though hers was [Seamstress]. She had decided to learn how to make clothing since Adam and Garyck could make armor and weapons. Adam had asked her reasons for this and she had said, *"Because it sounds fun! You make our equipment and I'll make our clothes! Tee-hee! We'll be the most fashionable guild around!"*

Susan's secondary class was [Cartographer] and Lilith had gained the [Chef] secondary class. He wasn't sure what Lilith would do with that class, but he knew Susan planned on mapping out the areas they explored, which would not only make it easier on them, but they could sell the maps she made. Adam planned on having them move on from here soon. They would make a lot of money if they could sell maps of unexplored regions.

At the moment, Adam was taking a break from smithing. He sat on the couch in the living room with a cup of tea prepared by Lilith. She stood behind him like a silent statue. He briefly considered asking her why she had decided to wear a maid outfit, but he was almost afraid of the answer.

"Oh, Adam. There you are," someone said from the entrance.

"Su," Adam smiled at the girl. "Were you looking for me?"

Susan nodded. She blushed a little and asked, "May I talk to you for a moment?"

"You can always talk to me."

"Thanks…"

Susan sat down on the couch beside him, closer than he was used to--at least, from her. Their thighs were touching and he could feel the warmth from her skin.

"I wanted to talk to you about Fayte," she said after a long pause. "Did something happen between you two?"

"I… suppose I shouldn't be surprised you noticed that," Adam said with a sigh.

Susan nodded. "Fayte has been avoiding you. It's not always obvious, but I noticed it the last time we went out. She used to confer with you all the time, but now she's making all the decisions on her own. I'm... a little worried. She seems very sad."

Adam wondered what he was supposed to tell this girl. Was it appropriate to let her know that Fayte caught him having a threesome with Aris and Lilith? He couldn't imagine that would help the situation, but he also wasn't sure lying to Susan was a good idea. Maybe... he should just be half-honest? No. She'd probably find out what happened eventually. It was better to be upfront about these things.

"Fayte... caught me, Aris, and Lilith in a, uh, a rather compromising situation," Adam confessed.

"Compromising...?" Susan didn't get it at first, but then she looked at Lilith, whose cheeks were now a little pink, then back at Adam. Her eyes widened and she raised her hands to her mouth. "Oh!"

"Yeah. Oh," Adam smiled humorlessly.

Susan blushed but continued. "I get why she's avoiding you now. Fayte... has never been a fan of polyamorous relationships. They remind her of Levon Pleonexia's lifestyle. You know Levon already has four wives, right? They never show up in public anymore, but they were all very famous for their beauty. Once they married Levon, they just seemed to vanish. They're only ever seen during social events."

Of course, that was the case. Levon was the kind of guy who couldn't abide other men coveting what he believed belonged to him. Items, money, women... he considered all of them possessions. That was why he didn't allow his wives out in public.

"And that's why she hates polyamory?" asked Adam.

"That is one reason. I believe the other is because Fayte's a romantic at heart. She wants to be swept off her feet by her knight in shining armor. She wants a man who will only look at her and no one else."

Adam nodded before his curiosity got the better of him. "And what about you? Do you want the same thing?"

"M-me?!" Susan squeaked.

"Yes, you."

"Well, I… I've never really thought about it." Susan fiddled with her fingers as they rested on her lap. "To be completely honest, I always assumed I would marry whoever my father told me to. It was only recently that I told him I would like to choose who I marry, so I don't really know what I want."

"There's nothing wrong with that. You should take your time deciding what you want. It's better to be completely confident in your choice than to make a choice you'll regret later."

"Hmm. I agree." Susan nodded, then her cheeks and ears turned pink as she looked away. "Th-that said, I do know what kind of qualities I'm looking for in a partner."

"Oh? Would you share them with me?"

"Well… they're…"

Susan wasn't able to get very far before someone appeared in the living room. It was Asmodeus, dressed in his typical ninja garb. He looked around for a moment, spotted Adam, and quickly knelt.

"Master, we have a situation," he said, and the dark undertones in his voice made Adam realize whatever he had to say was dire.

"We'll continue this discussion another time," Adam said to Susan.

Susan looked disappointed, but she nodded. "O-okay."

To Asmodeus, Adam asked, "What is it?"

"Levon Pleonexia has discovered your real identity. He's planning to launch an attack on you tonight."

Adam closed his eyes. He didn't know how Levon had found out about him. He was sure that he had been careful to mask his identity, but the hows and whys could be solved later. They wouldn't help him solve their current situation.

A midnight assault, huh? It looked like he wouldn't be getting any sleep tonight, and sadly, he wasn't staying up late for the reasons he preferred.

MIDNIGHT
ASSAULT

ADAM CALLED ARIS AND LILITH AND HAD THEM ALL LOG OFF. He would have called Fayte too, but she wasn't online. Susan also logged off. She had asked if she could help, and he promised he would let her help him. He planned to use her skills as a hacker to assist them.

After logging off, Adam explained the situation to both women. Lilith accepted his explanation with a simple nod, but Aris bit her lip and looked at her feet, seemingly bothered.

"Aris, what's wrong? Why do you look like someone just killed your cat?" asked Adam.

"I'm sorry… this is all my fault," she mumbled.

Adam sighed as he reached over, grabbed the back of her head, and pulled her into his chest. "You can't blame yourself here. Everyone starts off with standard equipment. You just happened to get unlucky. None of us could have known Thor would see what you look before you got a veil to hide your face."

"Mmm."

Had this happened before they became estranged from Fayte, Aris would not have been this hung up. Adam believed she felt so guilty because the guilt over her reckless actions prior to this had led to the rift between them and Fayte. Unfortunately, there wasn't much he could do about her feelings beyond providing emotional support. She would have to overcome that hardship herself.

"Since it's come to this, we need to come up with a plan," Adam let go of Aris and walked over to a table. It looked like a regular dinner table, but when he pressed a button underneath it, the table transformed. The brown surface turned back, then lit up, and a 3D holographic map of the surrounding area appeared before them.

"Should we ask Asmodeus to come and provide backup?" asked Lilith.

Adam shook his head. "No. The Grim Reapers are our trump card, and the moment we reveal them here, they'll lose their effectiveness as spies and saboteurs. We can handle this on our own."

"How are we going to fight them?" asked Aris. "I don't think I need to tell you this, but *Age of Gods* aside, I'm not much of a fighter."

"Then it's a good thing you won't be fighting," Adam began with a wry smirk. "Our goal here is not to fight, but to flee. I'm going to distract their main forces. While I do that, I want you and Lilith to escape through the alleys. Also, while I don't plan on using the Grim Reapers to fight, I do plan on having one of them meet up with you. He'll take you to one of our safe houses."

"Are you thinking of calling Leviathan?" asked Lilith.

Adam nodded. "He's the best driver in the group. I'll have him come pick you two up."

His cell phone began ringing at that moment, so Adam picked it up. He looked at the caller ID. After seeing who it was, he put the phone on speaker and set it on the table.

Susan's voice came over the speakers the moment he did.

"Adam, I've hacked into the security cameras surrounding your apartment, but I'm afraid I can't access the recording program. Levon has a very skilled hacker on his side. They have disabled the ability to record video footage. I also can't send data to the Department of Safety. I suspect Levon has a mole there who shut off the security feed to those cameras."

The security cameras were a two-way road that sent data in the form of video footage and received instructions via the security network within the Department of Safety's many relay stations. Each station was dedicated to specific city blocks. The information was then routed from the relay stations to the main headquarters, which was not located in New York but the American Federation's government center--the Trihexagon--which was located smack in the center of the nation.

The only way to shut off a security camera's ability to send video footage to a relay station was for someone to manually shut it off.

"Have you informed your dad about what's going on?" asked Adam.

"I did as you instructed and told him the gist of it. He's pretty livid, but he's agreed not to stir up the hornet's nest. Um, he did say he would like to see you though..."

Adam furrowed his brow. "Tell him... I'll see him if I can, but it might not be possible for a while, given the situation."

"I'll let him know."

"Thank you."

Adam was about to say more, but a ping alerted him to a text message from Belphegor. He read the message and sighed. Craning his neck to glance out the window, he saw that darkness had already crept upon the land.

"I just received a message from my informant inside Levon's forces. They've already mobilized their troops."

"What?! Already?!" came Susan's startled voice.

"Isn't this bad? We haven't finished planning yet," said Aris. For once, she looked worried.

Adam remained calm. "There's no need to worry. Fortunately, Levon can't bring out a large task force to deal with us. Five elite squads of ten members have left the Pleonexia Alliance headquarters and are on their way here. Susan, I'm going to give you their license plates. Can you track them for me?"

"O-of course! Please leave it to me!"

"Thank you."

Adam copied the information Belphegor had sent, then pasted it into a text message, which he sent to Susan. Silence reigned in the room for several seconds. Even Aris didn't dare to break it. She was even holding her breath as though worried just breathing would cause the situation to snap.

"I'm currently tracking their location. It looks like each vehicle is taking separate routes. Based on their route, I think their intention is to surround you."

Adam nodded. That was a standard attack formation when you wanted to keep someone from escaping, but it was also a terrible idea when you were fighting against an enemy like him.

Of course, it wasn't like Levon could have known that dividing his forces in this manner would only weaken his position. He didn't know Adam's strength. He had no idea that Adam had taken on entire battalions by himself.

Susan sent over the data showing their locations. Adam uploaded the data onto his map. The vehicles showed up as red blips that were traveling swiftly toward his location from five separate directions. Just like Susan had said, they were planning to surround his location.

"It looks like we don't have much time. They will be here in about fifteen minutes," Adam muttered, then looked at Aris and Lilith. "Lilith, put in the call to Leviathan and ask her to come pick you and Aris up at location Delta. I'll head out now. I'm going to cause a big distraction, once I begin making noise, you two will begin moving. Susan, you'll be their guide. I want you to use the security cameras to keep them abreast of any suspicious activity. There's a very good chance the forces we can see aren't the only ones Levon has sent to deal with us."

"You think there are more?" asked Aris.

"It's a standard tactic to hide a smaller, more powerful force behind a larger one," Lilith said.

Adam nodded. "I wouldn't be surprised if Levon sent a sniper squad on top of the five squadrons. It would be a hidden squad sent from a different location to avoid detection. Anyway, Lilith, you should suit up. You too, Aris. I have equipment for you both."

Aris blinked. "Did you know this would happen?"

Adam shook his head. "No, but I always try to plan for every scenario."

Adam, Aris, and Lilith went into another room. It seemed empty at first, until Adam pressed a button, revealing several mannequins with skin-tight outfits and racks full of weapons.

Aris stared in shock at the armory before her. "How come I never knew any of this existed?"

Adam shrugged. "Because there was never a need to reveal it?"

"That's not a good answer."

"Just get dressed."

Lilith quietly stripped her clothes off and suited up. These black suits were designed to help them blend into the night. They came with a variety of features like camouflage and heat masking. Lilith also put on a pair of sunglasses, then tapped a button on them, which activated the HUD. Like the suits, the sunglasses came with a variety of features such as night vision and heat vision.

Aris and Adam also put on a suit. While Adam went over to a weapon's rack and grabbed a spear, several knives, a pistol, and a submachine gun, Aris began feeling herself up.

"This suit is so weird. It feels like I'm not wearing anything," she murmured.

"It's called a Knull Suit. It's symbiotic clothing that mimics your biorhythm to create a suit that provides protection against both physical and energy attacks by distributing the inertia from such attacks evenly across the suit. It won't stop an explosion, but it can withstand anything else, including sniper fire. Of course, that doesn't mean you should let yourself get hit. These suits can only take a certain amount of damage before they stop working."

Aris nodded seriously. "Got it."

Another ping caused Adam to look at his phone. "It seems they're here. Looks like they plan to blockade the main streets and travel the rest of the way on foot. I'm gonna head out and stop them."

"I will protect Aris," Lilith said.

"Adam… be careful," Aris added.

He smiled at them. "Don't worry. I will."

***

Jack Davis grunted as their vehicle stopped moving. He looked at the empty street ahead of them, then at the eight people sitting in the back.

"We've arrived. Everyone, get out and get ready. This operation is beginning now."

"Sir!"

Jack and the driver left the vehicle along with the others, who opened the trunk door of their vehicle—a Ford Transit Custom. One of their men had already opened the bottom hatch on the floor, which revealed a large variety of weapons. There was everything from SMGs and assault rifles to standard 9mm pistols.

"Don't forget to attach your suppressors," Jack reminded them.

"We know. Don't worry. This isn't the first time we've done this," said one of his men. He was a blond man whose bright gold hair was currently covered with a cap. Like everyone there, he wore clothes designed to hide his identity, including a mask that hid his face.

"But it has been a while since our last mission," added another. He sounded older than the first person who spoke.

"I'm actually excited. We don't get to go on very many missions," said a man with a scratchy voice. Jack made a note to tell him to lay off the cigarettes.

Jack add a suppressor to both his pistol and assault rifle. While the pistol was a standard issue, the rifle was a Smith and Wesson that fired 5.56 nato-caliber bullets. It had an adjustable scope and was very versatile. He had been using this particular weapon for close to fifteen years now and it had never let him down.

"I can't believe you're still using that old gun, captain," one of his men said.

"Right?! We've got all this new tech and awesome weapons, but he's using something from twenty years ago," laughed another.

Jack scoffed. "Say what you want. Older weapons are more reliable. The current weapons might have automatic aim adjustments, but they're too heavily reliant on their computer chips. What would you do if the chip malfunctioned? You'd be shit out of luck. I'll stick to weapons that require real skill to use."

"So you say, but I think you just don't like using new technology. You're like a stubborn old man who likes to talk about how things were back when you were younger," said the one who first mocked him.

Jack would have said something, but a scream cut off any conversation. Everyone reacted quickly. They spun around and aimed their weapons at where the scream had come from, but even they were unable to hide their shock when they saw one of their own squealing like a gutted pig.

And the reason he was screaming was the spear that had impaled him from behind.

Jack had seen many polearms, but he'd never seen something quite like this. The spear wasn't pure black, but it was so dark it blended in with the night, and it had a streamlined shape that made it seem like more than just a spear.

Two more of his men went down in less time than it took to blink. Someone had shot them from behind. He and the others spun around and aimed their guns at where they thought the perpetrator had come from, but all they saw was their vehicle.

"Everyone, stay alert! We've got an enemy hiding somewhere around here!" Jack shouted.

"Yeah, no fucking shit," said another.

"Did anyone see who did it? I feel like I blinked and missed it."

"I didn't see anything."

"Someone alert HQ," Jack ordered.

"We can't. Our signal has been jammed."

"Fuck."

Jack was just about to suggest they move when someone opened fire from their left. Two more of his men went down in a hail of automatic fire. He wasn't able to see or hear the bullets, which meant their enemy was also using a suppressor.

Jack and the others quickly went behind their vehicle for cover. His heart was hammering in his chest as he realized whoever was attacking them was good. Very good. They had attacked before he could spot them, and even now, he could not actually see who was attacking them.

"There's a good chance our enemy has already changed locations. Activate infrared sensing to spot him," Jack ordered.

Everyone did as they were told. Jack also followed his own orders. Yet even when he looked around with infrared, he could not see anything, which meant their enemy was wearing something that masked their body heat.

"We won't find him this way. Switch to night vision."

It would be harder to spot their enemy with night vision, but so long as they were alert for any movement, they should be able to find him before he found them.

"Do you think the person attacking us is that Adam guy?" asked someone.

"Don't know, but they're a pro, whoever they are," said another.

Jack didn't say anything as he looked around. He didn't see any movement. Either they were very good at staying still, or they were a master of stealth.

A soft ping made him twist his head. His eyes widened. Even though he couldn't see anything, his sense of danger was screaming at him to retreat.

"Everyone! Step away from the—"

He never got to finish his sentence as the van they had been hiding behind went up in flames. The last thing he saw was a blazing inferno as it engulfed him, and the last thing he felt was the pain of a searing heat burning him up and shrapnel tearing apart his body.

***

"Squad 2? Come in. Squad 2, report!"

Levon sat in the command center as the operation to remove Adam from the board of life took place. He was not making any decisions regarding this operation. He was simply there to witness it.

However, it seemed not everything was going as planned.

It all began when squad 1 stopped moving. The holographic map in the center of the command center showed a real-time 3D representation of the area where the operation was taking place. All members of their elite force were represented as green dots.

The green dot representing Squad 1 had stopped moving several minutes ago, even though they should have been traveling toward Adam's apartment to help enclose the net around him. They had sent Squad 2 over to investigate. The controller had been communicating with them until several seconds ago, when their communications cut out.

"What's the situation with Squad 2?" he asked in a calm voice.

"I don't know," the controller said, voice on the verge of panic. "I wanted to see if they could figure out what happened to squad 1, but they cut off mid-sentence."

Could it be Adam?

"Have the other squads converge on the last known location of where Squads 1 and 2 disappeared. Also, bring out our reserve units and have them surround the apartment. Have several checking alleys and side streets," Connor ordered. He stood beside Levon, calm as could be as he handed out commands.

"All of them, sir?" asked the controller.

"All of them," Connor confirmed. "We have greatly underestimated our enemy. Also, send out the drones. I want real-time footage of what's happening."

Everyone quickly followed Connor's commands. Controllers began speaking to the various squads, the reserve squadrons were sent out, and several drones were released. Holographic screens appeared above them. They showed live footage of New York from an overhead view.

The drones began moving. Levon watched with narrowed eyes as they closed in on the location of Adam's apartment.

"Are we in the clear?" asked Levon.

"Don't worry," Connor assured him. "The reason we didn't send them out at first was to avoid causing a potential problem with the government, but I just informed our man on the inside about what's happening. He said he'll take care of it."

Levon nodded as he shifted his gaze to the map. Squads 3 and 4 were converging on the location of Squads 1 and 2. It wouldn't be long before their dots overlapped.

Just then, an explosion ripped through the video feed for one of the drones. Levon swung his head up and stared in shock as plumes of fire rose into the sky. The drone quickly oriented itself to close in on that location.

What they saw caused every person there to suck in a breath.

Corpses littered the streets. Levon could tell at a glance they belonged to his men, as they were wearing the camouflage uniforms of his elite units. The vehicle they had used to transport themselves was now a flaming pile of wreckage.

Standing in the middle of this scene of carnage was a man, his silver mask illuminated by the fire's light, body wreathed in a skin-tight dark suit. He carried a spear. About as long as the man was tall, the spear was covered in blood.

The man whom Levon could only guess was Adam raised his head. Levon froze. The man was looking right at the drone. Could he see it? Surely not. That was impossible! But as if to disabuse him of that notion, Adam drew a gun, aimed, and fired.

The live feed went dead.

"Dammit! He just shot our drone! Send the other ones to that location, but have them keep their distance," ordered Connor.

Several other drones began moving, encircling the area where Adam was located. They kept their distance this time. Adam was using a 9mm, and while he didn't know what type, most pistols of that caliber only had an effective firing range of fifty meters.

And yet, once again, as if to disabuse Levon of his common sense, the drones were shot down. One by one, the screens went dead.

"What is going on down there?!" Levon demanded to know.

Connor's lips were drawn into a thin line. "That's what I'd like to know. Either Adam is a much better shot than is humanly possible, or he has someone working alongside him. Either way, we can't use drones for this."

"Dammit!" Levon swore. This whole situation was turning into a nightmare. "What about our other squads? What are they doing?"

"Several are moving to intercept Adam," Connor said. "The others say they've found a pair of women fleeing the area. We've confirmed that one of them is Aris. We don't have confirmation on the other, but suspect she may be the one called Lilith."

Levon's eyes gleamed. "Have your men capture those two alive if possible. We can use them as hostages against Adam."

Connor went about ordering their troops to follow his commands. Levon gripped the seat of his chair as he glared at nothing in particular. The ember that had been burning inside of his chest was turning into a blazing inferno.

He would kill Adam today. And if possible, he would take those two women and make them his slaves. It would be the best way to punish Adam from beyond the grave.

***

Just as I thought, they had more forces in reserve.

Adam looked at the map on his phone, which displayed the location of every one of Levon's forces in real time. Susan was hard at work constantly sending him and Lilith data on their enemies' movements. He would really have to thank her later.

Maybe I should give her a kiss. She'd probably die of embarrassment.

The thought amused him, but he shook those thoughts aside and quickly ducked into an alley just as several people in dark clothes drove down the street on motorcycles. They wore the same gear as the men he had been killing.

Adam took to a knee and took aim. Time slowed down as he took a deep breath in, or that was how it seemed. It was, in all actuality, his perception of time that was slowing down. This was one of his numerous esper powers. The ability to perceive time more slowly. It made his reactions seem far faster than they really were.

He pulled the trigger once. Twice. Three times. Each shot struck the gas tank of a motorcycle, igniting the fuel inside and causing the bikes to explode, taking their riders with them. Adam was too far away to feel the heat, but the other four bikers were forced to swerve to avoid the wreckage.

Adam blew up their motorcycles too.

He moved on after taking out the motorcycle squad, traveling down the alley as he pulled out his phone once more. Most of Levon's forces were converging around the area he had just left. He grinned. The forces Levon employed were good and had a quick response, but so long as he was able to monitor their movements and they were unable to monitor his, they could do nothing against him.

They were sitting ducks.

Just as he thought that, Adam's instincts took over seconds after he emerged from the alley. He ducked back in as something struck the ground and gouged out a large chunk of the sidewalk.

He checked the phone and saw that there was a red blip about 1,200 meters southeast of him. A sniper. Adam furrowed his brow. That would be hard to deal with. He didn't have the equipment necessary to shoot a sniper at this range, which meant he needed to find a way around.

And they're coming from behind now…

"There's someone there!"

"Open fire!"

Adam turned quickly, raced forward, and ran up the wall just as six people opened fire. He used the strength in his legs to push off the wall and leapt to the other wall. The sound of automatic rifles echoed all around as the men missed their target.

"He's too fast!"

"What the fuck is he?! A spider monkey?!"

"I can't get a lock on him!"

Adam closed the distance and descended just as the men ran out of bullets. His first victim was the man in front, whom he impaled through the throat with his spear. He quickly pulled it free, then swiped the spear across another man's neck, ignoring the bloody spray splattering his mask as he moved on.

The remaining four men tried to retreat, but Adam was having none of it. He killed his third victim by shooting them in the knee, where they had no armor, then stabbing them through the gap between their armpit. The fourth screamed in agony as Adam removed his arm, tearing through the armor with the force of his swing. He died when Adam kicked him so hard in the face that his neck snapped.

"He's a monster!"

"Retreat!"

"Call for reinforcements!"

The last two almost escaped the alley, but Adam drew two throwing knives, channeled energy into the blades, and tossed them. He used all the strength in his arms and even put his body weight into the toss. Cracking sounds echoed as his knives penetrated the men's helmets. Both flopped to the ground.

I can't go back the way I came. Reinforcements will come from that direction. But I can't go the other way either because of that sniper. Guess I gotta go up.

Adam ran toward the wall, then ran up the wall. His momentum soon slowed, but he leapt to the other wall, then leapt back, and repeated the process, until he reached the roof. He quickly glanced in the direction of the sniper, channeling energy into his eyes to increase his vision. He could just barely see them. Like he thought, they were looking at the alley exit.

He took off in the other direction, traveled into another alleyway, and emerged from that entrance.

The quietness of the street was unnerving. He tapped his earpiece and spoke into it.

"Susan, I noticed no one has come out to see if there's a commotion. Where are all the residents?"

Adam had bought out his entire apartment for privacy, but the surrounding buildings were not his. This place was on the outskirts of New York City. Even so, there were a lot of people living here.

"Hold on. Let me see if there's a reason... I'm checking the news... ah. Found it. Looks like the government issued a gas leak warning and ordered all civilians to vacate the area about twelve hours ago."

"So there's no one here. Guess making all that noise was useless."

Adam had been hoping to cause a commotion so the civilians staying in their homes would check out what was going on. Humans were curious. The moment they saw the fires and fighting, he didn't doubt several would begin recording it on their phones, then upload it to the internet. That would have put some serious political pressure on Levon and would force him to divert resources toward putting out the flames.

But they had already prepared for that.

"This is what I get for living off the grid…"

This was an issue of his own making. To avoid being bothered, Adam abstained from all forms of government contact. Even his phone had any and all forms of government tracking removed. They couldn't find his location, and they couldn't issue announcements to him, which meant he missed the warning.

"Susan, it looks like Levon is bringing more forces to bear against me. I won't be able to use my phone anymore, so I'll be counting on you to provide accurate, up-to-date information. Can you do that?"

Adam didn't want to put more pressure on Susan, whose primary task was helping Aris and Lilith retreat to safety, but he would need support now if he wanted to avoid serious injury.

"Of course! Please leave this to me! Oh! Several squads are coming from both sides of the road!"

Adam had Susan hack the security of a nearby building and ducked inside. It looked like he entered a clothing store. A variety of handmade clothing hung from racks along the walls. Adam remained low to the ground and crept toward the back, where a door led into the employee room. There should also be a door through there leading out to the back. Light appeared just outside of the window. The two squads had already converged and were searching the area.

"Thanks. By the way, how are Aris and Lilith? Have they escaped?"

"Aris and Lilith? They're…"

LIGHT UP
THE NIGHT

ARIS FOLLOWED CLOSELY BEHIND LILITH AS THEY RAN DOWN A LONG TUNNEL.

They had taken an underground passage that brought them several about a kilometer away from their previous location, but Levon's blockade was much larger than they had first assumed. On top of bringing out his elite squadrons to deal with Adam, he had brought out several thousand members of his forces to create a net that would prevent his escape.

Aris and Lilith had run right into one of the patrolling squadrons mere moments after opening the hidden entrance. The two sides had stared at each other in surprise for several long seconds.

"Hey, don't those two girls look familiar?"

"I don't know about the masked woman, but that petite chick is Aris! I recognize her from the description!"

"We were told to capture her alive!"

"Get her!"

"Get back inside that passage and don't come out until I tell you to," Lilith commanded as she pushed Aris into the passage and shut the door behind her.

"Lilith?! Don't take them on by yourself! Let me… let me help!" Aris shouted as she banged on the hidden exit. Yet no amount of banging and shouting would get the door to open. She tried using the access panel to open the door like Lilith did, but she didn't know the code. All she could do was wait and worry.

The hidden entrance eventually opened. Aris smiled when she saw Lilith standing in the doorway, but she gasped when she noticed the blood running down her face.

"Y-you're injured!" she exclaimed in shock.

"It's just a minor injury," Lilith assured her.

"A-are you sure you're okay?"

"Yes. Let's keep going."

Aris had no choice but to follow Lilith. She stepped outside and grimaced when she saw the corpses littering the street. All of them had died from either bullet wounds or a slit throat. The amount of blood pooling on the ground made her want to vomit.

This was her first time seeing a dead body in real life, and it was an honestly terrifying experience. Aris didn't want to ever see something like this again. She knew, however, that this might not be the last time it happened, especially tonight.

They moved on, slipping into an alley.

"Susan, where do we go from here?" asked Lilith.

Static crackled in Aris's ear before she heard Susan say, *"Your rendezvous point is Montefiore Cemetery. You'll want to head south down Springfield Boulevard. It will be on your right."*

"Got it." Lilith ended her communication and looked back at Aris. "Follow me."

"M-mmm." Aris nodded and raced after the woman.

They soon reached the end of the alley, but they didn't head out immediately. Lilith removed a device from a pouch at her hip. It looked like one of those bendy straws. Attached to one end was a flatscreen, which Lilith quickly turned on.

The device turned out to be a camera. Lilith used it to look around the corners for signs of passing patrols. It was dark out, so the camera had been switched to night vision mode.

"They've blockaded the area, so we won't be able to head that way. We need to find another route," Lilith said.

"Um... what if we went through that door? Could we bypass their forces by traveling through the buildings?" asked Aris, pointing to a door off to the side.

"Maybe. It's worth a shot."

Lilith went over to the door and removed something from her pouch. It looked like a small square. She placed it next to the door. Then she hacked into the door's security, opened it, and slipped inside. She gestured for Aris to follow her.

This building was a general store. Aisles filled with rows of food supplies and basic necessities lined the store. Lilith crouched low to the ground and used those aisles for cover, and Aris tried her hardest to mimic the woman as she followed. They soon reached the end of the store, exited, and entered another building. This one was a clothing boutique.

It looked like they might be able to travel past the blockade. Aris felt like they might really make it without having to fight anymore.

Because she wanted to make sure there wasn't anyone near them, she looked out the window near the store entrance. A light chose that moment to shine into the window. It froze on her, and Aris felt a moment of panic as she and a person holding a flashlight stared at each other.

"Get down!"

Lilith grabbed Aris's arm and yanked her down just as gunfire shattered the glass and filled the room. Aris screamed and tried to cover her ears, but Lilith quickly pushed her toward the counter, which they hid behind.

The gunfire soon stopped. It happened so fast that Aris could still hear the sounds of gunfire in her mind. Her ears were ringing.

Lilith took a deep breath as she grabbed the SMG slung around her shoulder. She checked the ammo and the suppressor. Her calm actions served to help Aris settle down. The younger of the two took a shaky breath.

"Lilith… I'm…"

"It's okay. It was just bad luck that a patrol was passing by at that exact moment," Lilith assured her.

"Mmm. So, what do we do?"

"They're going to call reinforcements, so we'll need to get out of here quickly. I'm going to provide a distraction. I want you to head for that door. I'll follow you once you have safely exited."

Aris thought this plan wasn't fair to Lilith, who would be taking on much of the burden, but she also understood how useless she would be. It wasn't a pleasant feeling. In *Age of Gods,* Aris was a valued member of Destiny's Overture. She was just as good as the other members. Real life was much different. She couldn't do anything here. She couldn't protect herself, her friends, or the man she loved.

She hated this feeling.

"I want you to move when I say now," Lilith said. Aris clenched her teeth and nodded as Lilith did one last minute check of her weapon. The muscles in her body coiled before she sprang into action. "NOW!"

Aris bolted as Lilith opened fire. Startled screams echoed from outside. Aris tried hard not to pay attention to them as she put all her effort into running. She needed to move as quickly as possible.

Perhaps it was just her perception of time dilating, but she felt like she was moving much quicker than she normally did. Barely a second seemed to pass before she reached the door. She exited and traveled down the alley, hiding behind a large garbage can to prevent anyone from finding her.

The wait felt like forever. The sounds of gunfire filling the air didn't help. Aris pressed a hand to her chest and tried hard to regulate her breathing, but the anxiety filling her left her unable to keep the panic at bay. What if Lilith was killed? What if she died protecting her? Aris didn't think she would be able to handle that kind of guilt.

Fortunately for Aris's sanity, Lilith eventually emerged from the door. She looked around as though looking for something. Aris realized the woman must have been looking for her. She was just about to stand up when a flash of movement caught her eye. There was someone at the opposite end of the alley, a man peeking out from behind the wall with a gun pointed at Lilith.

Aris didn't know how she could see the man, but that hardly mattered. Lilith hadn't spotted him yet.

Something seemed to happen inside of Aris. Everything was moving in slow motion. She could see the man's finger as though she had the ability to zoom in on objects. It was slowly moving as he prepared to pull it.

Panic erupted from Aris as she ran out from behind the trash can and attempted to reach Lilith, even though she knew the woman was too far away. There had to be at least a dozen feet distance between them. She would never make it in time.

And yet she did.

Aris didn't quite understand it, but the world became a blur as she raced forward, slammed into Lilith, and sent them both tumbling to the ground. Gunfire filled the air. Aris gritted her teeth to avoid screaming.

She soon found herself being rolled over. Now on her back, she watched as Lilith raised her SMG and pulled the trigger, peppering the man who had fired upon them with a short burst of bullets. Aris tried hard not to look as the man's face became riddled with holes.

Lilith stood up and held her hand out to Aris, who took it and allowed the woman to help her up. She immediately noticed the expression on her friend's face.

"W-what is it?" she asked.

"Nothing." Lilith shook her head. "Let's keep moving."

They left the area quickly. It was a good thing, too. Several more people had arrived not long after they left. Aris and Lilith watched them from another alley before quickly darting through an emergency exit door that led into an apartment building.

Lilith relied on Susan to hack into the security cameras and gather data on their surroundings. It took longer than either of them would have liked. Susan could only hack into a few social cameras at a time, but she was able to give them accurate, up-to-date information on enemy formations, which allowed Aris and Lilith to bypass most of the patrols and blockades.

There were still a few patrols they met by pure coincidence, but Lilith was able to take care of them. She used a combination of gunfire and throwing knives to kill every enemy they ran into.

She's so cool...

Even though she still found it terrifying when people died, Aris felt like her admiration of Lilith was beginning to overpower her fear of violence. The older woman was graceful, elegant, and deadly. There was something sexy about that, Aris thought.

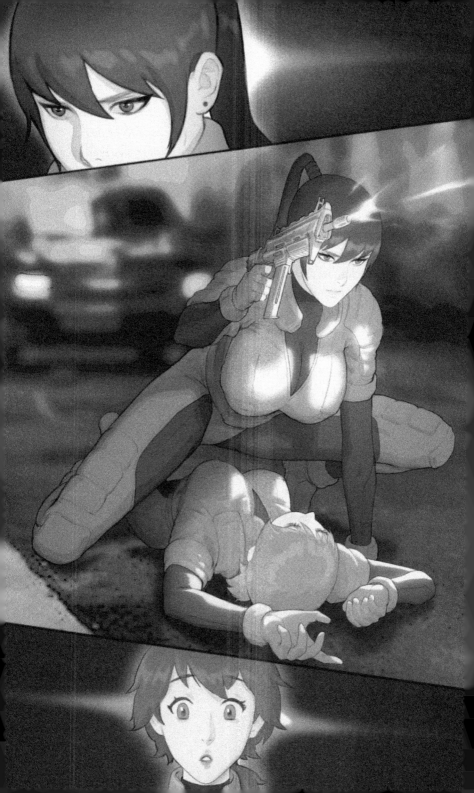

Wait. Am I... getting aroused right now?! Th-that can't be, can it? I'm not into violence! Why am I getting horny over this?!

Aris could not figure it out, and she wasn't given time to analyze her feelings because they were constantly on the run.

They eventually reached Montefiore Cemetery. It was right across the street, but they couldn't get to it because there were several people blockading the road. It was a full force. There weren't just men in uniforms carrying guns. Aris didn't know much about military vehicles, but she at least recognized the hummers with guns mounted on the top for what they were.

"I don't think we can get past this," Aris murmured.

"We can. We just need to create a distraction," Lilith said.

Aris turned to her. "How are we going to do that?"

"Don't worry. I've already done it."

"What?"

Before Aris could further question the woman, Lilith removed an object from her pouch. It was just a small cylinder with a button. She pressed the button, and several explosions suddenly lit up the night sky. Aris snapped her head in that direction.

"That's where we came from…"

"I planted several explosives on our route here," Lilith said.

"Oh…"

Aris didn't remember her doing that, but she wasn't good at paying attention.

One of the members standing outside the hummer began talking on a phone. When he got off, he gestured toward his men. They all got in the vehicles and took off toward the source of the explosion.

"Now is our chance," Lilith said, standing up.

Aris and Lilith raced across the street and reached the cemetery. It was an old building with a red-bricked roof. The worn-out appearance demarcated it as something that had survived World War

III. A small parking lot sat off to the side, and a single car was parked there.

The car was a very inconspicuous van, the kind you might find anywhere. Lilith walked up to the van. Aris followed cautiously behind her. As they reached the vehicle, one of the doors slid open and a person smiled at them. He was a man with slightly messy hair, dark skin, and big muscles.

"Lilith, I'm glad to see you made it. And this must be Aris."

"Ah. Um. Hello," Aris said.

"Leviathan, sorry to keep you waiting," Lilith said.

"No worries. You ran into some trouble, right? I saw the explosions," Leviathan said. "Anyway, hop inside. Now that you're here, we can go ahead and pick up Adam."

"Yes," said Lilith.

The older woman walked inside and Aris made to follow, but she paused and turned around to look at the scenery. It was getting close to morning. The sun was beginning to rise. Aris hoped that meant a new day would come--one in which she and her loved ones weren't having their lives threatened.

DAWN

.

"AAAAAAH?!"

"M-my arm?! My arm is gone?!"

"It hurts… it hurts so bad…"

Adam stood in the middle of a scarred battlefield. Bodies littered the ground. Most were dead, but some were still alive.

He was unharmed, but that was not because he had not been injured during this intense battle. All of his injuries had already healed thanks to his regeneration factor. It was one of several esper powers that had been forced on him through inhumane experimentation. He was kind of grateful to them now. Without the ability to heal from even fatal wounds, he would never have been able to get out of this situation.

Adam briefly considered killing the people who were still alive. They had attacked him, so death was certainly something they deserved… but no. They were merely following orders. Most of them didn't even know who he was. He was sure some of them had family, too. They had chosen the wrong side, but that didn't mean they deserved death.

Losing a limb was enough.

A vehicle pulled onto the street. Adam looked up, then stood and walked toward the oncoming vehicle. It was impossible for it to reach him because of all the bodies.

"Adam!!!"

A black blur flew out of the vehicle before it had even stopped. Adam caught the blur, which turned out to be Aris. She wrapped her arms around him in a tight hug, then did the same with her legs. She was like a koala now. He looked at the top of her head, then at Lilith. She gave him an uncertain smile when he raised an eyebrow as though asking what this was all about.

This is her first time experiencing something like this in the real world. Even if the violence in the game is very realistic, there's no comparison when you know death is permanent.

"You okay?" he asked.

Aris nodded against his chest. "… I was worried."

He brushed her hair as the passenger seat window was rolled down and Leviathan snuck her face out. She wore a mask, so Adam couldn't see her face, but he was almost positive the woman looked smug beneath that mask.

"Look at you, Mr. Lady's Man. I never would have expected the quiet kid who came to Eden all those years ago would one day become capable of seducing women so easily."

Adam shrugged. "I never imagined you'd become so talkative."

"That's true!" Leviathan laughed. "I was always the quietest one in the group. I never had much hope for survival back then… anyway, you should hop in. We need to leave before reinforcements come."

"Right."

Adam climbed into the vehicle and sat down. He readjusted Aris so her legs weren't behind him. She sat lengthwise across his lap, legs off to the side. Lilith took a place next to him.

"Where to, Boss?" asked Leviathan.

"Let's head to Delta One," said Adam after a moment of thought.

"Got it."

As Leviathan began driving away from the battlefield, Adam took his phone from his pouch. It had miraculously survived the battle, though the screen was cracked. He would have to get a new one. He found Susan's phone number, hit dial, and placed the phone on speaker.

"Adam?! Is everything okay?"

"Everything is fine. Sorry for cutting out. The situation got hectic for a while there, but we managed to escape. We're heading toward one of my hideouts now," said Adam.

"Oh, thank goodness. I was really worried when you suddenly disappeared."

"Sorry about that."

"It's fine. So long as you, Aris, and Lilith are okay."

"It's good to hear from you, Su," said Aris.

"It's good to hear from you too! I'm so happy you're safe!"

"Anyway, the reason I'm calling you is because it's too dangerous for us to remain in New York. We're planning to leave soon."

"... You're leaving?"

Adam pretended not to hear the devastation in her voice. "Unfortunately. Now that Levon knows my face, I'm sure he'll stop at nothing to have me killed. For now, at least, we need to leave New York. Anyway, the reason I'm calling you is because I have something I'd like you to give your father."

"What do you want me to give him?"

"I'm sending it now."

Adam accessed his gallery, selected a video, and sent it over. It was a large file, so it took several minutes to finish sending. Another minute passed before Susan spoke again.

"This is…"

"It's the video of my battle. My helmet is installed with a camera. Anyway, while there are no identifying marks on their uniforms, it should still be enough to threaten Levon with."

The Pleonexia Alliance was the only power in New York with a militia of its own. This was common knowledge. So if it got out that a military force operated a night raid on someone, thereby violating the treatise that stated all grievances must be settled in the game, it would be a huge blow to their reputation.

"I'll go give this to my dad right now."

"Thanks. I'll contact you again soon. I need to make a few other phone calls."

"Okay… goodbye, Adam."

"Yeah. Bye for now."

Adam hung up the phone and sighed. What should he do about Susan? It was obvious to him that she had feelings for him, and he was certain the idea of him leaving devastated her. He wouldn't mind making her his. However, he felt that her place right now needed to be at Fayte's side. That woman would need someone to stand by her since he could not right now.

"Guess I'll call Fayte," Adam said.

Aris nodded. "She needs to know what happened too." She paused. "Are we really leaving New York?"

"Yes. While the video I sent Susan will keep Levon in check, it won't stop him from using a more covert means to eliminate us. And now that he knows we're not a force he can deal with easily, he won't underestimate us. He'll begin using his contacts in the underworld next time."

Even with the treatise in place, crime still existed, the criminal underworld still existed. It would continue to exist so long as humanity did.

"What if we… eliminate him?" asked Aris hesitantly.

"Out of the question." Adam shook his head as Leviathan turned down another street. "We could assassinate Levon, but the moment we did, we would bring the entirety of the American Federation Government down on our heads. We'd be persona non grata. And don't forget, Levon now has our information. He knows what we look like. If he died, that info would go to the government. If that happened, we would have to seek asylum in another country, and there's no guarantee anyone would take us. There's also one other reason we can't kill Levon."

"What's that?" asked Aris.

"Devin Pleonexia," Adam answered. "He's Levon's father, and he's ten times more cunning and vicious than his son. When the rest of the world wanted an end to the violence after nuclear weapons eradicated more than half the world's population, he was one of the few who believed we should continue. It was also thanks to him that powerful families are allowed to own a militia even though there should be no need for one anymore. The only reason we're dealing with Levon and not him is because Devin stepped down from his position as the Pleonexia family head several years ago."

"He's not a man you want to cross lightly," Leviathan added.

"Anyway, I'm going to make a call to Fayte now," Adam said as he pulled up Fayte's contact information.

***

Fayte had not slept well last night. She had tossed and turned, woken up several times, and when morning came, she felt like she hadn't gotten any sleep at all.

Currently sitting on the couch with her knees drawn up to her chest, Fayte thought back to what happened between her and Adam. The plate of eggs and hashbrowns on the table before her sat untouched. She kept going over the incident in her mind, doubting. Had she made the right decision? Should she really have sent them away?

Knowing that Adam had been sleeping with Lilith and Aris hurt her immensely. A part of it was just her own feelings on loyalty. A man should always be loyal to his woman. He should not look at other women, sleep with other women, or engage in otherwise questionable activities with other women. Any man who would engage in sexual acts with someone who they weren't dating was scum.

Or so she thought.

But Adam wasn't a bad person, and he certainly wasn't scum. He had spent years of his life looking after Aris. Anyone else would have given up on her, but not Adam. He had desperately sought a cure for Mortems Disease. Had Fayte not shown up when she did, she knew he would still be looking.

None of that changed how much it hurt Fayte to see the man she had tried so hard not to love sleeping with another woman who wasn't Aris. Her own feelings had become a jumbled mess because of that moment. She couldn't even tell if she was upset that Adam had slept with Lilith, or if she was upset that he hadn't slept with her.

As Fayte was commiserating, her phone suddenly began vibrating. She picked it up and frowned. Adam was calling. Fayte was not sure she wanted to answer, but she didn't think he would call her for no reason--not after what happened between them.

"Hello?"

"Fayte, sorry to bother you. A situation has happened. Myself, Aris, and Lilith will be leaving New York."

"What?! Why?! What happened?!"

Fayte shot off the couch and began pacing as she bombarded Adam with questions. He let her, then carefully explained in detail the attack last night. Fayte pressed a hand to her mouth and listened, horrified as she realized how close to death Adam, Aris, and Lilith had been. Mixed with her fear for their safety was guilt.

Would they have been placed in the same situation if she hadn't kicked them out?

Was this her fault?

"None of this was your fault."

"E-excuse me?"

"You were thinking this was your fault, right? Don't think that way. What happened was simply the result of bad luck. It seems Thor saw what Aris looked like before she was able to acquire a veil. That's how Levon tracked us down."

"But... if I hadn't requested your assistance..."

"Then Aris would likely be dead already. Never forget that. You saved Aris, and you saved me. You have nothing to apologize for."

Fayte's lips trembled. She felt like crying, but she forced her tears back. "Where... are you going to go?"

"I was thinking of heading to Los Angeles."

"Los Angeles...? Oh, you're going to seek Asylum with Daggerfall Dynasty, aren't you?"

"As the second largest guild in the American Federation, they have the power to protect us. And I'm sure Daren will appreciate having me on his side."

Fayte agreed. Levon and Daren were bitter rivals, constantly fighting for the position of top guild, and yet, Daren had never once been able to claim that position. Adam could very well help him do what he had been attempting for years now. He had that kind of power.

"Um... what will happen..."

Fayte wanted to ask Adam what would happen to them, but she wasn't sure if she should, or indeed, if she even deserved it.

Adam intuited her question, however. *"Nothing will change. I'm still firmly in your camp. I'm going to help you, even if you don't want me to."*

"I do want you to help me," Fayte said with a sniffle. She wanted to cry so badly right now. Both relief and guilt filled her. "Thank you, Adam. I... I can't tell you how much this means to me."

"You don't have to. Fayte, regardless of what's happened between us, you will always be important to me. Anyway, I have to go now. We're reaching one of my hideouts and phone signals can't get through it. You stay safe."

"Okay. You too."

Fayte stared at the phone after Adam hung up and bit her lip. Even if he told her not to worry, or that this wasn't her fault, she still felt responsible for what happened. She wanted to make it up to him somehow.

"But what can I do?" she wondered out loud.

The silent room had no answer for her.

To Be Continued...

AFTERWORD

Man Made God 005 is currently the longest volume of the series. There's a lot going on and so much more that I wanted to add, but it was becoming so long I needed to find a good place to end it. I hope no one minds the ending being on a small hook for the next volume.

This is one of the hardest series to write for me. I'm not good with numbers. Any time a story involves precise calculations and numbers, I just get lost. It's bad enough when I have to write out measurements, but stats? Yeah. I'm screwed. Despite that, I am doing my best.

I think 005 had the most plot twists of the entire series so far. You could probably combine all the previous four volumes and they still wouldn't be as twisty as this one. Lilith got with Adam, the Pleonexia Alliance got their ass handed to them in a Guild War, Lexi is alive, and Levon has finally discovered Adam's identity IRL. With everything going on, I do wonder what will happen next. What's that? You say I should know what happens because this is my story? Dear reader, I am a pantser, not a plotter. Whenever I write, I write by sheer instinct, leaping keyboard first into the fray without a second thought as to what sort of word vomit is going to come out next. I almost never know what I am going to write until I actually sit my ass down and write it.

Anyway, while I am a pantser, I do have some ideas about the next volume. They aren't fully formed plans and I might just trash them and do something else, but I have ideas. Oh, do I have ideas. I'm sure they're bad ones, but I like to think most of my ideas are bad, so there.

One thing I want to focus on will be what's happening with Adam, Fayte, and Susan now that Adam has been separated from the two. There was a lot of drama between Adam and Fayte this volume. I would like to resolve that by the end of volume 6.

Anyway, I got some last minute thank yous to give.

To Abbey, my proofreader who helps find the mistakes in my manuscript. Arigato. I appreciate you helping fix my bad Engwush.

I also wanna thank Lonwa. We went out of contact for a long while, but he was game to come back as my artist when I contacted him.

Lastly, readers. Have I told you that you're awesome? If not, then let me tell you now. If I have, then let me tell you again. You're awesome. I really appreciate the support. Thank you so much for sticking with me. I hope you'll be around when 006 comes out. It's gonna be fire.

~Brandon Varnell

BRANDON VARNELL IS WRITING STORIES AND CRE- ATING COMICS ON PATREON!

https://www.patreon.com/BrandonVarnell

Severing Time & Space

Chapter 1: The Weak Clan Heir

WU JIAN CRIED OUT AS HE WAS STRUCK IN THE FACE. The world tilted as he spun like a top. He struck the snow-covered ground with a harsh thud, crying out once more as he smacked his elbow against the cold surface. A stinging sensation spread from his cheek to his jaw. His elbow stung fiercely, blood trailing across his skin, dripping to the ground. He reached up to touch his cheek and jerked it away with a hiss of pain. The sudden movement caused his elbow to cry out in pain.

Tears gathered in his eyes.

"Ha ha ha! Look at this wimp! Check it out! He's actually crying!"

"Can you believe this pathetic shrimp is the heir of our clan?"

"There's no way we can let a baby like him remain the clan heir. He'll bring shame to our forefathers. I think you should be the clan heir, Master Yong."

Three people stood over Wu Jian. All of them looked similar. Wu Yong, Wu Ming, and Wu Fei were all members of the Wu Clan, like Wu Jian. Wu Yong was Wu Jian's older half-brother. He had dark hair like Wu Jian, but his eyes were cyan instead of black. At ten years of age, he was two years older than Wu Jian, which meant he was bigger and stronger too.

Because he was the son of their father's second wife, Wu Yong was not the clan heir despite being stronger. That could change when they both came of age. He could challenge Wu Jian for the position, but this was how things were right now. Wu Jian wondered if that was why Wu Yong constantly tormented him. Was he jealous that someone much weaker than himself was the clan heir simply for being the son of their father's first wife?

He often bullied Wu Jian whenever no one else was around. That was why Wu Jian tried to stay in places that were crowded, but Wu Yong and his lackeys caught him when he was coming back from the restroom.

Snow fell from the sky as Wu Jian lay on the ground, tears pricking his eyes. Freezing cold trails of water caused his cheeks to tingle, mixing with the sting of where he had been struck. His hands and shins felt like they had been turned into blocks of ice as white powder gathered on his body. Perhaps he should be grateful to winter's chill, for the coldness had numbed his cheek and elbow to the point where he couldn't feel the pain as acutely.

"What's the matter? Get up. Stop acting so pathetic!"

"Wimp!"

"You shame our clan by looking like a girl! Are you a man or a woman?!"

Wu Jian sniffled and tried not to cry. Their words cut deep. What made them worse was how nothing they said was false. With his pale skin, glossy black hair, and delicate appearance, he really did look like a girl. Everyone always said so. Even his father often said he wished Wu Jian could be manlier.

As his three bullies continued to taunt and tease him, someone leapt onto the snow and rushed over to them. It was a young girl about the same age as Wu Jian. She had pure white skin, long dark hair, and eyes that were the color of the sky. She stood in front of Wu Jian and spread her arms wide as though to protect him. With her back turned to him, he could not see her expression, but he could well imagine the glare she was directing at the three boys.

"What do you three think you're doing?!" asked the girl. Her voice was young and girlish, but her tone was sharp and cutting like a drawn sword.

The three boys froze.

"N-now, now, Meiying, we weren't doing anything," Wu Yong began, stuttering. His cheeks were red. "We were just giving my younger brother some pointers. That's all."

While Wu Meiying was considered an oddball by most members of their clan because of the strange things she often said, her pretty appearance was enough to earn her the admiration of all the boys their age. Even some of the older boys were smitten with her. Wu Jian often got many jealous glares thrown his way because they were always together.

Wu Jian couldn't see Wu Meiying's face, but then she turned around and looked at him. Her vibrant eyes gazed into his, then looked down at his bruised cheek and the blood dripping from his elbow, and her face flushed with anger as she whirled back to the three boys. Her glare must have been powerful because all three took a step back.

"You are giving pointers to someone outside of the training hall? Do you take me for a fool? I know what you are doing. You will stop bullying Wu Jian right now, or I will tell Uncle Wu and Aunty Àilián about this," she declared.

Wu Ming and Wu Fei looked toward Wu Yong like they didn't know what to do and were waiting for his orders. On the other hand, Wu Yong gazed at Wu Meiying with a face that Wu Jian couldn't place. All he knew was that he didn't like it. He didn't want other boys looking at Wu Meiying like that.

"Tch. Come on, you two. We're leaving," Wu Yong said at last. He gave Wu Jian a glare and said, "You really are a disgrace. Someone who hides behind a girl for protection isn't worthy of leading the clan. I promise you, I will take away the position of clan heir once you come of age."

"That is not for you to decide." Wu Meiying bared her teeth at the older boy.

Scoffing to hide how unsettled he was, Wu Yong turned around, gestured for his two lackeys to follow him, and walked off. Wu Meiying waited until she was sure Wu Yong was gone, then turned to Wu Jian. She knelt and gave him a kind smile.

Despite being the same age as him—eight years old—she seemed so much older than he did. The way she stuck up for him was just one example. She was a lot better than him at their lessons, was better than him during their combat training, and acted so mature most of the time. She always knew what to say, what to do. It was like she could do anything she put her mind to.

That was why he looked up to her. It was why he always relied on her for protection even though he felt ashamed doing so.

"Are you okay?" she asked.

"I'm… fine…"

Wu Jian wiped his nose and tried to suck in his tears. The truth was he felt pathetic. Wu Yong might have been a bully, but he was right about one thing. Wu Jian was always hiding behind Wu Meiying for protection. Whenever someone picked on him because of his girly appearance or because he was weak or for any other reason, she would be the one who saved him. He was happy that she cared so much, but he also felt weak because he needed her to protect him.

Wu Yong is right. I am pathetic. How can someone as weak as me be the clan heir? Maybe it would be better if I let Wu Yong become clan heir.

"Come on. Let's go to the hospital wing and get you patched up," Wu Meiying said as she stood up and held out her hand. Despite his conflicted feelings, Wu Jian took her hand and let the girl lead him away.

While everyone else in the clan looked very similar to each other, Wu Meiying alone looked different. Her face, hair, and general appearance had none of the similarities shared by members of the Wu Clan. She was not a member of their clan. His mother had found Wu Meiying one day, abandoned in a basket, and taken her home. She was then adopted into the clan and named Meiying.

The name Meiying meant "beautiful flower." It had been his mother's hope that she would grow up to be a beautiful young woman, and it looked like her wish was coming true. Wu Meiying was easily the prettiest girl in the entire clan. Even the people who didn't like her because of the odd things she said often expressed admiration for her beauty.

The hospital wing was located in a building not far from where Wu Yong had bullied him. It was a big building. They walked across the walkway, entered through the shoji door, and came into an empty room. It had beds and medicine cabinets. Nobody was there at the moment, but Wu Meiying didn't let that bother her as she led Wu Jian over to a bed, sat him down, and walked to the medicine cabinet. Wu Jian said nothing as he watched her rummage through the cabinet. She came back moments later with cotton pads and ointment.

"Hold still, okay?" she instructed.

Wu Jian nodded. "Okay."

Wu Meiying dabbed the cotton in the ointment, then applied some, first to his elbow, then his face. He flinched when an itchy sensation spread across his elbow and cheek, but it was soon replaced by a soothing warmth. As she applied ointment to his face, Wu Meiying spoke again.

"Did those three hit you anywhere else?"

Wu Jian shook his head. "Just my face."

Wu Meiying huffed. "It's not 'just' your face. It's the ultimate disgrace to slap someone like they did, and they did it to you. I cannot believe they would hit their clan heir in the face like that. Hmph. The nerve of them! I'll show them what happens when you hit my Jian next time we spar. I'll beat them to a pulp."

Wu Jian looked down and said nothing. Since he was so small, his feet didn't reach the floor. He kicked them listlessly and let Wu Meiying finish spreading ointment on his face. She finished by placing a patch made from bamboo leaves over it. His elbow was similarly patched up.

"You know... maybe if you learned to stand up for yourself, they would not pick on you so much," Wu Meiying said hesitantly.

"How can I do that? Wu Yong and his friends are so much bigger than me. Even if I did stand up for myself, I would just get beaten more. That's what happened the last time I tried to stand up for myself," Wu Jian said. It wasn't like he hadn't stood up for himself before, but the last time he had done so, it resulted in a much more violent beating. He had learned his lesson and never tried to stand up to his bullies again.

"Maybe at first, but you can always... get... get..."

"Meiying? What's wrong?"

Wu Jian looked worried as Wu Meiying trailed off. Her eyes had become vacant and glassy. She swayed where she stood like she was dizzy. Wu Jian had seen her get like this before. While not frequent, it happened enough times that Wu Jian understood what was going on. Wu Meiying was about to predict the future. A shiver ran down his back. Every prediction she had ever made came true. He wondered what she would predict this time.

He waited for a few minutes, but when she just remained standing there with that glassy look in her eyes, he became worried. It had never taken her more than a few seconds to come back. That she was staying like this made him worry that she might have lost her soul.

"Meiying? Are you okay?" He placed his hands on her shoulders and lightly shook her.

Blinking several times, Wu Meiying's eyes regained their original clarity. She looked at him with a soft gaze that made his face heat up. He didn't know why she was staring at him like that, but then she cupped his cheek and stroked it with her thumb.

"Do you love me?" she asked.

"Of course I do," Wu Jian said without hesitation.

"And you want to marry me, right?"

"Yes. Of course. Didn't we... didn't we promise we would get married when we grew up?"

Wu Meiying nodded, her face more serious than he ever remembered seeing it. A chill ran through him. Why was she looking at him like that?

"Listen, Wu Jian. Please listen carefully. If you want us to get married, to stay together like this forever, then you must become stronger. If you don't..."

"Will something bad happen if I don't?" asked Wu Jian, a tremor in his voice.

Wu Meiying's lips trembled. "If you don't become stronger, then I'm afraid... I will be taken somewhere very far away, somewhere you'll never be able to reach me. I don't want to be taken away from you. I want to stay with you forever. So, please, promise that you will become strong. Become so strong that even if I am taken away, you will be able to reach me."

Wu Jian did not know why Wu Meiying was saying all this, but he had a very bad feeling about it. He believed her. If she said she would be taken somewhere he couldn't reach her unless he was strong, then it was probably true. Wu Meiying often made predictions like this, and they always happened just like she said they would. That she would say something like this shook him up. He swallowed heavily and nodded once.

"Okay. I promise. Starting now, I'll train hard and become stronger."

Wu Meiying's smile reminded him of the cherry blossoms that bloomed during the new year. It stole his breath. For the sake of that smile, Wu Jian would gladly walk through fire and lava. He would tear apart the heavens themselves if it meant he would get to see her smile like this all the time. As he looked at her smile, only one thought occurred to him.

I have to get stronger!

HAVE YOU EVER EXPERIENCED ONE OF THOSE LIFE-CHANGING INSTANCES? AN EVENT SO MOMENTOUS THAT, YEARS LATER, YOU'RE STILL MARVELING AT HOW IT CHANGED YOUR LIFE?

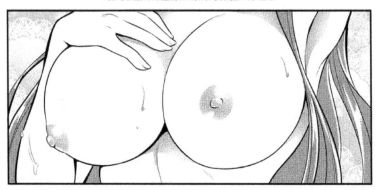

I HAD ONE OF THOSE. IT HAPPENED A WHILE AGO

EVEN TO THIS DAY, THROUGH ALL THE CHANGES THAT HAVE HAPPENED, THROUGH ALL THE EXPERIENCES THAT I'VE BEEN THROUGH, I STILL CAN'T BELIEVE HOW THIS ONE MOMENT CHANGED MY LIFE FOREVER.

NO MATTER WHAT CAME AFTER, OUR FIRST MEETING IS SOMETHING THAT I'LL ALWAYS REMEMBER.

ESPECIALLY SINCE, AT THE BEGINNING OF THIS TALE, I THOUGHT SHE WAS NOTHING BUT AN ORDINARY FOX WITH, UNORDINARILY ENOUGH, TWO BUSHY RED TAILS.

LIFE

.

.

.

.

.

.

.

.

.

.

IT HITS YOU WHEN YOU LEAST EXPECT IT TO.

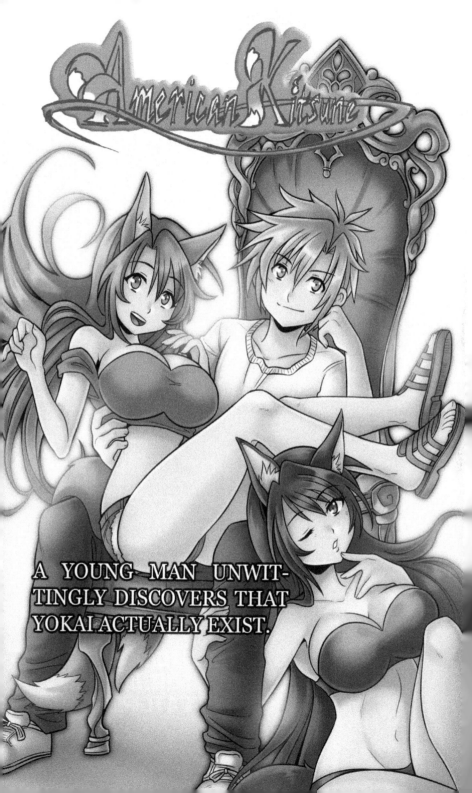

American Kitsune

A YOUNG MAN UNWIT-
TINGLY DISCOVERS THAT
YOKAI ACTUALLY EXIST.

catgirl doctor

THE STORY OF A YOUNG DOCTOR-IN-TRAINING AND CATGIRLS.

MMG:001
A MAN DESPERATE TO SAVE HIS LOVER JOINS FORCES WITH A WOMAN LOOKING FOR A WAY OUT OF AN UNWANTED MARRIAGE.
MAN MADE GOD

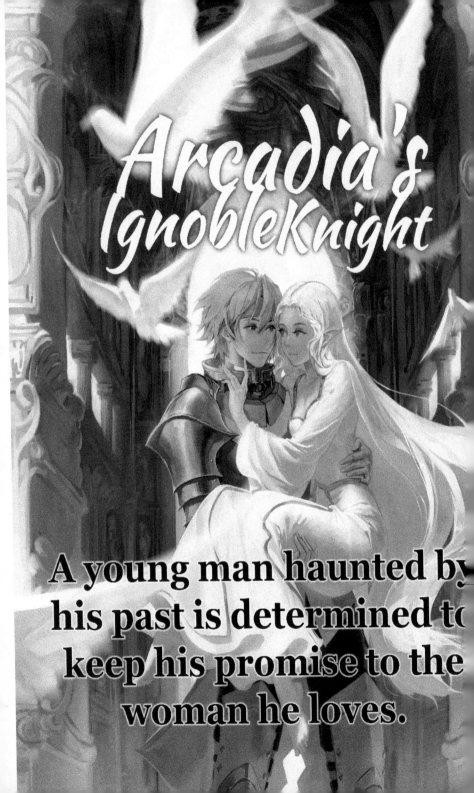

Arcadia's IgnobleKnight

A young man haunted by his past is determined to keep his promise to the woman he loves.

A hero betrayed...
A princess dethroned...
These two will join forces....
All for the sake of finding
a place to call home

JOURNEY *of a* BETRAYED HERO

A former Marine running from his past.
An angel with nothing left to lose.
A succubus at the bottom of the food chain.
What do these three have in common?
A goal: To escape the hellish nightmare
they've found themselves in. Together.

Swordsman Of the Rift 2

WIEDERGEBURT

LEGEND OF THE REINCARNATED WARRIOR

HE RETURNED TO THE PAST IN ORDER TO CHANGE THE FUTURE.

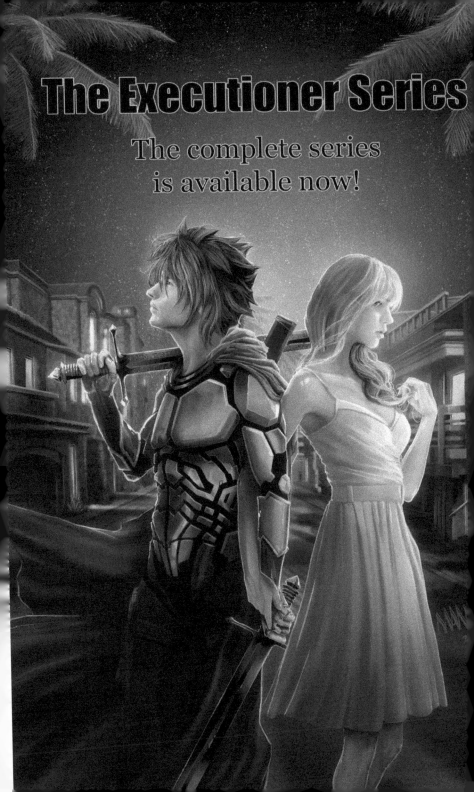

Want to learn when a new book comes out?
Follow me on Social Media!

 @AmericanKitsune

 +BrandonVarnell

 @BrandonBVarnell

 http://bvarnell1101.tumblr.com/

 Brandon Varnell

 BrandonbVarnell

 https://www.patreon.com/
BrandonVarnell

Ingram Content Group UK Ltd.
Milton Keynes UK
UKHW021824170323
418736UK00015B/745

9 781951 904715